Body & Soul

Also by Sheila Norton

The Trouble With Ally
Other People's Lives

Body & Soul

Sheila Norton

PIATKUS

✿ Visit the Piatkus website!

Piatkus publishes a wide range of bestselling fiction and non-fiction, including books on health, mind, body & spirit, sex, self-help, cookery, biography and the paranormal.

If you want to:
- read descriptions of our popular titles
- buy our books over the internet
- take advantage of our special offers
- enter our monthly competition
- learn more about your favourite Piatkus authors

VISIT OUR WEBSITE AT: www.piatkus.co.uk

Copyright © 2004 by Sheila Norton

First published in Great Britain in 2004 by
Piatkus Books Ltd of
5 Windmill Street, London W1T 2JA
email:info@piatkus.co.uk

The moral right of the author has been asserted

A catalogue record for this book is available from the British Library

ISBN 0 7499 0705 3

Set in Times by
Action Publishing Technology Ltd, Gloucester

Printed and bound in Great Britain by
Clowes Ltd, Beccles, Suffolk

Acknowledgements

Sincere thanks to the unknown doctor who once ordered doughnuts by taxi . . . and gave me an idea . . .

For all my friends and colleagues – past and present – on the staff of St Andrew's Centre, now at Broomfield Hospital and previously at Billericay, Essex. I promise *none* of you are portrayed by any of the characters in this book – whatever you might think! You are all beyond imitation!

Chapter One

The Old Armchair Bites Back

It was purely a coincidence that on the same day I went to the Body and Soul lecture, PJ told me I looked like an old armchair. And the trouble with pure coincidences is that no matter how much you rationalise and tell yourself there's nothing sinister about them and certainly nothing meaningful or spiritual about them, you can't help building them up into a big deal.

I wasn't feeling great about myself, to be totally honest, even before subjecting myself to Body and Soul. I only went along because of Sara's nagging. Sara does that to people. She doesn't call it nagging, of course – she calls it caring about people, and to be fair that's probably what it is, but in the course of her caring she manages to get them to do things they don't really want to do at all. Body and Soul was a good example. Who in their right minds, working in a hospital as we do and surrounded all day every day by the sick, wounded and mortally miserable of this world, would want to spend even half an hour of their spare time listening to a lecture with a title like that? Fun and Games, or even Peace and Quiet might perhaps have attracted a more enthusiastic cross section of the staff, and if I'd been responsible for promoting the monthly Occupational Health lecture (which thank God I wasn't – I had more than enough on my plate already), I'd have seriously contemplated calling it Kinky Sex and Threesomes to trick people into attending, and only giving out the leaflets about bodies and souls when the doors were locked.

'*Body and Soul* – Help for a Healthy Lifestyle', Sara had read out to me enthusiastically a few days earlier. 'There you go, Rosie!'

'Where?' I responded sourly. 'Where do I go?'

'To the Occupational Health Department. For their talk, Friday lunchtime. It sounds just exactly what you need!'

I wasn't offended. I'd spent most of the past few weeks (or maybe the past few months ... or was it beginning to run into years?) complaining about my life, so she couldn't be blamed for suggesting that I needed something. Anything. Even an Occupational Health talk in my lunch break.

'I don't. I don't need anything. I'm fine, thank you.'

'You're not.'

She looked at me with this look she gives people who aren't fine. It's a look that's hard to describe, but it would break the heart of anyone in the throes of a personal tragedy and would probably make a baby animal roll over and lie on its back with its tongue hanging out.

'You keep on saying,' she reminded me in her gentle, caring Mother Teresa voice, 'about your life being crap.'

'Yes, well, that's because it is. I don't need a half-hour lecture to tell me about it.'

'But it says here,' she jabbed at the computer screen, pointing out the words of the e-mail as if they were messages from Heaven rather than mistyped, badly spelled communications from Occupational Health, 'It says *Change Your Life*. It says *Help for a Healthy Lifestyle*.'

'Yeuk. I don't do healthy. I don't do lifestyles.'

'You haven't tried, Rosie.' She looked at me accusingly, as if I was hurting her. 'You've never really tried, have you, if you're honest?'

2

I have so!

I bloody have!

I've tried eating fruit, I have! I've tried cutting out chips and chocolate, and walking to the pub instead of taking the car!

'Piss off,' I said.

'Well, I don't see what harm it could do,' responded Sara, walking away from me with a sigh that would have had any weaker person running after her, feeling like shit, begging for forgiveness, wanting only to be given a copy of the e-mail and details of where to go for the lecture.

'Give me a copy of the e-mail, then,' I said when I caught up with her. 'Where do we have to go?'

At this point, before we go any deeper into Body and Soul, I suppose I should tell you about PJ and how the whole armchair scenario came about.

PJ had been working at the hospital for more than a year at this time, which was a reasonable length of time as medical contracts go, so we knew each other well enough to trade the odd insult or two. We could have a joke, we could have a laugh. We'd got past the stage of polite deference. But there still should have been a line beyond which it wasn't acceptable to go, and I'll tell you what that line was – or should have been, if it was there: a line of *understanding*. Understanding a person's feelings, and what might hurt them. What might make them feel small, or insecure, or lie awake at night worrying about themselves.

The thing about PJ was that he had two serious social problems. One, he was young, and two, he was male. He couldn't help it. He didn't mean anything by it. It just had the effect of making his mouth open without his permission, allowing a stream of total crap to emerge and devastate all around him. He was also a surgeon, and believe me, having worked with dozens, possibly hundreds, of them over the years I can tell you that this is another serious social disad-

3

vantage. They get used to telling people the brutal truth with no holds barred.

I'm afraid this is going to hurt you quite a lot.
We're going to have to take your leg off.
If we don't operate you're going to die.

'The nice thing about you,' said PJ on the day I amazed the Occupational Health Department of East Dean General Hospital by going to their lunchtime lecture and actually listening to it, 'is that you make me feel comfortable.'

He settled himself into the seat next to me with a self-satisfied grin as if he'd just paid me the greatest compliment he could imagine.

'Comfortable.' I tried to smile but felt the muscles in my face resisting the effort. '*Comfortable*? It makes me sound like an old armchair!'

'That's it exactly!' he agreed with far too much enthusiasm. 'A comfortable, cosy old armchair where I can relax after a hard day. That's how you feel, to me.'

I was sitting, at the time, on not exactly a comfortable, cosy old armchair but the green vinyl bench seat that served for comfort in the outpatient staff coffee-room, drinking something pink and disgusting that was supposed to make you lose weight without hunger pangs. It was only eleven o'clock and I was already hungry, so not only was it disgusting, it wasn't working and it was making me bad tempered. Or perhaps it was the hunger making me bad tempered.

'Thanks a *lot*!' I snapped, shaking off the hand he immediately laid on my arm and the apology he immediately tried to force on me. A *laughing* apology, which to my mind wasn't any nicer than the original insult.

'Come on, Rosie! I didn't mean ...'

I took the glass with the dregs of the pink shit to the sink and rinsed it out briskly, running the tap too fast and getting sprayed with water in the process. I could hear him behind me, still sniggering.

4

'I was trying to be nice!'

'Well, you need to try harder,' I responded, flouncing out of the room – a bit theatrically, I suppose, in retrospect, but well – how would *you* have felt? The last thing I wanted, at the age of forty-four, was to discover I was perceived as *comfortable*. It sounds so middle-aged! It sounds like Women's Institutes and Jam Making, Knitting Patterns and Cocoa. It's got a smell of fear about it; the fear of growing older that I'd been trying to ignore ever since I turned forty. I didn't want to be comfortable! I wanted to be interesting, and exciting, and alluring, and even fascinating. Nobody thinks of comfortable old armchairs as fascinating, do they?

Oh, God. Forty-four and my life was over.

'I'm sure he didn't mean it like that,' Becky tried to soothe me when I got back to my post and told her about it.

All very well for her to talk – all thirty-two years and eight stone of her.

'He's just being a normal thoughtless male.'

Men could be excused anything, in Becky's book, as long as they were good-looking and charming. Charming to *her*, that is – which most of them were, of course, what with her short skirts, her long dark hair and two-inch-long fluttering eyelashes. It wasn't even, quite honestly, as if PJ was particularly good-looking; he was on the skinny side, with big brown eyes that made him look a bit like a frightened rabbit. But at least he didn't look like an armchair.

Becky and Sara were my two colleagues on the outpatient reception desk. Unlike doctors, our job involved us being sweet, welcoming and diplomatic to people all the time, every day, no matter how rude they were to us or how we felt ourselves. It didn't mean we had to be sweet and diplomatic to each other, of course, and sometimes having a gripe and a bicker amongst ourselves was the only way to relieve the strain of being constantly nice. Trouble was, we had to bicker quietly so the patients couldn't hear.

5

'It'd be nice if you took *my* side for once!' I hissed at her, dumping a pile of patients' records on the desk in front of her, making her move her hands out of the way with a startled jump.

'Side?' she muttered. 'Who's talking about taking sides? Since when have you and PJ been at war?'

'Since now. Since he called me an old armchair.'

Wars have been fought over less serious things, if you ask me. PJ had better watch out.

'Well, anyway,' interjected Sara, who'd been half listening to our exchange whilst dealing with the problems of a pregnant woman who'd somehow turned up at the surgical clinic instead of the ante-natal clinic, 'perhaps you'll feel better about yourself after we've been to the talk.'

'Talk? What talk?' I asked her tetchily.

'You know. The Occupational Health one. At lunchtime. *Body and Soul.*'

'Oh, great. That's all I need. Insults and boredom, all in one day.'

'You said you'd come ...' she reminded me, looking at me over the top of her glasses.

'Yeah, OK, OK, I'll come.'

Anything for a laugh. It couldn't make me feel any worse than I felt after being called an old armchair, could it?

Well, yes, as it happened, it could.

Sara and I were a bit late getting to the talk so we sneaked into seats in the back row and tried to hide behind the people in front. The Occupational Health nurse, who was tall and muscular and looked as though she went to the gym twice a day and spent her spare time climbing mountains, was writing on the whiteboard at the front of the lecture room. The board was divided into two halves and BODY was written in big capitals at the top of the left hand side, and SOUL on the right hand side. Underneath BODY were two words so far: SIZE and WEIGHT. Should I get up and go now, or would that immediately attract so much

6

attention to my *Size* and *Weight* that it would be better to crawl out on all fours?

Someone near the front put her hand up and called out: 'Fitness!' and Mountaineering Woman nodded enthusiastically and wrote FITNESS on the board under SIZE and WEIGHT. I shuffled further down in my chair. It appeared this was a class participation exercise.

'For the benefit of those who've just joined us,' she said in a booming cheery voice, obviously developed during the course of years yodelling across mountain ranges – putting paid to any hope I still had of crawling out of the room, 'what we're doing here is, we're sharing suggestions of words that talk to us about our Body Image.'

There was an expectant silence in the room. I gradually became aware of the fact that everyone was looking round at Sara and me. That, in fact, Mountaineering Woman was staring straight at us herself.

'So!' she boomed. 'Any suggestions, you two at the back?'

How unfair is that? Just because someone arrives late at the lecture, probably already stressed out because they've had trouble getting away from the queue of patients waiting to abuse them at the reception desk, why pick on them like that and show them up in front of the whole class? I glanced sideways at Sara, who was smiling back at Teacher with a look of pleasant, interested co-operation and obviously no intention whatsoever of contributing. Sara turned to me and raised her eyebrows.

'Rosie?' she asked out loud.

Well, thanks, friend! With the spotlight now fully and solely concentrated on me, I said the first thing that came into my head – which, perhaps not surprisingly, was:

'Armchair!'

'*Armchair*?' repeated Yodelling Woman, rubbing her head as if for inspiration. 'The word *armchair* speaks to you about your body image?'

'Yes.'

'How very interesting . . .' she lied, turning to write it on the board nevertheless. 'Can you . . . er explain . . .?'

'An old armchair,' I told her, feeling my voice rising with indignation as I recalled the insult again, 'is something comfortable to collapse on.'

A titter went round the room. Did I say something funny?

'*Comfortable*,' repeated Teacher, writing that on the board too. Must have been short of suggestions before we came in. She turned to look back at me. 'So you feel comfortable about your body?'

'No!' Are you joking? Does anybody? 'No,' I repeated sadly, and the tittering died away and more heads turned to look round at me. Who was this madwoman, anyway, who came in late and started ranting about armchairs? 'What I feel is . . . old. Old and battered and not . . . not very exciting.'

The heads all turned back to the front again, probably embarrassed now. There were a few coughs and then one or two more hands went up, one or two more suggestions were called out – sensible suggestions, about diet, and dental hygiene and the prevention of constipation. Nothing else about items of furniture. But I noticed Mountaineeress looking at me once or twice and I could almost have thought she was smiling.

'What we're looking at here,' she announced finally, having filled the left hand half of the whiteboard with what (apart from ARMCHAIR) looked like the jumbled up chapter headings of a Family Medical Encyclopaedia, 'is the sum of your insecurities about your physical selves.'

There was a murmur of protest from some of the ranks.

Insecurities? retorted the surprised expression of a particularly beautiful young nurse in the front row who quite obviously didn't have any.

Insecurities? muttered a burly porter sitting just in front of me who didn't seem too sure what it meant.

8

Insecurities, I thought with a nod of agreement. She's hit the nail on the head. Every single word on that board made me feel insecure, even the date at the top. I sat up a bit straighter and began to take more interest. Perhaps the mountain air had sharpened her brain after all.

'Now, perhaps that gives you a clue,' she called out with a fresh burst of enthusiasm, 'to what I'm looking for, for the right hand side?'

She tapped the blank half of the whiteboard with her pen and looked around the room expectantly. Silence. Everyone had become too insecure to speak. She looked at me. I was trying to duck behind the porter's head but he kept moving.

'Rosie?' she prompted.

Trust Sara to announce my name to the world. That was it, now – I was marked for life.

I shrugged.

'Not sure what you mean by *soul*,' I admitted.

'Soul, mind, heart, call it what you will. I'm talking about the *you* inside your body. Your personality. Your spirit. Give me a word that sums up your own image of yourself . . . *inside*.'

Jesus, God, this was like being stripped naked and put on display in a shop window. I could feel myself cringing. Why me? Hadn't I already been punished for being late? Ask someone else, please, Teacher – let someone else go first . . .

'Kind. Fair,' called out a low-grade manager from personnel with a nervous tic that resembled an attack of the hiccups.

I stared at her. How did she get the guts to go first, when that was all she could come up with? *Kind*? *Fair*? What sort of a self-image was that? I'd rather die than admit to having such a mealy-mouthed, pathetic, nondescript self-image. I'd rather think of myself as . . .

'Dynamic! Creative! Charismatic!'

Where the fuck did *that* come from? I felt myself blush scarlet as the tittering started up again all around me. Sara was nudging me.

'Well done!' she said, pointing to the Mountaineering Woman who was writing my words on the board with pleased, decisive strokes.

'Good,' she announced. 'Anyone else?'

As the right hand side of the board gradually filled up with the equivalent of a psychiatric report on a patient with a multiple personality disorder, I sat in stunned silence, seeing only those three words:

Dynamic – Creative – Charismatic.

I listened, genuinely interested, as Mountaineering Woman explained her theory of *Help For a Healthy Lifestyle*. It didn't matter, she explained, how much attention you paid to the left hand side of the board, if you didn't get the right hand side sorted out at the same time. Think what your own self-image was telling you. If you thought of yourself as slim and fit on the left hand side, but the stuff on the right was all negative, perhaps you were too obsessed with your physical appearance and should go to the gym less and make a few more friends at the pub. If your physical self-image was bad but you were happy in yourself, maybe all you needed was a good diet.

'All a bit obvious, really,' whispered Sara, looking disappointed.

I lingered behind at the end of the lecture.

'All right, Rosie?' asked Mountaineeress as she passed me on the way out of the room.

'Yes. Thanks.'

I hesitated.

'Can I ask you something?'

'Of course!' she smiled.

Must have done her self-image a power of good.

'What would you say,' I asked, quietly, in case anyone was listening, 'to someone whose body image was an armchair and whose soul image was Creative, Dynamic and Charismatic?'

'Get out of the armchair,' she said at once, looking at me

10

so directly that I suddenly felt as if I was in church, talking to the vicar. 'And get creative, Rosie! Get dynamic! Be charismatic!'

Well, I probably would if I knew how, wouldn't I?

'Would you call me dynamic?' I asked Barry while we were getting in each other's way in the kitchen that evening.

We always got in each other's way if we were both in the kitchen at the same time. Or anywhere else at the same time, come to that. Right then I was trying to peel things and chop things for a stir-fry. He was trying to fill up the kettle to make a coffee, and seemed to have to do a lot of elbowing me, dripping water over my hands, and knocking cupboard doors against me in the process.

'Mm,' he said, sitting down at the kitchen table with the newspapers to wait for the kettle to boil.

Couldn't do anything else whilst the kettle was boiling, of course, being a man.

'What do you mean, *Mm*? That's not an answer. I want an answer. Am I dynamic, or charismatic?' I paused, waiting for him to show some sign of listening, and then went on regardless: 'Or would you think of me more in terms of being . . .'

He raised his eyes slowly from the paper. Possibly listening, possibly wondering whether the kettle was boiling.

'. . . comfortable? Like an old armchair?'

He stared at me blankly.

'Well?' I demanded, waving a half peeled carrot at him. 'Well?'

There was a resigned look about him, the look of someone who knows he's got absolutely no chance of saying the right thing, that he's a doomed man and he might just as well give up now.

'What's brought all this on?' he asked, trying to buy some time.

I sighed and turned back to chopping the carrots. I didn't want to tell him that a guy at work, ten years my junior,

11

had called me an old armchair. He'd find it far too difficult not to laugh out loud, and far too tempting to use it as ammunition in future arguments.

So what if I'm lazy and selfish and bad-tempered – at least I don't look like an old armchair!

'I don't want to get middle-aged,' I said instead, crossly, throwing bits of carrot into a pan.

'What are you talking about, you silly girl?'

A little, healing, wave of warmth began to creep back into my old, cold, frightened bones. Perhaps I was worrying unnecessarily. At least Barry didn't see me as an old armchair. It's true he didn't ever really look at me at all any more, but maybe if he did, if he made the effort and really thought about it, he wouldn't just see me as Rosie, plain, dumpy, mousy-haired, boring old Rosie, but someone dynamic and charismatic that he fell in love with all those years ago.

'Of *course* you're middle-aged!' he went on calmly, returning to his paper. 'We all are, aren't we? You have to face it sooner or later, Rosie, old girl!'

Old girl! Bloody *old girl!*

I stomped around the kitchen, throwing vegetables into the pan with increasing venom, watching them spit in the hot oil and wanting to spit back at them. I elbowed Barry back, hard, when he got in my way again getting the milk out of the fridge.

'What's up with you?' he asked aggressively. 'Bad day at work?'

What's up with me?!? How could he have forgotten already, after only about three and a half minutes, that he'd just called me middle-aged *and* old within the space of two sentences? Could he really not see that he'd just insulted me, done irreparable damage to my self-esteem and then just carried on reading a news report about high winds and storms in western France?

*

'So how long has this been going on, then?' I demanded eventually, halfway through the meal which we'd eaten up till then in silence.

'What?' He looked at me warily. 'How long has what been going on? And what's the matter?'

'How long have I been an *old girl*? How long have you thought of me as old, and boring, and . . .'

'Oh, I see.' He nodded with satisfaction, proud of himself for working out what the problem was. 'For God's sake, Rosie – you *ask* me what I think, and when I tell you, you don't like it.'

Of course I don't, you idiot. You're supposed to lie.

'I didn't say you were boring,' he added, looking at me as if he was considering it. 'But what's the point of pretending? We're middle-aged, both of us.'

'Well, I don't want to be,' I retorted, childishly.

'What about me?'

Just like a man. Turn the conversation around to himself when he's not getting any attention.

'What do you mean, what about you?'

'Well, you can't tell me you don't think of *me* as middle-aged.'

Fortunately I had a mouthful of dinner. I slowed down my chewing and swallowing so I had time to think of a response. Here was the difference between us, you see: I was far more considerate of his feelings. I didn't want to stick in the knife and twist it, the way he did. But there was no getting away from the fact that he'd hit the nail on the head. Of course I thought of *him* as middle-aged! Barry had been middle-aged since he was about twenty-five! He pottered about in his greenhouse muttering to himself. He talked about the 60s as the Good Old Days. He moaned about teenagers and pop music and people not talking properly. Sometimes I felt like I was still living with my father.

I finished my mouthful. I had to say something.

'Well, if I'm middle-aged then you must be, too,' I allowed, resentfully.

He smiled and got back to his dinner, quite happy with this.

'I'm not putting up with it!' I told him, throwing my fork down. 'I don't want to be middle-aged and I *don't* want to be comfortable!'

'So what are you going to do?' he asked with a sigh, looking at me as if I was a rather wearing pupil in one of his remedial classes.

What indeed?

What do you do about an old armchair? Buy new cushions for it? Cover it in red velvet? Have it re-sprung and re-upholstered?

'I'm going to re-invent myself,' I declared, with a lot more confidence than I felt and ignoring the fact that it sounded absolutely ridiculous. 'I'm going to become a new person. I'm going to become dynamic, creative and charismatic.'

'Well, bloody good for you,' said Barry mildly, getting up to put his plate in the dishwasher. 'Is there any of that pudding left over from yesterday?'

I'd better say at this point that I realise you must wonder why I was over-reacting to this whole armchair and middle-age thing in such a Prima Donna fashion. *Why the big deal?* you must be asking yourself. *What's so terrible about going through life as a comfortable armchair, when there are people in the world who don't know where their next crust's coming from and haven't got a pot to piss in?* Well, I take your point. But in fairness to me, you should perhaps understand that, Barry aside, everything about my life was very youthful. For a start I had three very youthful children, one and a half of whom were still living at home. Emma, the eldest, had already flown the family nesting-box and settled in a far more interesting tree – a house-share in London, the sharees being her boyfriend, Tom, and an assortment of other bright young things. The half-flown fledgling was our second daughter Natasha – in her first year at Leicester University and making brief but colourful weekend appearances in the house from time to time, followed by longer stays during the vacations when she reclaimed her bedroom, her stereo system and rights of ownership over the dog. This ownership had been in fierce dispute since she left for university, when Stuart, our youngest, decided that as he was expected to feed, walk and entertain him whilst Natasha was away, Biggles would henceforth be known as his dog. Biggles by the way was also very youthful, having been born out of wedlock to a cocker spaniel mother and a large brown shaggy father of indiscriminate breed only a few months before the departure for university.

When the kids had all been little helpless creatures, crying in prams and throwing up on rugs, I used to have a vision of the days ahead when they'd all be grown up, charming, sensible people who'd take their cups out to the kitchen, offer to put the rubbish out, and have conversations. You know, proper family conversations about serious, interesting things. Politics, religion and whose turn it was to put out the rubbish. Instead, at this point in my life Stuart and a succession of his friends spent their time racing in one door of the house and out of another, dropping school bags and football bags as they went, the conversation never really progressing much beyond:

Where are you going?
Out.
When will you be back?
Dunno.
What about your homework?
'nt got any.

Their youth, energy and verbal penury wore me out. I watched them, and felt my life ebbing away. I spoke to them, and heard my words echoing in an abyss of wasted breath.

And then I went to work and was confronted by the young and lovely Becky, and the younger-than-me, lovelier-than-

15

me Sara, and about a hundred attractive young men and women in white coats who didn't look old enough to be medical students never mind fully-fledged doctors.

All right, I admit it. I had a problem.

Got the picture? See where I was coming from?

I didn't want to be the old battered armchair in a life full of beautiful modern furnishings.

I wasn't going to sit back and accept it; I was going to fight back!

At some point in the future I was going to look back on this day and think – that was the turning point: the day of the Body and Soul lecture.

I loaded the dishwasher, went to bed and dreamed that the Mountaineering Woman was chasing me round the hospital car park and everyone was laughing at me.

But I'd show them! You see if I didn't!

Chapter Two

Enter the Gorilla

'What,' asked Natasha during the course of one of her regular calls from the phone hanging from the landing wall in her halls of residence, 'did you spend your Boots voucher on?'

We'd been discussing the cost of a pint of cider at the Student Union on a Friday night, when this question was flung at me apropos-of-nothing. I'd like to say there was a stunned silence, but given the blood-curdling shrieks at Tasha's end of the line (*'Just a couple of the girls trying to study in their rooms'* apparently), silence was something I wasn't going to encounter again until my ears had stopped ringing about four hours after the termination of the phone call.

'Boots voucher?' I asked, dazed.

What Boots voucher?

'The one we bought you for Mother's Day!' she retorted in wounded tones.

Oh, that one, of course, of course. Where the hell did I put that?

'Yes, of course,' I soothed hastily. 'No. I ... er ... I'm still looking. I've got a few ideas in mind.'

'Well, don't spend it on boring stuff like you usually do,' she said without much enthusiasm.

Boring. That word again.

'What do you mean, *boring*?'

'You know. Boring toothpaste. Tissues and toilet paper. Boring Economy Shampoo.'

'They're the things I *have* to buy. For the family,' I said, stung.

'Yes, well. Not with your Mother's Day voucher, you don't. Treat yourself to something you really want, Mum.'

'But . . . I don't know . . . what do you think . . .?'

'Listen, Mum, I've got to go, OK? Lots of stuff to do – you know. Essays to write. OK, Helen, just got to get my purse! Which pub are we going to? Bye, Mum!'

I held the phone to my ear for a while, listening to the dialling tone change to the snotty-voiced cow saying *Please Hang Up*, wishing a dozen different impossible and selfish things along the lines of Natasha still being a little girl, living at home under my jurisdiction and not being subject to the whims and fancies of the male students, bartenders, nightclub owners and drug pushers of Leicester, and too far away for me to march over there and bring her safely home by midnight.

'Kids,' I muttered to myself, putting down the phone and getting wearily to my feet. 'Never stop bloody worrying you.'

Now I sounded like my mother, as well as being middle-aged and boring.

To take my mind off my daughter being mugged, drugged, raped and murdered, I began a search of my dressing-table drawers which resulted in the discovery of four pots of the same shade of pink pearl nail polish (all half used), eleven keys of unknown origin which didn't fit any lock in the house, seventeen shillings and ninepence-halfpenny in pre-decimal money, and two Boots vouchers. One was for ten shillings and sixpence; the other, for £25, was this year's Mother's Day present from my three kids – put in a safe place until I decided which boring shampoos and tissues to

18

spend it on. I looked at it, running my fingers briefly over the three names they'd signed with love, and smiled at the thought of the arguments they'd undoubtedly had over it. Most of this princely sum would certainly have been contributed by Emma, the only one in gainful employment, but Tasha and Stuart would probably have put in their opinions, along with their fiver or whatever, about what sort of voucher I ought to have. Stuart would probably have favoured one for the CD and video shop, whilst Tasha would have suggested one of her favourite fashion stores. But Emma, sensible and practical as always, had obviously had the last word.

'Mum would rather have a Boots voucher,' I could almost hear her saying. 'So she can spend it on something useful.'

I can't really explain what came over me at that point. Perhaps it was the thought of the Economy Shampoo and toilet paper. Perhaps it was being called boring once too often. Perhaps I just had some sort of hormonal crisis. I picked up the three pots of boring old-fashioned pink pearl nail varnish and chucked them in the bin. Then I tipped the contents of the dressing table drawers – pre-decimal money, keys to mysterious long-defunct locks and dried-up, old-fashioned, hardly used bright red lipsticks and bright blue eye shadows – straight into the bin after the nail varnishes and looked at the empty drawer with satisfaction.

'Not enough,' I decided with the zeal of a convert.

Next was the underwear drawer. Out went the old grey bras and the baggy knickers. Anything with holes in, anything stretched so big it looked like a maternity garment. Anything matronly. Anything used to be white but wasn't any more. Anything I could remember owning when the children were babies. Didn't leave a lot, but hey, wasn't it better to have two nice bras in the drawer rather than seventeen hideous items I'd have been embarrassed to be run over in?

The wardrobe had to be next. Off their hangers came

dresses that hadn't fitted me since the 80s. Out of the shelves came trousers I wouldn't be seen dead in even if they *did* still fit me. Into the bin-bags went shoes so outdated my granny would have cringed at them.

By the time I'd finished, I had enough black sacks to keep Oxfam busy for about three years.

Now what?

A £25 Boots voucher wasn't exactly going to replace my entire wardrobe.

Here I was, on a Friday evening, sitting in my bedroom surrounded by the relics of my life, and if Prince Charming had stepped out of the fairy story and asked me really nicely to go to the ball with him, I'd have had to decline on account of having nothing to wear. Where was the fucking Fairy Godmother when I needed her? Come to that, where was Prince Charming anyway?

'Fancy popping out for a beer?' asked Barry, appearing in the bedroom doorway yawning and scratching his stomach.

'Yeah. Got a pumpkin and a couple of white mice?' I said, laughing only slightly hysterically.

'Sometimes,' he said, 'I wonder about you, Rosie. I really do.'

'So what did you buy?' asked Becky enthusiastically.

It was half past eight on Monday morning, we were preparing for one of the busiest clinics of the week whilst staving off the first few premature patients, keeping them almost literally at bay with one hand and setting up our computers with the other. I'd been telling the girls the story of my Friday night blitz on my wardrobe and my consequent Saturday shopping trip.

'A couple of bras,' I said cheerfully. 'Could you take a seat over there, Mr Wilson, please, until we call you? Thank you. And a couple of pairs of knickers.'

'Is that it?' she retorted. 'Why didn't you treat yourself to a new outfit?'

'Have you noticed anything about your pay slip recently? Surprisingly enough, mine's much the same as yours. There aren't any six-figure sums on there. Thank you, Mrs Smith. We're not open yet but if you like to leave your card there and we'll give you a call ...'

'At least you've made the first step,' Sara enthused. 'Chucking out all your old stuff. Well done. That's so symbolic and dramatic.'

'No it's not. It was pretty stupid, really. I don't know what came over me. Now I've got hardly anything to wear and absolutely no make-up or stuff.'

'But what about your Boots voucher?'

They both turned and looked at me. I could see them working downwards from my hair to my toes. Obviously hadn't spent it on beauty products, had I?

'Not toothpaste?' said Sara. 'Not toilet paper, Rosie, for God's sake?'

I sneered mysteriously.

'Please tell me you didn't spend it all on Tampax?' groaned Becky. 'No, sir, this isn't the cardiac care department. Just turn right out of this door and carry on to the end of the corridor. You're welcome. Not panty-liners, Rosie? Not a supply of cystitis remedies?'

'Or those creams they sell for vaginal dryness?' sniggered Sara.

'You're gross, you two, do you know that?' I huffed. 'If you can just raise your minds out of the gutter for five minutes, I'll tell you.'

Silence. Obviously difficult raising their minds out of the gutter.

'I bought a camera,' I said.

Still silence.

'A camera,' I prompted. 'You know. You hold it to your eye, look through it, press a button and you get a picture ...'

'Yes, yes, we get the ... er ... we get the ... idea,' smiled Sara.

'But why?' asked Becky, frowning. 'I don't understand. Why a camera?'

It would hard for Becky to understand the concept of spending money on anything that didn't, either directly or indirectly, help you to attract a man.

'I just wanted . . .' I began. 'I don't know. I just decided I wanted . . .'

Three pairs of eyes watched me, waiting to hear what it was I'd decided I wanted. One pair belonged to Mr Wilson, eighty-five years old and such a regular patient he might as well have had his own chair, if only he'd stay sitting in it for five minutes. He preferred to lean on the reception desk and try to join in our conversations.

'OK, Mr Wilson,' I smiled. 'Yes, we're open now. Let's see your card. Who's your appointment with this morning?'

Monday morning was up and running.

It wasn't until the morning clinics were coming to an end and things were quietening down a bit towards our lunch breaks that I managed to tell the full story of my shopping trip. I'd actually spent a long time in Boots. It's really quite difficult, walking round a shop with £25 in your pocket which you don't want to spend on anything boring. Exciting things mainly seem to come in multiples of £100. I looked at perfumes. I even sprayed a few on my wrists and sniffed them, trying to look as if I knew what I was doing, but within only a couple of minutes I was finding it hard to remember which was which and they were all starting to smell the same. I wandered into the babycare aisle by mistake and got completely sidetracked for a good fifteen minutes marvelling at all the products that weren't available when my kids were born, or perhaps they were but no one ever told me about them. Still, not much point spending £25 on colic treatments now they were all grown up just because I missed out back then. For a while I hesitated over hair colourants. For £25 I could go blonde, add red streaks, go completely auburn a few weeks later and still have enough to do the roots when they came through. Or I could easily blow the whole lot on anti-ageing remedies. Creams and lotions to make my hands soft, my face smooth, my eyes bright and my hair sleek and shiny. But what's the point when my bum would still be huge and my stomach and legs would still be flabby? Who's going to look at a huge-bummed, flabby-bellied woman and say, 'Wow, your soft hands, smooth skin and shiny, healthy hair have transformed you into a raving beauty!'? Unfortunately liposuction isn't available with a £25 Boots voucher.

And at that point in my deliberations, feeling far more dejected than someone spending a gift voucher ought to be, I turned into the photographic section. It might surprise you to know I've never owned a camera. Of course, we have one in the family – it's Barry's – and of course, I've used it over the years to take the usual holiday snaps and pictures of the babies all looking much the same staring cross-eyed at the camera sucking their dummies. But photography's not something I ever got into properly, and looking at the prices of some of the cameras padlocked and chained to the display stands, I didn't think I was ever likely to.

'Can I help you?' smiled a young boy who looked as if he was probably just about due to go up to senior school.

'Er . . . no, thank you. Just looking,' I smiled back.

And for some reason, perhaps because he reminded me of Stuart and he brought out my maternal instinct, not wanting him to feel discouraged on what must surely have been his first day at his first Saturday job, I added by way of polite conversation:

'Very expensive, aren't they?'

'Those ones there are, yes,' he agreed with another of his charming smiles. 'But there's a huge range of prices in cameras nowadays. It just depends what you want. How much are you thinking of spending?'

'Twenty-five pounds,' I said.

Why did I do that?

Why did I tell him that, as if I was seriously contemplating spending my £25 on a camera? It hadn't even entered my head. I was only trying to keep him happy. I didn't even know whether there *were* cameras that cheap.

'But of course, there probably aren't any . . .' I added quickly, laughing, ready to walk away.

'Twenty-five pounds, Madam? Not a problem.'

He was already sliding glass doors, taking out cameras and putting them on the counter.

'Seventeen ninety-nine this one. Autofocus, red-eye reduction, autoflash and lens cover. Or this one here is nineteen ninety-nine, comes complete with case, film and batteries. Were you looking for one with a self-timer? Tripod socket?'

'Er . . .'

'Well, this one's only twenty-four ninety-nine, large viewfinder, low light indicator, includes batteries . . .'

I tried to look impressed. How soon could I thank him for his trouble and get him to put them all back, without hurting his feelings?

'Or, of course . . .', he went on, reaching behind him again into another cabinet, '*If* you could go up to thirty-four ninety-nine, *this* one is really the very best of all the small less-expensive cameras. Look: built in flash, motorised film advancement, wide angle lens, low battery indicator. And fully guaranteed, of course, Madam.'

He held the camera out to me.

I looked at him. He wasn't really eleven years old, of course, now I looked at him properly: he was probably about seventeen. He had blond hair cut very short, blue eyes and a fresh, close-shaved complexion. Somewhere he had a mother sitting at home wondering how he was getting on in his first day at his new job. He turned the camera round so the viewfinder was facing me and put it into my hands.

'Try it!' he smiled.

I held it up to my eye and squinted through it. It was surprisingly light. I clicked the shutter.

24

'Don't worry – there's no film in it!' he laughed.

I clicked it again. It seemed easy enough. I had a sudden vision of myself taking this camera out and about – not to family gatherings, not to take the usual groups of inebriated cousins at weddings and fortieth birthday parties – *Smile please! Whoops, Auntie Edna wasn't looking! I'll just take another one. Can you all squeeze in a bit? Audrey, can you lean nearer to Rod? Watch the birdie! Oh, the flash didn't go. Hold on, I'll just try again* . . . No, I was going to go out and about in the countryside and take proper nature photographs. I was going to become . . . an artist. I'd never been able to draw or paint, but I'd always had a feel for what a picture should look like. I felt a sudden surge of excitement. This was it! This was something I could do! This was something I could become! I was going to be a photographer!

'I'll take it!' I shouted at the young lad, who to his credit only raised his eyebrows very slightly before grinning his pleasure at the speed of the sale.

'I'm sure you've made the right choice,' he told me smoothly, as he packed the little silver camera into a box with its carrying case, film, batteries and instruction booklet. 'Here's your guarantee card. That'll be thirty-four ninety-nine please, then, Madam, thank you very much.'

The deal completed, the voucher and extra cash handed over, I left him to go and phone his mum about his success-ful morning whilst I rushed home to show Barry and Stuart my purchase.

'What d'you need a camera for?' asked Barry predictably.

'Can I borrow it to take to school on Monday?' asked Stuart.

I locked it in my half-empty wardrobe and looked through the local paper for photography classes. No one was going to deter me. I'd show them! I wasn't going to be boring for much longer! Photographers were surely in the Creative and Charismatic bracket, weren't they!

*

'So didn't you buy anything else?' asked Becky, looking disappointed. 'Anything . . . you know. For yourself?'

Who did she think the camera was for?

'Anything pretty,' she added desperately.

'Oh, well, yes,' I remembered. 'Just this nail varnish.'

I got it out of my handbag and showed her. Hadn't had time to put any on, yet.

'Wow!' she exclaimed. 'Bright blue!'

She looked at me with surprise.

'Yes. I'd had enough of boring Pink Pearl.'

'Actually,' she said, showing me her nails – beautifully, and probably professionally, done in Pink Pearl, 'actually, Rosie, bright colours are very *out* now, you know. But whatever turns you on, of course.'

'Nice nail varnish!' PJ called as he rushed past the reception desk during the afternoon.

I'd spent my lunch break putting on the bright blue and ignoring the little voice in my head telling me I was now very *out*. I also ignored PJ, who needn't think for a minute that he only had to compliment me on my nails and I'd forgive him.

He lingered for a while, looking surreptitiously at Becky, who was looking surreptitiously back at him.

'Yes, *doctor*?' I said, not in any mood to watch them flirting with each other, and needing Becky to get on with stamping up case notes for the next day's clinics. 'Was there anything you wanted?'

'Just wondering if you wanted to come out for a drink tomorrow night.'

This was a bit brazen, wasn't it? I mean, he might at least have waited till he got her on her own. He might at least have let her finish the stamping up. We'd never be able to do a thing with her for the rest of the afternoon while she preened and giggled and wondered what underwear she was going to wear on their date. I watched her, waiting for her reaction. Not that I'd ever known her to say no, to be honest, apart from that one time with the lesbian body-builder who used to come to the gynae clinic.

'Well?' said PJ. 'Anyone?'

I looked back at him in surprise. He wasn't looking at Becky. Well, not *just* at Becky. He was looking from one of us to the other – all three of us – even me.

'It's a birthday drink for Henry,' he continued. 'He's thirty tomorrow.'

Thirty. I was working with doctors who were only just turning thirty. How bizarre. When I first started working at the hospital (half a lifetime ago) the doctors, even the most junior of their ranks, seemed like god-like figures to be looked up to. Now I was starting to look upon them as slightly mischievous children who needed to be kept in line.

'That'd be nice,' said Becky inevitably, smiling coyly and looking at her pink pearl nails. Maybe she thought she'd pulled. Maybe she had – how would I know?

'Yeah – great!' agreed Sara. 'I'll see if I can get a baby-sitter.'

At this, there was a pause. I know those kinds of pauses. They're the pauses where you look around and suddenly realise everyone is looking at you, waiting for you to say something, something you've been too thick to think of on your own.

Oh, sorry, is it my round?

Oh, dear, look at the time! I'd better be going then, as you've put your pyjamas on, put the cat out, made yourselves some cocoa and switched your electric blanket on.

Oh, I've just had an idea! Why don't I baby-sit for you! Wouldn't that be fun if I sat in your house all night with your attention-deficit-disordered three-year-old psychopath who never sleeps, trying to padlock him to the furniture and stop him killing the budgie, while you go out to the pub and on to a night-club and come home too pissed to put him to bed? Great idea!

'What time does it start?' I said. 'I think I'll come too.'

*

'I can't get over it,' said Sara for the twentieth time as we packed up to go home. 'You *never* come to parties, Rosie!'

'It isn't a party,' I said defensively. Actually I'd been to more parties than she'd had hot dinners, but they were mostly in my previous existence (pre-motherhood) when I was less dumpy, less boring, and had more clothes and make-up. 'It's just a drink at the pub.'

'But you never ...'

'Good! It's good that she's coming!' interjected Becky. 'You keep telling Rosie she should do something about her life, Sara. Now she's got blue nail varnish and she's coming to the pub, you don't like it!'

Blue nail varnish and the pub are *not* the mainstays of my life, young lady. Never let it be said. But thanks for the support.

'I do! I do like it, I *do so* think she should wear blue nail varnish and come to the pub!'

Why have these two things suddenly become the focus of conversation? Why, in fact, have I suddenly become so interesting to everyone? Could it be anything to do with my unavailability as a baby-sitter? Don't get me wrong, I have baby-sat Callum before, many times, much as I dislike the little sod, and I do have a certain amount of sympathy for Sara's situation, having acquired Callum without really trying during the course of a two-week holiday in Magaluf after her marriage broke up. She thinks his father was on a package deal from Manchester and called either Gavin or Kevin, but she doesn't even hold that against him.

'Can you get your mum to look after Callum?' I asked her now, interrupting the argument about my right to wear blue nail varnish to the pub. Poor woman already looked after the kid all day while Sara was at work. She must have chalked up her place in heaven by now.

'I'll ask her,' she shrugged doubtfully.

'Fine. See you tomorrow then, girls!'

I could feel their eyes on the back of my head as I walked

out to my car. Strange. They never normally watched me like that. I had a feeling I liked it.

'You don't normally *do* that,' said Barry, more in puzzlement than in protest, when I told him about the drink at the pub.

'Well, I am tomorrow night.'

'Why?'

'The fact that you have to ask that question should be answer enough.'

This was too deep for him. Come to that, I think it was too deep for me as well. I'm not sure I knew what I meant, but it certainly shut him up.

'It's just a couple of drinks,' I told him more gently, a bit taken aback by the look – stricken but brave – on his face. 'I'm not leaving home! I won't get knocked over the head and carried off into slavery. I doubt I'll even be very late home; I'll be driving, after all.'

'Not much point going for a drink then, is there?' he put in, moodily.

'You don't have to get plastered to have a good time. I can still enjoy myself drinking Coke.'

And if you think I sounded like a Mother Superior addressing the Convent School at the beginning of Lent, you might be pleased to know that I was to regret uttering that remark pretty soon, along with a lot of other regrets, none of which had anything whatsoever to do with Coke.

'Should be interesting tonight,' PJ informed us the next morning. 'How many patients have we got in Mr McFarlane's clinic?'

'Seventy-eight. Why?'

'Seventy-*eight*? Christ! Why – because I want to get away early. If the clinic runs late, the operating list this afternoon will run late and ...'

'No, I meant why will it be so interesting? What's happening?'

'Well, *you're* all coming for a start,' he leered at us – particularly at Becky, who simpered and stuck out her tits a bit more. 'And also,' he went on as I ignored him, 'I've arranged a little surprise for Henry's birthday.'

'Oh, God,' groaned Sara. 'Not a stripper. Please tell me it's not. I'm not coming if it's a stripper, PJ. It's so degrading, so . . .'

'All right, keep your knickers on – no it's not a stripper.'

'So what is it?'

'Secret,' he whispered, grinning as he walked off to his consulting room. 'You'll find out soon enough!'

'Can't wait!' I said sarcastically.

'Oh – if any of you have got a camera,' he called back, 'bring it along!'

I had to study the instruction booklet first.

EASY-START GUIDE said the first page in large bold letters, followed by a diagram that didn't bear any obvious resemblance to my camera. FIRST GET TO KNOW YOUR CAMERA.

I turned the camera round and held it up against the diagram. Nothing like it. Maybe I'd got the wrong booklet.

'You've got it upside-down,' said Stuart, giving me a fleeting glance en-route to his bedroom.

I knew that really.

Twenty minutes later I'd identified the lens, the viewfinder, the bit that zoomed, and the places where the batteries went in and the film came out. I was ready to roll. I held it up to my eye, feeling every bit the professional.

'Back to front,' Stuart reminded me on his way back downstairs.

'I know!' I grunted. 'Stuart, where are you going?'

'Out.'

'Yes, but . . .'

'Won't be long. N't got any homework.'

Amazing. A notebook came home every Friday with a full write-up of the week's homework assignments in it, all ticked by Stuart, all duly signed by me. When did this mythical homework get done? The age of miracles is still with us.

'Yes, but Stu ...'

'If I give you a ring from Andrew's place, can you pick me up before *Big Brother* comes on?'

'No, I ...'

'Aw, come on, Mum, please! You said I could stay up for it tonight if I did all my homework ...'

What homework? Am I dreaming? Have I just stepped out of a parallel life where I have a son whose homework gets done before he goes out with his mates?

'No, Stuart, I'm not picking you up from Andrew's tonight. You'll have to come home earlier. I'm not having you out at all hours of night ...'

'Mum! You said you'd pick me up! Please, Mum!'

He stood in the doorway, arms spread in bewildered supplication, his face a picture of hurt and disbelief, unable to contemplate the possibility of a mother who wasn't available to jump to his every need.

'I don't remember saying anything of the sort,' I told him firmly, standing up and putting the camera down carefully. 'And whether I did or not, I'm sorry, but tonight I am NOT available to be your personal taxi service.'

Stunned silence.

'Why not?' he asked eventually, his voice hoarse with shock.

I'd spoilt him. It was my own fault. Fourteen years old and he still expected the world to revolve around him. Then again, he was a male; I suppose he was going to spend the rest of his life believing it anyway.

'Because I'm going out.'

'What? You and Dad? It isn't your anniversary, is it?'

'No. Not Dad. Me.'

He gulped. For a minute I thought he was going to cry.

'Is ... everything OK, Mum? Are you and Dad ... OK?'

31

One night out on my own, and he thought we were headed for the divorce courts. See what I mean? It was my own fault. I'd been far too available for him. It was time things changed, before he grew up thinking every woman was put on this earth purely to satisfy his whims. We've all met husbands and employers and serial rapists who think like that, haven't we. I didn't want my son being one of them.

'Everything's fine,' I said brusquely. 'I'm going out, on my own, with some people from work, and I might not be back in time to pick you up. You can either ask your Dad to pick you up, or you can come home on your bike before it gets too late. OK?'

'OK,' he whispered, looking like he'd just been told his life was over.

'And when you get in,' I added, a bit meanly, 'you can do your homework.'

'I'll pick you up,' said Sara, phoning me about three seconds before I was about to leave the house.

'Are you sure? It's not on your way, is it?'

'It is now. I've just taken Callum back to my mum's. I'll have to pass the end of your road.'

'Oh. Well . . .'

'Don't worry, Rosie. I'll take you home afterwards – I won't be drinking. But at least we can stay as late as we like, can't we. Mum's keeping Callum all night.'

'All night? Oh, good.'

I meant, of course, that it was good for her, good that Callum was being kept all night. But I saw Barry look up from his newspaper, and the look he was giving me reminded me of Stuart half an hour previously. Spoilt little boys! What had I been doing all my life, allowing them to get themselves into this state of dependence? It suddenly, and briefly, irritated me beyond all reason. If I wanted to go out and have a drink, I bloody well would! If I wanted to have a good time, and get as pissed as a newt, and stay out all night, just watch me!

'Yes – thanks!' I told Sara. 'That'll be great. See you in a few minutes, then.'

'Don't wait up,' I told Barry as I picked up my bag to leave.

He didn't answer.

I nearly said something about homework, but thought better of it.

The Spread Eagle wasn't a very special pub. It just happened to be the nearest to the hospital. It also had the advantage of having a very large bar – which until a couple of decades ago had been three smaller bars: the Public (domain of men, darts and dominoes), the Saloon (ladies allowed, carpet included) and the Snug (small, cosy, full of smoke, the place to hide in a dark corner with an illicit partner). These days, of course, the fashion is for carpet and upholstery everywhere, piped music, bar meals, and even children allowed in to roam the place freely looking for crisps and play stations as if they were in an extension of their own cosseted homes. Thankfully, there wasn't any of that going on in the Eagle. Perhaps that was why, on a Tuesday night, the huge bar was empty apart from two sullen-looking regulars sitting on bar stools staring into their pints, and a large, ragged and rapidly growing group of assorted personnel from East Dean Hospital. Sara and I elbowed our way to the bar and ordered a couple of lager shandies.

'Is that all you're having, girls?' called PJ over the heads of a group of nurses from the renal ward. 'Come on, it's a birthday party! Let Henry buy you something a little stronger!'

Henry, who looked as if he'd already drunk enough to keep him pleasantly pissed until the middle of the next week, grinned vacantly in our direction and turned his pockets inside-out to indicate that he'd either spent his entire fortune, such as it was, or been mugged.

'I'm driving, thank you,' said Sara primly, sipping her

shandy and giving Henry a look of faint distaste.

I sometimes wondered how Gavin from Manchester ever got close enough to her to get Callum started.

'What about you, Rosie?' continued PJ, pushing his way to my side. 'Come on, have a drink and be nice to me. You've been ignoring me since I insulted you the other day.'

'Oh! You noticed, then? You knew you insulted me?'

'I didn't mean to, for God's sake. Here.' He passed me a glass of champagne, completely overlooking the fact that I was holding a half pint of shandy in one hand and my camera in the other. 'You took it in the wrong way. It was meant to be a compliment.'

'Yeah, well, let's not go down that road again,' I sighed. 'The damage is done. And how do you propose I'm going to hold that glass? What's in it, anyway?'

'Champagne. Drink your beer and give me the empty glass. Henry's spent his entire pay cheque on champagne all round. He seems to think turning thirty is something to celebrate.'

'Shelly-brate!' agreed Henry with a horrible smile, swaying towards us at an alarming angle. 'Got to shelly-brate!'

'I think he already has!' I muttered to PJ. 'He's not going to last the evening, is he?'

'Give him time. He'll get his second wind in a minute. Either that or he'll go outside and throw up, then he'll be fine.'

Bless him.

'You've made up with PJ, then.' Becky had arrived while we were talking, and was now watching the back of his head as he weaved through the crowd handing out glasses of champagne.

'Well. You know what they say. Life's too short to bear a grudge against a moron.'

And talking of morons . . .

34

Henry, surrounded by a group of giggling nurses, was demonstrating his ability to drink from the wrong side of the glass. Unfortunately, he was the only person who thought he had the ability. His shirt was wet with a mixture of sweat and champagne and his face was red with the effort of not choking himself to death.

'Yeuk,' said Sara, turning her back on the spectacle.

'Not exactly your perfect male specimen,' I agreed.

'Take a photo, then,' laughed Becky.

'What?'

'A photo, go on – you're standing there holding your camera!'

'Yeah, come on, take a photo!' chorused the gang of nurses who by this time were holding Henry up between them.

Well, what it is to be in demand.

CLICK!

Recorded for posterity, for all it was worth, was the sight of Henry finally falling into an untidy heap on the pub floor, taking two nurses down with him, and:

CLICK!

There was a good one for the album, of PJ hauling Henry to his feet, posing for a minute with him draped around his shoulders before dragging him outside to the fresh air amid screams of maniacal laughter from the nurses still sitting on each other's laps on the carpet, and:

CLICK!

I was getting carried away with this now, getting into the swing of it – there was a good one of Sara and Becky raising their glasses and smiling cheesily at the camera, and:

'ROSIE! OVER THERE, ROSIE! QUICK, LOOK OVER THERE, COMING IN THE DOOR NOW, WHERE'S YOUR CAMERA, ROSIE – QUICK!'

CLICK!

There, before I had a chance to even think about it, I'd captured the first time in living memory that a consultant orthopaedic surgeon had entered the Spread Eagle dressed as a gorilla.

The evening could only deteriorate from now on.

Chapter Three

Steamy Windows

Let me tell you a little bit, at this juncture, about Mr Ashley Connor. Mr Connor, as well as being a gorilla on this particular evening in question, was an orthopaedic consultant of not very much experience. That's not to say he didn't have much experience as a surgeon, of course – or indeed as a human being if we're talking experience in general terms – but he certainly hadn't had much as a consultant, this being his first post at that exalted level, and this night's festivities being the culmination of his second week at East Dean.

The elevation of a person to the rank of consultant often seemed to change them almost overnight from being relatively agreeable and amiable colleagues to being supercilious and somehow untouchable, as if by tossing aside their white coats and donning a pinstriped suit they'd joined an exclusive club which not only refused entry to anyone below their status but generally refused any dealings with us whatsoever. When this happened with registrars from within our own ranks, who'd been happy to steal our biscuits and tell us dirty jokes and then suddenly came over all snotty and superior the day after a successful interview, it was particularly galling but we tried to ignore it and let them get it out of their system – often the novelty of behav-

37

ing like the lord of the manor wore off at about the time of their first real crisis as a consultant, when they suddenly realised they still needed help from colleagues who might be on their side, and they underwent a sudden and welcome recovery of the memory of their roots.

In a lot of ways, it was easier to bear when new consultants arrived, as Ashley Connor had done, from outside the area. We could form our own judgements of him without being influenced by remembering him, say, collapsing on the pub floor pissed at his thirtieth birthday party. And the judgement most of the female staff at East Dean had made of Mr Connor so far, I can tell you, was: *'PHWOAR!'*

He was (when not dressed as a gorilla) drop-dead gorgeous: tall, slim, with dark hair just beginning to go prematurely grey in streaks, in that annoyingly attractive way that would look bloody awful on a woman – and (I couldn't help noticing) very unusual eyes – green-grey and kind of piercing. He'd already melted many a heart with his disarming little-boy smile when he asked for the help he needed in settling into a new hospital.

Sorry to bother you, girls – is this the right form for MRI scan requests?

If it's not too much trouble, could you give me an idea of the size of the next six weeks' clinics? I know you're very busy but you don't mind, do you?

You wouldn't have a minute to run over to the canteen for a chicken sandwich for me, would you?

Would you go to the ends of the earth for me and back? If I smiled at you like this? Yes, I thought you would!!

OK, so he knew what he was doing, he knew he had us all eating out of his hand, but at least we knew he knew! And, of course, the fact remained that he was still, at the end of the day, a consultant.

'Strictly off limits,' pronounced Becky on his very first day, whilst we were still lusting after his back view as he left the building. We all sighed and shook our heads.

'Pity he didn't come to work here as a registrar,' she

added regretfully. 'I'd have had him then, whether he liked it or not.'

And I dare say he would have done, but she was never going to know now, was she?

Ashley Connor's appearance at the pub that night dressed as a gorilla achieved two very distinct results. The first was that everybody there, (and everybody not there who heard about it afterwards), decided that he was a Great Bloke. Our first impressions had been favourable, and now they were confirmed beyond any shadow of a doubt. He was willing not only to mingle with lesser mortals and buy them drinks, but to do so whilst looking ridiculous. On a scale of 1 to 10 for social acceptability, he'd scored an easy 20. And the second achievement was me making a fool of myself.

'I think he's a Great Bloke,' I told Becky and Sara, slurring only very slightly, 'And I think I'm going to tell him.'

Sara lunged at my arm to try to hold me back as I pushed my way through the crowd towards Ashley Connor.

'Rosie! Are you mad? Are you drunk? Come back here and behave yourself!

Now, contrary to anything you may have been smugly thinking, and anything Sara and Becky were certainly smugly thinking – no, I wasn't drunk. OK, I wasn't very used to alcohol these days, and the second very large glass of champagne which I'd just downed swiftly, far too soon after the first one which had been far too soon after the shandy, had definitely made my brain feel slightly numb and had triggered a temporary paralysis of my common sense, but it was nothing I couldn't cope with. I was compensating for the loss of my reasoning powers with a sudden and urgent feeling of self-confidence. It was amazing! I felt no inhibition whatsoever! I shook Sara's hand off my arm as if it was an attack by an irritating insect, and waded on through the crowd towards the Gorilla Man.

39

'Hello,' I told him without waiting for a pause in the conversation. 'I'm Rosie. And I think you're great!'

He turned towards me. I'd like to have said he was smiling but who can tell with someone whose head's inside a gorilla suit?

'Well, hello, Rosie,' he responded. 'Thank you very much!'

'You're welcome,' I said automatically. 'Want a drink?'

'I'm fine, thank you,' he said.

To my surprise, he took off his head. I mean, you know – his gorilla's head. And yes, he was smiling.

'Now, then,' he said, looking at me as if he was giving me his full attention. 'You'll have to help me out, since I'm still the New Boy. I know you, Rosie, but I'm having trouble placing you ... it's outpatients, isn't it?'

'Yes! The reception desk!' I told him proudly. 'I'm the supervisor.'

'Ah. A difficult job. And you must do it very well, as it seems to run like clockwork. Well done.'

I felt my cheeks go warm with pleasure at this unaccustomed praise.

'Well,' I said modestly, 'It's difficult at times, yes. You know what it's like. It must be much the same for you, Mr Connor ...'

'Ashley, please,' he smiled again.

'Ashley, it must be difficult for you sometimes, I expect. You know, getting the junior doctors to do what you want. I have the same sort of trouble with my colleagues. It's difficult to be their supervisor and stay their friend at the same time, isn't it? My problem is, you see: we all used to work together when Doreen Price was supervisor, and then when she retired ...'

'*ROSIE*!'

I looked round in surprise. People were frowning at me. What was the matter with them? Becky was glaring, Sara was hiding her face behind her hand, and PJ was looking worried.

'Come and get another drink, Rosie,' prompted PJ, who,

it seemed to me, was obsessed with getting alcohol down my throat tonight.

'I'm talking to Ashley, thank you very much,' I replied haughtily. 'Go and get one yourself.'

I noticed Ashley was laughing. It was easier to tell now he'd taken the gorilla head off. I laughed along with him, pleased that he was enjoying my sparkling wit.

'And how are you settling into East Dean?' I asked him politely. 'Do you like it? Have you got plenty of patients? Is your office nice? Have you got your own secretary?' I lowered my voice slightly. 'Some people have to share them, you know.'

'Yes, I know ... fortunately I have ...'

'And the nurses: are they looking after you? I expect they are, of course, because—' here I raised my voice again, to give everyone around me the opportunity to hear and profit from my amusing repartee '—because you're such a *SEX SYMBOL* around here!'

This didn't get the round of laughter I was expecting. In fact, the only one who did laugh was Ashley.

'Thanks, Rosie! That's good to hear!' he told me, putting his hand briefly on my arm before deciding to move on to talk to a couple of the registrars who were hanging around behind him presumably hoping to get good references.

'Oh, my God,' wailed Sara, from behind her hand, as soon as he was out of earshot. 'You are *so* embarrassing.'

'I can't believe you just told him he was a sex symbol,' echoed Becky. 'For God's sake, Rosie!'

I looked from one of them to the other, feeling hurt and offended. You see what I mean? I was supposed to be their supervisor but they spoke to me like this. It was hopeless. It was much easier before Doreen Price retired and I didn't have to try to maintain this dignified stance all the time.

'Fuck off,' I told them.

'Rosie,' said PJ, still looking worried. 'Come on, come with me and I'll get you another drink.'

*

41

'I don't want another drink,' I told him after he'd led me by the hand to the bar and sat me on a barstool. 'I've only had ... two or three ... but I'm not used to it.'

'I can see that. I'll get you a soft drink, shall I?'

'OK. Thanks.' I watched him as he was served with the drinks. 'But I'm not drunk!'

'I know. I didn't say you were, did I?'

'Sara and Becky are pissed off with me.'

'Well, that's what you wanted, wasn't it?'

I stared at him.

'What? No! Why?'

'What was it all about, then? Were you showing off to me, by any chance?'

'*YOU*?'

'Rosie, don't just sit there staring at me innocently like that. You were chatting up one of the consultants ...'

'I wasn't *chatting him up*!' I gasped. 'I was just talking to him, and if you think ...'

'Look, I know I upset you and you're pissed off with me, and fine, if you want to go and chat up the new consultant, the new *Sex Symbol* ...'

'PJ, I think you're drunk,' I decided. 'And I also think you're mad.'

'Yes, probably,' he agreed. 'Look, when I said you were like an old armchair I didn't mean it rudely ...'

'How else can you call someone an old armchair? There isn't a nice way of saying it, PJ. Old armchairs aren't exactly attractive, are they? They're saggy and tatty and all their springs stick out.'

I felt ridiculously like crying, just thinking about myself in this context. See what irreversible harm he'd done to my psychological well-being? It wasn't good enough to start apologising now, just because he was drunk, or mad, or both.

'Well, I'm sorry,' he said nevertheless. 'I *like* old armchairs, Rosie. I really do. Can we kiss and make up, do you think?'

And probably because he was very drunk and I was very slightly drunk, we did. It was only the sort of kiss you give your brother or your uncle or your drunken work colleague, but it didn't go unnoticed, of course, by Sara or Becky or the nursing staff of the entire hospital. And it didn't, I realised as I held onto PJ's shoulders to stop me falling off the bar stool after the kiss had been accomplished, go unnoticed by Mr Ashley Connor either.

'Hello Rosie. How are you?'

It was the Mountaineering Woman from Occupational Health, walking towards me in the staff car park and greeting me like a long lost friend. I hadn't seen her since the day of the Body and Soul lecture, over a week ago now.

'OK, thanks,' I said a bit brusquely. 'I'm rather late this morning so if you don't mind ...'

'I'll walk with you.'

Great. She legged it off at about sixty miles per hour, expecting me to keep up with her and talk at the same time.

'Did you think any more about the lifestyle changes we discussed?' she asked me brightly.

Didn't remember actually discussing any. Couldn't answer her, anyway, being out of breath from the speed of our trek across the car park.

'About doing something to fulfil the dynamic and creative side of your personality?' she prompted me.

'Oh – that,' I puffed. 'Er ... I bought a camera.'

'Wonderful!' she enthused. 'Wow!'

I couldn't help thinking that if she found this as exciting as her expression implied, she couldn't be getting out much.

'And are you enjoying using it? Are you building up a portfolio?'

A *what*?!?

'Um ... I took some pictures down the pub the other night,' I offered lamely as we slowed down to wait for the sliding doors to the outpatient entrance to open for us.

'Wow,' she said again, with perhaps slightly less enthusiasm. 'You must let me see them some time, Rosie!'

'OK. Thank you,' I responded a bit uncertainly.

'Just give me a call ... Heidi Hampton, extension five-five-four-two.'

How unreal was that? Heidi of the mountains?

And off she jogged to her lair in the nether regions beyond Radiology, leaving me feeling an infinitely less worthy person than I'd felt when I got out of bed that morning. Not only was I so unfit that I couldn't walk across the car park at breakneck speed without having melodramatic thoughts about an incipient cardiac arrest, but I wasn't even capable of sustaining a relationship with my new camera. Dynamic and creative? Clapped out and useless was more applicable. I unlocked the door to the Reception Office, hung up my jacket and began idly sorting out papers that had been dumped on my desk since I'd gone home the night before.

'You looked pissed off already and it's only five past eight,' commented Becky, hanging her miniscule red leather bomber jacket on the hook next to my anorak.

Thanks, friend. Good morning to you, too.

'I'm OK,' I grunted. 'Just thinking about photography.'

'They don't open till nine o'clock. Do you want me to go down there when they open? Which patient's photos do we need?'

I looked up at her sharply. Such conscientiousness could only mean one thing.

'I wasn't talking about the Medical Photography department. But which member of their staff do you fancy?'

'New guy called Dave. Have you seen him? Tall, blond, wears his camera in a sort of sexy way.'

How can you wear a camera in a sexy way? I sighed, feeling older and more out of step than ever.

'No, I haven't seen him, and yes, next time we need any patient's photos I'll make sure I let you know. But for now can you go through the ward bookings from yesterday and

44

make sure we've got all the notes ready for Urology while I start on Medical. And . . .'

'And what?'

Becky waited for a moment, shrugged and went out to the reception desk to start on Urology, probably assuming I'd just had a 'senior moment' and forgotten what I was going to say. But I'd actually had a sudden and interesting thought. I don't get them very often and they need close attention when they come along. I'd had this thought about the sexy camera-wearing Dave the Medical Photographer. Not the sort of thought that Becky was obviously having about him, but an interesting one in its own way, and far less disturbing to the equilibrium!

Everyone had been treating me with a kind of amused despair since the evening at the pub. I'd sobered up completely after downing a couple of orange-and-lemonades, and the only memory that stuck in my mind the next day with any degree of embarrassment was when I nearly fell off the bar stool whilst kissing PJ. However, it didn't take long for my supportive and understanding colleagues to reassure me that I'd made a complete and utter prat of myself by chatting up Ashley Connor and almost boring him to tears in the process.

'I suppose everyone was laughing at me?' I'd asked Sara gloomily.

'No, Rosie. No one was laughing. Everyone was too embarrassed.'

Oh, well, that's all right, then.

I couldn't waste too much time worrying about this, or indeed thinking about my future as a dynamic and creative photographer, as I had enough worries with the pile of paperwork on my desk.

'Who brought these in?'

I waved a wad of letters at Sara and Becky, who barely took their eyes off their computer screens and the queues of patients forming at the reception desk to glance at me.

'What are they?' asked Becky.

'Referral letters, for new patients. But . . .'

I hesitated. I couldn't discuss this in front of the hordes of elderly Medical follow-ups coughing and wheezing their way through their booking-in.

'Didn't see anyone bring them in,' said Sara.

And she'd been the first in that morning. So they'd been delivered after we'd all left the previous evening, as I suspected, and just dumped on my desk. Lovely.

'What's wrong?' asked Becky. 'Not been date stamped?'

Oh yes, they'd been date stamped all right. That was just the problem.

I showed the letters to Monica, the Patient Services Manager and my immediate superior, later that morning.

'Christ!' she exclaimed, pushing her hair back off her forehead and exhaling with a sharp 'pff' of shock. 'Who's been hoarding these?'

'I don't know. I asked the secretary; she says she's never seen them; but she hasn't been here very long, and some of these letters go back . . .'

'Yes, I can *see* how long they go back. For God's sake!'

She got to her feet with a noisy scraping of her chair and pushed her office door shut.

'For God's sake, Rosie, we're going to get roasted alive if this gets out!'

If it gets out?

Where else is it going to go?

I felt a shiver suddenly go down my spine, and a strange and cowardly desire to open that door and run out, leaving her with the neglected letters sitting on her desk with their incriminating date stamps.

'What do you mean, *we*?' I said.

I was surprised at how assertive I sounded.

'It isn't my fault, Monica, and it isn't yours. We just have to tell Sylvia Riley about it straight away.'

Sylvia Riley was Director of Operations and a total, utter cow. She could reduce people to tears with a single word and nod of her head, and seemed to enjoy it. Monica was scared shitless of her. 'She'll go ape,' she said now, looking at me bleakly. 'She'll have somebody's guts for garters.'

'She can go as ape as she likes!' I retorted, impatience beginning to make me braver. 'The only thing that actually matters here is that we've got a batch of patients waiting for appointments with the orthopods. I'll get on and send them out, shall I?'

'They'll be outside their thirteen week limit.'

Government regulations are turning us all into blithering idiots. Some of us more than others.

'They've already waited more than thirteen weeks,' I pointed out. 'So the best we can do is to send them urgent appointments, now. And let's thank God they're not cancer patients,' I added grimly.

This seemed to make no impression on her at all.

'You know what Sylvia Riley's like about patients waiting more than thirteen weeks. Our position in the hospital league tables . . .'

'Stuff the league tables!'

I spent half my working life thinking it, but rarely had the nerve to say it. Monica, with her pale anxious face and rows of files on the shelf about regulations and procedures, suddenly represented, for me, all that had gone wrong with the NHS over the past decade.

'Stuff waiting times, stuff the figures, and stuff Sylvia Riley!' I added for good measure. 'There's no point wasting time worrying about it, Monica – *I* don't know why this lot got overlooked, neither do you, but they need appointments.'

'Leave them with me, then,' she said curtly.

'You'll tell Sylvia Riley?'

She nodded.

'And then I'll get the letters back to make the appointments?'

'Rosie, I said leave it with me!' she snapped, opening the door for me and glaring at me as I went out.

Why did I suddenly feel like I was the one to blame around here?

Dave the Medical Photographer was indeed tall and blond and did indeed wear his camera in what could possibly be construed as a sexy way if you were as young and impressionable as Becky.

'What can I do for you?' he asked me in a charming manner which could also be construed as borderline sexy.

But it wasn't his sex appeal I was interested in.

'I wondered,' I said, a little hesitatingly, half afraid that he'd burst out laughing at me, 'if anyone here would give me a few lessons? You know, very basic photography. I'd pay you!' I flushed, embarrassed by his smile and his lack of immediate response. 'I mean, you must be good, and it would save me going to lessons ... if I could find any ...'

'What camera have you got?' he asked, still smiling.

I decided the smile was friendly rather than mocking, and began to calm down a little.

'A quite cheap one,' I admitted. 'And I've only taken five or six photos so far. I don't know how they'll come out. I ... just aimed and fired.'

'That's pretty much all there is to it!' he replied lightly. 'There's nothing very clever about it, Rosie. What sort of photographs do you want to take?'

'Well!' I warmed to my subject. 'I had this idea of taking nature photographs. You know – flowers, trees, birds, animals ...'

I supposed he knew what nature was.

'Close-ups, perhaps. Or views. Landscapes. I've always liked hills. And mountains. Rivers. And seascapes.'

'Well, that narrows it down!' he laughed. 'Not many mountains and seascapes around here, though!'

He had a nice laugh. I laughed along with him.

'So – can you give me any advice?' I added abruptly, noticing the time. I'd taken longer than usual for lunch, and I didn't want Becky getting suspicious about where I was and who I was talking to. Couldn't cope with her interrogating me about the angle of his camera.

'Of course I can. But nothing formal – I don't want your money! Just bring your camera in and we'll have a chat about it. Tell you what, though – why don't you finish off your film first, and then you can show me your photos and I'll see what they're like – see if you're doing anything wrong. Practise the sort of things you were saying you'd like to try – flowers and trees and so on. Who knows – you might be a natural and not need any help!'

'Nice of you to say, but I doubt it somehow! Thanks, Dave, that's a good idea; I'll go out and use up the film and get it developed . . .'

'Even better, bring it to me and I'll develop it for you.'

'Oh! Do you do that too?'

'Hobby of mine,' he explained. 'I don't go in for the digital stuff like my colleagues here. I prefer messing about in a dark room!'

Eat your heart out, Becky!

I was home reasonably early and found Stuart doing something intricate and greasy with his bike in the back garden.

'Has Biggles had his walk yet?'

This was Stuart's job, and one he made surprisingly little fuss about, probably because it underlined his rights of ownership, at least while Natasha was away.

'Yes,' he grunted from beneath the back wheel.

'Shall we take him for another one?'

He stopped fiddling with the spanner and stared up at me through the wheel spokes.

'Another one? What for?'

'It's a nice day. It's spring. The birds are singing and the flowers are coming up . . .'

'Mum. Are you feeling all right?'

'Yes, I just fancy a walk. Somewhere nice. Don't you want to come?'

'Not really. I'm going over Andrew's on my bike when I've got this wheel back on.'

I looked doubtfully at the collection of tools all over the ground and the grease all over Stuart's arms. He *seemed* to know what he was doing.

'Is it safe?'

He shot me a withering glare.

'It will be. When I've finished.'

Only fourteen and he's already got that male trait of being in a bad mood while he's doing any DIY.

Biggles definitely thought it was his birthday: two walks in the space of two hours. He looked at me with astonishment when I got his lead off the hook behind the door, and then ran round and round my legs in such a state of excitement I couldn't get hold of him to do his collar up.

'Calm down, you stupid mutt, or you'll trip me over! See you later, Stu!'

No response, not even a grunt. The bike project wasn't going well, then.

We went to Bluebell Woods, about twenty minutes walk away. It was far too early for bluebells, but there were daffodils out in startling bright patches where the sunlight streaked through the trees, and here and there a straggling, shy little show of late snowdrops, protected from the trampling feet of dogs and foxes by the root of a large tree. There were rooks circling high above the trees, rabbits darting suddenly into their holes and squirrels freezing like bright-eyed statues on branches as we passed, hoping we hadn't seen them. Biggles ran here and there, sniffing the ground and the air, pawing at the undergrowth, wagging his tail, delighted with life and all the wonderful sensory experiences it provided for him. I followed, camera at the ready, aiming and firing in much the same way as I'd done at the pub. The air was cool and bright with the promise of warmth to come. I swung my arms as I walked and breathed deeply, imagining the worries of the day lifting off my shoulders and flying up through the treetops into the sky. If only Heidi the Mountaineeress could see me now! This was great! In fact, this was not only photography practice, it was exercise too! If I did this every night ... or even every other night ... I'd soon be as fit as her, if not fitter. I was doing my bit, in fact, for my Body *and* Soul! She'd better watch out or I'd be doing her lectures for her.

I'd almost used up the film by the time I'd reached the other side of the wood. I came out of the trees into a clearing where, during the summer, there were normally a few cars parked and sometimes an ice cream van. Today there was only one car, in the corner of the clearing between the trees, with its windows steamed up. Didn't take a lot of imagination to guess what was going on there.

The view from here was particularly good on a clear day, even at this time in the early evening when the sun was just beginning to go down behind the hills. I stood back and used up my last couple of photos, concentrating on getting the sunset and the hills and the rooftops of the town in the distance. There. They should be good. Dave might be impressed. I might even get offered a job in Medical Photography, although I suppose they don't often need to take landscapes.

As I turned to head back home the way I'd come, I was busy watching my camera wind back its film from thirty-six to zero, and it was only as an afterthought that I had another sneaky look over my shoulder at the car between the trees. The windows had been wound down, presumably to de-steam the interior after the activity had been concluded, and in the hastening twilight I could see the shape of someone's face turned towards me, watching me. I looked away, feeling uncomfortable about being seen snooping, and for some reason kept the dog closer to me as

I walked back quickly through the woods, my heart beating a little faster than the exercise necessitated.

'Where the hell have you been?'

Barry was crashing saucepans around in the kitchen.

'Walking the dog. Sorry. Didn't Stuart tell you?'

'Don't know where *he* is, either. Nobody bothers to leave me a note, or tell me anything ...'

'*Sorry*! God, I've only been ...'

Why didn't I want to tell him I'd been in the woods?

'... walking the bloody dog,' I finished lamely.

'I get home from work, the house is deserted, no dinner on ...'

'Ah. I see.'

We faced each other over the cold cooker with its cold saucepans, and its cold implications.

'I didn't mean it like that,' he said defensively. 'Not that I *expect* ...'

'No.'

I hung up the dog's lead and my anorak and started rummaging in the freezer for an instant meal.

'I'll do it,' he said. 'Just tell me what to do ...'

'Just put the kettle on,' I sighed. 'It's what you do best.'

'No need to be like that,' he grumbled, leaning over me to fill up the kettle. 'I had to supervise 9F in class detention for an hour or I'd have been home early and I could have got something started. Some chops or something.'

The idea of Barry getting anything started in the kitchen without full written instructions wasn't even worth arguing about. We drank tea in silence, waiting for the microwave to thaw and cook a Chicken Korma with Mushroom Rice.

'So what had 9F been up to?' I asked eventually.

'Nothing out of the ordinary. A riot in the boys' toilets.'

'So how come the whole class was in detention? The girls too?'

'The girls were outside the toilets, inciting the riot,' he

52

replied wearily. 'Something to do with the comparative sizes of the boys' penises.'

Christ. It was never like that when I was at school. Boys used to fight about football teams and girls would have rather died than gone anywhere near their toilets. I'd still rather die than go anywhere near a boys' toilet, come to think of it.

Stuart's bike, in two pieces, came through the back gate a short kicking distance ahead of Stuart, just as we were finishing eating.

'Dad!' he shouted, stamping into the kitchen. 'The wheel's off again! Guess what happened to 9F in the toilets today? Is there anything to eat?'

I was too amazed by the sheer volume of this narrative to attempt a response beyond a wave in the direction of the remains of the Chicken Korma with Mushroom Rice congealing in the microwave.

'They got done for showing the girls their dicks,' he went on cheerfully, sitting down with the polystyrene Chicken Korma tray on his lap and a fork in one hand.

'I know,' said Barry. 'Eat properly.'

'Andrew's sister said Michael Horrocks had the biggest.'

'Put your food on the table. Use a knife and fork, Stuart. Just because we're not having proper food is no excuse to eat like ...'

'Just because we're not having *what*?!' I put in. 'Is that supposed to be a dig at me? What do you think Chicken Korma is, if it isn't proper food?'

'It's nice, Mum,' said Stuart, with his mouth full.

'See?!' I shot at Barry.

'Did I say anything?' he sighed. 'Was I complaining?'

'Forget it,' I retorted, putting the plates in the sink.

The thing was that his whole manner, his voice, his tone, his actions, seemed to have *implied* complaint, ever since my night out at the pub. It wasn't as if I'd stayed out all night, or even come home drunk, incapable, singing rugby songs and reeking of another man's bed. For God's sake, I'd just been out for a couple of drinks. My life recently had been so utterly predictable that my attempted change of status from Old Armchair to Dynamic-Charismatic seemed to have rocked his sense of security; threatening to undermine his image of himself as The Man Around Here. Barry wasn't any more charismatic and fascinating than I was. His hair was thinning and greying, his stomach had gone from washboard flat to washing-up-bowl round, he needed glasses but kept leaving them around the house and forgetting where he'd put them. But we didn't have a bad marriage. I'd seen a lot worse. We got on each other's nerves, but how can you expect anything else when you've spent so many years hanging around each other, blaming each other for things and sharing the same toilet? To my fairly certain knowledge, neither of us had ever yet thought about throwing in the towel and heading for the divorce courts. We were still on speaking terms. After all this time together, shouldn't he have been sympathising with my identity crisis and supporting me in my quest for a new life, rather than watching me with that surly expression as if everything I did was a personal insult to him?

'I'm going upstairs,' I said. 'Don't let the light in.'

It was probably unnecessary. The little boy in Boots had told me that nowadays you didn't have to be in pitch darkness to change films. But I was still a bit nervous about opening the camera; what if the film hadn't wound back properly? What if I got it out and discovered it was still in the middle? I wasn't exactly expecting gasps of admiration and promises of an exhibition as a result of my first thirty-six photos, but if I failed I didn't really want it to be on account of over-exposure by the bedroom light. As it happened, all it took was a swift slide of (a) *the film compartment shutter* and a quick press of (b) *the film ejection button* and the film popped out of (c) *the film*

54

compartment like a pea out of a pod. Easy. I put the film back into its little plastic pot and popped it into my handbag to give to Dave the next day at work. Then I lay down on the bed in the dark and couldn't be bothered to move. For some reason, as I closed my eyes, I found my mind wandering back to the car in the woods with the steamed-up windows. I hadn't been in a car with steamed-up windows (apart from during a heavy shower when my heater-blower packed up) since I was a teenager. It took quite a bit of effort of memory, now, to recall how it had felt. How uncomfortable. How hurried and difficult. How undignified. How . . . absolutely fantastically exciting. I fell asleep and dreamed about Michael Horrocks showing me his big dick.

During the night, Barry rolled over, stretched, farted and started fiddling with my clothes, with his eyes still closed. I lay there trying to remember why I hadn't got undressed.

'Are you awake?' I asked him as he was trying to get my pants off.

His eyes flew open.

'Awake? 'Course I'm awake. What do you think, I'd do it in my sleep?'

How would I know the difference?

'It's just . . .'

'What?' he asked, irritably, moving away from me and trying to look at me in the dark. 'What's the matter?'

'It just feels, sometimes, like . . . well, like I'm just part of a wet dream, to be honest.'

'Well, thanks,' he said huffily, turning over and going instantly back to sleep as if to prove my point.

I got up and got undressed quietly before getting back under the covers, but I lay awake for most of the rest of the night. I couldn't honestly have said what was wrong with me. But I knew something was. Something definitely was.

Chapter Four

Little Robyn Red Breast

The next day at work, I had a call from Trudy, who was Ashley Connor's secretary. She hadn't worked at the hospital for much longer than he had, and had inherited a backlog of work that had been building up since the previous consultant had been forced into early retirement after suffering a couple of heart attacks.

'I've had two phone calls this week from people asking about their appointments,' she told me. 'And I can't find either of them on the computer.'

'Tell me something surprising,' I muttered.

'Both supposedly referred by their GPs way back before Christmas.'

'Letters must have gone astray. Get the GPs to fax over another copy and we'll make urgent appointments.'

'Yes, I have done. But it's getting a bit much.'

'A bit much? What is?'

'There were a couple of these last week, too. I mean, I know things were left in a bit of a muddle, but ...'

'Oh, hang on – yes, I know what this is!' I suddenly remembered. 'You know that pile of referral letters that turned up on my desk? I bet these are those patients, starting to phone up wondering about their appointments. Don't worry, Trudy – Monica's sorting it out. Give me the names of the patients that have phoned in, and I'll check with her.'

'Thanks, Rosie. Can I leave it with you, then?'

'Yeah. If any more phone, tell them their appointments are in the post. Hopefully none of them will complain about waiting over thirteen weeks.'

'It bothers the administrators more than the patients.'

'But who are we here for, after all?' I replied sarcastically.

I wrote the names of Trudy's patients on a stick-it note and took it to Monica's office, but she was at lunch. Her desk was clear apart from two files labelled neatly PROTOCOLS and PROCEDURES. I stuck the stick-it note on her computer screen and went to Medical Photography.

'Here's my film,' I told Dave proudly. 'I took flowers and trees and squirrels in the woods. And some landscapes.'

'Well done,' he said. 'I'll get it developed and printed for you during the next few days. I'll give you a call when it's done and we can have a look at the prints together, if you like?'

'Thanks – that'd be great,' I smiled, feeling excited.

Monica still wasn't in her office. I'd have to phone her later.

'Mr Connor was here,' Becky told me when I arrived back at the reception desk. 'Asking for you.'

She gave me a suspicious look, as if it was my fault.

'Did he say why?' I asked her.

'No. I asked if I could help, and he said no, he wanted you.'

The look was now quite plainly resentful.

'Have I got to call him, or anything?'

'No. He said he'd come back. He said that yesterday, too.'

'Yesterday? You didn't tell me ...'

'Sorry,' she said, not sounding it. 'Must have forgotten.'

'Well,' I said, only faintly puzzled, 'if it's urgent he knows where I am.'

We got stuck into the afternoon clinics and didn't have a lot of time to chat until the last few patients had been booked in at about half past four.

'Is it OK if I go now?' asked Sara. 'Only my mum phoned to say Callum was running a temperature.'

'Christ, Sara – why didn't you say?' I looked at her in alarm. We all took for granted the fact that we worked too many hours that we didn't get paid for – but she was a mother, and her child should take priority. 'Is he OK?'

'I don't know.' She was pulling on her coat, turning off her computer. 'Mum's given him some Calpol and I said I'd get home as soon as I could.'

'You should have gone straight away!'

'It was Gynaecology, though, wasn't it. It was busy. I couldn't just . . .'

'Go, Sara. Just go,' I interrupted her. 'I hope he's all right. Kids often run temperatures for no reason . . .'

'Yeah. Thanks.'

She dropped her purse as she was leaving. Her hand shook slightly as I picked it up and handed it back to her.

'Don't worry,' I said, touching her hand briefly. 'And don't come in tomorrow if he's not a hundred per cent. OK?'

'Thanks,' she said again, rushing out.

Why did I feel like shit? Why did I feel like it was my fault? If I'd known, I'd have told her to go earlier, wouldn't I?

Why did I suddenly feel like I wasn't cut out to be a supervisor?

'What are you doing still here?'

I looked up with a start from working on the clinic outcomes. Ashley Connor was leaning against the desk and watching me. It was just after six o'clock. I rubbed my eyes and sighed.

'One of the girls had to rush off. Her little boy wasn't well. We'd normally have done this between us . . .'

'Can't it wait till tomorrow?'

'Rules are rules,' I smiled. 'Clinic outcomes have to be entered onto the computer the same day.'

'Or what?'

'Or I get the sack, probably. Or at the very least, a dressing-down by Sylvia Riley.'

'I can't believe you're the type to be intimidated by someone like her,' he retorted, smiling into my eyes.

Something about that smile made the muscles in my stomach go into a sudden spasm. Confused, I looked back down at my work quickly and asked, without looking at him:

'Did you want me for anything? Becky said you'd been asking for me.'

'Nothing to do with patient outcomes,' he replied.

At this I had to look back up at him despite the cramp in my stomach muscles. He was staring at me, a lazy, slightly amused stare, as if he was just waiting for my reaction but he wasn't in any hurry, he'd stare all night if necessary.

'What, then?' I said, feeling a sudden heat flaring in my face. Did I look as hot and red as I felt? Had the heating suddenly been turned up in here?

'Just a social call, really,' he said, without altering his stance or his stare even a fraction.

'That's ... nice!'

Nice! *Nice*?!

What the hell was I talking about? It wasn't nice – it was strange! It was weird, it was odd, it was *freaky*! Since when did a consultant surgeon hang around the reception desk like some sort of pervie psycho patient, staring and going on about social calls?

'Anyway,' I said, flustered now, shuffling patient records into a pile, standing up, smoothing down my skirt, looking at my computer, at my shoes, at anything but him. 'Anyway, as you say, it's late, and I shouldn't be still here. And it can wait till tomorrow, can't it, so ...'

'Drink?' he said.

I hit the switch on the computer, buying time, hoping the tiny sound it made would deaden the noise of my heart banging against my ribs in alarm.

'Quick one?' he went on, 'On the way home?'

'OK, then,' said a squeaky, timid little voice I didn't even recognise as my own.

Just a drink.

A social call.

Nothing strange about that, was there? Nothing strange at all.

Strange or not, by the time I'd got to my car to drive to the appointed meeting place (Ashley Connor having gone in the opposite direction, of course, to the Consultants' Car Park which was appropriately placed next to the main entrance, well away from anything unsightly like parking meters, or patients driving around all day looking for parking places), I'd convinced myself that this was nothing to write home about – nothing whatsoever to make a big deal about. Two colleagues, on their way home, stopping off for a quick drink at a quiet pub half an hour's drive out of their way in the countryside – what could be more natural and normal? There really wasn't any need for the palpitations I was having, or the difficulty I was experiencing with breathing as I struggled to unlock my car door.

'You OK?'

I looked up and saw PJ watching me from across the half-empty car park. He was half in, half out of the driving seat of his Fiat.

'Having trouble?' he called.

'No, no! I'm fine!' I shouted back overly-enthusiastically.

To prove how absolutely fine I was, I got the car door open and plonked myself into the driving seat, taking a few deep breaths and looking at myself for a full two minutes in the mirror before remembering that I needed to insert the key to start the engine.

As I pulled out of the car park and onto the main road,

I glanced in the mirror again and saw PJ following me, pulling faces at me. I tipped the mirror up so I couldn't see him any more. When I turned off to the rendezvous with Ashley Connor, he sped past on the main road with a blare of his horn and a very obvious stare.

'Piss off, arsehole,' I muttered as I trundled down the country lane, suddenly alone with the dark sky and my jumbled thoughts. 'Don't ask, PJ. Just don't ask.'

Ashley was waiting for me in the pub car park.

'Nice place, this,' he said, holding my car door open for me. 'Been here a couple of times with James.'

James MacFarlane was one of the other orthopaedic consultants – very senior, very close to retirement age and very much into the attractions of neat whisky, or so the stories went.

'I can't stay long!' I almost snapped, heading for the pub door at a fast trot and without waiting for him.

'No. Of course. We both have to drive home.'

Again, he held the door open for me and indicated a table for me to sit whilst he headed for the bar.

'What will you have?' he asked, smiling at me. 'Shandy? Or champagne?'

'I don't normally drink,' I responded, finding myself smiling back despite my embarrassment at the memory of Henry's birthday party.

'So . . .?'

'Diet Coke,' I said. 'Please.'

As I sat at the table in the alcove by the chimney and shrugged out of my anorak, I began to relax. This was really quite nice. Civilised. Pity we didn't do this sort of thing all the time. Probably if Sara and Becky had still been there, working late with me, he'd have invited them too. It really wasn't anything to get stressed about.

So why was I chewing my fingernails when he arrived back at our table with the drinks?

'What's up?' he asked, smiling.

'Nothing! Why?' I retorted sharply.

'You look edgy.'

Edgy, me? Hell, no, I was totally cool and in control of the situation. I had a drink with a consultant every night of the week, me.

'OK,' I admitted, looking down at the table, down at my feet. 'About that night at the pub . . .'

'I know what you're going to say. Fair enough, I looked a prat in the gorilla suit.'

I laughed, spluttering into my drink.

'No, no . . . I was going to say . . . *I* was the one being a prat . . . I'd had a drink . . .'

'Rosie,' he said, touching my hand briefly to make me look up at him. 'Don't apologise. Don't ever feel you need to apologise. You were charming.'

'I was?!' I asked, amazed.

'Utterly. Believe me.'

Oh, I believe you. If you looked at me like that for long enough, I'd believe you if you said you were King Kong himself.

'So what was wrong with the kid?' he asked, changing the subject abruptly.

It took me a minute of backtracking through our conversations to realise he was talking about Sara. 'I don't know, yet. Running a temperature – you know what it is with kids. Could be anything, could be nothing . . .'

I tailed off, looking at him dismally and realising he probably didn't have the faintest clue what it was like to have to go out to work whilst your sick child was being cared for by your mother. He probably didn't even have a clue what it was like to have a child, never mind a sick one, never mind one who'd never met its father.

'Poor girl. She must have been worried. She shouldn't have to leave him. How does it work? Will she get paid, if she has to stay home to take care of him?'

Pleasantly surprised by this degree of empathy in a man, any man, I warmed to the subject of NHS pay and conditions whilst he listened, seeming genuinely interested, and we slowly consumed our drinks, and I suddenly realised with a guilty start that I'd been doing all the talking, that I'd relaxed in his company to the point of forgetting who he was, and that it was now a quarter to seven and I ought to be getting home.

'Sorry,' I said, banging my empty glass down on the table with a nervous glance at my watch. 'But I'm going to have to dash. My husband ...'

'Yes, of course. I hope he won't be upset that you're late?'

'Oh, no, of course not!' I laughed gaily, far more gaily than I felt. 'He'll probably have the contents of the freezer in the microwave by now and if I take my time he might even have worked out how to open the dog food.'

He laughed, probably thinking I was joking.

'It's been nice to talk to you, Rosie,' he said as we got to our feet.

He held my elbow as we walked out to the car park – a strange, old-fashioned thing to do, making me feel torn between feeling like a lady, and smacking his hand and telling him to fuck off.

'Thanks for the drink,' I replied at length, 'And for asking me.'

'My pleasure. We should do these things, shouldn't we – more often.'

Yes, we should. All of us. It helps the daily grind, if we take a few minutes to unwind socially together, get to know each other, all of us, at all levels – break down the barriers, learn what makes each other tick, understand our colleagues ...

'You and I. We should do it again. Perhaps one night next week?'

I was still feeling shaky when I turned the car into my road. I had to sit on the driveway for a few minutes in the dark after I'd turned off the engine, going over the conversation again

63

in my head, trying to decide whether I'd misunderstood, read too much into it, whether it had been the result of a long day at work, too much Diet Coke and a fevered imagination. Or whether Mr Ashley Connor had actually been coming on to me – me, a married woman, a mother of three huge children nearly as grown up as him. Until my recent clear-out, I'd had knickers and lipsticks that were probably older than him. He was gorgeous. Everyone fancied him. He could have young nurses falling at his feet just by clicking his fingers. It was ridiculous. I must have imagined it. He was just being polite.

I slammed the car door shut and let myself into the house. I could hear the TV playing in the lounge.

'Hello?' I called out tentatively. 'Barry?'

He appeared in the doorway, rubbing his eyes as if he'd just woken up.

'Sorry I'm a bit late.' Why did I feel the need to make excuses? 'Sara had to go home early because of Callum. I had to stay and do the outcomes on my own.'

'I was thinking about getting something out of the freezer,' responded Barry without having listened.

'Only thinking about it?'

'Well . . .' He looked hurt. 'I didn't know what you'd want.'

'Pizza. I'd like pizza. There's a new pack in the top of the freezer. Thanks.'

I went upstairs to get changed, leaving him standing in the hall looking after me, slightly puzzled.

After a few minutes I heard him rummaging in the freezer.

'Whereabouts?' he called.

I ignored him. He'd find them eventually.

PJ arrived early for the surgical follow-up clinic the next morning.

'Where were you off to last night?' he asked me as soon as he saw me.

'What's it to you?' I prevaricated, feeling short of breath again just at the thought of it.

64

Becky looked up with interest.

'Last night?' she asked, radar system all a-twitch for some gossip.

'I was driving home by a different route, and PJ wants to make something of it. Hasn't got anything else to occupy his tiny mind,' I told her as calmly as I could with my pulse and heart rate threatening to send me into a seizure.

'Driving home by the same route as Mr Connor, by any chance?' he said very softly, almost under his breath.

I looked up sharply and to my consternation, found him looking straight back at me, holding my gaze, without a flicker of amusement.

'Mr Connor?' I retorted. 'How would I know what route he takes?'

I turned to the rack of case-notes waiting behind me for the morning's clinic.

'Have you got patients to see, *Mr* Jaimeen, or are you just going to hang about here causing trouble all day?'

'Come on, Jamas, let's get this show on the road!' called Matthew, the registrar, heading for the consulting rooms, and I watched from behind my computer terminal as they loped off together, discussing (probably) the patients they'd just seen on the ward round and certainly not the question of where the new consultant, or the old reception desk supervisor, went after leaving work.

If I'd been hoping for a reprieve, though, it certainly wasn't going to last for long. At the end of the clinic, I was chatting to a couple of the outpatient nurses in the coffee room and trying to resist tucking into a chocolate cake someone had brought in for a birthday celebration, when PJ plonked himself down on the seat opposite me, stretched out his legs and began:

'So ... what's the goss, girls?'

I got to my feet, ignoring him, and gave in to the temptation of the chocolate cake.

'Goss?' giggled Linda, one of the nurses. 'We don't get

a chance to hear any, do we, Hayley? We're *far* too busy, aren't we!'

'Yeah, we're not all like you, Jamas!' said Hayley, giggling back. 'Hanging around here chatting up the girls!'

PJ smiled and shrugged. I cut deeply into the chocolate cake and shovelled a piece onto a plate.

'Give us a bit, Rosie,' he called.

'Ooh!' exclaimed both the nurses together, collapsing with laughter at the supposed double-entendre.

I glared at them and handed the plate to PJ, cutting another piece for myself.

'Thanks. Whose cake is it, anyway?'

'Sister's,' said Hayley. 'She said to tell everyone to help themselves.'

'Bit late now,' said her friend nastily. 'Rosie's had half of it already!'

'No she hasn't,' said PJ mildly. 'I've got the biggest bit.'

'Ooh!' went the chorus again. 'Jamas has got the biggest bit! Ooh, Jamas, show us your biggest bit, come on!'

'I'd rather see Mr Connor's, wouldn't you, Hayley? Phwoar!'

'Yeah! Phwoar!'

They convulsed with silent laughter, looking flirtatiously up at PJ every few seconds to make sure he was still watching them. He and I ate our cake in silence, not looking at each other.

'Seems like Mr Connor has a fan club,' he commented at length, picking up the last few cake crumbs off his plate. 'What do you think, Rosie?'

'Me? Think?' I retorted, still avoiding his eyes. 'What about?'

'What do you think about the sexual charms of Mr Ashley Connor? Eh?'

'Yeah – would you give him one, Rosie?' sniggered Linda. 'I would, Jamas, I can tell you that for nothing!'

'Come on, Linda,' said Hayley, suddenly, looking at her watch. 'See you guys later, OK?'

'See you,' replied PJ as they scurried out of the room, late back from their break. 'She'd give just about anybody one, anyway,' he added to me.

'You'd know that, would you?' I smiled at him.

'Maybe,' he smiled back.

I put the plates in the sink and started to rinse them up.

'Want a coffee?' he asked companionably.

'No, thanks. Got to get back to work. We're short today – Sara's off. Callum's got tonsillitis.'

'Ok. See you, then. Probably pass you on the way home again.'

I stopped, half in and half out of the door, and looked back at him. He was looking at me directly again, and not smiling.

'What's it to you?' I asked, feeling rattled.

'Just be careful.'

'I don't know what you're talking about,' I retorted, feeling myself blush scarlet.

'Don't you? OK, fine. Bye.'

'Bye, *Jamas*,' I said, crossly, knowing he hated his imposed nickname. I just, but only just, avoided the temptation to slam the door behind me.

I was left feeling as if I'd admitted to something I wasn't even doing.

'Everything OK?' I asked Becky when I arrived back at Reception.

'It depends what you mean by OK,' she said mysteriously.

'Why? What's the problem?'

'Oh, nothing much.' She shot me a look of undisguised annoyance. 'Just that in the half hour you've been gone, I've had – first – *Medical Photography* on the phone, asking for *YOU*.' She stated this in tones of great significance. 'Then, second, I've had *Mr Connor* turning up at the desk, asking were we still having to manage without Sara, and had we heard how her little boy was, and by the way did I know where *you* were?' She paused for effect, watching me carefully to see how I would react. I picked up a piece of paper and concentrated on not reacting. 'And *then* I've had Sylvia Riley on the phone, demanding that as soon as you got back, you give her a ring and arrange a Very Important Meeting with her.'

Sylvia Riley. Hmm. Must be serious. I went to pick up the phone.

'And your husband phoned,' added Becky, almost as an after thought. 'Said it was urgent.'

There are times in life when you wish you hadn't stayed for the chocolate cake.

I must have been holding on the phone in the reception office for at least ten minutes whilst they sent some kid to look for Barry.

'Sorry,' he panted at length. 'I was on the football pitch.'

'But you left a message – you said it was urgent!'

'It is. Well, it *was*. But I didn't know when you were going to phone back. I couldn't leave year seven out on the football pitch without anyone . . .'

'Barry, will you just tell me what the fuck you phoned for?' I hissed, cupping my hand over the receiver.

'It's Stuart. He's had an accident . . .'

'*WHAT*!' I stood up, still holding the phone, holding my head with my other hand. I felt like it was going to explode with shock and fright. 'What's happened? What sort of accident? Where is he? Why . . .'

'Calm down, calm down,' he said, infuriatingly. 'He's OK. They're taking him in the ambulance. He'll probably be there by now.'

'Where – here?!'

'Your place, yes. Casualty. Might be a fracture, but you know, might be nothing . . .'

'Fractured *what*, Barry? For Christ's sake! Why aren't you with him? Why didn't you tell Becky to find me, and tell me? Why didn't you bring him here yourself . . .?'

'Year seven . . .' he began, patiently, 'Are . . .'

68

'On the fucking football pitch. Well, screw year seven, Barry! And screw you, too!'

I threw down the phone, shaking with anger and frustration. What sort of a father put year seven football before his own son?

'Stuart's in A&E,' I told Becky abruptly, interrupting her booking-in of a bored-looking teenager for the dermatology clinic. 'I've got to go ... I'm sorry ... I'll let you know ...'

'God, Rosie! Is he all right? What happened?' She swivelled in her chair and watched me heading for the door. 'Are you OK?'

I didn't stop to answer.

He was pale and looked a bit battered and shaken, but everything appeared to be intact, at least from the distance of the doors of the A&E Department. No severed extremities, nothing hanging off at an unusual angle. His left arm, though, was lying across his chest in a makeshift sling.

'Mum,' she said, his lip and chin quivering as he tried to maintain male bravado.

'Stuart!' I cried, with no attempt whatsoever at any bravado at all. 'What happened? What have you done? Are you hurt?'

'It's ... just ... my arm ...' he managed between great gasps of breath, swallowing frantically to stop himself from crying. 'They think ... it's probably broken ...'

'I'm Robyn Dainton,' announced a small, blonde girl with breasts rather too large for her sweater, who was sitting next to Stuart. She held out her hand to me. 'From the school.'

'From Stuart's class?' I asked, confused, wondering why she wasn't in uniform.

'I'm one of the Student Welfare Officers,' she responded, giving herself Capital Letters and smiling pityingly at my stupid mistake. 'I came with Stuart in the ambulance.'

No need to sound so bloody chuffed about it. Obviously

no other bugger was going to volunteer, not even his own father.

'Have you been to Triage yet?' I asked.

'Sorry?'

'Triage. Assessment ...'

'Oh! The nurse in that room over there? Yes, she had a look, and sent us to X-Ray.'

'You've been to X-Ray already?'

I saw the X-Ray envelope lying under Stuart's chair, grabbed the films out of it and held them up to the light.

'I really don't think you should ...' said Miss Robyn bloody Dainty, watching me with prim disapproval.

'I work here,' I told her brusquely. 'I'm allowed.'

'Is it broken, Mum?' asked Stuart, trying to get a look at the X-rays over my shoulder. 'Is it bad?'

'Oh, pretty bad, I should think,' replied an amused male voice behind us. A young A&E houseman was holding out his hand for the films. 'Can I take these over to the light box and get a better look? Thanks.'

I got up and followed him to the light box.

'It's a compound fracture of the ulna,' he said, pointing to the place. 'I suspect it's going to need pinning. How did he do it?'

'He hasn't even told me yet. It happened at school. Sports, I suppose,' I began, and then I looked back at Stuart and realised he was still in his school uniform. Not football gear. Not even gym clothes. School uniform, with a rip in the knee of his trousers and dirt all down one side of his blazer, a graze on the back of his hand and dried blood on his face.

'Have you been in a fight?' I demanded.

'Sort of,' said my son sheepishly.

'Sort of? How, sort of?'

'Sort of fighting, on bikes. Only my wheel came off again. I *told* Dad about my wheel!' he added accusingly. 'I came off, and hit the wall ...'

'How can you fight on a bike? Where were you? Why were you on your bike?'

70

'It was lunchtime,' he said, moodily. 'Me and Steven Porter got into an argument . . .'

'What about?'

'It doesn't matter, Mum!'

'Can we save this till later?' interrupted the doctor. 'Stuart's going to have to be admitted, I'm afraid. I'll call the orthopaedic team and we'll get him up on a ward as soon as possible. How old are you, Stuart?' He checked his notes. 'Fourteen, yeah? We'll get you on the kids' ward, then, and Mum can stay with you if she wants . . .'

'I work here, on the main outpatient desk,' I told him. 'I just need to go and tell my colleague what's going on.'

'Sure. Stuart can wait here with his sister . . .'

'She's not his sister!' I exploded, looking back at the Robyn the Welfare Officer, who was studying her lipstick in a handbag mirror. 'She's from the school, and she can clear off back there as soon as she likes!'

'I'll be all right,' said Stuart. 'I'll wait here, Mum. Is there a TV in the kids' ward?' he asked the doctor hopefully.

'Yeah. And a playstation.'

'Cool!' The pain in his arm seemed to have been forgotten. 'Steven Porter's gonna be *so* in trouble for this!'

'What *were* you arguing about?' I asked him as the doctor walked away.

'Katie Jenkins,' he replied with a shrug.

I found myself hoping she was worth it.

'Don't worry,' said Becky, looking worried.

'I'll get back over here as soon as I can. Once he's settled on the ward.'

'Don't be daft. Stay with him. Is he going to need surgery?'

'Looks like it. But he's not a baby, I don't have to stay on the ward the whole time. And with Sara being away . . .'

'She phoned a little while ago. She's hoping to be back on Monday. Callum's started on the antibiotics so her mum should be able to cope with him now.'

'Oh, that's a relief.'

Poor bloody mother. It was hell's own job to cope with the little sod, tonsillitis or otherwise. But I'd be glad to see Sara back, in the circumstances.

On the way back to A&E, I met up with Heidi, the Mountaineeress of Occupational Health, again. Bad things always come in batches.

'Oh, hello, Rosie! How's the photography going?' she yodelled.

I was instantly reminded that I hadn't returned the call from Medical Photography.

'Don't know yet,' I replied a bit shortly. 'I haven't seen my first lot of prints.'

'Keep it up, keep it up!'

She marched off, leaving me wondering whether she'd ever been a sergeant on a drill parade. Unfortunately, no sooner had I seen the back of her than I was confronted once more by Miss Robyn Dainton, who'd finished doing her lips in a perfect red to match her jumper, and was now sitting with her legs stretched out in front of her, admiring her shiny tights and shiny black shoes as she told me importantly:

'We're just waiting for someone to take us to the Penguin Ward.'

'Puffin,' I said.

'Sorry?'

'Puffin. It's Puffin Ward. And now that I'm back, *Robyn*, there's absolutely no need for you to hang around here any more.'

Unless you were hoping to play with the toys on Puffin Ward, of course.

'You can get back to school.'

I sat down on the other side of Stuart, who was reading a comic he'd picked up from the selection on the table. She didn't move. Couldn't she take a hint?

'Thanks for your help,' I added grudgingly.

'Well, that's OK. But I can't go back to school, actually.'

She sounded a little less sure of herself now.

'Why not?'

Didn't know the way? Couldn't remember which school it was? Wet her knickers and didn't have a spare pair in the bag?

'I ... er ... came in the ambulance, you see. With Stuart.'

'Yes. So ...? Oh, I see. You haven't got your car here.'

'No. Well, I haven't actually *got* a car, you see. I ... er ... get a lift to school and back every day, so I don't have to ... you see ...'

Yes, I see! Spoilt little madam.

'The bus stops right outside here. They're every twenty minutes. Any bus will take you back into town, you can get off at the shops at the other end of ...'

'But I haven't got any money.'

Wonderful. A welfare officer who can't drive and doesn't carry any money!

'Here,' I muttered, fumbling around in my bag for my purse. 'It won't be more than a couple of quid. If it is, you'll have to walk part of the way,' I added nastily.

'Thanks,' she said, having the decency to flush the colour of her jumper as she took the money and got to her feet. 'I'll pay it back – to Stuart, when he comes back to school, if that's OK? I hope you're soon better, Stuart. I'll let Mr Watkins know they're keeping you in ...'

'Never mind the headmaster. Perhaps you'd better tell my husband!' I said sarcastically.

She gave me the strangest look.

'Stuart's father,' I explained. 'Mr Peacock, Maths and PE?'

'Yes, yes, I realised that,' she said, gathering up her cash-free handbag in a fluster, dropping it, picking it up again and finally heading for the exit. 'Bye.'

'Strange girl,' I commented to Stuart, watching her departure.

'Yeah. She's the one we take to school.'

Stuart turned a page of his comic, rubbed the scab forming on his chin, fidgeted in his chair, unaware that he'd just casually delivered something only marginally less destructive than an atomic bomb.

'You *WHAT*?' I hissed at him, making him jump and look up at me sharply.

'We take her to school. Me and Dad. Well, Dad does, and sometimes when I don't go on my bike, when it's raining, when I go with Dad, I ...'

'Every day?'

He shrugged.

'I guess. She only lives down Hillside Road, and ... Mum, why are you looking like that? You're freaking me out! Dad *told* you, ages ago, that he takes her to school!'

Far be it from me to freak out my fourteen-year-old son, especially while he's sitting in A&E with his arm in a sling. I rearranged my features, with difficulty, into the expression of a benign and unfreaky mother.

'He did, didn't he?' said Stuart a bit less confidently.

'Yes.'

I didn't trust myself to say any more. Yet.

'I told you, didn't I?'

Barry's defensive tone was only slightly less suspicious than his refusal to meet my eyes.

'You told me you sometimes give some woman from the school a lift, Barry, yes. You didn't say it was Little Robyn Red Breast.'

'What? What difference does it make ...? You didn't even know who she was.'

'Exactly.'

He looked up at me, warily. We'd got fish and chips on

74

the way home from the hospital and we were sitting in the kitchen eating it out of the paper.

'What's that supposed to mean?' he asked, shoving a handful of chips into his mouth.

'You *know* what it means.'

Come on. We all know the difference between 'some woman from the school', and a tart in a tight red sweater who looks about fifteen.

He shook his head and sighed. Oh, yes, he might very well pretend he didn't understand what all this was about, but I wasn't that stupid. I knew what this was all about; I knew perfectly well what it was all about. He was having an affair with Miss Robyn Dainty, wasn't he – as sure as the sky was blue, as sure as her hair was dyed and her bra was padded.

'Rosie,' he began, 'I don't know what you're thinking, but ...'

'Yes, you do,' I interrupted him. 'And I don't want you to treat me like an idiot.'

He pulled a face. I didn't like that face. It was sarcastic.

'Don't look at me like that!' I snapped, gathering up the fish-and-chip paper with the remains of his chips still in it. He reached out a hand, feebly, to try to stop me, but I snatched it away and thrust it into the bin. How could he worry about his last half dozen chips, when he was in danger of losing his marriage! 'Don't you dare look at me like that, when I've just told you I know about your *bit of stuff.*'

'I haven't *got* a bit of ...'

'*And* you don't even care enough about your own son – you didn't even care enough, when he was lying in agony, when he was being taken to hospital by ambulance, to leave year seven's bloody football match to go with him!'

'That's not fair. I've already told you, I couldn't ...'

'Yes, you could. You should have done! You should have got someone else to sort them out, and come with him. But no, that was fine, wasn't it – that was OK, because you could send him with Miss Chirpy bloody Cheep Cheep Robyn ...'

75

'It was OK, Rosie, because you work at the hospital! I knew you'd be there!'

'Don't shout! Don't shout at me, just because you've been found out ...!'

'Don't be so *fucking* ridiculous! There's nothing to be found out about! You just don't like it because Robyn's an attractive young woman, that's what this is all about! Isn't it?'

We glared at each other over the cod crumbs and the grease stains on the kitchen table, and the air between us hummed with anger, and the distance between us groaned and stretched, until it felt like the depth of the ocean, the breadth of the continents, like an expanse of outer space that could never now be crossed. And my ice-cold heart shrivelled into the torn and tatty cushions of my old armchair self.

Chapter Five

Bun Crumbs of Comfort

'Is he all right?'

Emma had been out when I'd phoned to tell her about her brother's accident, and the message I'd left with her flat-mate had propelled her into returning the call as soon as she got home.

'He's cheerful enough. We stayed with him on the ward till he was running out of computer games and beginning to look sleepy.'

'But they've got to operate?'

'Yes. The fracture needs pinning. He's on the trauma list for tomorrow morning, so he'll be nil by mouth from midnight and . . .'

'Mum, you're not at work now.'

'Sorry.'

I gulped, suddenly aware that I needed, badly, to cry. I was covering up my anxiety about Stuart by talking hospital-language.

'Will he be all right?' asked Emma in a small voice.

'Of course!'

Mum isn't allowed to cry. She has to be the one to reassure and comfort everyone else. Anyway, it's only a broken arm, nothing to get upset about – of course he'll be all right. What the hell am I crying about?

'Don't worry, Mum,' said Emma. 'Stu'll be back out on his bike again before you know it, won't he. Go and have a cuddle with Dad.'

Not an option, unfortunately. We're floating light years apart in outer space.

We went to bed in stony silence and drove in stony silence to the hospital early the next morning. Stuart was already in a theatre gown and was sitting on his bed looking mutinous.

'Why can't I just have it put in plaster? Why do I have to have an operation? When Andrew broke his wrist, they just put it in plaster. I want to go home.'

'It's a bad break, Stu,' I said, sitting next to him on the bed and stroking his hair back off his face. 'They have to repair it with a pin to hold it in place. It's the only way.'

He turned his head away angrily, but not quickly enough to stop me seeing the look in his eyes. He was frightened.

'Come on, lad, soon be over – don't make a fuss,' said Barry.

Thanks. Very helpful.

'Everyone feels nervous about having an operation,' I told Stuart quietly. 'Everyone. No matter how old. It's only natural.'

'I'm not nervous! I just want to go home!'

'I know you do. You will soon. Hey, just think how Steven Porter's going to feel when he sees you back at school with your arm in plaster.'

'Yeah!' said Stuart, brightening visibly. 'He's gonna be *well* jealous.'

'You can get all the girls to sign your plaster.'

'Yeah!'

'That ... er ... Katie whatsername – the one you were fighting over?'

'Oh, *her*,' he scowled. 'I'm dumping her when I get out of here. She can go out with Steven Porter for all I care, if that's what she wants. I don't give a shit.'

'Don't swear,' I told him automatically.

And don't think I'm fooled, son. Not for a minute. You'd give your (broken) right arm to keep going out with Katie Jenkins – it's written all over your poor little face. It's a bastard, isn't it.

'She's a right little tart, anyway,' said Barry while we were waiting for Stuart to be brought back from theatre. 'That Katie Jenkins.'

This was the first thing he'd said to me since the previous evening so I felt compelled to make an effort to say something more constructive than 'Well, you're the expert in these things, apparently,' which was burning the tip of my tongue.

'Boys always go for them, I suppose,' I said instead. 'The more obvious, the better.'

'I had to talk to her myself the other day about the length of her skirt,' he said with a sigh. 'Practically showing her knickers. And love-bites all round her neck.'

'Christ! Do you think Stuart ...'

'No, she was hanging around with a boy from year eleven. I saw them outside the school, practically having sex in the street. I think Stuart's still too naïve to realise what some of these girls are like. Raging nymphos, half of them. He thinks if a girl kisses him it means she's his girlfriend.'

How things have turned around. In our day, it was the girls who were innocent and naïve and the boys who treated us like shit. I felt a sharp pang of maternal sympathy for my awkward adolescent son who just wanted a nice girl to go out with. Or perhaps a not-nice girl.

Since we appeared to be talking to each other again, I asked Barry guardedly, 'Does he talk to you about sex?'

I'd done my bit with the two girls, and had felt it only fair to leave any necessary discussions with Stuart to his father.

'Yeah, a bit. He's at the curious stage, you know. He hasn't dipped his wick yet.'

For God's sake, I should hope not!

'He's only fourteen!'

'Yeah. Virginity becomes a burden to kids at a very early age these days, Rosie.'

He saw the look on my face and added defensively, 'We do our best, at school. Talk to them about relationships and safe sex and everything. There's only so much we can do. Chastity belts aren't an option ...'

'Doesn't he find it awkward confiding in you – you know, you being a teacher at his school?'

'Well, we've kind of got into the habit of chatting a bit in the car. On the journey to school and back.'

I froze. A tableau came, unbidden, into my mind, of Barry and Stuart and Little Bobbin' Robyn having cosy little chats in the car.

So tell us about your girlfriend, Stuart. How does she make you feel? Like this? What would you like to do to her? This? Or this?

'No!' I said, shaking my head, trying to clear the scene, clear the soundtrack from my mind. 'No!'

'No what?' asked Barry mildly.

'No, I won't have it! I will *not* have you discussing sexual matters with my son, in front of that ... your ... that *woman*!'

'Oh, for God's sake! Are you still on about that? I thought we'd established that there's nothing going on ...'

'*You* might have established something, Barry – who knows what you've established! All *I* know is you give a lift to this ... this *person* ...'

'She sits in the back of the car and hardly says a word. I talk to Stuart, he talks to me. Robyn's usually doing her hair or her make-up or whatever and doesn't take any notice of us.'

'Yeah, right!'

'Rosie, I'm not going to argue with you about this, it's too ridiculous ...'

We were interrupted by the ward doors being swung open and Stuart being wheeled back in.

'Hi, Mum,' he said, looking up at me sleepily. 'Can I go home now?'

Barry and I sat in silence either side of the bed while Stuart lay watching TV cartoons until the after-effects of the anaesthetic gradually sent him back off to sleep again.

'Why don't you go home, have a break, and I'll stay here till he wakes up,' said Barry gruffly without looking at me.

'Why don't you. You go, and I'll stay here.'

He stood up and stretched, obviously relieved.

'OK. Do we need any shopping?'

In normal circumstances I'd have jumped at an offer like this and written him a list, but it was as much as I could do to grunt, 'No', and let him go.

'I'll come back later and take over, then.'

'OK,' I grunted.

Is this what happens to people whose marriages hit the rocks? Do they stop talking and start communicating in grunts, like pigs? Part of me felt ashamed and stupid. Whatever the problems in our marriage up till now, and there had certainly been plenty – we'd managed to talk, even if at times the talk had been grudging or angry or even scathing and sarcastic. How had a little tart in a red top, who couldn't even drive and had to borrow her bus fare home, managed to reduce me to this level of grunting child-ishness in such a short time? Did I really believe she and Barry were having an affair? Or was Barry right – that I was just miffed because she was 'young and attractive'?

Or was I miffed because he THOUGHT she was young and attractive?

And thought I wasn't?

'He's out for the count,' smiled a young nurse, stopping by Stuart's bed.

I'd almost been out for the count myself. It's terribly hard to stay awake when you're sitting by a hospital bedside.

'Why don't you pop off and get yourself a cup of coffee and something to eat?' she suggested.

That's the other thing about hospital visiting. You use up less energy than anyone in the world apart from the person in the bed, but you fantasise about food the whole time. No wonder hospital canteens are always so crowded. All the visitors are eating for England. It's the boredom, and the anxiety. If your relative or friend is in hospital for more than a week you have to join Weight Watchers afterwards.

'Yes, I think I will,' I whispered. 'If he wakes up . . .'

'I'll tell him you'll be right back. Don't you worry, now. He'll probably still be sleeping it off for a while yet.'

Of course. No self-respecting teenager surfaces from sleep much before eleven on a Saturday morning, even without a general anaesthetic!

I sat in a corner of the canteen, near a window, with a coffee and a buttered bun. It was strange being here on a Saturday – seeing people, doctors and nurses that I recognised from during the week. It felt odd that they were working normally, in their normal roles, whilst I was here in a different capacity – as if I'd stepped out of my own life and into theirs. I could see them but they couldn't see me . . . because today I wasn't me – Rosie Peacock, Outpatient Reception Supervisor – but just some woman visiting her son on the children's ward. If I were to attract their attention and say hello to them, they'd look at me blankly and try to remember where they knew me from. Which patient, which relative, which case? Was I going to be a nuisance, ask awkward questions, demand to see the consultant? I'd see that guarded expression come over their face, that professional, polite smile, that look that says 'I really do care about your problem and I'm listening and sympathising, but I've only got three and a half minutes to spare . . .'

'Hey, Rosie! What the hell are you doing here?'

PJ, with an expression that was anything but guarded, professional or polite, was legging it from the other end of the canteen towards me. He vaulted the back of the chair opposite me and landed with a crash, nearly sending my coffee flying.

'You recognised me!' I said.

'What? Why wouldn't I? Have you been in for a face-lift or something?'

'Very funny. Do you think I need one, then?'

'Hey! Jesus, Rosie, what's the matter?'

It was the thing about the face-lift, you see. I know, I *know* it was a joke, but I suppose it was just the last straw, what with Barry finding Robyn Dainty young and attractive, and probably having sex with her in his car even as we spoke, whilst I was sitting in the hospital with our sick child, waiting for him to not do any shopping. And what with all the stress of Stuart's accident, coming just at the same time as my marriage had degenerated into a series of grunts. And what with still falling into the category of old armchair, despite the Body and Soul lecture and taking up photography to make me more dynamic and charismatic and everything. It just suddenly all got to me, all at the same time, and all in the most embarrassing manner, mid-buttered bun.

'Here,' said PJ, grabbing a handful of serviettes out of the container on the table. 'Spit.'

As if it wasn't bad enough to be blubbing in the canteen, I had to choke on bun crumbs at the same time.

'Better?' he asked me surprisingly gently. He was behind me, holding my airway clear with one hand and the wad of serviettes and partly digested bun in the other. 'Take a breath, Rosie. You've gone a very funny colour. That's it. OK?'

I nodded, tears running down my face.

'OK, don't cry, then. We can always buy another bun.'

'Idiot.' But I was laughing and crying at the same time. 'Is that how you talk to all your patients?'

'Only the pretty ones.'

'Not funny, PJ.'

'Wasn't meant to be.'

He regarded me carefully as I took a swig of coffee and a few more deep breaths and finally wiped my face with a clean serviette.

'What is it? Why are you here today? Can I help?'

I shook my head.

'No. I'm OK, thanks. It's Stuart – my son – he's on Puffin Ward. Fractured his ulna. He's just come round from surgery to pin it.'

'He's OK, though – yeah?'

'Fine. Sleeping it off. I don't know what came over me . . .'

'Yes you do. Emotional stress. He's your son, you're bound to feel it. Just because we work here doesn't mean we're immune from normal reactions to traumatic situations.'

'Thanks, doctor.'

'You're welcome. The bill's in the post,' he smiled. 'Want another coffee to wash the mucus down?'

'You say the nicest things. But I'd better get back to the ward.'

'OK. Take care.'

I had a strange feeling that he wasn't, for once, being sarcastic.

Emma and Natasha both came over on Sunday. They arrived together, Emma having met Tasha off her train from Leicester and driven her the rest of the way home.

'There wasn't any need,' I told them, pouring out tea and doling out biscuits as I struggled with my messy and conflicting feelings – pleasure at seeing them, gratitude and satisfaction that they cared enough to come rushing home at the suggestion of a crisis, guilt at feeling pleasure and gratitude and satisfaction when they really shouldn't have been worried enough to come. Who'd be a mother? We never stop tormenting ourselves with guilt and paranoia from the first day we stab a bum with a nappy pin or inflict vomiting by overfeeding.

'Yes, there was,' retorted Emma, giving me a quick hug and a chocolate biscuit flavoured kiss.

'You were worried,' agreed Tasha through a mouthful of digestive. 'You needed us.'

'I could tell how worried you were, on the phone,' insisted Emma as if I'd disagreed.

'And Dad wouldn't be any use,' said Tasha with a shrug. 'Men never are, in a crisis.'

I decided that now probably wasn't the best time to tell them that their father and I were barely talking, on account of his friendship with an underage floozie who couldn't even afford to buy clothes that fitted properly.

'Well, it *is* lovely to see you both,' I conceded. 'But Stuart's fine. We're bringing him home this afternoon.'

'Great!' said Tasha with surprising enthusiasm for one who normally treated her brother with a kind of resigned tolerance at the very best. 'We'll come with you! Help carry him out to the car!'

'It's his arm that's broken, not his leg,' I reminded her. 'And you'd better try not to provoke him. He's not exactly feeling very cheerful.'

'Poor little bruv,' said Emma indulgently. 'Thought he'd grown out of brawling with his mates?'

'It was over a girl,' I confided, dipping into the biscuit tin.

'NO! NEVER!' responded his sisters in unison.

'Mm. A Katie Somebody.'

'Bloody hell, she should be so lucky! Two guys fighting over her, and she's only what? Fourteen? Has she been up at the hospital tending his wounds?' asked Emma.

'No. I think she's going out with the other boy.'

'Typical! Poor Stu.'

'Any trouble in the world,' Natasha mused, stirring her tea, 'and there's always sex behind it. Arguments, fights, riots, fucking world wars ... they reckon it's politics or religion, but if you ask me it's sex every time. Causes all the problems in the world.'

85

I always did think that girl was wise beyond her years. Absolutely amazing what they learn at university these days.

We took Biggles out for a walk while we were waiting for the allotted hour of Stuart's discharge from hospital.

'Can we go to Bluebell Woods?' asked Emma. 'I haven't been over there since I left home. There aren't any woods in Hackney Wick.'

'Good idea. I'll bring my camera.'

About time I had some more practice.

It was cold. We walked briskly, companionably, without the need for much more talking, our heads down against the wind and our hands (apart from Tasha's holding the dog's lead) deep in our pockets.

'Let him have a run off the lead,' said Emma when we got to the woods.

Released, Biggles bounded off joyfully, tail wagging, to investigate all the sights and smells he'd forgotten investigating on the previous occasion. I got the camera out and concentrated on taking some really artistic shots this time.

'Mum!' exclaimed Tasha as I lowered the camera from taking a good one of her leaning against a tree trunk waiting for us. 'You got the dog in that, having a crap!'

Oh, great. So much for artistic photography.

We turned back before we got to the clearing where I'd seen the car with the steamy windows. I didn't feel like thinking about it. But of course, the very fact that I'd made the decision to turn back made me realise, uncomfortably, how much I still *was* thinking about it. It had almost got to the stage of being a fantasy. If it wasn't for the fact that Barry and I weren't talking, I'd feel inclined to suggest going out and having sex in the car somewhere, just to get it out of my system. But of course, he was probably doing that with Robyn Red Breast, anyway.

*

'Did you want to come with us to pick up Stuart?' I bellowed when we got home.

Barry was watching football on TV with the sound turned up so loud my ears were pulsating. Why do blokes do that? Can't they hear the idiot commentator above the noise of the crowd? Or are they trying to listen for the sound of an individual boot kicking the ball?

'No, it's OK, you go ahead,' he bellowed back. 'Won't be room in the car. Oh, shit! You stupid fucker, how the fuck did you miss that penalty?'

We left him to his simple innocent pleasures and set off for the hospital.

'Hi, Mum!' called Stuart cheerfully as we walked into the ward. He was playing on the playstation with his good arm and using his plastered left arm to deflect the attention of a small boy of about six who was trying to take over. 'Just a minute, Adam! You can have a go now – I'm going home ...' He turned round again and exclaimed: 'Hey, Tash! Em! Didn't know you were coming home!'

'Hi, little bruv!' laughed Emma. 'Been up to no good again, I hear?'

'Yeah – what's all this ... fighting over some bird?' demanded Tasha.

Stuart smirked.

'Didn't want her anyway. She's a right old slapper.'

'Stuart!' I protested, shocked. 'Don't talk like that about girls ...'

'Well, she is!' he retorted. 'She snogged William Bayliss, David Curtis *and* Steven Porter. All on the same day!'

'Bloody hell, boy,' commented Emma, whistling through her teeth. 'No wonder you were fighting over her.'

'Wonder how she does it!' mused Tasha.

'No sports, no playing around – no *fighting*,' said the staff nurse pointedly to Stuart as we left the ward. 'And he has to come back to se Mr Connor on Thursday.'

'Mr *Connor*?'

'He's the consultant.'

'I know. Sorry, I know. I just . . . didn't realise he was . . . that Stuart was under . . . Mr Connor.'

She looked at me strangely for a minute and then her eyes widened.

'Oh, *Rosie*! It's Rosie, from outpatients, isn't it! I didn't recognise you out of context!'

'I know. People don't. It's like – we're in a different role, you know. Patient, parent, visitor, instead of staff . . .' I tailed off, flustered. 'Mr Connor's fracture clinic on Thursday, then.'

'Yes, that's right, Rosie,' she said, much more warmly now that she'd recognised me. 'Well, I don't need to ask you to phone up for an appointment, do I? Ha ha ha!'

'No. I'll just . . . bring him to work with me, I suppose. I'll sort it out, anyway. Thanks, Jean.'

'You're welcome. Take care, Stuart!'

He pulled a face.

'She's only being nice to me now she knows you work here. She was a right moaney old cow a little while ago when I wanted the football on the TV.'

Can't blame her. Probably didn't want her ears to explode.

From the point of view of Tasha and Stuart being nice to each other, the honeymoon was over almost as soon as we got home.

'Get out of my room!'

'Give me my Dido CD back then, *arsehole*!'

'Haven't got it! Do me a favour! Wouldn't *want* it!'

'You little liar! I know you had my Blue one . . .'

'It was *my* Blue! I had it for my birthday! Get out of my room, Tasha, or I'm telling Mum!'

You don't have to tell Mum, thank you very much, she can hear every delicate syllable already and there's no way she's getting involved. I put my feet up on the sofa with determination and raised my eyebrows at Emma above the Sunday paper.

'Kids, eh?' She smiled at me ironically.

'You'll find out some day,' I replied automatically.

'Oh, I don't think so,' she replied quietly. There was a sudden scary silence. It was scary because it was coming from upstairs, where Tasha and Stuart had probably killed each other over the Dido CD, and it was scary because it was being echoed down here in the lounge, where Barry had dozed off in front of *The Antiques Roadshow* with the dog asleep at his feet, and Emma had picked up the supplement and started thumbing through it at great speed, very obviously not looking at any of the pages, and very obviously trying to disguise the fact that her mouth was going wobbly and her eyes were blinking much too fast.

'What did I say?' I asked her softly.

'Nothing, nothing,' she muttered, turning the pages even faster. Adverts, pictures, book reviews, articles about celebrities having therapy, all passed her by in a blur. None of it was quite as important to her as the *nothing* she didn't want to talk about.

'You and Tom,' I said, daring to go there – to push uninvited into the empty space she'd left in the conversation by her page turning and her silence – because I was her mum and I couldn't bear not to *know* what was hurting her, 'you're very young, and you've got all your lives ahead of you . . .'

'No we haven't,' she replied curtly, throwing down the supplement at the same time as she turned her head away from me and did a quick wipe of her eyes. 'Tom doesn't want kids.'

'But he'll change his mind, Em. He's not much older than you – he's too young to be thinking about children. He'll feel differently about settling down and having a family when he's had a chance to grow up a bit.'

'No. He doesn't want any, ever. He really means it,

89

Mum.' She stared ahead of her, shaking her head sadly. 'I don't know what to do. I love Tom, but I've always wanted to have kids one day. If I wait for him to change his mind, and he doesn't, I could still be sitting here crying about it when I'm forty and it's too late!'

I put my arm around her and gave her a hug. They'd been together for nearly four years, but they were still only kids, really – twenty-three and twenty-six. I thought they'd just been having fun and enjoying their lives, and putting off any discussion about marriage or children until they felt ready for it.

'I didn't realise you'd started discussing it,' I told her.

'Well, you have to *discuss* it, don't you,' she said reasonably. 'It's not like years ago when babies just came along by accident whether you wanted them or not . . .'

'We did have the Pill when I was young, too,' I smiled at her.

'Yes. Well, sometimes I wish the Pill had never been invented. Then there wouldn't be any choice in the matter, would there? We have too much choice, Mum, to be honest! It makes life difficult, complicated!'

But choice is the greatest gift we've given your generation! We worked, we protested, we fought bloody hard to get you the choices you enjoy so casually these days!

'Young women only had one choice, generations ago,' I reminded her gently. 'They had to rely on a man for everything. They couldn't support themselves financially, never mind leave home and share a flat . . .'

'I know, I know – I realise I should be grateful we've got so much freedom. But it takes away the option of leaving things to fate.'

'Leaving things to fate? Do you think that's the best way to start a family?'

'Probably not. But if one of you wants kids, and the other doesn't, it isn't exactly an issue you can compromise on, is it? You can't agree to have half a child! You can't decide to have one and then change your mind and send it back.'

'You *can* agree to wait a while and then discuss it again – in a year or two or whatever.'

'We could go on like that forever. He's adamant. I've even told him I've thought about finishing with him but he says if I only want him as a sperm donor I can't really love him.'

The bastard! What makes him think his sperm's so bloody precious? Perhaps he should stop screwing my daughter if he feels like that! Perhaps he should stick his miserable little dick somewhere else ...

'And *I* sometimes wonder,' she went on sadly, 'Whether he really loves *me* – if he doesn't care about my needs at all.'

'Then perhaps you're right. Perhaps you should both be considering whether this relationship is worth going on with. Start considering it now, Em – not in another ten years' time when you've got so deep into a rut you can't begin to climb out of it.'

She sniffed, blew her nose loudly and said in a quiet little voice: 'But I might never meet anyone else I love. Perhaps I'll just have to accept that I'll never have ... you know ... what you and Dad have got.'

I glanced at Barry, who by now was competing with the dog for Snorer of the Week Award, and resisted the urge to congratulate her.

'Of course you will,' I said, instead. 'You've got all the rest of your life! Of course you'll have a family one day – but at your age, you should just be enjoying yourself – either with Tom, or without him!'

'I suppose so. Thanks, Mum!' She gave me a quick kiss on the cheek and darted out of the door to add her contribution to the CD Wars. However serious her worries about the future were, it was just as important to settle arguments about Dido and Blue.

'Get *out*, Emma – mind your own *fucking* business!' came Stuart's voice, on the verge of tears, 'Or I'm telling Mum, I mean it! Mum! *MUM*!'

The joys of parenthood! Eat your heart out, Emma!

Monday morning. Sara, thank God, was back from her enforced spell of childcare, having handed the convalescent demon child back to his long-suffering grandmother. And here were the same arthritics, the same coughers and wheezers, the same miserable old gits and the same sweet little old ladies, queuing up again for the Medicine For The Elderly clinic.

'*Please* take a seat, Mr Wilson. We'll call you when we're ready for you.'

Sometimes I think we should make a recording of our most frequently used phrases, and play it very loud for the sake of the hard of hearing.

'What's that you say, Miss?'

'You know perfectly well what I said, Mr Wilson,' I shouted a little louder. 'Please just sit down in the waiting area until we're ...'

'Hi, Rosie. How's the patient?'

PJ was smiling at me over the top of a pile of patients' records.

'Very deaf and a bit obstinate,' I replied more quietly.

'No – not *him*!' he laughed. 'I mean your son. Still on the ward? Still giving you digestive reflux?'

'No – he's home, thanks. Sorry about the thing with the bun,' I smiled back.

'No problem. Glad to be of service. Are you OK now?'

I nodded.

'Apart from trying to stop Stuart doing anything to injure himself any worse. He seems to think a plaster cast's a perfect weapon for a fight, or a tool to hammer pieces of bike together.'

'Well done, Rosie. You've produced a normal fourteen-year-old boy!' He rested his pile of notes on the desk and I looked at them with suspicion.

'What're you doing with all these? Not taking them out of the hospital, I hope, doctor?'

'No,' he shrugged. 'Just a little light reading. I suppose you could call it Prep.'

'Prep?' I asked, even more suspiciously. 'Preparation for what?'

'Surgery, dear. These are patients on Wednesday's operating list.'

'So? Since when have you studied pre-op patients in your spare time?'

He grinned, obviously pleased that I'd asked the right question.

'Since I became an orthopaedic registrar as a matter of fact!'

'Really? Well done, PJ!' I told him, warmly, all thoughts of old armchair insults forgotten. Then, thinking the situation through a bit more, I added: 'How come?'

'Nice of you to have such confidence in me,' he sighed. 'How come, is that I've been asked to act up while there's a registrar position vacant.'

'Good for the CV, though?'

'Yeah. Good experience. Bit scary, though. That's why I'm studying these in advance.' He lifted the pile of notes again. 'Ashley Connor may be Mr Nice Guy, but he has a reputation for taking no prisoners in theatre.'

'Ashley Connor?' I asked, giving him a sharp look.

'Yes, I'm Mr Connor's registrar as from today, Rosie. So you can address me with a bit more respect in future if you like!'

'No thanks. Wouldn't want you to get delusions of grandeur.'

'Oh, well ... worth a try!' he responded with a grin, walking off in the direction of the doctors' mess. 'See you around. Any messages you want me to pass on to Mr Lover-boy Connor?'

I screwed up a piece of paper and threw it at the back of his head as he departed.

'Idiot,' I muttered.

'Oh, that reminds me, Rosie!' said Becky, who'd been

quite openly listening to every word of our conversation whilst fluttering her eyelashes at PJ. 'Mr Connor was looking for you on Friday when you were over at A&E with Stuart. Again!' she added pointedly.

'Oh. Thanks,' I said, trying to ignore the thumping of my heartbeat.

She gave me a curious look.

'So aren't you going to try and page him or something? It might be important.'

'If he needs to talk to me, he knows where to find me,' I responded as calmly as I could, not looking at her. I could feel her eyes on me, though, as I started booking patients in, and I could feel a hot flush creeping up from my neck. Surely I wasn't starting the menopause already, was I? That was all I needed!

He arrived at the desk just as were finishing the morning clinic. He leant over the counter, so that his head was very close to mine, and whispered against my ear:

'Fancy lunch?'

A deathly hush had fallen over the whole reception area. Sara, Becky, and probably the entire staff of Outpatients, to say nothing of the patients, were probably straining their ears, their eyes out on stalks. The hot flush was consuming me.

'OK!' came a hoarse little squeak of a whisper from somewhere deep in my throat.

'Meet you at the consultants' car park ... say about fifteen minutes?'

'OK!'

I only dared to raise my burning face from the desk in time to see him leave by the main doors.

'You all right?' asked Becky, managing to make it sound like an accusation.

I nodded.

'You sure?' echoed Sara, watching me closely, hands on her hips.

'Yes. Thank you. Everything's fine. He ... Mr Connor ... just needed to check something with me – about a patient. Can you go through the non-attenders, please, Becky and Sara – would you start on the outcomes and make sure all the notes are stamped up ready for this afternoon. I'm going to lunch early – got a few bits of shopping to get.'

'Right,' said Becky.

'OK,' said Sara. She gave me a direct look. 'Don't forget to get something to eat, though, will you.'

I didn't bother to reply.

I sank down as low as I could in the soft leather seat of Ashley Connor's Jag as we pulled out of the car park and onto the main hospital drive. Glancing fearfully out of the window, I ducked my head and covered my face with my hands.

'Maybe you'd like to sit on the floor?' said Ashley with amusement in his voice, 'Or get in the boot?'

'It's not funny. What would anyone think if they saw me in your car?'

'That we were going to have lunch together?'

'Exactly! I'm a married woman! I've got a reputation!'

'Well, I'm pleased to hear it! But as far as I'm aware, Rosie, lunch between consenting adults hasn't been made a criminal offence yet in this country.'

'I don't know why I agreed to this!' I continued, miserably, still darting glances to left and right as we drove out onto the road and headed towards the pub. 'I don't know why I let you talk me into it!'

'As I recall it, you didn't put up a whole string of protests! Maybe you're hungry?'

I laughed, despite myself. Despite the fleet of butterflies swooping and diving in my stomach.

'Actually I'm not hungry at all,' I admitted. 'Not sure I could eat a thing.'

'Me neither,' he smiled. 'Shall we just cut to the chase and go somewhere for a quick shag?'

I gasped.

'Joking, Rosie!' he said, laughing out loud. 'Come on, stop looking like you're being kidnapped by a serial rapist! We got on well the other evening, didn't we – so where's the problem? Let's just have a drink and a chat, if you're really not hungry.'

Once again, I felt myself beginning to relax. He was right. Where was the harm in two colleagues – two *friends* – having a lunchtime drink together? People did it all the time. It didn't mean a thing. If Sara and Becky wanted to look so prim and proper and disapproving, that was their problem.

'Brazen it out,' advised Ashley, when we were installed in a corner of the pub with a glass of wine each and a packet of nuts in case I changed my mind about the anorexia, and I'd told him about their shocked and suspicious faces after he'd spoken to me at the reception desk. 'Just tell them the truth – that we're popping out for a quick drink. People never get suspicious when you tell them the truth. It's when you act shifty and nervous that they imagine you're in the throes of some dirty and desperate affair.'

'You sound as if you know all about it.'

'Everyone loves a bit of gossip, don't they – especially in hospitals. And the gossip currency gets more priceless the higher up the ladder you climb. Plus I'm still pretty new here, so people are watching my every move.'

'Doesn't it bother you?'

He shrugged.

'If the worst they can say about me is that I had a drink with you in the pub, they'll soon get bored with talking about me!'

I sipped my wine in silence. He was right – people wouldn't bother to gossip about him if they saw him coming out for a drink with *me*. Why would they? I was being ridiculous even imagining it. After all, he was young and handsome and a consultant, and I was ... well, older, and married, and overweight, and a receptionist with blue fingernails. He'd been trying to reassure me, but all he'd done was stir up all my Old Armchair feelings again.

'You've gone very quiet,' commented Ashley eventually, having talked for a while about his previous post at a London hospital. 'Why don't you tell me about your weekend?'

'It wasn't much fun,' I admitted. 'My son broke his arm and got brought in to Puffin Ward. He's under your care, as it happens.'

'Why didn't you say!' he exclaimed.

'Haven't had a chance – it only happened Friday. He's home now, coming back for review on Thursday.' I proceeded to tell him the whole story – leaving out Robyn Red Breast and Barry's possible involvement with her in the car – and was so gratified by his sympathetic reaction that I forgot I was an old armchair and warmed to my subject, even relating the tale of the walk in the woods and the photo of the dog having a crap.

'So is it a hobby of yours – photography?' he asked with interest, once he'd stopped laughing.

'A new hobby, yes. I've only just bought the camera.'

'And you often go walking in the woods?'

'I take the dog there. It's a good place to practise my nature photography,' I explained, pleased with myself. See? I was a much more interesting person now I had a hobby to talk about.

'That's fascinating, Rosie,' he said.

I looked at him sideways to make sure he wasn't taking the piss. Fascinating?

He drained his glass, looked at me again and smiled. Then he put his hand over mine – firmly, very firmly, like there was to be no argument about it – and, doing that thing again where he spoke very close to my ear, close enough to make it tingle and give me a shiver right through to my bones, he added: '*You're* fascinating.'

*

OK, call me vain. Call me a sad, pathetic, silly vain old cow. But the world, as far as I can tell, is made up of two types of people – those who get called things like fascinating on a regular basis, who get used to it right from when they're very young and don't think anything of it, who yawn and groan with boredom when they get called it and wish people would shut up because they *know* they're fascinating and isn't it just a waste of time to keep telling them? – and those who only ever get called old armchairs. Who've never been called fascinating in their lives before and when they hear it for the first time, want it repeated over and over, whether it's true or not, because it's so exciting to even *pretend* to believe it. That's what I did, I suppose, sitting in that pub that Monday lunchtime with Mr Ashley Connor, consultant orthopaedic surgeon, who had no more business to be buying me wine and telling me I was fascinating than I had to be skiving off work pretending I was shopping for my family: I made a decision that I was going to pretend to believe him. If he wanted to tell me I was fascinating, I wasn't going to look too deeply into his reasons. He was making me the gift of a compliment – and who was I to look a gift horse in the mouth?

'Thank you,' I said, smiling straight back into his eyes, for all the world as if I agreed with him.

And from that moment, I knew we were going to be seeing each other again.

Chapter Six

A Burden of Dishonesty

'Did you get all your shopping?' asked Becky when I walked back into work without any obvious signs of carrier bags.

'In the boot,' I replied, smiling at her.

Think what you like. Do I look like someone who gives a shit? I am, after all, considered fascinating in some quarters.

'Two phone calls for you!' announced Sara. 'One: Dave from Medical Photography. Says he has something to show you.' (Out of the corner of my eye I saw Becky frown and pout.) 'Two: Sylvia Riley. She says . . .'

'Oh, *shit*!' Suddenly I didn't feel so fascinating. I'd completely forgotten about Sylvia Riley's demand for a serious meeting.

'She says why haven't you returned her calls, and please would you meet her in her office at half past one.'

I looked at my watch. One thirty-five.

'What calls?' I called back over my shoulder as I made for the door. 'There was only the one . . .'

'She called again when you were in A&E,' said Becky. 'Sorry. And this morning when you were at coffee . . .'

'Thanks a million!'

I was tempted to run all the way to her office, but

resisted the temptation. Arriving late's bad enough. Arriving late gasping, panting and soaked in sweat definitely tends to put you at a disadvantage.

Sylvia Riley was a small, squat woman with wild scary hair and wild scary eyes. If she ever lost her job as Chief Frightener at the hospital, she'd have no trouble getting work as an extra in horror movies. Her office, unlike Monica's obsessively tidy domain that looked like no one ever worked in it, was littered with papers from wall to wall. The papers pinned to the notice board had long since overgrown their borders and encroached onto the surrounding walls, fixed haphazardly with drawing pins, sellotape, Blu-Tak and even stapled to each other to form a kind of paper-chain running down the wall, message clipped to message clipped to message. I found myself staring at them in horrified fascination. How did she know which ones to deal with first? From where I was standing, in front of her desk like a schoolgirl summoned to the headmistress, they all appeared to be marked URGENT or IMPORTANT or annotated with stars, exclamation marks and heavy red underlining. I shivered with apprehension at the very thought of the weight of responsibilities she must have to face every day. No wonder she always seemed so foul-tempered and vindictive. Maybe underneath it all was a heart of gold, a sincere and caring personality desperately trying to surface.

'Sit down!' she snapped at me without even looking up. 'I said one-thirty!'

On the other hand maybe she was just an aggressive, grouchy old shrew.

'Sorry.' I pulled up a chair and attempted a pleasant, neutral tone. No point being too apologetic, putting myself in the wrong before I even found out what she wanted. 'I'm afraid I've only just got the message that you asked to see me. My son was in A&E on Friday with a broken arm and one of the girls had to have a day off with her little boy, he had tonsilli ...'

'I didn't bring you here to discuss the day to day running of your staff and your family!' she interrupted me, almost spitting the words across the desk at me. 'It's up to you, Rosemary, as supervisor, to make sure things run efficiently. I don't expect to have to leave more than one message.'

'No. Quite.'

Sympathy and consideration out of the question, then, along with the heart of gold and the caring personality.

I waited while she finished signing some papers on her desk, shuffled them into a pile, stuffed them into a folder and then, finally, looked up at me.

'Rosemary,' she said, with a huge sigh, and shook her head, staring at me.

I wasn't quite sure how to react to this, since there wasn't any denying that it was my name.

'Yes?' I tried, tentatively, after a moment of silence.

'I suppose you *are* aware of what East Dean Hospital NHS Trust is all about? What we're all here for, what *exactly* our priorities are?'

'Patient care,' I replied automatically, wondering if it was a trick question. As she didn't reply immediately, but continued to look at me, shaking her head slightly with her mouth clamped shut with disapproval, I added for good measure, hoping to impress her: 'The *best possible* patient care.'

'Yes, yes, yes, we all know about that,' she retorted impatiently, brushing it aside like a irritating itch. 'But as you quite well know, Rosemary – or you *should* do, in your position – our priority is to ensure we meet all the government targets!'

Oh, of course, silly me. There was I, thinking I was working for a hospital.

'If we don't meet the targets, we don't get the funding.'

'I know.'

No point in pretending I thought life in the NHS these days was like childhood games of doctors and nurses. Even

101

without the sexual connotations. I wasn't particularly politically minded but as far as the Health Service was concerned the lunatics had taken over the asylum several general elections ago and things had gone from daft to ridiculous to impossible with every successive government plan.

'You say you know – but do you *care*?' demanded Sylvia Riley.

This was the point at which I changed tactics. Not deliberately, you understand – not as a conscious decision but because she'd seriously pissed me off. I could put up with her being a moody old cow, I could accept her being unapproachable, unsympathetic and unpleasant, and still retain the polite, deferential air of a subordinate who senses they're in trouble without knowing what the hell they've done. But I was *not* going to stand there and listen to her – her of all people – suggest that I was *uncaring*.

'That's not fair!' I shot back at her, having the satisfaction of seeing her blink with surprise. 'Of course I care! I care about my job and I do it well.'

'Perhaps you do,' she returned calmly.

'What's that supposed to mean? What have I done wrong?'

She lifted another buff folder from a tray on her desk and opened it. Out of its depths, like a conjurer producing a rabbit, she took a pile of papers. I recognised them immediately as the out-of-date referral letters I'd left with Monica.

'Oh! I see what this is all about! Why didn't you say!' I exclaimed with relief. Was this all? I thought it was going to be something really serious.

'So you admit you knew about these letters?'

'Yes, of course. I expect Monica told you it was me that found them ...'

'Monica has gone on Long Term Sick Leave,' said Sylvia Riley with a tone of such dramatic finality that I had a horrible half second of dread that she was going to tell me she'd died.

102

'Oh!' So that was why I hadn't seen her in her office for a while. 'That was a bit sudden – I didn't know she was ill,' I added.

'Yes.'

OK, I supposed it was none of my business what was wrong with her. Just when I needed her to back me up: typical!

'But she did tell you about them, obviously,' I added, suddenly feeling that chill running up my spine again.

'The letters,' said Sylvia Riley, ignoring this and looking daggers at me over the top of her glasses, 'were in an envelope. An internal envelope, Rosemary, sent to me in the internal post. By somebody who knew they were over the thirteen weeks maximum wait to meet the government's target for outpatient appointments. Somebody who knew it was serious – *very serious*, Rosemary – and who didn't even have the decency to let anyone know. Somebody who didn't even have the courtesy to put their name on the envelope or a note inside ...'

'Well, that person wasn't me!' I retorted, getting to my feet, glaring at her across the desk. I was not that sort of person! How dare she sit there, behind her desk, behind her glasses, throwing insults at me – implying that I wouldn't even have the balls to own up to finding a few letters that were a little bit outside some silly arbitrary deadline that everyone knew was meaningless? 'I'm not spineless and pathetic like some of the people you seem to think so highly of!' I stopped abruptly, realising I was describing Monica – perhaps unfairly now that she'd suddenly gone off Long Term Sick.

And, sitting back down with a thump of my old tired bones and a screech of the metal chair on the polished floor, I realised with complete clarity that I only had two choices here: drop Long Term Sick Monica straight into the shit, where she doubtless belonged in this particular instance but where she'd haunt me all through my nightmares with visions of her suffering from some unspeakable

103

incurable debilitating illness and on top of that, enduring the taint of guilt, or even worse the threat of dismissal from her job, for sending Sylvia Riley an anonymous brown internal envelope containing incriminating referral letters. Or I could plead ignorance.

'I've got no idea,' I said, pleading ignorance, 'how the letters got in that envelope, how they got to your desk, or who sent them. I found them on my desk – and I don't know who left them there, either.' That much was true, anyway.

'I find that hard to believe,' she said stonily.

'Well,' I responded heatedly – immediately pissed off again, 'I can't help how hard you find it! Let's be honest, *Ms* Riley, all that matters now is that the patients should be sent urgent appointments, and let's be grateful,' I found myself repeating what I'd said to Monica, without much hope of it having any more effect, 'that they're not cancer patients!'

'That is *not* the point.' Not to some of us, apparently. 'I'm not impressed with this, Rosemary. Not impressed at all. In future, if you find something like this, get *straight* on the phone to me – do you understand?'

Only too well, unfortunately. I nodded, cursing Monica and her Long Term Sickness inside my head.

Can I go now, teacher, now I've had my telling-off? But hang on, there was more:

'We need to find a way of dealing with this situation, now, Rosemary. The best way we can of dealing with it.'

'Certainly. I'll make the appointments right now, this afternoon, and send them out first-class ...'

She sighed as if I was a particularly stupid child.

'I *mean*, the ... unfortunate date stamps on the letters.' She hesitated, looking at me over her glasses again. 'If these letters had gone astray in the post, of course, and we had to ask the GPs to send us duplicate letters about the patients now – it wouldn't be a problem.'

'But they didn't go astray in the post.' You see? I *was* a particularly stupid child, wasn't I?

104

'But perhaps they did,' insisted Sylvia Riley sharply. 'Perhaps you could phone the GPs today and sort this out, Rosemary.'

'Are you asking me to ...?' I began, horrified.

'I'm asking you,' she replied in very measured tones, 'to sort out a problem which was your fault in the first place. And perhaps then we'll say no more about it. Is that clear, Rosemary?'

Clear as air. Clear as water. Clear as cold, hard, ice. As cold and hard as the feeling in my heart. In return for keeping the heat off Mousey Monica, safe at home with her Long Term Sickness, I was paying the price not only of presumed guilt but also of the weight of a burden of dishonesty. Oh, I didn't mind telling the occasional little lie, in the interests of a quiet life. I wasn't averse to a bending of facts, sometimes, into shapes that fitted my convenience. But this? It was lying unnecessarily, and it was lying at someone else's command. It stunk.

'What's the matter?' asked Barry the fifth time I changed channels.

It wasn't often I won the battle for possession of the TV remote, and when I did I normally hung on for dear life to any programme I could find that didn't look like football. Tonight, though, because I couldn't settle, I was flicking from University Challenge to EastEnders to a documentary about the police and back to University Challenge again like a tourist trying to cram in as much British culture as possible in a half hour of prime time TV.

'Nothing,' I muttered, switching back to EastEnders and pretending to watch its closing minutes with avid attention. Barry and I had gone back to communicating only at the most basic level – the level required for survival, i.e. food, drink and shelter. I cooked the food and put it in front of him, he poured out the drinks and handed them to me, one of us locked the front door at night and the other one made sure they'd done it – each sequence of actions accompanied by an appropriate exchange of grunts. Instigating a conversation about my channel flicking and its possible root in what was the matter with me was a sudden, startling departure from this and I wasn't sure whether I was ready for it.

'You're not really watching this,' he said, his hand poised to reach over and grab the remote control. 'If you don't want to watch it, I'll have the football on, on Sky.'

Oh no you won't, sunshine. I want, badly, to watch this documentary just starting, about the decline of Britain's aristocracy. Sounds like just the sort of thing I'd need to know about.

'I am watching it,' I said, gripping the remote control firmly. 'And since when have we been back on speaking terms?'

'Speaking terms?' He looked at me with genuine surprise. 'Have we not been speaking?'

I suppose that says it all, really.

'What's the matter, Mum?' asked Stuart. He was lying on the kitchen floor, using his plastered arm as a bat to knock a ball to the dog, who watched him with startled confusion. 'Come on Biggles! Come on, boy! Catch!'

'He doesn't want to play,' I said, mildly, spooning coffee into mugs. 'He thinks you're crazy. There isn't a place in the Guinness Book of Records for the most uses for a plaster cast on the arm, you know.'

'Pity! That'd be cool!' He sat up and looked at me again. 'So what's the matter?'

Comes to something when even a fourteen-year-old boy notices.

'Nothing much. Just a bad day at work.'

'Thought so. Either that or whatsit-called. PMD.'

'PMT,' I smiled. 'And what would you know about it?'

'Dad told me.'

I carried the coffee mugs into the lounge. Barry had seized control of the remote, the minute I got up, changed channels to the football and was watching it nonchalantly as if it had suddenly appeared on the screen without his knowledge or permission.

'What do you know about PMT?' I asked in what I hoped was a deceptively pleasant voice, putting a mug down in front of him with a thud.

'Eh? I dunno – never get a chance to watch telly in the mornings.'

'I didn't say GMT. I said PMT. What have you told Stuart about it, from your vast experience?'

He looked up warily.

'Can't remember. Probably he just asked me a few questions and I told him what I thought he needed to know.'

'Well, I don't suffer from it, OK? You've known me for over twenty-five years, and in that time I've never suffered from it. If I'm upset, or I'm in a bad mood, it's got nothing to do with my hormones, OK? It's because I've got a *reason* to be upset. So please don't tell Stuart stuff you know nothing about.'

'Well, if you'd *tell* me the reason you're upset . . .!'

'I've just had a bad day at work. If *you* have a bad day at work, do you want to come home and talk about it? No, you just want to sit in front of the football and fall asleep,' I said, a bit unfairly I suppose in view of the fact that I'd refused to let him watch it. 'So can I please just be left to have my bad mood in peace, without everybody wanting to accuse me of hormonal imbalance?'

'Suit yourself,' said Barry with a shrug, picking up his coffee. He took a mouthful and spluttered it back into the mug. 'It's cold! You didn't boil the water!'

Shit. Must be my hormones.

'What's the matter, Rosie?' asked PJ the next morning.

I'd hardly even got out of my car. He was waiting for me to catch him up and walk across from the car park with him.

'Do I look that bad? Everyone keeps asking me what the matter is.'

'I didn't say you look bad. Just preoccupied. Worried.'

'Well, congratulations, doctor, your diagnosis is spot-on.'

'Want to talk about it, or want to tell me to piss off and mind my own business?'

I hesitated. The temptation to tell somebody was overwhelming, but I wasn't sure how likely PJ was to spread the gossip.

'I shouldn't really tell anyone,' I began, looking over my shoulder.

'You're involved in a bank robbery? You're pregnant by Michael Jackson? What? You're looking very shifty, Rosie. No one's going to creep up on you in the hospital car park and arrest you. If they do, I'll hit them with my stethoscope.'

'Thank you.' I smiled weakly. 'Perhaps I'm just being silly – over-reacting. But I don't like being asked to do something ... *immoral* ...'

'So it *is* Michael Jackson!'

'PJ! Please! This is serious!'

'Sorry.' He gave me a naughty puppy look. 'Come on, then, I won't tell anyone. I promise.'

'It's Sylvia Riley. I seem to have got myself into trouble with her without even doing anything wrong.'

By the time we'd walked to the hospital entrance, I'd given him a brief synopsis of the situation, including how I'd covered up for Long Term Sick Monica.

'You're mad,' he said quite affably. 'You should have split on her and left her to fight her own battles. I bet she gets paid a lot more than you do, for taking the strain.'

'Yes, but I don't think she *can* take it. That's probably why she's off sick.'

'Not your problem, Rosie.'

'Fine – but what do I do now? Phone these GPs and pretend we didn't get the original referral letters? We're not just talking about half a dozen – there's a stack of them! I don't feel comfortable about it, but ...'

'Then you shouldn't have to do it!' PJ exclaimed, more angrily than I was expecting. 'You're quite right, it's *bloody* immoral and it's *not* right for Sylvia Riley to expect you to do her dirty work for her!'

'I don't know what else I can do, now. At the end of the day, she's the boss.'

As he opened the door for me, I glanced at his face and was surprised to see how hard he was frowning.

'Don't do anything you're uncomfortable with,' he told me quietly. 'Think about it, Rosie – you've got to live with yourself, and go on doing your job. It's OK for her – she's washed her hands of it. Devious cow.'

I watched him stride off in the direction of the orthopaedic wards and realised I didn't feel any better for confiding in someone. PJ was right. I had to live with myself, and ultimately I was the only one who could decide what to do.

By lunchtime, I still hadn't stopped worrying, and I still hadn't done anything about the letters, which were sitting in their buff folder in a locked drawer of my desk.

'I'm going to lunch,' I told the girls at twelve-thirty, before they had a chance to ask me what I was worried about. I'd seen them looking at each other and raising their eyebrows in my direction all morning. I know all about that sort of eyebrow raising. My daughters and I used to indulge in it all the time when they lived at home.

'Going out *shopping* again?' asked Becky with an unnatural emphasis.

'No. Just popping over to Medical Photography,' I replied calmly. I then felt so stricken with remorse by the look of anguish on her face that I felt obliged to add quickly, 'Purely on business. No pleasure involved whatsoever. Do you want me to give Dave any messages for you?'

'Like what?' she asked, pouting.

'Your phone number?' I suggested.

'Already given it to him,' she retorted, to my surprise.

109

'And he hasn't even bothered to call me.'

So it's true, then – you can't win 'em all!

'Maybe he's gay,' suggested Sara kindly.

'There you are! Not bad for a beginner!' said Dave cheerfully, spreading my photographs out over a desk and standing back so I could look at them. 'Who's the plonker in the gorilla suit?'

'Mr Connor. He's not a plonker, he was just being a good sport,' I admonished him. And what was this? Me sticking up for him, defending the ape-man?

'Looks like *he* was being a good sport, too!' smiled Dave, pointing at the picture of Henry collapsing into a pool of nurses.

'It was a bit of a night,' I agreed.

'They've come out well,' Dave said. 'And I specially liked your nature shots. Next time, you might try experimenting more with light and shade. Get some different angles – looking straight down on flowers from above, looking between branches of trees – try to be original. Don't always have your subject in the centre of the picture.'

'You're a bit of an artist on the quiet, aren't you,' I commented, looking at him with renewed interest and wondering whether Sara was right about him being gay. 'How come you're working in such a scientific field?'

'Difficult to get good jobs in photography – unless you set up your own business. That's what I'd like to do, one day.'

'You won't earn enough to do that while you're working for the NHS.'

'Tell me about it!' He started gathering up my photos and putting them into an envelope. 'Anyway, Rosie, well done – your first lot of prints are really good. Bring me your next film when it's finished!'

'Sure you don't mind?' I thought about the next film. 'Can you do anything about a dog crapping in the foreground of a good picture?'

He laughed. 'Yes, probably! If it's only on one edge, I can crop the photo before I print it. It's easy. I did it on some of these prints – cut out a litter-bin you got in the foreground of one shot, and part of a car on the edge of another one. And someone's arm in one of those pictures in the pub.'

'So you do some editorial work too!'

'Yeah – we all like to play God a bit, don't we!' he laughed.

I turned to go.

'Oh, Rosie,' he called after me. 'Your negatives – sorry, I left them at home. I'll bring them in . . .'

'OK, no rush. I won't be needing them.'

'Right. Say hello to Becky for me, then!'

I looked back at him and he winked, a definite twinkle in his eye. So maybe not gay after all?

I stayed late that evening. I didn't actually do anything – I just kept opening my drawer, taking out the folder of referral letters and looking at them. Twice I got as far as booking appointments on the computer for the first couple of patients, but then I chickened out and cancelled them. Twice I dialled the number of the first patient's GP, to pretend I was investigating a referral letter that had gone astray – but both times I hung up. I couldn't do what I should have done and wanted to do, and I couldn't do what Sylvia Riley wanted me to do either. I rested my head in my hands and stared at the desk. Was I going to spend the rest of my life dithering pathetically like this?

'Is it that bad?' asked a familiar voice, familiarly close to my ear, making me jump.

'Yes,' I admitted abruptly. I closed down the computer and stood up to get my coat. Not much point sitting here the rest of the night if I was going to dither pathetically. Might as well dither pathetically at home, where nobody took any notice of me.

111

'Want to talk about it?' asked Ashley, watching me. 'Over a drink perhaps?'

When you've been married for the best part of forever, to someone who barely notices whether you're there or not unless you're putting a plate of hot stew in front of them, there's something very tempting about a suggestion of talk over a drink, with the prospect of actually being listened to. So tempting, I could quite understand people turning their backs on home and family for it. I looked at my watch. Home and family could wait a little longer, and probably still not miss me. And anyway – hadn't I already decided I was going to be brazen, as well as fascinating, in future if the opportunity arose?

'OK,' I said, putting on my coat and following him out of the building. 'Usual place?'

We weren't a couple, we weren't even having an affair, but we already had a usual place. At this rate we'd have a song, an anniversary and a whole album full of memories before we'd even found out what each other's middle names and star signs were.

'What's your middle name?' I asked him as we settled down at our *usual* table. 'And what star sign are you?'

'What's this?' He looked mildly amused. 'Some sort of compatibility test?'

'No!' I fidgeted uneasily in my seat. Compatibility? Since when did you need compatibility to have a drink after work with a colleague? 'No, I just realised we hardly know anything about each other.'

'Don't we? Well, we both know quite a bit about each other's jobs. We know what cars we drive, and what we like to drink. That's a start, isn't it?' He smiled and then added as an afterthought, 'And hobbies – I know, for instance, that you like photography.'

'Oh yes. I forgot I'd told you about that.'

'You must show me some of your photos, some time.'

'Why?' Well – be fair! Why all the sudden interest in my

photos? I really preferred it when he was on about *me* being fascinating, rather than just my interest in photography.

'You took some at Henry's party, at the pub, didn't you. I haven't seen a picture of myself as a gorilla recently.'

Ah. Right. Like most men, I suppose – can't resist a photo of himself.

'I've just had them developed, actually. They're not bad.' I rummaged in my bag. 'Left them at work. I'll show you tomorrow – remind me.'

'I will.'

'And what about you? Do you have time for any hobbies?'

'I do a bit of amateur dramatics.'

'Ah! That explains the . . .'

'Gorilla outfit, yes. From a pantomime at my last hospital. Most people tend not to have them hanging in the wardrobe!' He paused. 'But apart from that – I suppose my only hobby is people. Getting to know them. Enjoying a quiet drink with someone I like. Like this.'

I felt an urgent need to finish the rest of my drink without looking at him. I could feel his eyes on me, but I didn't want to look up in case they were saying anything I was afraid of seeing, afraid of responding to.

'So – there you have it!' he said at length with a laugh. 'We do know quite a bit about each other – don't we. But just for the record, it's Capricorn. And Edward.'

'Thank you,' I smiled. 'Mine's Cancer. And Ann.'

'Well. Now we've cleared that up . . .' To my great surprise and consternation, he took hold of my hand across the table. 'What is it that had you worried enough to stay late at work and sit with your head in your hands looking like the world was coming to an end?'

For what seemed like about half an hour, I looked at his hand holding mine on the pub table. I couldn't say anything; I tried, I even moved my lips and pushed hard from the back of my throat so that a noise of some description might come out even if it wasn't a recognisable English word, but it was no good, I'd been struck dumb and senseless at the same time. Senseless because the only thing I could think, the only thought that kept bouncing around in my head was that this changed everything. A hand holding a hand – a simple gesture of comfort, friendship, support, call it what you like – and I'd divorced it from reality and imbued it with such completely illogical significance in my own mind that all I could do was stare at it as if it belonged to someone else – not my hand being held, not Ashley Connor's hand doing the holding but some alien hands that just happened to be lying in front of us on the pub table. Then his hand suddenly gave mine a squeeze, surprising me so much that I almost flinched, and he repeated:

'What is it? Are you going to tell me?'

And, partly because it was still bothering me enough to want to talk about it to somebody, anybody, who might listen and understand, and partly because everything was now changed for ever because of those two strange hands lying in front of me, I once again poured out a brief résumé of the Story of Sylvia Riley and the Late Referral Letters.

Ashley listened intently until I'd finished. In the silence that followed, he sighed, shook his head, collected up our glasses and went to the bar for another round of drinks. It wasn't until he'd sat back down again, had a mouthful of his drink and *resumed the holding of my hand* – which had become so sweaty during the previous hand-holding, I'd had to wipe it quickly on my coat while he was at the bar – that he finally commented:

'This is all very disturbing. *Very* disturbing.'

I waited. Disturbing was all very well and good, but it didn't do much to reassure me, or to point me in the right direction next time I was sitting at my desk staring at the buff folder and dithering pathetically.

'Leave this with me, Rosie,' he went on, looking at me very seriously. I allowed myself, at last, to meet his gaze, and then immediately regretted it because the Very Serious look he was giving me was also a Very Sexy look, and it made the hand holding my drink shake en route to my mouth, miss my mouth and deliver a serving of Coke over the two alien hands lying on the table in front of us, holding each other.

'Whoops,' I croaked, mopping Coke desperately from the back of my hand with a tissue out of my pocket. I nearly passed the tissue to Ashley to wipe his hand with, but remembered just in time how long it had probably been in my coat pocket. Anything could have happened to it, and long since dried, during that time.

'Don't worry,' he smiled, taking a Proper Hanky out of his jacket pocket and wiping his own hand, his eyes with their sexy look never leaving mine during the process. I wasn't sure whether he meant not to worry about the spilled Coke or about the referral letters, but it didn't seem to matter very much any more. I was past worrying. The look in Ashley Connor's eyes suddenly seemed much more important than whatever it was I'd been worrying about during the previous forty-four years.

We finished our drinks and walked back to our cars slowly, as if we didn't really want to get into them. Well, I don't know about him – if I'd had his car I'd probably have wanted to get into it, but I certainly wasn't in any hurry to get into mine. It wasn't particularly welcoming on account of the smell of wet dog that seemed to linger, no matter how many weeks it was since I'd last had a wet dog in the car. He watched me unlock the driver's door; I waited, not wanting to open it too wide while he was still standing so close, in case the wet dog smell wafted out and knocked him over.

'So I'll see you at work tomorrow, then,' he said, leaning against the car. It shuddered in protest.

He was a big buy and it was a little car. It was probably feeling as overwhelmed as I was.

'Yes. At work. Of course.'

'I'll be in theatres, but I'll come and see you between cases.'

'Will you?' I asked in alarm. God, this was really handing Sara and Becky the gossip opportunity of a lifetime, right on a plate.

'Yes, of course. You promised to show me the photos!'

'Oh. Right.' I'd forgotten about that. 'Well, don't worry, if it's difficult for you to get out of theatre ... there'll always be another time.'

'No, it shouldn't be a problem. I've got a new registrar, so I'll need to see whether he's fit to be let loose on a patient first, but hopefully he can at least be trusted with closing incisions.'

'Oh yes – it's PJ, isn't it!' I exclaimed before I could stop myself.

He looked at me curiously. 'Paresh Jaimeen. They call him *Jamas*, don't they?'

'Yes, but he doesn't like it, so I just call him ...'

'Oh, well, we all get called things we don't like, don't we. Boys will be boys,' he interrupted dismissively. 'So how well do you know Mr Jaimeen? Is he any good, do you think? Any better than most of the other useless trainees we get lumbered with these days? Half of them can barely put a sentence of English together, much less recognise a major blood vessel when they see one.'

'PJ speaks perfect English,' I replied. 'He grew up in this country. And I'm sure he'll be an excellent registrar.' I didn't think it was appropriate to add that he'd taken all his patients' medical records home to study, he was so afraid of Ashley Connor's reputation in theatre.

'Quite a good friend of yours, is he?' said Ashley, frowning slightly.

'He's a nice guy, and he's really keen to do well.' I smiled at him. 'Be nice to him, Ashley. Please!'

'Hm.' He put an arm casually around my shoulder and pulled me closer to him. I let the car door go. It was either that or we both fell over. 'As a favour to you, I suppose, I could *try* to be nice to him. Or perhaps I should be jealous of him?'

'Of course not!'

Jealous? Mr Ashley Connor, sex god of the hospital, *jealous* – because of *me*? Me and *PJ*? The very thought of it was so ridiculous, it made my head spin. Or was it his arm around me that was making my head spin? He turned me to face him and quickly, very quickly before I had time to protest (and anyway *would* I have bothered to protest?) kissed me, just the once, very lightly on the lips. With that, and before I'd even had time to blink, let alone lick my lips to savour the taste of it, he opened the car door for me and retreated, in the face of the blast of wet-dog air that emanated from inside, to the warmth and safety of his Jag. Without a word, he got into his driver's seat, started the engine, gave me a wave and began to back out of his parking space.

As I drove home, a couple of challenging questions were nagging at me. One – how was it that I'd gone to that pub in such a state of consternation, about something posing such a serious threat to my job, and yet here I was leaving an hour later with nothing more pressing on my mind than how soon I might get Ashley Connor to kiss me again, preferably more thoroughly and somewhere more private. And two – where was I going from here? And I don't mean the journey home. You know what I'm getting at here, don't you. People don't go from being called fascinating, to being kissed in a car park, to being just good friends. Even I knew that, and I had absolutely no experience outside books and films of anything remotely like it. I knew where this looked like leading, and I knew where I wanted it to lead, too. And only a very small part of it was the justification I was giving it in my own mind – that if Barry was having it off with Bobbin' Robyn in the back of the car when they were supposed to be coming home from school, then why shouldn't I allow myself the same privilege – especially as I appeared by some miracle to have become fascinating to someone? I couldn't really do anything else in the circumstances, could I? It looked like it was going to be a *fait accompli*.

Chapter Seven

Doughnut Therapy

'Guess what?' Becky hissed at me under her breath the next morning while we were setting up the clinic.

'What? You want to go to coffee already? You want the day off tomorrow?'

'Rosie!' she protested, looking hurt. 'My whole life doesn't just revolve around my next break.'

'No,' I smiled at her. 'Sorry. So who's the man?'

'*HIM*!' she exclaimed.

I looked up at the ageing, overweight arthritic slowly making his way to the patient toilets.

'Well, looks aren't everything ...'

'No, no – not *him*, Rosie. *Him*! You know! Dave, in photography! He phoned me last night!'

'Oh!'

Well, now, there's a turn-up for the books. Definitely not gay, then.

'He's asked me out tomorrow night!' she went on excitedly. 'He said he was too shy to phone me at first.'

'Be gentle with him, then. Where's he taking you?'

'I don't know. He said he'd pick me up straight from work. OK if I finish a bit early, Rosie?'

'Why? What time does he finish?'

'The same as me. But I need half an hour in the loo

to do my make-up and stuff, don't I!'

Oh, of course – silly me. How did I know this whole conversation was going to lead to time off?

'Whatever. Work through your lunch break and you can finish whenever you need to.'

'Thanks, Rosie. Ooh, I'm so excited about this! He's really cute, don't you think?'

'Mm. Lovely.'

'Well, of course,' added Becky with a sly smile, 'some of us only have eyes for Mr Connor, don't we?'

'Yes,' agreed Sara without looking up from her work, 'some of us seem to be *very* interested in Mr Connor these days, don't we, Rosie?'

I shrugged and smiled what I could only hope and believe to be an enigmatic smile. Think what you like, girls. Some of us don't need half an hour in the loo to make ourselves *fascinating*.

'Talk of the devil,' said Becky loudly about ten minutes later.

'Morning, Rosie. Morning, girls!' said Ashley. 'How are you all?'

'We're fine, thanks,' said Becky, giving him an appraising look.

He was worth appraising, I had to admit. Even if I wasn't already headed into something of a *fait accompli* with him, I'd have found it difficult to take my eyes off him.

'What do we owe this early morning visit to, Mr Connor?' asked Sara.

'I thought I'd just call by and see if Rosie had her photos to show me,' he said, leaning on the desk and treating me to a dazzling smile.

'Oh, yes!' Bloody photos again. It was nice of him to take an interest, but I'd have felt a bit more special if he was calling on me this early in the morning because of my fatal powers of attraction, rather than my photos of himself in his gorilla outfit. 'Hang on, I'll just get them out of my drawer. I didn't expect you till later.'

'Well, I've only got a few minutes before I'm due in theatre so I thought, if it's OK with you, I'd borrow the photos now, have a quick look later on, while your friend Mr Jaimeen practises a bit of suturing, and hopefully call back and return them around lunchtime?'

I went into the office behind the reception desk, unlocked my drawer, took out the envelope of photographs and sorted out the ones of Henry's birthday party, putting them in a separate envelope for him.

'Here they are,' I told Ashley. 'If you like any of them, I could always get you copies.'

'Thanks. See you later, then.'

'Yes. See you later, Ashley.'

I watched his back as he walked away.

'*See you later, Ashley*,' mimicked Sara and Becky together with soppy looks on their faces.

'Shut up,' I retorted mildly.

'*See you lunchtime, Ashley. I'll have my knickers off ready ...*'

'Shut up, Becky, or you can work till six o'clock tomorrow night.'

She grinned and leaned back in her chair.

'Don't worry, Rosie, your secret's safe with us.'

'Secret? What secret?' I returned, the hairs on the back of my neck standing up.

'We know you fancy him,' she smiled condescendingly. 'But don't worry. We won't tell him.'

Oh, is that all. I thought for a minute she'd read my mind about where it was all leading.

There was a serious-looking e-mail on my screen when I switched on my computer.

To: Rosemary Peacock
From: Sylvia Riley
Re: Orthopaedic referrals
I need to speak to you again today about the above

matter. Please come to my office at 1.00 pm.

'Oh, great,' I sighed, deleting it.

'What?' asked Sara. 'Are you all right? You look a bit stressed, Rosie, and we haven't even started yet.'

'I'm OK. But I've got another meeting with Sylvia Riley later.'

'How nice for you. She's getting a bit friendly, isn't she? That's twice this week!'

'Sylvia Riley, friendly? You must be joking. I bet she isn't even friendly with her own family. She probably barks orders at them and makes them stand to attention in front of her.'

'Yeah. She probably orders her husband into bed when she wants a bit of nooky,' agreed Sara.

'Or maybe not,' put in Becky. 'Perhaps that's why she's so bad-tempered – she's not getting it.'

'That doesn't make you bad-tempered!' protested Sara, going a bit red. 'That's just male propaganda, Becky – men like to tell each other we can't live without it.'

'We can't – can we, Rosie?' said Becky, winking mischievously at me.

Sara ignored her and got on with her work. Becky raised her eyebrows at me but I shook my head, warning her off the subject. Sara was quite obviously not bothered whether she ever repeated the experience that had landed her with Callum, and who could blame her?

'It's over-rated, if you ask me,' I said.

'Depends who you're doing it with,' persisted Becky. 'And, of course, if it happened to be Mr Ashley Connor you might feel different . . .'

I threw my pen at her and we all laughed. But Becky's words had triggered off a series of images in my mind which were hard to ignore despite the hustle and bustle of the morning's clinic. And it was one o'clock before I remembered I was supposed to be in Sylvia Riley's office.

*

'Come in, Rosemary. Sit down.'

She was already looking at her watch. For God's sake, I was only three minutes late! She was tapping on her desk with her pen while I sat myself down. She was going to give herself an early heart attack at this rate, with a bit of luck.

'Rosemary.' She fixed me with a steely glare. 'Have you taken any action yet with regard to our conversation on Monday?'

Conversation? I'd thought of it as more of a lecture. I didn't remember getting much of a word in.

'No,' I admitted, trying to avoid her eyes. 'I've ... er ... been a bit busy with the clinics ...'

'Good!' she said, to my amazement. 'Don't.'

'Don't?' I repeated stupidly. 'Don't what?'

'Don't take any ... further action ... along the lines we discussed.'

We discussed? Again, I didn't remember there being a lot of discussion about it, but apparently my memory was playing tricks.

'You mean you don't want me to phone the GPs and pretend we didn't receive the referral letters?' I asked, relief beginning to wash over me.

She looked down at her desk and pretended to be doing something very important with a piece of paper.

'I mean that I merely want you to make those patients urgent appointments. Is that understood?'

'Completely.' I smiled. 'And we're not going to worry about them being outside the thirteen weeks deadline?'

'Worry?' she retorted sharply. 'Of *course* we're worried about it, Rosemary! We're *very* worried about any instances of failure to meet targets, as you must surely realise! And in future, I expect you to be *vigilant* in picking up on this sort of thing and bringing it *directly* to my attention! Is that clear?'

Oh, perfectly, thank you! I'll be as vigilant as you like. In future, I'll bring anything that looks or smells remotely

123

out of date *directly* to your office, Ms Riley, and let you deal with it yourself, believe me.

'Yes. I'll make the appointments immediately,' I said, getting to my feet.

'Thank you, Rosemary.'

She picked up her pen and pretended to write something important on her blotter. The interview was concluded. I'd had a reprieve. Sylvia fucking Riley had backed down – something that had never happened before in living memory – and why? Someone had intervened on my behalf, hadn't they – and I knew who that Someone was! And further-more, I knew exactly how I wanted to thank him!

I was still floating on a cloud of light-headed relief when I bumped (almost literally) into PJ that evening in the supermarket. We were both leaning into one of those silly frozen food cabinets with the doors that slam shut on you as soon as you let them go. I had a packet of sausages in one hand, and he was reaching for the chicken pies, when I let go of the door and heard a sharp intake of breath at my right ear.

'Don't worry, Rosie. I've got nine other fingers. I didn't really need my right thumb tonight.'

'PJ! Sorry – I didn't see you ...'

'You were miles away. Concentrating on what to cook for hubby's dinner, I suppose?'

I didn't think it would serve any particular purpose to tell him I'd actually been imagining what Ashley Connor would look like without his trousers on.

'What are you doing here, anyway?' I asked instead, dropping the frozen sausages into my trolley.

'What, apart from getting my thumb amputated? Shopping, Rosie, strange as it may seem. Unlike some fortunate people, I don't have a nice wife to trot around the supermarket for me, stocking up on my favourite sausages. I have to forage for myself, or starve.'

'My heart's bleeding for you, PJ. Here, let me get you

your pies, while you nurse your sore thumb. Chicken or minced beef? Economy or Finest?'

'Economy chicken, obviously. We don't get paid for another two days, do we?'

'I thought perhaps you were going to live it up a bit. What with getting the Acting Registrar job and all!'

'Don't remind me!' he grimaced, taking the packet of pies from me and adding them to a basket holding a bag of frozen chips and two tins of baked beans. 'Your Mr Ashley Connor reduced me to a heap of shit in theatre today. You see before you a quivering wreck of humanity!'

'Well, that's nothing new!' I looked at him more closely and added: 'Seriously, PJ – are you all right? You *do* look like shit, to be honest.'

'Thanks, Rosie.'

An elderly lady nudged me with her trolley and I lurched out of the way, ending up blocking the aisle and making two more women tut and shake their heads. It's a jungle in Tesco at six o'clock in the evening, I can tell you. Show any fear and you're as good as dead.

I looked again at the pathetic contents of PJ's basket, looked back at my own trolley, full of sliced white loaves, family sized packets of cornflakes and toilet rolls, tins of dog food, duos of special offer bourbons/custard creams – all the trappings of family life – and I suddenly felt a heart-stopping moment of pure sadness for him, living on his own with his economy chicken pies and baked beans and no one to heat them up for him or share them with him.

'Come on,' I told him fiercely, tugging at his arm so that the wire basket nearly tipped its meagre spoils out onto the supermarket floor. 'Come and have a coffee in the café.'

'Coffee in the café?' he repeated wonderingly, following me obediently as if in a daze. 'It sounds enticingly French, Rosie. What have you got in mind?'

Just coffee, PJ. Don't get carried away.

We sat at a table in the window, overlooking the trolley

return at the edge of the car park. A burly looking guy who was obviously proud of his uniform was pushing a roped-together wagon train of about five hundred trolleys blindly across the path of speeding vehicles towards us. PJ smiled at him from the safety of our window seat.

'There's a lucky man,' he said glumly. 'Nice easy job, no worries, no responsibilities.'

'Hey!' I unloaded his coffee from the tray and put it down heavily in front of him, along with a doughnut on a plate. 'What's all this?'

'Looks like a doughnut. I didn't order it.'

'No, I did, you fool. You look as though your blood sugar needs a boost.'

'Who's the doctor here – me or you?'

I ignored this. 'I meant – what's all this about? It isn't like you to be moody.'

'Sorry. It's just working with your Mr Ashley Connor . . .'

'Do you have to keep calling him that? He's not *my* Mr Ashley Connor.'

But I felt myself growing hot, all the same, at the idea that he might be. Might be, very soon, if I had anything to do with it. I took a huge bite of doughnut and tried to chew on it nonchalantly.

'Maybe not. But you'd like him to be, wouldn't you. I can see it written all over your face. You're even eating that doughnut in a lascivious way, just thinking about him.'

'*Lascivious*? I don't even know what it means!' I protested.

'Look it up, Rosie,' he said with a sigh.

I put down the doughnut – the *lascivious* doughnut – and stared at him.

'You're worrying me now. What happened today in theatre?'

'Nothing in particular.' He smiled – it looked as if it was an effort – and picked up his doughnut. 'I think I'm probably just tired. Stayed up too late last night studying the case notes!'

126

'I expect it's been hard, hasn't it – working with Mr Connor,' I sympathised. 'I've heard he can be quite demanding in theatre. But he's very fair, too, you know. I told him about my problem with Sylvia Riley – you know, about those referral letters – and he must have spoken to her straight away. She's changed her mind – backed down – I haven't got to lie to the GPs.'

'Good,' said PJ, looking down at the sugar on his fingers. 'Bloody right too.'

'It was a relief, I can tell you. So I'm very grateful to Ashley.'

'Yes, I bet you are. Good old *Ashley*,' said PJ, licking his fingers.

'PJ, you're sounding very bitter. It's not like you.'

'Sorry, Rosie.' He took a bite out of his doughnut and finally looked up at me. 'Thanks for this – it's just what the doctor ordered.'

'Well, it wasn't much,' I said awkwardly. 'What I'd really like to do is take you out for a nice big meal, with wine and everything.'

Where did *that* come from? I frowned to myself, immediately regretting it, but fortunately PJ laughed and retorted:

'Now *you're* worrying *me*! You don't need to come on too strong with the sympathy, Rosie – I'm not a patient! I'll be fine when this dosage of doughnut therapy kicks in.'

'Good.'

He took another bite and we both laughed as the jam in the middle oozed out over his fingers, covering them with bright red like a surgical wound.

'And can I have a repeat prescription?' he smiled at me as he licked off the jam. 'Next time you feel like giving me a crush injury in the frozen food cabinets?'

I looked up *lascivious* as soon as I got home. *Lustful, wanton, inciting to lust*, pronounced my Concise Oxford Dictionary *circa* 1968, whose sad and battered volume had stood faithfully on my bookshelf since it had left the relative excitement of my school life round about the same time as Barry had come into it. I held the dictionary against my heart and savoured the feel of the words in my mind. *Lustful. Wanton.* Oh yes. I could certainly give Mr Ashley Connor some lasciviousness, all right.

'What you reading, Mum?' asked Stuart with uncharacteristic filial interest. I snapped the dictionary shut and put it back on the shelf.

'Nothing. Just looking up something for my crossword.'

'Crossword? Never knew you liked things like that!' he remarked, heading out of the door with Biggles at his heels.

Oh, but there's a lot you don't know about me, boy. There's a lot even *I* don't know about me.

The phone started ringing as I headed for the kitchen to start slaughtering vegetables ready for dinner. Stuart got there before me.

'Hi, Robyn,' I heard him say, before holding the receiver away from him and bellowing up the stairs, 'DAD! ROBYN FOR YOU!'

Stuart dumped the receiver on the table and sauntered off to watch TV. I stood in the hall, staring at the phone, itching to pick it up and say something. But what? What could I possibly say that would be helpful in this situation? Presumably if I called her a bitch or a whore she'd hang up. If I asked her whether, as she seemed to like my husband so much, she'd like to help him pay our mortgage and council tax so I could give up work and stay in bed all day, she'd probably think I was joking. I even considered offering to do a deal with her – she could have Barry if I could have her red jumper and the phone number of her hairdresser – but by the time I'd decided this was perhaps fairer on me than her, Barry had appeared at the top of the stairs in his underpants, with a T-shirt half on and half-off, scratching his head. Definitely fairer on me.

'Who?' he asked, looking from the phone to me and scratching his head again.

'Who? Who do you think?' I snarled. 'Little Miss Muffett. As if you didn't know.'

I turned and went into the kitchen, but couldn't quite bring myself to close the door. Yes – I wanted to listen. And I was watching, too, while I was pretending to stab potatoes.

'Oh, hello, Robyn. Yes. Yes, of course.' (Some laughter.) 'Yes, I know. Of course I haven't forgotten. (More laughter.) 'I know, but you should trust me by now – silly girl!' (More laughter.) 'OK, see you tomorrow. Yes! Yes – me too. Bye, then!' He hung up, wiping his mouth as if he'd just kissed her.

'Me too, what?' I called from the kitchen doorway as he was trying to sneak back up the stairs. Men should never try to *sneak* while they're wearing their underpants. It looks horribly undignified.

'Eh?' he turned back to look at me – a look of baffled innocence. Yeah, right.

'*Me too, Robyn! Ha ha ha!*' I mimicked. 'You laughed more during that phone call, Barry, than you've laughed during the whole of the last fucking year!'

'Well,' he retorted, suddenly raising his voice enough to make me jump, 'Perhaps I haven't *heard* or *seen* anything during the last *fucking* year to make me feel like laughing!'

'Don't shout!'

'And don't you *insinuate!*'

We stared at each other, bristling with hostility, me with a potato in one hand and a knife in the other – him halfway up the stairs in his underpants with the T-shirt now pulled down as far as his stomach.

'So when are you seeing her?' I asked, with a sigh. As least if he gave me dates and times, I could arrange to see Ashley on the same nights and not feel guilty about it.

'Tomorrow morning, as normal. I'm taking her to school, *as normal*, Rosie. She just wanted to remind me that we need to go in early for a staff meeting, that's all. OK? Can I finish getting changed, now?'

I gave the potato another hard stab for good measure, missed it, dropped it, and stuck the knife into my hand instead.

'Shit!' I leant against the sink, allowing the tap to run cold water over the wound, shock and self pity bringing tears to my eyes.

'You're not supposed to do that,' said Stuart, getting up from the kitchen table and turning off the tap. 'It makes it bleed more.'

I wiped the tears with the back of my good hand.

'What, then? It's dripping blood all over the ... and I feel a bit ... funny ...'

'Sit down, Mum. Put your head down. Lift your arm up and let me press on the cut. Are there any clean tea towels?'

'Where did you learn all this?' I asked – but fortunately I didn't have time to hear my son tell me he'd learned it from Robyn Dainton, the school welfare officer, who gave first aid lessons during wet lunch hours, before I fainted out cold on the kitchen floor.

'You ought to see a doctor,' fussed Sara the next day at work.

'No, thanks. I see quite enough of them, every day.'

'But it might need stitching,' pointed out Becky.

'Stuart stopped it bleeding. It's fine.' I smiled at Stuart, who was sitting in the reception office reading his physics homework while we were waiting for his fracture clinic appointment.

'Yeah, but Mum, I did say it looked a bit ...'

'It looks fine,' I repeated firmly. 'It isn't very deep.'

I flinched slightly as I picked up a pile of patient records, smothering the flinch quickly with a nonchalant yawn as I was aware that everyone was watching me, waiting for me to shout out in pain so that they could whisk me off to A&E. It's a funny thing about hospital staff. I suppose I'm as guilty as everyone else – as soon as any of our colleagues has anything wrong with them more serious than a slight headache or a runny nose, we all want to leap into action, get them admitted to a ward and preferably on an operating table within the hour. I think it's our way of reassuring ourselves that the system works efficiently.

'What have you done?' asked Ashley Connor, frowning at my bandaged hand when I took a list of patients round to his consulting room.

'It's nothing. Just a little scratch with a knife . . .'

'A clean knife? Is your tetanus immunity up to date?'

'Yes! Yes, it was clean, I'd only been stabbing a potato with it.'

He looked at me curiously.

'Well, if you want to see one of the hand surgeons . . .'

'No, honestly, Ash—' I glanced at the nurses around me, ear-wigging our conversation, and corrected myself quickly, '—Mr Connor, it's nothing. But I've got Stuart here today, for his fracture check . . .'

'Stuart?'

'My son. He was on the ward over the weekend. Fractured ulna.'

He nodded vaguely. Fair enough, he had hundreds of patients, why would he remember one more schoolboy who'd fallen off his bike fighting over a girl?

'I've got him here with me . . .' I explained.

'Oh – OK, Rosie. Sure – I'll see him first. Take him for an X-ray, will you, and bring the films back with you.' He looked up from the papers he'd been studying and gave me a smile that almost made my knees buckle. 'By the way, I liked your photos! Did Sara tell you I brought them back?'

'No. Must have been while I was with Sylvia Riley yesterday. Guess what – she's backed down about those referral letters! She said . . .'

'I wondered about the other photos, though.'

131

'Other photos . . .? I think I gave you all of them,' I said, puzzled.

'No – not just the ones from the pub. I'd have liked to see what else you've done. Your nature photos. They weren't in the envelope.'

'Well – I didn't really think you'd be interested. I . . . I'll have to remember to bring them in again. I've taken them home, now.'

'Yes. I'd like to see them,' he said, smiling again so that I forgot the whole thread of my story about Sylvia Riley and the referral letters.

By the time we'd waited around in the X-ray department for Stuart's arm to be x-rayed through his plaster, waited around again for the films, and finally taken them back to the clinic, Ashley was seeing another patient.

'She could be some time,' one of the nurses warned me. 'It's that girl with the multiple fractures from the parachute jump.'

'I need to get back to school,' complained Stuart, looking at his watch anxiously. 'We've got a maths test, and I haven't handed in my physics homework, and . . . oh, hi, PJ!'

I followed the direction of his grin. PJ was at the door of his consulting room, showing a patient the way to physiotherapy.

'How do you know PJ?' I whispered.

'He came to see me when I was in the ward. He was really cool! We had a game on the playstation. I beat him!'

'Hi, Stuart!' said PJ now, loping over and slapping him on the back as if he was a guy of his own age. Stuart visibly grew in stature. 'How's the arm?'

'OK, I think. Got to see the consultant.' He pulled a face. 'Waste of time, but *Mum* says . . .'

'Mum's right,' PJ smiled at me. 'We need to look at the X-ray and make sure the fracture's mending in the right position. Otherwise you'd *really* know all about waste of time!'

132

'Can't *you* look at it?' returned Stuart hopefully.

PJ glanced at the closed door of Ashley's consulting room, looked around him, assessing the number of patients waiting, and shrugged.

'Don't see why not. Come on, then, mate.'

Beaming with pleasure at being called *mate* by his new hero, Stuart followed PJ into his room, where PJ held the door open for me, giving me a mischievous grin as I entered.

'Maybe I should look at your hand while we're at it. Everyone's saying you tried to do yourself in with a potato knife.'

'She was pretending to stab my dad,' put in Stuart, showing off for PJ's benefit.

PJ raised his eyebrows questioningly at me. I shook my head.

'Just a stupid accident. It's OK. No worse than your crush injury of the thumb by freezer door!' I reminded him with a smile.

He held up his hand and extended the thumb, looking at it with surprised interest.

'Hey, that's amazing! I'd forgotten about it! The dough-nut therapy must have worked! Perhaps we should try it for your hand, Rosie!'

'Perhaps,' I agreed. I handed him Stuart's envelope of X-rays and he took them over to the light box.

'This looks absolutely fine,' he said. He turned to Stuart. 'Come and have a look.'

I smiled as I watched him point out the bones of the forearm and the place that had been pinned.

'Cool!' exclaimed Stuart enthusiastically. 'Could I get picked up by a magnet?'

'If it was big enough and strong enough, I suppose,' laughed PJ. 'OK, Stuart – you can get back to school now. We'll see you after about six weeks and hopefully get the plaster off then. All right?'

'Yeah! Thanks, mate!'

'Stuart!' I admonished him.

'That's OK,' laughed PJ. He said something quietly to Stuart, who grinned, shook his head and went a bit red.

'What did he say to you?' I asked curiously as we walked back to the reception desk.

'Asked me whether the girl we were fighting about was worth all this trouble.' He pulled a face. 'No *way!*'

What a transient thing is human affection sometimes. One day you fancy someone enough to risk life and limb in a fight, the next day you can't stand the sight of them. And so the world goes on.

When I saw Ashley again, at lunchtime, he stopped dead and stared at me as if he was trying to remember something.

'Oh yes! Rosie – your son! What happened – I thought you were bringing me his X-rays?'

'It's OK. PJ looked at them for us ...' I began.

'Oh. He did, did he?'

'Yes. He says Stuart's arm's doing fine.'

'Good,' he muttered, frowning. 'And you? Are you OK?'

'Yes, I'm fine too, thanks – but listen, I was trying to tell you about Sylvia Riley! Thank you so much for getting me off the hook ...'

'Sorry? What?' he said, looking at me vaguely.

'About those referral letters. I realise you must have spoken to her. It certainly did the trick – she's completely backed down; I haven't got to lie to the GPs. Thanks, Ashley.'

'No problem.' He waved this aside, and then added with an abrupt change of subject: 'What are you doing over the weekend?'

Shopping, dusting, hoovering, changing the beds, washing, ironing, cooking, cleaning the windows ...

'Nothing,' I said, smiling in anticipation, wondering where he was going to invite me and how I was going to make my excuses at home.

'D'you want to come to a football match?'

My dreams of a romantic drive in the countryside, a cosy lunch or a candlelit dinner for two faded into stunned silence. Football? *Fucking football?* I hated football! It was bad enough having it on TV every waking moment – why the hell would I want to give up any of my weekend to go and stand out in the cold and watch it *live*? I'd rather do the dusting and hoovering! I'd rather do everyone else's dusting and hoovering down the street ... *and* their washing ... *and* look after their incontinent toddlers ...

'I'm playing on Sunday afternoon – consultants versus junior doctors! Fund raising for the hospital charity fund.'

'*You're* playing?' The picture in my mind changed abruptly from a grey dreary scene of faceless boring men chasing a ball around each other's legs, to one of Ashley Connor in football shorts. I felt my spirits lift somewhat. So maybe football had its interesting moments after all.

'Sure. I'll be there,' I smiled back at him.

'You're going to a *football* match?' repeated Barry, mouth open wide in disbelief. 'You hate football!'

'Can I come, Mum? Is PJ playing? Please can I come?' begged Stuart.

'No!' I snapped. 'It's only for staff.'

This was such an obvious lie that I had to look away. Restricting an event to staff when it was supposed to be a fundraiser would make no sense to anyone. Stuart and Barry both pulled faces and turned back to the telly in silence. Sulking. Why should they worry – either of them? If there was football on TV on Sunday afternoon, they wouldn't even notice I'd gone out until it became necessary to make themselves a cup of tea.

'See this?' Becky asked me the next day, pointing to a poster on the wall of the outpatient waiting room.

*

EAST DEAN GENERAL HOSPITAL
CHARITY FOOTBALL MATCH
Consultants v Junior Doctors
SUNDAY 30th MARCH 2003 : Kick-off 3pm
Memorial Park, West Dean Road
Admission £3 by programme (Children half price)

'Mm,' I replied nonchalantly.

'D'you fancy coming?' persisted Becky.

'Er . . . I dunno,' I lied, not wanting to admit I'd already agreed to it. 'I don't really like football.'

'Nor do I,' she shrugged. 'But it'll be a laugh, Rosie. Loads of people are going.'

I hesitated. It'd certainly be more fun standing at the side of the pitch with Becky, and probably a crowd of the girls from outpatients, having a laugh with them and enjoying their company, rather than standing on my own trying not to make it obvious that I'd gone with Ashley Connor and pretending to concentrate on a game I knew nothing whatsoever about.

'OK,' I said with a smile. 'Who's selling the programmes? I'll go and buy them.'

PJ phoned me on the reception desk just before I finished work.

'Rosie! Thank God – thought I might have missed you.'

'What's the matter? Is it something important? I was just about to go home.'

'Of course it's important!' he retorted. 'Wait there!'

He hung up, leaving me to put on my coat, looking at my watch in irritation and wondering whether I should just go. Two minutes later he burst into the deserted outpatient department, white coat open and flapping behind him, stethoscope trailing out of his pocket, hair askew as if he'd just got up.

'There you go!' he said triumphantly, placing a paper bag in front of me on the desk.

136

'What is it?' I asked, fingering the greasy looking bag suspiciously.

'Doughnut therapy, Rosie! For your poor hand!' He smiled at me as I opened the bag and laughed at the rather squashed contents.

'That's a nice thought, PJ! Thanks!'

'You're welcome. One to be taken twice a day before meals. Listen, I've got to dash – I was in the middle of examining a patient on the ward . . .'

'That's OK. Have a nice weekend, PJ.'

'What are you doing Sunday? D'you want to come and support me and the boys playing football against the consultants?'

Blimey. First time in my life I'd ever been invited to the same event by three people.

'Yes – I'm already coming. I've got my programme.'

'Excellent. I'll see you there, then. Oh – and bring your camera!'

Good point. It might be nice to have a few photos of Ashley in shorts, if only to look at in my old age when I'd forgotten what it was all about. If I'd even managed to figure out what it *was* all about, by then.

'Shall I pick you up on Sunday, Rosie?' asked Ashley Connor five minutes later, as I was heading for the car park. 'For the football match?'

I tried to picture the scene at home. Ashley's Jaguar pulling up outside our house. Ashley stepping over the dog to get into our hallway to wait for me, while Barry watched the telly and sulked about me going out and having to get his own tea, and Stuart whinged and whined about wanting to come with me. No – no way. It just wasn't going to happen.

'Thanks,' I said, 'But Becky's picking me up.'

'See you there, then.'

'Definitely.'

I smiled, trying to look fascinating. We walked outside together into a blast of cold air and a squally icy shower, and *fascinating* immediately gave way to *shivering physical wreck*. I realised with alarm that the clothes I possessed that were suitable for wearing to a football match on a cold March day were all about twenty years old and reminiscent of a bad day in an Oxfam shop. Why hadn't I got any further with the major renovation of my wardrobe? Come to that, why didn't I have at least one daughter who (a) lived at home and let me borrow her clothes, and (b) wore the same size clothes as me? Was it right or fair for daughters to grow taller but slimmer than their mothers? I heard other women talking about borrowing their daughters' clothes and it gave me the same sorrowful feeling of missing out that I used to get about not having a sister when I was a teenager.

'Hope it's nicer weather than this on Sunday,' I said to Ashley between my chattering teeth as the rain drove needles of sharp pain into my face.

'Oh, I don't know,' he responded with a lazy smile. 'I don't mind playing in rough conditions. Sorts out the men from the boys!'

'Or the consultants from the juniors,' I pointed out.

'Same thing,' said Ashley, resting his hand briefly on my shoulder as we parted company. 'But then I don't need to tell you that, do I, Rosie? I'm sure *you* know which you prefer, don't you!' With a grin and a wave, he strode off to the consultants' – or perhaps I should say the *men*'s – car park, leaving me standing there looking after him and wondering once again how it had come about that I, Rosie Peacock, forty-four years old and only recently likened to an old armchair, had attracted the attention of someone like Mr Ashley Connor to the extent where he was flirting with me outside the outpatient building on a Friday evening in the rain.

'Don't forget your camera!' he called back to me just as I was walking away.

That was it. The camera. Ever since I'd bought it, my life seemed to have been changing. Either the camera had

138

magic powers, or men found female photographers irresistibly sexy.

'I won't forget!' I shouted back.

'Forget what?' asked a voice behind me. It was Dave the Medical Photographer, collar turned up against the downpour, holding a big black umbrella protectively over the head of Becky (whose consternation at emerging from her half-hour in the toilets attending to her hair and make-up, to see the rain and wind threatening to undo all her work, could only be imagined).

'My camera,' I said, walking with them towards our cars. 'On Sunday, for the football match.' I glanced at Becky. 'So where are you two off to, tonight, then?'

'I don't know – where are we going, Dave?' asked Becky in a Little Girl voice. *I can't make important decisions like that – I need a big strong man to make my mind up for me!*

'I thought perhaps we'd start off with a couple of drinks and then go on for a meal somewhere?' he suggested tentatively.

'Lovely!' She smiled at him as if that was the cleverest, most original thing she'd ever heard.

'Have a nice time, then,' I said, getting into my car, envying them their couple of drinks and their meal, their shared umbrella, their new relationship. 'See you on Sunday, Becky!'

'Yes – OK!'

I'd started the engine when I realised she was saying something else. I wound down the window, getting rewarded by a spitting of rain in my eyes.

'What?' I called back above the rising strains of Red Hot Chilli Peppers on my car radio.

'Your camera, Rosie!' she repeated, laughing, as she got into Dave's car, showing enough leg, in the process, to put him off his driving, his drinks and his dinner. 'Don't forget your camera!'

139

Chapter Eight

Football and other games

Sunday afternoon was cold, overcast and blustery.

'At least it isn't raining today,' said Becky, trying to sound cheerful but not convincing anyone. We'd arrived at the park late because she'd been out for lunch with Dave and forgotten the time, but the match hadn't started yet. Groups of nurses were hanging around the sidelines, huddled together against the wind, chatting and laughing and calling out in the direction of the hut where the players were apparently getting changed.

'*Why are we waiting* ...?' joined in Becky as we approached the rest of the crowd. Just at that moment, the door of the hut burst open and out ran ... a gorilla. The spectators immediately went wild, jumping up and down and screaming with appreciative laughter as the gorilla charged onto the pitch followed by the rest of his team ... a chimpanzee, two cats, a penguin, a chicken, two tigers and three white mice. They roared, grunted, meowed and squeaked as they did a circuit of the pitch, playing up to the crowd and passing the ball between them, paw to paw. The gorilla stopped in front of me and performed an elaborate bow, before being urged on by a large tiger pushing him from behind.

'Excellent!' laughed Becky. 'I bet that was Mr Connor's

idea! He's the captain – he's such a good sport, isn't he, Rosie!'

'Yeah,' I agreed unenthusiastically. Well, sorry, but I'd been looking forward to seeing Ashley Connor in his football kit and the gorilla outfit was no substitute. 'I don't think the penguin's going to be able to kick the ball very well, though.'

'No – and the chicken looks like he's the goalie! He could have trouble with those wings ...'

'Where are the other team?' people around us were asking.

'*Come on, come on! Come on, come on!*' they began to chant, clapping their hands and staring towards the hut, as the consultants' team, still making their animal noises, continued to limber up on the pitch.

Suddenly there was a cheer as a figure emerged from the hut. It was PJ, in white football shorts and a red top, followed by a motley crew of registrars and house officers dressed the same. As they trotted onto the pitch, the spectators fell silent. By comparison with the team of pantomime animals, they looked uninspiring, and they knew it. It showed on their faces, it showed in the way they ran, even in the half-hearted way they lifted their arms to greet the crowd.

'Boring!' yelled a young male nurse from the children's ward.

'Where's your costumes?' called Becky.

'Ssh!' I nudged her. 'Don't! Look at their poor little faces! They didn't know – you can see they didn't. The consultants didn't tell them they were going to dress up.'

But by now the crowd had taken up the call:

'*BorING, borING, borING!*'

The junior doctors jogged around the pitch, trying to laugh off the cat-calls and insults.

'Poor things,' I said indignantly.

'No – they should have made more effort,' retorted Becky unsympathetically. 'They knew it was a charity match.'

141

But I was watching PJ's face as his team limbered up, and all I could think was – he feels defeated before it's even started.

Sure enough, by half time the juniors' team was two-nil down.

'What did you think of my goal?' asked Ashley, joining us on the sideline as he gulped greedily from a carton of orange juice.

'Yeah. Very nice,' I said awkwardly. Despite having just watched the first forty-five minutes of live football I'd ever seen in my life, I still wasn't at all sure about the rules and was far more interested in his legs than his goal. Needless to say, the animal costumes had come off as soon as they'd done their intended job of winning the crowd's support, and Ashley's team were now clad in a blue and white strip, and all looking very pleased with themselves.

'I'll see you later,' said Ashley, touching my arm briefly and smiling into my eyes. 'Wait for me at full time. Don't go away.'

Becky raised her eyebrows at me as he jogged off – but even her eyebrow raising was nothing compared with the looks I was getting from across the pitch. Heidi, the yodelling mountaineeress from Occupational Health, was there with a group of her friends. They were all dressed in blue and white and holding a banner that proclaimed (in large blue letters and with no attempt whatsoever at originality): COME ON YOU BLUES. She continued to glare at me as Ashley jogged over to her side of the pitch, stopping briefly to talk to her. As I watched, he turned towards me, following her glare, and I saw him shrug and shake his head. For some reason it made me feel very uneasy.

'So who are you supporting, girls?' asked PJ, sauntering over to join us, half an orange dripping juice between his fingers. 'The menagerie or the real footballers?'

'Unfortunately for you,' pointed out Becky callously,

142

'It's the menagerie who seem to be playing the real football today.'

'Maybe we just need a bit more support,' he grinned, taking a noisy suck of his orange. 'We need some cheer girls in short skirts and red and white knickers, waving pom-poms and shouting out for us ...'

'*Two, four, six, eight, who do we appreciate? R–E–D–S, Reds!*' chanted Becky and I together, waving imaginary pom-poms in the air.

'Yes. Still prefer the idea of the short skirts and the knickers though!' laughed PJ.

'Bit cold for that, thanks,' I retorted.

'Saving it for after the match, eh? For the benefit of the captain of the opposition?'

There was an uncomfortable silence. Becky glanced at me and then looked away, pretending to be suddenly very interested in something on the ground.

'Well, he's certainly got *all* his fans here today, hasn't he,' added PJ when I didn't reply. He stared very pointedly across the pitch at the blue and white banner now being waved very energetically as the players began to trot back onto the pitch. 'Just hope he appreciates it. See you later, Rosie.' And, tossing his orange peel into a rubbish sack, he ran off, his thin brown legs in their grubby white shorts suddenly making me feel sad.

'I'm not supporting *either* team!' I called after him. 'PJ! I don't even understand the rules!' But he didn't show any sign of having heard me.

'So is it true?' asked Becky, ten minutes into the second half. We were both standing in a kind of dazed silence watching the game without much interest.

'What? Is what true?'

'You know, Rosie. What PJ was hinting at. What we've *all* been hinting at. You and Ashley Connor. Are you making a play for him?'

I turned to her indignantly.

143

'*Me*? Me making a play for *him*? What do you think I am
– crazy? It would never have occurred to me, never in my
wildest dream – I wouldn't have dared – I wouldn't have
had the nerve . . .'

'But *he* showed an interest in *you*. Didn't he! All this
hanging around the reception desk, talking about your
photos, talking about lunch . . .'

I shrugged, feeling my face burning. OK, Becky – go on,
tell me it's ridiculous, that I'm making a fool of myself,
that he's just having a laugh at my expense . . . say what
you're obviously thinking, don't spare my feelings . . .

'Good for you,' she said, very quietly, making me spin
round in surprise to find her looking at me with the utmost
seriousness. 'Good for you, Rosie, if it makes you happy.
Have a bit of fun for once.'

'You don't think I'm making a fool of myself?'

'Why should you be? Anyone can see he's keen. If he
fancied *me*, I'd be in there like a shot, I can tell you!'

'But Becky – I'm forty-four, and married, and . . .'

'And bored, and not very happy, and looking for a bit of
adventure. Aren't you!' She smiled. 'Go for it, Rosie – but
don't take it too seriously, eh?'

I shook my head, completely at a loss as to what to say
to this. Here was Becky – young, beautiful Becky who
could have any man she wanted and who I'd always felt
looked on me with a mixture of pity and disdain – Becky,
of all people, encouraging me quite openly to proceed
towards my *fait accompli* with Ashley Connor. I watched
Ashley now as, to the accompaniment of cheers and whistles from the crowds of Blues supporters, he dribbled the
ball expertly around Henry's feet and passed it down the
midfield.

'He looks like a professional, doesn't he,' she said
gently, slipping an arm through mine.

Surprised still further by this unexpected display of
affection, I drew in a deep breath and admitted: 'He looks
. . . *gorgeous*. He *is* gorgeous!'

144

'Don't waste any time, then, Rosie. You've only got one life.'

But before I could reply, PJ had scored for the Reds and the park suddenly came alive with the rather belated sound of cries of support for the junior doctors, encouraged by which they promptly scored again.

'Lover boy's lost his golden balls now, eh!' smirked PJ as he ran back to his position.

'Hey! It's supposed to be a charity match! Where's your charity?' I rebuked him – but my admonishment was drowned out by the whistle, and within a few minutes PJ had taken possession of the ball and scored the hat trick.

The crowd went wild.

'*Two, four, six, eight* ...' began Becky, laughing. 'Come on, Rosie, fair play! They deserve to win – they've come up from nowhere ...'

But I was watching Ashley's face – and not *just* because I couldn't take my eyes off him, either. As the referee blew the final whistle and the players began to slap each other on the back, collect up their animal skins and make their way to the hut, he could barely look at PJ as they exchanged a cursory handshake and nod of congratulation.

'Good match, wasn't it!' said a voice at my side. It was Heidi, her blue and white banner screwed up in her hands and the blue ribbons in her hair looking somewhat sorry and bedraggled. 'Didn't quite imagine you as a football fan.'

'I'm not. But it's for charity, isn't it.'

'Yes. I suppose you came to take photos.' She indicated my camera. 'Get some good shots?'

I flushed. The only shots I'd bothered to take were several of Ashley in his shorts.

'Yes, thanks.'

'We must get together some time – I'd like to see them.' Great.

'In fact, I think it would be good to have another chat, anyway, Rosie. I'd be very interested to hear how you're getting on with the changes to your lifestyle that we discussed.'

'Mm. OK. Maybe some time . . .'

I looked around desperately. People were beginning to drift away to the car park. Becky was looking at me questioningly.

'Are you waiting, Rosie? For . . .'

He appeared from the hut just at that moment. He'd changed into casual trousers and a jacket, and was heading towards us but appeared to hesitate slightly and slow down when he saw us talking together.

'I'd better go,' said Heidi, very loudly. 'I've got friends with me and I'm supposed to be giving them all a lift home. See you.' She turned and began to stride off. 'See you,' she repeated as she passed Ashley, without looking at him.

'What was all that about?' he asked me, watching her as she disappeared out of sight.

'Don't know,' I shrugged. 'Just one more person interested in my photography, it seems.'

'Want a lift home?'

I glanced at Becky.

'Go ahead,' she said at once. 'I'm . . . er . . . I've got to get straight home – I was just going . . .'

She smiled at me and whispered something under her breath that I didn't dare ask her to repeat.

'See you tomorrow.'

We walked slowly back to the car park together. Nearly everyone had gone.

'Did you take any photos today?' he asked as I got into the passenger seat of the Jag.

'Er . . .' I looked at him a bit sheepishly. 'Only a few.'

'Action shots?'

'No. Mostly of you,' I admitted before I could stop myself.

He laughed. 'Always knew you had good taste.' And he leaned over and kissed me quickly as he started the engine.

146

I resisted with some difficulty the urge to grab him round the back of the neck and snog him good and hard – but only because I didn't want him to crash the Jag.

We pulled out of the car park and onto the main road.

'So where to?' asked Ashley. He glanced at me and smiled. 'You don't have to go straight home, do you?'

My heart missed a beat.

'Where did you have in mind?'

'Pub? Wine bar? Nice restaurant somewhere?'

My life flashed before me. Pub? Yes, there'd been a few – but mostly the sleazy one on the corner of our road, where I tended to sit on a stool chatting to the barmaids and nursing a gin and tonic while Barry played darts at the other end of the bar. Wine bar? I'd been to one once, with Emma, after we'd been out late-night shopping together. Nice restaurant? Barry and I normally went to a Harvester on our anniversaries. That's twenty-four anniversaries, twenty-four visits to a Harvester, twenty-four versions of a prawn cocktail or melon starter, a steak dinner, and apple pie or banana split for afters. Apart from that, we only frequented the local Indian and Chinese.

'I'm . . . not much of a connoisseur of restaurants,' I said a bit limply.

Then I looked down at my old jeans (worn with two pairs of socks and my old, warm boots), and the hefty grey fleece I'd zipped up over the purple sweatshirt, topped off with the old anorak and pink woolly hat.

'In fact I think I'd better go home!' I almost shouted.

'What – right now? Can I at least go to the next round-about or do you want me to do an emergency three-point turn?'

'It's not funny,' I muttered. 'I've just realised what I look like.'

'Sorry. I'd have covered the mirror if I knew you were suffering from an identity crisis . . .'

'Look at me! For God's sake! All the oldest things in my wardrobe!'

147

'Rosie, you've been standing for nearly two hours in the cold wind watching me play football. If you'd been dressed up to the nines in glamorous fashion gear, I'd have called the psychiatric on-call instead of asking you out for dinner.'

I pulled off the pink woolly hat and tried desperately to smooth my hair down. I didn't want to look in the mirror because my nose would, quite obviously, be bright red and my ears would be a funny shape from wearing the hat. What was the matter with me? Was I mad? Any other woman in the world would have died with embarrassment if someone as gorgeous as Ashley Connor had kissed them while they were looking like a cross between a scarecrow and a Yeti. Me, I just puckered up and closed my eyes as if it was no less than I deserved.

'You must be mad,' I told him fervently. 'No one in their right mind would want to be seen with me, looking like this.'

'Don't put yourself down,' he laughed lightly. 'You look fine to me.'

This wasn't reassurance enough for a Scarecrow-Yeti, even without the pink hat. There probably couldn't be reassurance enough in the world. Even if Prince William had appeared, as in a dream, and announced that the age difference meant nothing to him, looks were irrelevant, dress sense was an overrated virtue and he wanted to marry me and make me the future Queen of England, I'd have had to go home and change first.

'I look like shit,' I insisted, still working frantically on my hair with my bare hands. 'I can't go anywhere. Sorry, Ashley. I forgot all about it.'

'About what?' he asked, sounding more amused than ever.

'What I look like!' I snapped, beginning to feel irritated by his lack of understanding.

He drove in silence for a minute or two. I began to panic that, on top of all my other concerns, I'd now offended him. But suddenly he took one hand off the wheel, laid it

148

lightly on my knee (very daringly considering the traffic conditions, not to mention the state of my jeans), and said quietly: 'That's the nice thing about you, Rosie.'

He'd lost me now. What was nice about me? The fact that I looked like a bad advert for outdoor pursuits for the over forties?

'You're so ... refreshing,' he went on, still smiling to himself, the hand still lying on my knee, which was beginning very scarily to tremble. Refreshing? It sounded like a bottle of spring water. I couldn't think of anything much less sexy, apart from of course an old armchair.

'I don't think I like that!' I retorted, unwisely. 'I don't really like the sound of being refreshing, Ashley! It really isn't very flattering to be compared with a bottle of water, thank you very much. It was bad enough PJ thinking of me as comfortable and cosy, without you thinking of me as *refreshing*.'

'PJ?' he replied, trying to look round at me without taking his eyes off the road or his hand off my knee. The Jag swerved dangerously, and he slowed down, indicated left and took the next turning off the main road. We pulled up into a parking area outside a parade of shops and he turned off the engine. 'What's all this about PJ?'

'Nothing. Only that he called me a comfortable old armchair, and I didn't like it very much.'

Ashley's mouth set with annoyance.

'The boy's an idiot. He's got no business calling you *anything*. What does he know?'

'Well,' I prevaricated, feeling awkward and defensive now. 'He was only being friendly. I just didn't like his metaphors. But then, I don't like yours very much either.'

He began to smile again.

'Well perhaps when you hear the word *refreshing* you think of a bottle of water. But I don't.' He put his arm around me and moved his hand a little further up my thigh. A shockwave of feelings I could barely remember from the earlier years of my marriage made me catch my breath,

149

shivering despite the layers of thick clothing. 'I think of an exotic cocktail – bright, sparkling, and original. And very intoxicating.'

His face was very close to mine now. I turned my lips towards his and closed my eyes. Intoxicating! Yes! This was good, this was very good. If he kissed me again now, I'd probably faint with pleasure, and it'd be well worth the loss of consciousness.

'I'll go and get some fish and chips,' he said, getting out of the car and slamming the door behind him.

We drove to a quiet spot beside the river. It was just beginning to get dark but the wind had dropped, and when Ashley lowered the electronic windows I was surprised not to be cut in half by an icy blast from outside. Of course, the layers of clothing, to say nothing of the heat of my own lust and embarrassment, probably helped.

'Here,' he said, handing me a wrapped parcel of cod and chips, and a can of Coke. 'Since you wouldn't risk a restaurant, I thought a picnic would be the next best thing.'

'Thank you,' I said primly, not unwrapping it.

'What's the matter?'

'Nothing. It's very nice of you. I appreciate it.'

'You don't like fish?' he asked anxiously. 'Or you're on a diet? Not that you need to be, of course,' he added quickly.

'I love fish. Thank you,' I said again.

This was ridiculous. Here I was, in his car, being called exotic and intoxicating, having my thigh touched up and fish and chips bought for me, and even Becky telling me it was obvious he was coming on to me and I should go for it. What was he waiting for? Me to make the first move, perhaps? There was no one around – this was a picnic spot and there were no other cars parked here at this time on a Sunday evening. I laid the parcel of fish and chips carefully on the floor of the car by my feet and said, without looking at him:

150

'I've had a fantasy lately. About having it off in a car.'

He nearly choked on a chip. I actually had to thump him on the back, and began to have worrying thoughts about the Heimlich manoeuvre.

'So tell me a bit more about this fantasy,' he managed eventually when the chip had come back up.

I leaned against him and tried to ignore what the gear stick was doing to me.

'If you want to get in the back seat with me,' I said, my heart throwing itself madly against my ribs in protest at my daring, 'I'll show you.'

We never did eat the fish and chips.

'What was it like?' squealed Becky, her eyes like saucers, her hand clamped to her mouth in excitement. Sara was on her lunch break and we were closing up the Monday morning clinic. Becky had been badgering me for the goss ever since I arrived at work, but I'd been reluctant to say much in front of Sara – who'd given me a disapproving look as soon as she heard I'd had a lift home from Ashley – or in front of the Medicine for the Elderly patients, despite their collective deafness. It's amazing how a deaf old patient will always hear the few words you really don't want them to hear. '*Back seat*' would have got them all frantically adjusting their hearing aids and '*knickers*' might have caused a few unexpected cardiac symptoms.

'We didn't do it,' I shrugged.

'You *didn't*?' gasped Becky.

Don't look at me like that. I'm as disappointed as you are, believe me!

For a start, it'd taken quite some time to get out of the various layers of clothing. It's not easy in the back of a car; I don't care who you are or how posh the car is. Between the two of us, we seemed to have too many feet and not enough hands. Then there was the problem of the leather

151

upholstery. It might look very nice, but have you ever tried taking a pair of jeans off whilst sliding about on it? It's just not designed for it. It's easy enough to sit still while you've got both feet on the ground in the normal way of travelling, but lift one leg off the floor and your arse slips off the edge of the seat. After a few minutes of this I got the giggles, which helped to control my nerves but didn't do a lot for Ashley's erection (I couldn't help noticing). I was just wondering how long he was going to watch me struggling with my own clothes and get the hell out of his own, when he commented somewhat sadly:

'It's not very dignified, is it?'

I stopped disrobing, halfway out of the inside layer of sweater, with my jeans still round my ankles.

'No, but it's exciting – don't you think?' I said. My heart was still going like a road drill and I wanted nothing more, at that moment, than to launch myself on top of him – preferably minus the remaining one arm and one shoulder of my sweater and the ankle-trailing jeans – rip off his smart shirt and trousers and shag the life out of him. It was difficult to think about anything else, even the possibility of sliding off the leather seat together at the most crucial moment – so I was completely bemused when the next thing he said was:

'Will you have to cook dinner for your husband when you get home?'

By now I'd got the sweatshirt halfway over my head, and I paused inside its purple darkness to mouth to myself: *What the fuck*?? before pulling it back down over my shoulders, sitting up and looking at him.

'You said that deliberately!' I accused him, needled beyond caring about any remaining niceties. 'To put me off! Just because you've lost your hard-on!'

'Rosie, please!' he protested, looking pained. He straightened himself up against the seat and we both sat there, staring at each other – him in his nice clothes and nice car, me in my pink flowery bra and non-matching knickers, with my purple sweatshirt round my neck and my

152

jeans round my ankles, and my sexual excitement slowly ebbing away.

'I'm just not sure ... this is such a good idea,' he said apologetically.

'Not now it isn't. Not now you've so *kindly* reminded me about my husband. Just as I was going to ...'

'Yes, yes, I know, I'm sorry,' he said hastily, picking up my fleece from the floor of the car and handing it to me as I put my arms back into the sweatshirt. 'But perhaps another time, another place ...'

'If you'd rather not,' I said, crossly, 'then forget it. But it wasn't *my* idea to park here in the dark with nobody around, giving me ideas, leading me on, getting me all ...' I wriggled uncomfortably into my jeans, 'worked up.'

'I know. I'm sorry,' he said again, looking suitably apologetic. He leaned over to kiss me but I turned away. There was an uncomfortable silence. My breathing was taking a while to return to normal but I wasn't going to let him see that.

'Tell you what,' he said suddenly. 'We'll go somewhere much nicer.'

'What, now? It's a bit late, Ashley, and as you've said, I have a husband at home and ...'

'No, no ... not now. In a couple of weeks' time I'm going to a meeting in Paris. You could come with me. What do you think?'

I looked back at him. Is this man completely mad? He knows I'll go scurrying home, with or without my clothes, if he mentions my husband while we're in the back of his car together, but thinks I can quite cheerfully leave home for a whole weekend away without ending up in the divorce courts?

'I'll think about it,' I said.

OK, OK, so I was completely mad too. But Paris! I'd never been to Paris. I'd never even looked at Paris in a brochure. The nearest I'd been was Calais – and then only to the hypermarket to stock up on vin rouge and cheap

153

lager. It would be nice to dream about it for a couple of weeks – to imagine Ashley and me in Paris together, walking arm in arm down streets with strange foreign names where nobody would recognise us, sitting in the bar of some chic and fashionable hotel where we could retire to our own room whenever we wanted without any fear of sliding off leather car seats.

'Think about it and let me know, then,' he said, as he got out of the car and came round to open the back door for me. 'Shall we ... er ... get into the front again?'

I trod on the fish and chips as I climbed back into the passenger seat. I bet it made an awful stain on the carpet.

'So what are you going to do?' whispered Becky just as Sara came back to the reception desk.

'Ssh!' I warned her. 'Well, I offered to pay for it to be valeted but he seemed to be OK about it ...'

'No, not about the fish on the carpet! About the weekend in Paris, for God's sake! Paris!!' She went cross-eyed with dreaminess. 'Ooh, I'd just *love* to go to Paris! With Dave ...'

'Who's going to Paris?' cut in Sara, looking at us suspiciously. 'You can't have time off during the Easter holidays, Becky – I've already booked it. I'm taking Callum to Spain while the playgroup's closed for the holiday.'

'What – and leaving him there?' said Becky without sounding particularly surprised.

'Don't be silly. It's important for him to understand his roots.'

Becky and I looked at each other in gobsmacked silence for a couple of seconds before Becky, sniggering, retorted in a half-whisper:

'His *roots*? His fucking *roots*, Sara? I thought his father was from Birmingham?'

'Not necessarily. I wasn't too sure about the accent. He didn't talk very much,' she said defensively.

154

'Well, he wasn't a native Spaniard at any rate, was he? I mean, you must have noticed whether he was talking in English or Spanish when he asked you to get your knickers off, even if you *had* had one too many Sangrias.'

'Quite a few too many actually,' said Sara sadly, beginning to look a bit sick just at the memory of it. 'But that's not the point. I consider him half Spanish. He was made in Spain, wasn't he. And I'd like him to grow up with a bit of understanding of his native culture. It's the best I can do.'

'So it's an educational visit to Magaluf?'

'Exactly,' smiled Sara.

'And you will be careful, this time, won't you, with the Sangria?' I pointed out anxiously. 'Or are we hoping for a little half Spanish brother or sister for Callum?'

'No, we are *not*, Rosie. I've learned my lesson, thank you! I don't want anything to do with men any more.'

Becky and I contemplated this in appalled silence.

'So who's going to Paris, anyway?' she persisted.

'I am,' I said. 'With Ashley Connor. For an orthopaedic conference.'

As an announcement, it could have been timed better. Like, for instance, not when PJ happened to be standing behind me.

Well, OK, I *wasn't* going to say yes to the Paris trip. I *so* wasn't going to say yes. It was a bad idea, it was a ridiculous idea. Having a quick shag in the back of Ashley's car would have been lovely; it wouldn't have taken long (especially if we'd slid off the seat) and I could have almost pretended to myself that it hadn't happened at all. It could have been a sort of accident, something that 'just happened' to me, like we used to say when we were teenagers and didn't intend to go any further than a kiss and a cuddle but events mysteriously overtook us. I wouldn't have beaten myself up with guilt about it because Barry would have still been watching the football anyway and it wouldn't have been any skin off his nose as he tended to prefer that to sex these days. But a weekend away in Paris was a whole new ball game. It would require tact and diplomacy – or to put it more accurately, lies and deceit – and I wasn't sure I had the energy for it. But events – of a completely different nature – had overtaken me when I arrived home that evening.

'If I drive you home now,' said Ashley as we left the picnic area minus the squashed fish and chips, which he'd managed to scrape off the floor and throw in a litterbin but the smell of which lingered on hauntingly, 'perhaps I can come in and wait while you have a look for those photos?'

Photos? Fucking *photos* again? But believe me, I was far too stressed out by the thought of Ashley coming into the house, to wonder very much about his continuing fascination with my photography.

'No, I don't think so! Definitely not!' I gabbled.

'You think your husband might be funny about it?'

About me coming home with someone I'd just tried to seduce in the back of a car? Yes, I'd say there was a fair chance he'd be funny about it.

'Absolutely. He's obsessively jealous,' I smiled, trying to look, despite the boots and the fleece and everything, like a person a man would be obsessively jealous about.

'That's not good,' frowned Ashley. 'Don't be blackmailed by jealousy, Rosie. It can kill a marriage.'

Considering Barry and I had managed, despite both of us suffering from various shades of every emotional handicap known to man or woman, to clock up nearly a quarter of a century of reasonably mediocre marriage without being able to kill it, this wasn't about to alarm me very much. Especially as, in reality, the most jealous I ever saw Barry was when I fed the dog chocolate biscuits.

'It's the next turning on the right,' I told him. 'Just drop me on the corner.'

'Don't be silly. I'll take you to the door,' he replied as he swung the Jag smoothly into my road.

'What number? How far down?'

'Shit,' I responded.

My house wasn't very far down at all, you see. And outside it, Barry was sitting in his car with the engine running and the passenger door open. And approaching the door from the direction of *my house* was someone I'd recognise only too well anywhere, even outside my own house, even wearing jeans and a sexy short black leather jacket instead of her tight red top.

'Drive past!' I hissed at Ashley, who, to be fair, had no idea what he was supposed to be driving past or why. 'Keep driving! Go to the end of the road! Don't look as if we know them!'

'Who? Why? I don't!'

But I was far too busy to explain. Far too busy watching as Robyn Dainton slid carelessly onto the seat next to my husband and, as he turned towards her, leaned over and kissed him casually on the lips.

It was the casualness that did it. OK, I'd have been *surprised* at a passionate kiss, if only because I didn't know Barry still had it in him. But that quick, nonchalant peck on the lips was the sort of kiss *I* usually got from him. It wasn't the kiss of a pair of illicit shaggers. It was the kiss of a couple who were actually *together*. Outside *my house*. In *my husband*'s car.

'Ashley,' I pronounced when he pulled up at the end of the cul-de-sac and, understandably enough, looked at me for further guidance. I felt dizzy and short of breath and I was aware that I probably had a mad glint of hysteria in my eyes. 'Ashley, I've made up my mind. If the offer's still on – I'm coming to Paris with you.'

Chapter Nine

Walking on eggshells

From my vantage point of forty-four years, looking back over a life consisting, generally, of month after month of mundane everyday activities punctuated once in a blue moon by something exciting or interesting, I feel qualified to make this observation: exciting things in life usually come with a down side. They're either expensive, scary, or they make you sick. And they tend to get you into trouble with either the police, or your doctor, your parents, or even your kids. There was so much on the down side of my excitement about the pending trip to Paris, and so much potential for trouble, that I spent the next couple of weeks veering between mania and panic like a hyperventilating psychiatric patient.

There were trivial things on the down side, like what underwear I was going to take to Paris, and there were annoying things like PJ getting on my case about why I was going and whether I ought to be doing so, and then there was the really serious thing – just in case you thought I might have forgotten – about the complete breakdown of my marriage.

The breakdown hadn't actually happened, but it was there in the wings, waiting to come on stage at the given moment. It was waiting, to put it more precisely, for a cue from me. I was looking at it kind-of obliquely, considering what it meant, what it would be like to live with, whether I could put up with it because once I'd taken it on board that would be it . . . no going back.

'I saw you,' I told Barry stonily, when he came back from wherever he'd been with Robyn Red-Breast in the car the previous afternoon, 'With *her*. In the car.'

'Taking her home,' he replied with a shrug. 'And I saw *you*. With Some Bloke in a Jag.'

'Bringing *me* home,' I retorted with a matching shrug.

We looked at each other across the kitchen, eyes narrowed, summing each other up, gauging the strength of our defences.

'She came to watch the football,' said Barry eventually. 'She phoned just after you went out. Her TV packed up. She supports the Arsenal.'

Oh, well. That makes everything all right, then. As long as she supports the Arsenal.

'Cosy,' I said. 'She kissed you when she got in the car.'

'She's a friend. Friends kiss. I suppose you don't kiss your smart friend in the Jag?'

'He's one of the consultants,' I retorted, trying not to blush as I realised how similar this was to 'she supports the Arsenal' in its irrelevance. 'He gave me a lift back from the football match.'

'Oh yes. The *football match*. How did it go?' asked Barry. His voice dripped with sarcasm. It suddenly occurred to me that he didn't actually believe that was where I'd been. Despite everything – despite the deceit and lies that were beginning to crawl nastily like maggots through the over-ripe fruit that was our marriage, I suddenly found this so funny I had to sit down and have a laugh.

'What's the matter?' he asked, looking perplexed and irritated.

'I need to go to the loo,' I spluttered. 'I can't stop laughing. I'm going to wet myself!'

'What's so bloody funny?'

'Look at me! Look at what I'm wearing! You don't think I'd go out dressed like this if I was on some sort of . . . *assignation* . . . do you?'

Then I had an involuntary mental re-wind to the back seat of Ashley's car, down by the river, and stopped laughing with an uncomfortable hiccup. I got up and made a dash for the toilet, aware that the conversation – and the accusations – had been shelved for the time being. By mutual and unspoken consent we didn't speak much during the evening. We both knew we were treading on eggshells. One wrong foot and the whole structure was going to crack wide open and all sorts of ugly and obscene things were going to break forth. Better not to jump around too much until we were really sure we wanted to release them.

As if I didn't have enough on my mind, I was finding it increasingly difficult to pretend my hand wasn't hurting. The cut was over the crease between my index finger and palm, and it hadn't healed very well because every time I opened my hand it opened the wound. I was holding something in the other hand while I was walking through the outpatient department that Monday afternoon when PJ came flying through the swing doors towards me, nearly knocking me off balance. I put out my left hand to ward him off and he stopped in alarm as he saw me flinch.

'Sorry, Rosie. Not looking where I'm . . . Hey, are you all right?'

'It's nothing.' I nursed my injured hand ruefully. 'Just a bit sore . . .'

'Let me see.' He steered me into the nearest empty consulting room, pushed me down onto a chair and peeled the dressing off the wound. 'Jesus, Rosie. Why the hell haven't you shown this to anyone?'

We both contemplated the red, angry swollen palm of my hand.

'It's OK,' I shrugged. 'It's just taking a while to heal . . .'

160

'Don't be fucking stupid. Sorry, Rosie, but look at it. It's infected. If the hand surgeons saw this they'd have you on the ward on IV antibiotics with your arm elevated before you could blink.'

'Why do you think I haven't shown them?' I retorted.

'Well you should at least have shown *me*.' Shaking his head at my stupidity, he rummaged in the desk drawer for a prescription pad and began to scribble on it. 'Here, take this to pharmacy and start taking the antibiotics straight away. OK?'

'Yes.'

'And put this cream on the wound twice a day. For God's sake!' He shook his head again as he handed over the scrip. 'I can't believe you. You should know better ...'

I accepted the prescription and the rebuke with a shrug.

'OK, I was going to ask someone about it soon if it didn't get better. I've been busy.'

'Yes, so I hear.'

'What's that supposed to mean?'

'You know. Ashley Connor. Don't give me that innocent look, Rosie Peacock. I heard you telling the girls this morning about going to Paris. You realise it'll be all over the hospital by tomorrow?'

'Only if you spread it around.'

'I won't. But your friends probably will.'

'No, they w ...'

'And anyway, it's not exactly going to be a secret, is it? When you turn up at the hotel with him do you really think all the consultant orthopods from all over Europe are going to just discreetly cough and look the other way? Their eyes are going to be out on stalks. They're going to be nudging each other and asking who's the bit of stuff old Ashley's brought along for a dirty weekend, wonder if his wife knows what's going on ...?'

'Wife?' I repeated, weakly.

PJ, who'd been re-dressing my hand, paused in mid-wrap of the bandage and looked me in the eyes.

161

'You didn't know he had a wife?'

'Well ... I don't know ... I suppose ...' I stammered. 'I suppose it just hasn't come up in conversation ...'

'He hasn't told you,' said PJ flatly, looking back down at his bandaging, which he finished off with a swift sticking of pink plaster. He held onto my hand for a moment, staring at it as if he was contemplating what a good job he'd made of the dressing. 'I don't think you should go to Paris, Rosie. It's really, really, not a good idea. Trust me.'

'Trust you?' I retorted, snatching back my hand and getting up. 'Why? What's it got to do with you? I *am* going to Paris, thank you very much, and Ashley's already arranged for me to be listed as his secretary so nobody's going to think *anything* of it, not that it's any of your business.' I paused at the door and looked back at him. 'Thanks for the prescription,' I added more gently.

'You're welcome,' he said in the same flat tone, without looking up at me. 'Take care.'

Looking back now, of course, I can't imagine how I'd got that far without even wondering whether Ashley was married. Would it have made any difference, anyway, if I'd known? I was married myself, and that didn't exactly seem to have stopped me from sliding about half undressed on the back seat of his car, did it?

'I think I've got serious problems,' I suddenly found myself blurting out when Becky and I were leaving that night, 'with my marriage.'

'Of course you have,' she agreed without missing a beat.

I looked at her in surprise.

'You knew? It's that obvious?'

'Only to me and Sara, probably. We've known you a long time, Rosie. We've heard you ...'

'Moaning? Whingeing?'

She shrugged.

'Everyone moans. But ... you just haven't been happy. Not for ages.'

I contemplated this as we walked out of the hospital together. Had I been unhappy for ages? I hadn't realised. I just thought it was normal – the tired, bored, dragging sense of life passing by, the lack of spark, the loss of interest in anything. Didn't other people feel like that, then? Didn't they wake up with a groan when they realised they were still the same person, still with the same old life, and hadn't changed overnight into a princess living in a palace somewhere tropical?

'I haven't been *that* unhappy,' I said slowly. 'I suppose we'd all like things to be different, wouldn't we, but . . . well, I just couldn't be bothered to try.'

'Exactly. You were too depressed. Sara's been on at you for years about doing something to change your life. Then you went to that lecture and started making the effort, and look at you now!'

'Look at me . . . how? How do you mean?'

'Rosie, don't you realise how different you've been? Everyone's noticed. It's like . . . you're more . . . alive. More dynamic!'

'Charismatic?' I prompted her excitedly. 'Fascinating?'

'If you like, yeah!' she laughed. 'Whatever!' She leaned towards me and whispered, 'Ashley Connor's certainly noticed, anyway!'

'That's half the problem,' I said, calming down. 'He's half the serious problem with my marriage, Becky. The other half is the girl Barry's been seeing.'

'I don't think so,' she replied calmly. 'Not really.'

'He is! She came round to watch football, and she kissed him in the car, and she looks about sixteen and wears . . .'

'No, no.' Becky stopped walking and took hold of my arm, turning me to face her. 'I didn't mean that. Maybe he is seeing someone, maybe he isn't. Maybe you're having an affair with Ashley Connor, maybe you're not. I meant, that isn't the problem. The problem was already there, Rosie. It's probably been there for years. You're bored with each

other. Ashley Connor, and this girl – they're not the cause
. . . they're just the symptoms.'

'How do you know all this stuff?' I asked her. I felt
light-headed and faint with alarm, like I'd been turned
upside down and shaken. I hung onto Becky's arm, swaying
slightly. 'What makes you so sure . . .?'

'You don't seem to realise it, but Sara and I are your
friends. We notice things. We try to help. But up till now,
you've always been too busy either complaining about your
life, or joking around, taking the piss, trying to cover up
how you really felt.'

To say I was staggered would be an understatement. I was
totally lost for words. Who was this person, this poor, sad,
strange wreck of a woman Becky was describing, who spent her
days feeling sorry for herself or acting like a clown instead of
appreciating that she had friends who cared about her? And
anyway, since when did I have friends? I never realised I had
friends! I thought of Becky and Sara as my colleagues. We got
on OK, we worked well together – even though I'd been
upgraded and was supposed to be their supervisor we never
argued seriously or did anything to upset each other, we
sympathised with each other's problems and tried to help each
other but . . . OK, I suppose we were friends! I'd just been too
thick to notice! What was the matter with me?

'I'm sorry,' I muttered against Becky's arm which had
suddenly appeared round my shoulders.

'Sorry?' she retorted. 'What for, you daft thing? I'm just
glad you've started to come out of . . . whatever cold dark
place you've been in for so long! You look like someone
who's just woken up, and started looking around and seeing
the world again.'

'Yeah – like seeing the cracks in my marriage,' I said
bitterly.

'If that's part of the reality you've been avoiding looking
at, Rosie,' she replied quietly as we walked on again, 'then
maybe it's time you *did* wake up to it.'

*

164

That night, I lay awake for a long time listening to Barry pretending to be asleep. I wanted to try to talk to him, to ask whether he'd been unhappy for ages, too, without realising it – or at least without *me* realising it. But I didn't really know how to start, and anyway I was worried about the eggshells we were walking on – I still wasn't sure about breaking them. Eventually I fell asleep and dreamed I was driving Ashley Connor's car while he and his wife had sex on the back seat.

'You didn't tell me you were married.'

We were at our Usual Pub the next day, having our Usual Quick Drink after work. Ashley put his drink down carefully, wiped his mouth and looked up at me, smiling, amused.

'Perhaps you didn't ask.'

'Perhaps not, but it tends to come up in conversation. I must have mentioned my husband to you within the first five minutes of meeting you. It's a normal thing to mention, Ashley.'

'Would it have bothered you? If you'd known, would it have stopped you meeting me ... like this ... or like the other day in the back of my car? Why would it have mattered to you any more than *you* being married?'

I flushed.

'At least *you* were aware of all the facts. If you'd told me, I would have understood why you weren't ...'

'What?' He picked up his drink again and looked at me over the top of it, eyebrows raised. 'I wasn't what?'

'Well. You weren't quite as keen as me, when it came to it, were you. I suppose you were thinking about your *wife*.'

I didn't mean it to come out quite like that – bitter, resentful, as if I had any right whatsoever to resent this poor woman when I'd never even met her and didn't even know of her existence a couple of days ago.

'My wife's got absolutely nothing to do with this,' he replied calmly before taking another mouthful of his drink.

'If I haven't mentioned her, it's purely because it's irrelevant.'

'What?' I persisted. 'Your wife's irrelevant to you? Your marriage is irrelevant?'

'Don't twist my words,' he said with a sudden laugh. 'Come on, Rosie – lighten up. OK, so we're both married. We're not teenagers, we know the score. We've both been around the block a few times . . .'

Well, I don't know about you. I haven't been around anyone else's block since long before I got married at the age of twenty.

I fiddled with my drink and watched him watching me.

'Have you got kids?'

'Two boys.'

'How old?'

'Six and eight. Rosie, can we stop this? I'm sorry if I didn't mention it but I suppose, when I'm with you, I'm trying not to think about home. Is that OK? Can you understand that?' He looked at me with a big-eyed, puppy-dog smile that made me shiver all the way from my ears to my toes. 'Am I forgiven?'

Obviously. You know perfectly well when you look at me like that all I want to do is grab hold of you and snog the bollocks off you.

'I suppose so,' I said with a pretend sigh.

'Still want to come to Paris?'

'Does your wife know?'

'Does your husband?' he shot back, with a grin.

'Not yet. I'm . . . er . . . waiting for the right moment.' Like when we're speaking to each other. I smiled back at him, excitement about Paris suddenly and briefly bubbling to the surface through all the anxieties about my marriage and my life in general. 'What happens at the conference? Will I have time to see the sights? Can I go up the Eiffel Tower?'

'Of course!' He took hold of my hand. 'We'll fly out on the Thursday night. The conference is on Friday. On

166

Saturday I'll show you Paris and on Saturday night we'll hit the town!'

'So ... what do I do on the Friday? Stay in the hotel? Not that I mind ...' I asked anxiously, wondering if there'd be a mini bar and if so whether I'd have to pay for my own drinks.

'Look around the shops if you like! I haven't met a woman yet who could resist French fashion.'

And *I* haven't met one yet who could afford it.

I smiled weakly, wondering whether I could save up for a pair of knickers at least by the time I got there.

'Great!' I said. 'And I suppose I could always take my camera and get some more practice in.'

'Excellent idea!' he enthused. 'Don't forget, by the way – I'm still looking forward to seeing the rest of your photos when you remember to bring them in.'

'Yeah, OK,' I agreed distractedly. I couldn't actually think off-hand whereabouts at home I'd put them. Somehow with everything else that was going on, my new hobby had taken a bit of a back seat in the order of life's essentials.

'And I'm looking forward to Paris, too,' he added softly, squeezing my hand again and giving me a long, meaningful look. 'To having a little more privacy than the back seat of my car.'

'Mm!' I agreed, returning his meaningful look and having to swallow hard to stop myself from dribbling disgustingly with anticipation. 'Yes ... I'm looking forward to that, too, Ashley. In fact I can't wait!'

The waiting was actually quite nerve-racking. I wasn't sleeping much at night, what with listening to Barry also not sleeping, wondering about whether we were ever going to get around to talking about our marriage, and imagining what it was going to be like actually being in bed with Ashley Connor. I was a mess of conflicting emotions – sadness, confusion, fear, guilt, excitement and lust. During the day I worked like an automaton, hoping desperately that

I wasn't making any mistakes, that I was remembering to smile at patients and make eye contact, that I wasn't calling people by their wrong names or sending them to the wrong doctors. I was vaguely aware of people talking to me – of Sara and Becky for instance, giving me worried looks and asking if I was OK, and PJ constantly prowling around making irritating comments about Paris – but their voices were on the periphery of my consciousness, faint and hazy compared with the terrifying sharpness of the thoughts and fears in the frontal lobe of my mind.

'Are you all right, Mum?' asked Stuart one evening when he'd gone to get some ice-cream out of the freezer and found it neatly stacked with bottles of detergent, shampoos and toothpaste. 'You seem a bit ... out of it, lately.'

'Sorry,' I said, vaguely, wondering whether I'd unpacked the frozen food into the bathroom cupboard. 'Got a lot on my mind.'

'You should have *my* life,' he retorted gloomily. 'Got a maths test tomorrow *and* I've got to sit next to Steven Porter.'

Life's a bitch. If only all I had to worry about was a maths test and sitting next to Steven Porter, I'd settle for being fourteen again!

'We ought to talk,' said Barry finally when we went to bed that night. We were getting undressed with our backs to each other to avoid having to look at each other. I turned and studied his face. I'd known that face intimately since I was eighteen, but now I felt like I was looking at a stranger. He had shadows under his eyes where he hadn't been sleeping. Did I look as bad as he did?

'No,' I said, turning away again. 'Not yet.'

'Stuart knows there's something wrong. It isn't fair. Drifting along, not talking, not saying anything to him ...'

'There's nothing to tell him.'

Yet.

'How serious is this, Rosie?' he persisted, sitting down

168

on the edge of the bed, looking at the carpet. 'How bad is this? I don't know. I need to know what you're thinking. Are you thinking . . .'

'I don't know!' I interrupted him crossly. 'I don't know what I'm thinking! If I did, I'd tell you, but I don't, and I don't want to discuss it till I sort it out in my head. OK?'

'Meanwhile we just go on like this . . .?'

I sighed and sat down too, on the other side of the bed, facing away from him.

'I'm going away next weekend,' I said. 'Maybe when I get back . . .'

'Are you?' I felt the bed bounce as he turned round to stare at the back of my head. 'Where are you going? You never go away . . .'

'There's a lot of things I never do,' I retorted morosely.

'I've never stopped you. I didn't know you weren't happy.'

'Nor did I,' I admitted. I sighed. Here come the lies. 'I'm going away with a couple of the girls from work. Just for two nights. Paris.'

'Lovely,' he said unenthusiastically.

'I think we need some space. Time apart, to think.'

'You're probably right.' The bed bounced again as he got up and went to hang up his trousers in the wardrobe. 'I suppose you and your friends will be out on the town, on the pull with all those Frenchmen.'

'Don't be silly,' I said wearily, climbing into bed. I turned over and closed my eyes, closing out the guilt and the worry and the fear and the sadness and concentrating instead on the thought of Ashley lying next to me. Frenchmen? Huh! Who needs them?

'Are you getting excited about Paris, Rosie?' asked Becky, nudging me gently and grinning in Ashley's direction. He was standing with his back to us, talking to one of the other consultants, and I realised I'd been staring at him for about five minutes.

169

'You've got your tongue hanging out!' added Sara.

'Yeah – put it away. You might need it next weekend!' laughed Becky.

'Stop it!' I said, smiling. 'You've got such a dirty mind!'

'Oh, and you haven't? I can read your thoughts right now ... just like a page of the Kama Sutra!'

'I can't stop thinking about him,' I admitted quietly, still staring. 'I think I must be mad. My marriage is crumbling before my eyes, and all I can do is fantasise about having it off with another man.'

'That's not mad,' said Becky. 'It makes perfect sense.'

'As long as you don't get hurt, Rosie,' cautioned Sara, giving me her Nun/Social Worker look. 'I don't suppose he's exactly looking for long-term commitment.'

'I know. I'm not stupid. He's married, anyway.'

'Bound to be,' nodded Becky, following my gaze. 'Probably got snapped up before he even finished medical school.'

'A fling is one thing,' went on Sara, 'as long as no one gets hurt ... as long as you're not expecting too much ...'

'As long as you have *fun*,' said Becky. 'Are you packing your sexiest black underwear?'

'I haven't got any!' I replied, suddenly panic-stricken.

'Well, it doesn't have to be black. Red, perhaps?'

'No, I haven't got *any*!'

'Well, that'll be even better, then!' laughed Sara. 'If anything's sexier than sexy underwear, it has to be *no* underwear ...'

'I mean, I haven't got anything sexy. I don't possess anything ... anything whatsoever that a man would want to look at. Barry never looks at me. He wouldn't notice if I walked around naked all day with *Fuck me senseless* tattooed on my belly.' I stopped, frowning, picking at my lips anxiously as I mentally took stock of my underwear drawer. Since I'd cleared it out a few weeks ago, I'd had so few items left that I'd had to wash bras and knickers out almost every night to avoid running out. I was beginning to

170

wish I'd kept all the old off-white baggy pants and greying bras with overstretched elastic – but on the other hand what sort of an impression would they have made on Ashley Connor when I got undressed in the hotel room? He'd probably take one look and beg me to put my clothes back on.

'I need to buy some!' I almost shouted, grabbing Becky's arm so hard I flinched from the pain in my bad hand. 'I need knickers and bras! Urgently!'

'You can buy some in Paris,' Becky reminded me.

'They'll be too expensive. I'll only be able to afford one knicker. And anyway, what about the first night?'

'Ooooh! The *first night*!' laughed Becky and Sara together, giving each other knowing looks. 'We mustn't forget the *first night*, must we!'

'It's all very well for you two to laugh,' I scowled. 'I've never done anything like this before. I'll probably mess it all up and make a fool of myself.'

'Of course you won't,' said Becky seriously. 'Don't worry, Rosie. Would you like to go out knicker-shopping tomorrow? I'll come with you if you like. I could do with some new stuff myself, now I'm seeing Dave!'

Fortunately this took the emphasis of piss-taking off me for a change and we spent a pleasant few minutes teasing Becky about her new relationship before getting back to work on the clinic outcomes.

'Everything all right, girls? Rosie?' smiled Ashley as he passed the desk a moment later.

'Fine, thanks, Mr Connor,' replied Becky, quick as a flash. 'We'll be setting up your private patients clinic in a knick ... whoops! I mean in a tick.'

'Yes, we'll have it all ready for you Mr Connor. Don't worry about a thong ... I mean, a thing!' joined in Sara.

He walked off, shaking his head at them in complete bewilderment as they collapsed, giggling over the desk.

'Very childish,' I pronounced, making them giggle even more. 'I wish I'd never told you!'

*

171

The knicker-shopping expedition took place the next day, a Saturday. I met Becky at Marks & Spencer because that was the only place I'd ever bought underwear before.

'No, no, no – not in here!' she exclaimed, steering me away from their comforting familiar glass doors and leading me instead towards the Anne Summers shop.

'Becky!' I hissed at her, recoiling in embarrassment. 'It's a sex shop.'

'No it's not!' she laughed, pulling me firmly by the arm. 'It's lingerie and ... well, *saucy* things. It's completely respectable!'

Forced to follow her into the shop, I lowered my head and my eyes, terrified that I'd be recognised by someone ... a neighbour, a teacher from Barry's school, someone from the hospital ...

'Rosie,' pointed out Becky, as if she were reading my mind, 'If we meet anyone we know, they're hardly like to disapprove or they wouldn't be in here themselves!'

Realising this was fair comment, I looked up – just in time to see Robyn Dainton disappearing into one of the changing cubicles.

'Becky!' I whispered again, grabbing her arm and shaking her. She was deep in contemplation of something flimsy, silky and purple that looked as if it had more holes and straps than I'd understand what to do with. 'Becky, I've got to go. Come on, I'm going!'

'What's the matter with you?' she asked peevishly as I dragged her unceremoniously back out to the street. 'I'd only just started looking ... there were some really nice things. I was going to show you the black ...' She paused, looking at my face. 'What is it?'

'Robyn. That little ... *girl* from Barry's school. The one he's been seeing. She's in there! She's trying on ... *stuff* ... to wear for my husband!!'

Becky took a deep breath and put her arm around me as we walked away from the shop.

'You don't know that,' she said calmly. 'You're jumping to conclusions.'

I didn't reply. As a conclusion, it didn't exactly require a pole vault.

'And when all's said and done,' she added with a sympathetic smile, 'Perhaps he's only doing the same as *you're* doing.'

'It isn't that!' I retorted. 'I'm not *jealous*. I'm not *unreasonable*.'

'What, then?'

I shrugged. I stopped dead in the middle of the pedestrian precinct of the shopping centre of the town where I'd spent my entire married life, and shrugged again, and tried without success to make sense of my scrambled emotions.

'It's just ... the underwear!' I exclaimed crossly. 'He's never shown any interest in underwear!'

'She's in for a disappointment, then, isn't she?' smiled Becky. 'Hope she isn't wasting too much money!'

'Yeah!' I laughed a little shakily. 'She still owes me two pounds for her bus fare!'

We ended up back at Marks & Spencer.

'I was thinking about getting my hair done,' I confided to Becky as we drank coffee in Starbuck's a little later. Carrier bags of black lacy bras and thongs lay beside us on the floor. I kept nudging mine with my foot so that it popped open and allowed me a glimpse of its contents, feeling the thrill of excitement as I imagined myself wearing it for Ashley.

'Go for it!' said Becky. 'What are you going to have done?'

'I don't know. Just a cut, I suppose.'

She studied me for a moment, her head on one side, as she sipped her coffee.

'Why don't you have some highlights put in? It'd suit you.'

'Would it?' I said doubtfully, fingering my thick, scruffy brown locks.

'Yes. Come on – new lifestyle, new underwear, new nail varnish, new man . . . a new hairstyle would complete the picture!' She put down her coffee cup. 'Drink up. Let's see if we can get you booked in anywhere!'

In a smart little hair salon by the multi-storey car park, a girl in a white coat pretending to be a health care assistant took out a huge diary from under her reception desk and pronounced that she could fit me in on Tuesday morning or Wednesday afternoon.

'I'll be at work,' I said, pretending to sound regretful. 'Never mind.'

'What about evenings?' insisted Becky, holding onto me to stop me from walking out.

'No . . . nothing at all . . . absolutely *manic* I'm afraid,' said the girl without a trace of sincerity.

'Never mind . . .' I began again.

The ornate gold and ivory phone on her desk began to trill loudly, its volume no doubt turned up to the highest pitch to make it heard over the noise of the dryers.

'Mrs Green? Four-fifteen?' rhymed the receptionist unwittingly. 'Oh dear. Well thank you for letting us know.'

She put down the phone and looked at me appraisingly as if weighing up whether or not to take a chance on me.

'That was a cancellation,' she informed me importantly. 'You could have four-fifteen today if you like. Wet cut and highlights? With Darren?'

It was nearly five to four. Wet cut and highlights with Darren it was, then. Becky wished me luck and I watched her from the salon window as she trotted back to the multi-storey with her Marks & Spencer bag, leaving me to pretend to read hairstyle magazines for twenty minutes while Darren finished a perm on an elderly lady in a bright green trouser suit.

'Shall I take your bag, Madam?' asked a new voice at my side suddenly, interrupting my in-depth study of *Before* and *After* pictures advertising hair gel. The models in the

174

pictures all had surprised expressions as if the gel had got into their eyes or up their arses. I clutched the Marks & Spencer bag tightly to my chest.

'It's OK. I'll keep it with me.'

'Fine,' said the girl, giving me a curious look. 'Would you like to put this on, Madam?'

She helped me into a blue, tie-at-the-back gown that reminded me of patients going to the operating theatre.

'Come this way, please, Madam,' she said, leading me to the row of sinks with depressions for the neck which never failed to remind me of executioners' blocks. I sat obediently with my neck bent backwards over the sink waiting for the axe to fall or cramp to set in, whichever came first, wondering as I always did how anything as basic and hygienic as a hair wash should need to be so undignified and downright uncomfortable. Finally, dripping and draped in towels, I sat looking at myself in the mirror and waiting for Darren to do his worst.

'Rosie! My God! Is it really you?'

Just my luck, just my fucking luck. The first person I see as I step out of my car on my first day back at work as a short-haired honorary blonde instead of a scraggy-headed mousey haired mouse, has to be PJ.

'Don't start,' I warned him, daring him with my eyes not to start. I was feeling insecure enough about my new image after spending most of Sunday fending off hoots of derision from my son and raised eyebrows from my husband.

'I wasn't going to start anything,' replied PJ. He put both hands on my shoulders and twirled me round. 'It's a good cut, Rosie. Very good. I like it.'

'Hmph. What would you know about good cuts?' I snorted, not wanting to admit I was pleased.

'I'm a surgeon, aren't I?'

I laughed despite myself.

'What about the colour? Too much, isn't it? Too brassy? Too young for me?'

'Don't talk shit. Of course it isn't. It's good. I like it,' he repeated. Then he frowned briefly as if suddenly remembering something and added, 'I suppose it's for the *Conference*. For Mr Connor's benefit.'

'It's for my own benefit, actually,' I replied haughtily, feeling myself flush slightly.

'Good,' he said shortly.

We walked in silence for a while, my blonde crop suddenly weighing heavily on my head as if it were a new hat. I imagined I could feel people staring at me from across the car park. If PJ assumed I'd had it done for the *Conference*, for Ashley, everyone else was obviously going to assume the same. And of course, they'd be right, wouldn't they. What on earth was I thinking of? Who was I trying to fool? What a silly, ridiculous old cow I was being. What difference was a new hairstyle and colour going to make? He either liked me, fancied me, *wanted* me, or he didn't. I'd spent a fortune, far more than I could afford, just to make an idiot of myself.

'I wish I hadn't had it done, now,' I said moodily to PJ.

'And *I* wish you weren't going to Paris,' he snapped back equally moodily.

'Oh, shut up,' I told him. 'Anyone would think you were jealous.'

'Maybe I am,' said PJ, giving me a sideways grin. 'Maybe *I* wanted to shag Ashley Connor in a hotel bedroom. Oh, and talk of the devil ...'

'Morning Rosie!' said Ashley as we approached him outside the hospital entrance. 'Morning Mr Jaimeen.'

'Morning Mr Connor,' replied PJ without smiling at him. 'Got to run, Rosie. Catch you later.'

'Your hair!' exclaimed Ashley quietly as PJ walked away.

I put my hand up to it ruefully.

'I know. It was a mistake. I wish I'd never ... the hairdresser made it too blonde ... cut too much off ... maybe I could sue him ...'

He put out a hand and gently touched my lips, stopping me in mid-flow.

'Rosie, what are you talking about? It's beautiful.'

'Is it?' I gasped, staring at him in open-mouthed wonder. 'Do you think so?'

'You don't know, do you?' he said. 'You really don't know.'

'Don't know what?' I mouthed back, the words getting stuck somewhere halfway down my throat. I realised I was still gaping at him, goldfish-like, so I swallowed hard and tried again. 'What? What don't I know?'

He shrugged, smiling at me.

'That you're beautiful. You're lovely.'

It was definitely the nicest thing anyone had ever said to me. That, anyway, was my excuse for kissing him passionately on the lips outside the main entrance, to his wide-eyed surprise and in full view of half the staff, and probably quite a lot of the patients, of East Dean General Hospital. And quite possibly causing our downfall.

Chapter Ten

Jungle Telegraph

Everywhere I looked, people were nudging each other, grinning behind their hands and whispering.

'You're just being paranoid,' said Sara. 'People grin. People nudge. People whisper. What makes you think it's got anything to do with you? It could be about anything. Or anyone.'

'It wasn't anyone, or anything, snogging Ashley Connor outside the hospital this morning. It was Rosie,' sniggered Silly Hayley, who shouldn't have been listening to our conversation, much less intruding into it.

'Piss off,' I told her calmly. 'Nothing to do with you.'

I slammed the door of the coffee-room fridge hard, catching the tip of her finger not-quite-accidentally as she was trying to retrieve a bottle of milk.

'Ouch!' she complained, giving me an evil look. 'Not *my* fault you've been rumbled, Rosie Peacock. You should have been a bit more discreet where you were putting it around!'

'Yeah, like not *everywhere* for instance!' joined in Linda, her sidekick, nastily.

'Give it a rest, Linda. We all know you're jealous. Mr Connor's probably the only male on the premises you haven't managed to screw yet.'

I looked round in surprise to see PJ standing in the doorway.

Linda went red and muttered a few obscenities under her breath before stalking out of the room, with Hayley scurrying after her.

'Not sure if I should thank you for that or not,' I told him, sitting down and stirring my coffee loudly.

He walked over to the sink and began to fill the kettle without looking at me.

'You must have expected this. You know how people talk. It's all round the place about the pair of you this morning.'

'Well, as you so kindly warned me,' I retorted sarcastically, 'they were going to find out anyway, so I thought I might as well save them the trouble of guessing.'

'No you didn't, Rosie. Don't give me that! I bet you weren't thinking at all. You just fell on his face like a sexmad hyena on heat!'

'I'll take that as a compliment.'

'I ... er ... I think I'll leave you two to it, then, to ... finish your little chat,' said Sara in the short silence that followed. She got up and left, looking back at me with a mixture of warning and embarrassment.

'We seem to have cleared the room,' remarked PJ as he sat down next to me with his coffee.

'Thanks to the insults you've been handing out so freely, yes.'

'You need it. You need someone to talk straight to you, try to keep you from going off the rails.'

I spluttered on my mouthful of coffee, about to rebuke him for talking to me like a Victorian grandfather chastising a slightly tarty chambermaid, when I realised he was smiling at me over the rim of his mug.

'You total bastard,' I said instead, mildly. 'Always winding me up.'

'You're such an easy target these days. Any mention of Mr Ashley Up-Himself has you falling apart at the seams. Oh well, I suppose at least the trip to Paris will get it all out of your system, if nothing else.'

'I'm looking forward to it. Can't you just be pleased for me? I've never been to Paris before.'

'I don't suppose you'll be seeing much of it, though, will you. I think you ought to know, Rosie, that when he talks about showing you his Eiffel Tower he might mean something other than a day of sightseeing . . .'

'I'm not rising to it, PJ – and don't start making another innuendo out of that, either – it's all been said before, believe me. Well, I don't care what you or anyone else thinks. I'm looking forward to it and you can all get stuffed.'

'Good for you,' he replied quietly, before downing the rest of his coffee in one go and thumping his mug down on the table. 'Bloody good for you.'

And just to round off a perfect day, Heidi came to see me as I was finishing work.

'I wondered if you had time for our little talk,' she said, parking herself at the reception desk just as I was about to close the shutter.

Little talk, little talk. What was the matter with the woman? Didn't she have any friends to talk to? Didn't she have a home to go to?

'I was just going home,' I said. 'Is it important?'

'Yes,' she said, giving me a very level look. 'Actually I think it is, Rosie.'

When you get a look like that levelled at you by someone who probably throws javelin and cricket balls for a hobby, you don't argue. I led the way into the reception office and cleared one of the chairs for her.

'What's up?' I asked. 'I've been trying, honestly – the lifestyle thing. I haven't forgotten. I just haven't had much time lately for walking, and there isn't much to take photos of around my house, but . . .'

'But you've been getting out and about more, haven't you.'

'Yes. Yes. I suppose that's all part of it, isn't it? Like

you said, get out of the armchair, and be charismatic and dynamic and stuff ...'

'And just *who* have you been getting charismatic *with*, Rosie, mm? That's the question.'

Is it? Who says?

'Sorry ... I don't quite follow ...'

'I'll come straight to the point. Ashley Connor. It's no good you trying to deny it.'

'I wasn't going to, actually,' I retorted. 'Since I didn't realise this was going to be an inquisition into my private life.'

'It stops being your private life,' she said in a very quiet, very deadly tone, 'when you decide to make a public show of it.'

'Is it any of your business?' I snapped, getting to my feet and feeling my legs trembling. I quivered my way to the door, holding it open, willing her to leave before I kicked her.

'My department's responsible for the well-being of the staff. Mr Connor's career could be jeopardised by gossip or scandal ...'

'And mine couldn't?'

'Yours too,' she agreed almost as an after-thought.

'So you thought it was your duty to come and poke your nose in?'

'To warn you, Rosie. Let's think of it as a friendly warning.'

Let's not.

'Thank you,' I said without any attempt at friendliness. 'I'm going home now.'

'You know he's married, I suppose?' she said as she passed me in the doorway.

'Thank you,' I said again, refusing to meet her eyes. I wanted so badly to kick her, I was having to do a little wriggly dance on the spot as if I needed the loo, to take my mind off it. If it came to a fight I'd come off the worst – her muscles bulged through her jacket so that even her shoulder pads rippled.

'Well, don't say I haven't warned you,' was her final shot.

'I won't, don't worry.'

For a long time after she'd gone, and long after I should have been at home, I stood at the reception desk staring out through the empty waiting room at the door where she'd flounced out, her back straight with indignation and her footsteps heavy with disapproval. What the fuck was all that about then?

Gossip's a funny thing, and never more so than in a hospital. Believe everything you see in the TV hospital drama programmes. For a day or two after a couple who shouldn't be together are spotted kissing outside the hospital entrance (just for instance), the jungle telegraph is so red-hot with it, you feel like we're all going to spontaneously combust at any moment. Then suddenly, it all goes quiet again. No one mentions it, it's old news, it's boring, everyone's heard it and everyone's fed up with talking about it. The kissing couple think it's safe to come out of the dark corners they've been trying to hide themselves away in. They stride around their lives again, gradually forgetting to look nervously over their shoulders and gradually becoming confident and daring again, foolishly believing people have forgotten about them. People haven't. People are quietly watching their every move, waiting for them to make the next mistake. And the minute they drop their guard completely, the minute they smile at each other in a certain way, or touch each other's hands slightly more than necessary or are spotted together in a car – just for instance – they might as well be stripped naked and paraded up and down the middle of every ward and department with ADULTERERS on signs hung round their necks. Not that people, in general, disapprove. They just like something to talk about, and most of them are pretty grateful to the couple responsible for giving them the opportunity.

182

For a couple of days Ashley and I followed the correct protocol. We laid low. We didn't go to the pub together. We didn't stop to chat when we passed each other in corridors.

'I'm not surprised people are talking. I wasn't exactly expecting you to launch yourself at me like that,' he told me on one of the few occasions that we managed to snatch a private moment.

'Like a hyena on heat?' I prompted him, a little stung by the implication that it was all my fault – that I'd forced myself on him against his will.

'Is that how you see yourself?' he grinned.

'No. It's how PJ described me,' I admitted.

His face darkened.

'Oh, did he.'

'He was only joking,' I added a little lamely.

'Yes. Perhaps if he spent a bit less time joking and concentrated on his work . . .'

At this point we were interrupted by a nurse coming into the consulting room.

'So make that patient another appointment, please,' said Ashley smoothly, handing me a file that actually had nothing to do with me.

'Certainly,' I said equally smoothly, giving the nurse a look of wide-eyed innocence as I went out. She didn't even give me a second glance. The gossip was dying down. We were old news, boring news. But we were waiting in the wings for a comeback.

The day before the trip to Paris, I was standing staring into my wardrobe wondering why everything in it shouted Middle-aged! and Dull! quite so loudly, and wishing someone from a TV makeover programme could arrive on the doorstep right now announcing that they wanted to transform my image for the sake of the viewing public, when Stuart ran into my bedroom and threw himself onto the bed, making it rock and shudder in a way that brought back memories of having sex in it.

183

'Get off the bed,' I told him without looking at him.

'What're you doing?' he countered, ignoring me.

'Trying to choose what to pack.'

'For your weekend away with your friends?'

'Yes.'

'When I went on the school trip to Paris,' he told me with an air of acquired wisdom, 'we had to take a clipboard and two pads of paper.'

'Yes, well, it was an art and culture trip, wasn't it.'

'Aren't you going to the Louvre? Aren't you going to Montmarte?'

'I don't know. It depends where my . . . friends . . . want to go. Stuart, will you please stop rolling around on my bed and . . . what's that?'

He'd rolled onto his side and flung out the arm with the plaster on it, so that the hand poking out of the top of the plaster was facing me as I turned to look at him. Quickly, but not quickly enough, he tried to turn his hand over and hide it out of my sight – as he'd obviously been managing to do quite easily up till now because the arm was supposed to be in a sling. I took hold of his hand by the fingertips, and turned it over.

'How long have all those bruises been there?' I asked him, shocked.

We both stared in silence at his purple-black knuckles and swollen sausagey fingers.

'Dunno,' he said with a sullen shrug. 'Since the accident, I s'pose.'

'No, it wasn't like that then. I'd have noticed. Does it hurt?'

He shrugged again, avoiding my eyes.

'S'pose the bruises have just taken a bit of time to come out,' he said.

'I don't know. I don't like the look of all that swelling. I think we ought to take you back to the hospital. There's something wrong. Perhaps the plaster's too tight, or . . .'

I tailed off, not being sure enough of my facts, just knowing my maternal instinct was firing on overdrive.

184

'Aw, no, Mum! I don't wanna go back to the hospital! It doesn't hurt that much, honest! Look, it's not that bad ...'

He tried to prove his point by flexing his fingers, but the tight shiny skin over the swollen joints resisted the effort, and his mouth contorted involuntarily into an Ouch of pain.

'You're coming back with me in the morning,' I told him firmly. There was no way I could fly off to Paris the next evening leaving him with his father and a possible problem.

'Anyway, *you* can't talk,' said Stuart sulkily as he slid off the end of the bed and out of my bedroom. '*You've* still got a bad hand too, but *you're* going off to Paris anyway.'

Hm, yes, that reminded me. I'd finished the antibiotics PJ had prescribed, but my hand still didn't look too great. Maybe Stuart had a point; maybe we *both* needed a bit of medical attention in the morning!

Ashley held Stuart's hand firmly by the ends of his fingers and gently prodded the bruised knuckles.

'How long ago was the accident?' he asked.

'Two weeks,' I said.

Ashley frowned.

'I think we'd better get the hand X-rayed.'

'He had check X-rays done last week.'

'Yes, but not of his hand,' said Ashley, checking in the folder of films inside Stuart's notes.

'Why – what do you think's wrong?' I asked, a bit alarmed.

'I think there are fractures of the proximal phalanges of the middle and ring fingers here,' he indicated, 'and it's causing swelling here ... and here ... Who did he see last week?'

'PJ. But last week it seemed ...'

Ashley strode to the door of the consulting room.

'Mr Jaimeen! Can you spare us a minute of your valuable time?'

PJ's head appeared round the door.

'Hi, Rosie. Oh, hello Stuart!' He glanced at the file of

185

X-rays open on the desk. 'Problems?' he asked, looking around at us all.

'Did it not occur to you, *Mr* Jaimeen,' said Ashley icily, 'to X-ray these badly contused fingers last week? Or were you too busy having a *laugh* and a *joke* with Mrs Peacock here?'

Even Stuart's eyes widened in surprise.

PJ walked over to the desk and studied his hand carefully.

'It wasn't like this last week,' he said quietly.

'No, of course it wasn't. The swelling's got worse since the fractures have been left undiagnosed with the boy no doubt trying to use his fingers, making matters worse all the time ...'

'No.' PJ straightened up and looked Ashley in the eyes. 'I mean, there wasn't *anything* to see last week. No bruising. No swelling. And Stuart didn't complain of any pain, otherwise of course I'd have asked for a hand X-ray.'

He looked to Stuart for confirmation but Stuart, inexplicably, was staring at the floor and swinging his feet as if none of this was anything to do with him.

'I didn't notice any bruising until last night,' I put in quickly, but was stopped in my tracks by a glare from Ashley.

'If there was any bruising or pain to the hand when he was admitted,' pointed out PJ, '*you'd* have presumably asked for a hand X-ray yourself at the time, Mr Connor.'

True though this undoubtedly was, it was enough to infuriate Ashley completely.

'Get the X-ray done now!' he snapped angrily. 'And in future you'd better refer all patients having fracture checks to me!'

He strode out of the room, muttering about having to do everything himself. There was an uncomfortable silence.

'Sorry, Rosie,' said PJ, sitting down at the desk to write out a radiology request form. 'Sorry, Stuart.'

''s all right,' muttered Stuart, still looking at the floor.

'Why does he talk to you like that?' I asked, still in a

state of shock. I stared at the door Ashley had all but slammed on his way out. 'It isn't very fair!'

PJ smiled bitterly.

'It isn't the least bit fair, Rosie, but he's the consultant and I'm the junior. He can't be seen to make any mistakes, so I have to take the can.'

'Is this his mistake?'

He shrugged as he handed me the radiology form.

'Who knows? He missed the fracture first, and it looks like I missed it second. I just don't remember seeing any sign of bruising or swelling to those fingers last week . . . but there you go. I must be cracking up. Pressure of work . . .' He gave me another tired smile.

'Sorry to be a pain,' I said, 'But I think I might need some more antibiotics for my hand, too.'

'Bloody hell, Rosie! What is it with your family and your hands? Let's have a look.' I took off the dressing and showed him the wound. 'Hm. It's certainly taking its time to heal, isn't it. Are you sure you took the tablets properly?'

'What do you take me for? A patient?' I grinned.

'Well, let's try you on something a bit stronger. You're not allergic to penicillin, are you?'

'Never been allergic to anything in my life.'

'Good. I'm giving you a high dosage of these. You'd better take them for a week. And keep using that cream. I'll prescribe you some more, OK?'

'Thanks, PJ.'

'Listen. If it's still looking red and weepy when you get back from this . . . this weekend away . . . the hand surgeons should probably admit you.'

'Don't be daft. It'll be fine. It's only a little cut.'

'You know better than that, Rosie,' he warned me solemnly. 'Here you go.' He handed me my prescription and Stuart's radiology form. 'You'd better take the films back to Mr Connor when they're done. He won't trust me to look at them. That's another nail in the coffin of my registrar career.'

*

187

Stuart and I walked to the X-ray department in silence.

'I don't understand it,' I said, as we sat down in the waiting room. 'PJ didn't notice those bruises last week, and I didn't even notice them till last night. Why didn't you mention it, Stuart? It's obviously painful. Why the big secret? You've been hiding that hand away . . .'

He shrugged. Suddenly I was irritated and annoyed by that shrug. How dared he sit there shrugging, looking sulky, staring at the floor, whilst two surgeons argued over him and his mother took time off work fussing over him when she really needed to be worrying about whether she'd packed enough clothes for Paris?

'What?' I demanded. 'What's the matter? What are you looking so moody about? We're going to get it sorted out now, OK?'

He nodded. I stared at him. His lip was wobbling as if he was going to cry.

'Sorry, Mum,' he said in a shaky voice.

Now I was *really* worried.

'Sorry?' I said. 'What? Why? I'm not having a go at you, I just don't understand why . . .'

He suddenly got to his feet and looked at me resolutely, his wobbly lip now under control, his mouth set firm.

'Can we go back?'

'Back where?' I asked, stupidly, still staring at him.

'To PJ. I want to talk to him again.'

'After the X-ray, Stuart. But he's very busy. And we don't want to get him into any more trouble with Mr Connor.'

'No, listen. I need to tell him . . .' He swallowed and glanced at the door. 'Mum, it's not PJ's fault. I don't want him to get into trouble and . . . and have a nail in his coffin. It's my fault. I should have told you.'

'Yes, you should. But that doesn't change the fact that no one noticed . . .'

'No one noticed because it wasn't there. I didn't have any bruises last week because I only fractured my fingers on Monday.'

He hung his head and looked at me from under his fringe. Suddenly he was a naughty little boy again, caught out in some misdemeanour at school. Please don't tell Daddy. Please don't smack me. Don't send me to my room, don't stop me going out with my friends, please, please, please – I promise to be good for the rest of my life . . .'

'How did you do it?' I asked him, quietly, on a huge sigh of understanding and, for some reason, relief.

'It was Steven Porter's fault. He keeps on having a go at me about Katie Jenkins. I chased him across the playground and swung my arm at his head.' He demonstrated swinging the heavy plaster at an imaginary target and I winced. 'But he ducked.'

'And . . .?'

'I hit the wall behind him. I caught my knuckles really hard on the wall.'

For a minute I couldn't think of a thing to say. I pictured the nasty Steven Porter ducking out of the way of Stuart's plastered arm, pictured him running off laughing as Stuart cried out in pain, and I wanted to chase him and hit him round the head myself.

'You should have told me,' I rebuked him.

'Thought I'd be in trouble.'

A girl in a white radiologist's coat came into the waiting room and called out:

'Stuart Peacock? This way, please.'

'Let's get the X-ray done first,' I said, leading Stuart by his good elbow.

'Then I can go and tell PJ I'm sorry?'

'Then I'll make sure you do. *And* Mr Connor,' I said grimly.

'Sorry, Mum,' he said again, giving me a pleading look.

Kids, honestly. The trouble they get you into!

'I've got maths at half past ten,' worried Stuart as we waited for Ashley to finish seeing a confused elderly patient who needed a hip replacement but thought she was at the dentist's.

'Every time he says anything to her,' giggled Hayley, who'd escaped from the consulting room for a few minutes to phone for some blood results, 'she opens her mouth wide and points at her molars.'

I expect he's had worse conversations.

'Well, you'll just have to be *late* for maths. They know you're at the hospital – Dad will have given your form tutor the message.'

'Yes, but we're doing those fractions again. The ones I can't do. I won't be able to do them and I'll get into trouble.'

'Stuart, you're fourteen. Your life's a continual struggle to stay out of trouble. You're in trouble here, now, if you don't explain yourself to Mr Connor and PJ, so don't think you're going to talk your way out of it.'

'What's up?' asked Hayley, nosily, pausing as she was about to go back into Mr Connor and his dental fantasy patient.

I don't know what came over me. I mean, everyone living within a twenty mile radius of East Dean Hospital must have known that telling Hayley Gibson anything was as effective as having it broadcast on five different radio stations in every language including the Morse code. Put it down to excitement about the Paris trip. Put it down to anxiety and exasperation about Stuart. Put it down to worry about the impending doom that was my marriage. I looked up at Hayley and smiled, and like Ashley's hip replacement patient, opened my gob not only wide but very foolishly.

'Stuart's got a confession to make to Mr Connor,' I said, as if it was a big joke and the sort of thing that happened every day. 'He's just given PJ a terrible telling-off and it wasn't his fault. Stuart didn't exactly tell the whole truth about his finger fractures.'

'Ooh,' said Hayley, obviously thrilled with this new piece of gossip. 'Yes, I *heard* Mr Connor going off at poor PJ.' I bet you did. I bet you were listening outside with your ear pressed up to the door. 'Again!' she added pointedly.

'Again? Again what?'

'He's *always* forever going on at poor Jamas. My friend Chloe – you know Chloe, short curly hair, loud voice, works in theatres? She says You Should Hear Him In Theatre!' Hayley did a very good imitation of Chloe's loud voice. Several patients looked round in alarm. 'Poor Jamas,' she repeated with a sigh, looking at me closely and shaking her head. 'Why do you think Mr Connor picks on him, Rosie?'

'How should I know?' I returned, suddenly and rather belatedly realising my mistake in talking to Hayley News-Of-The-World at all, never mind about anything to do with Ashley Connor.

'Can't you work on him a little bit,' she whispered in a loud hiss against my ear, making me shudder and jump at the same time. 'You know ... try to put him in a better mood? Eh, Rosie?'

'I'm sure *I* haven't got any control over Mr Connor's moods!' I said heartily, with what I hoped passed for a laugh of amazement – just as the consulting room door opened and Ashley stepped out, looking for the blood test result Hayley was supposed to be delivering. His frown of impatience, as he took the form out of her hand, suddenly changed to a beaming smile as he caught sight of Stuart and me sitting behind her.

'Ah – Rosie! Stuart's had his X-ray? Good! I'll be with you in just a couple of minutes!' he said cheerily, and began to whistle softly to himself as he returned to his hip patient.

'*Just one look, that's all it took, yeah, just one look ...*' sang Hayley, grinning at me very pointedly until I felt myself beginning go red.

'What was *that* all about?' asked Stuart as she skipped back into the consulting room after Ashley and closed the door behind her. 'Is she mad?'

'Absolutely,' I told him. 'Raving. They all are, here. It's the pressure of work.'

191

He nodded solemnly.

'You should change jobs, Mum – while you still can.'

By the end of the day I was beginning to think he was probably right.

Ashley was so laid back in his response to Stuart's apology that it was quite bizarre, after his annoyance earlier.

'Don't worry, lad,' he said, laughing out loud as he viewed the new X-rays. 'I was young once myself! These things happen, don't they – eh!' He looked at me and winked. 'Fighting over a girl, I suppose?'

'Well ... er ...' Stuart fidgeted uncomfortably in his chair.

I found myself hoping he wasn't going to tell Ashley that the girl in question was a slapper.

'Your secret's safe with me, boy. Look, Rosie, these aren't bad fractures and I think they're going to mend perfectly well. We'll just buddy-strap the fingers together. He'll need some anti-inflammatories. And don't even think about using this hand to punch anyone for a while – OK, Stuart?'

Stuart nodded, looking suitably chastened.

'I need to say sorry to PJ, too,' he reminded me as Ashley scribbled on a prescription pad. 'I don't want him getting his coffin nailed.'

Ashley turned and frowned from Stuart to me.

'What? What's this about coffins?'

'Just a joke,' I replied at once, trying to kick Stuart but missing and stubbing my toe on the chair leg. 'Ouch.'

'No need to talk to Mr Jaimeen,' said Ashley, still frowning. 'He's busy with a patient. I'll tell him what happened. And by the way, Rosie, how's *your* hand now?'

'Oh – not so bad, thanks. PJ gave me some stuff ...'

'Oh did he? Perhaps *I'd* better have a look at it. Knowing him ...'

'No, it's fine, honestly, Ashley. Fine. Thank you. See you later.'

I hustled Stuart out of the room quickly.

'Mr Connor's a bit weird, isn't he,' he commented. 'Why do all the nurses smile at him all the time?'

'I don't know, Stuart,' I said, trying to wipe the smile off my own face. 'Probably because he's very good-looking.'

'Huh! Talk about *shallow*!' he said in disgust.

'Yes, I know. Terrible, isn't it.'

'And he's *horrible* to PJ. Mum, I want to say something to PJ myself about this.' He indicated his strapped-up fingers. 'It *was* my fault he got into trouble.'

'You don't want to get him into more trouble, do you? You heard Mr Connor – he's busy with a patient. And you need to get back for that maths lesson.'

And I had to get back to the reception desk. The queue was almost out of the door.

'I've got a problem,' said Sara, looking up at me with the hint of tears not far away.

'What? Are you OK? You look a bit ...'

'I'm all right, Rosie – but it's Callum. He's had a relapse. He was poorly last night – I gave him Calpol and asked Mum to call the doctor this morning ...'

'Why didn't you *say*?'

'Well, you were busy, with Stuart, and obviously I was hoping ... but Mum's just phoned – the doctor's been round. Callum's vomiting and really feverish and getting dehydrated and ...'

'Sara, you'd better go straight home!'

'The doctor says they might have to bring him in and put him on a drip if he can't keep the antibiotics down ...'

'Go *home*, Sara. For God's sake!'

'But Rosie! You're going off to Paris later, aren't you! Becky can't possibly manage on her own – and all day tomorrow ...'

Shit. Shit, shit and shit again. Of course she couldn't. And I was never going to get a temp organised at this short notice.

'Don't worry about it. I'll sort something out.'

'Are you sure?' She was already picking up her bag, putting on her coat.

'Of course. Just go. Hope he's all right . . .'

I looked at my watch. Eleven-fifteen. Five and a quarter hours until I was due to be at Gatwick, a third of the workforce down, the facture clinic running late and a gynaecology clinic due to start at two o'clock. Maths wasn't my strong point, but it wasn't going to add up. Something was gonna have to go.

'I don't think I'm going to be able to make it,' I told Ashley abruptly when he finished the clinic at lunchtime. 'You'd better go without me.'

'What? Don't be silly – it's all arranged. Why . . .?'

'Sara's off. Her little boy's ill again. There's no way I can leave Becky on her own for half the gynaecology clinic. And tomorrow! It's General Surgery. I just can't do it, Ashley.'

'Rosie, you're entitled to time off. They'll just have to manage somehow. Tell Sylvia Riley she's got to find someone to cover you.'

Oh, yes, sure. I might as well fall to my knees and pray to God to send me an angel.

'She'd go mad,' I said sadly. 'She already hates me.'

I suppose I was hoping he'd say – leave it to me, I'll phone Sylvia Riley myself and tell her to sort it out. But after all, why should he? It was my problem, and he was probably busy right at that moment, tending to someone's broken ankle or preparing to operate on their arthritic knee. He'd probably got enough problems getting away, without taking mine on board.

'Sorry, Rosie, but I've got to run,' he said. 'I'll be in theatre until it's time to leave for the airport. Leave a message with one of the ODAs when you've made up your mind. Hope you can sort it out.'

'Can I speak to Sylvia Riley, please?'

194

I'd practised for about five minutes, trying to make my voice sound polite but firm. I needed to get on the right side of her without coming across as grovelling or begging.

'She's very tied up at the moment,' said her snooty-voiced PA. 'Can *I* help at all?'

Yes, you stuck-up pretentious bitch, you can get your arse out of your smart chair, leg it across your thick pile carpet and tell your boss to put down her newspaper and her sandwich and talk to someone who needs to grovel to her.

'No – thank you,' I said, trying not to snarl. 'I really need to talk to Ms Riley. Can't she be interrupted?'

The PA gave a huge sigh and said '*Just* a minute,' in the tone of someone whose patience has been sorely tried by a demanding child for forty-eight hours without a break. There was a click on the phone and then silence – and just as I'd decided she must have cut me off there was suddenly another click and the strained voice of Sylvia Riley asked me with thinly veiled annoyance and probably half a ham sandwich in her gob: 'What can I do for you, Rosemary?'

'I'm so sorry to interrupt you,' I gabbled, immediately forgetting my practised tones of firm non-grovelling politeness, 'but I've got a serious problem on the reception desk this afternoon. And tomorrow!' I added quickly.

'What sort of serious problem?'

What could I say that would sound serious enough? An earthquake, a flood, a riot? A sit-down protest by gynaecology patients?

'A staffing problem,' I said flatly. 'I've got one member of staff off, and I'm due to go early tonight, and take tomorrow as a day's leave.'

'Well, it doesn't sound as if you'll be able to, does it,' she said with evident pleasure.

'But I'm going away,' I said, hating the whine I could hear in my voice. 'I need to get to Gatwick by four-thirty!'

'I don't think it's acceptable to leave one member of staff responsible for the desk on a busy afternoon, do you?'

'No. Of course I don't! That's why I've phoned you!' I replied desperately.

'Do you expect *me* to come and man the desk?' she retorted sharply.

I shuddered at the thought of it. She'd probably have all the patients lined up in alphabetical order and shoot them if they complained.

'I was rather hoping you could find me someone who could.'

Your nasty little PA for instance. Make a change for her to do some work, although the culture shock might be the finish of her.

'I've got *more* than enough to do, Rosemary,' she said with the weary voice of someone whose burdens the rest of us can never presume to imagine, 'with the waiting list figures being outside the government limits *yet again* and as for the *expenditure budgets* . . .!'

Oh, the expenditure budgets! God save and preserve us all from the expenditure budgets.

'So you can't help me?'

I had a sinking feeling in my stomach. I might as well have been watching the plane leave the Gatwick tarmac with Ashley on board it, waving goodbye to my dreams of Paris and a good shag. I thought seriously about asking Sylvia Riley if she realised how much I'd spent on new underwear.

'It's not a holiday – not strictly speaking,' I said instead, on an impulse I'd probably live to regret. 'It's an orthopaedic conference I'm going to.'

The silence lasted so long, I began to wonder if Ms Riley had fallen asleep, choked on her sandwich or just put down the receiver and got on with her expenditure budgets.

'Well!' she said suddenly, making me jump in surprise. 'Perhaps Mr Connor will have to manage without your *help*.'

So the gossip had even reached the outer limits of the management offices. Amazing how people who don't seem

196

to have any connection with the human race whatsoever will prick up their ears at the suggestion of anything remotely carnal. Probably still trying to work out what it's all about.

'He won't be very pleased,' I said with a sigh.

So that was that. Defeat. No Paris, no shag, and I might as well take the underwear back to the shop.

'Stay tonight,' barked Sylvia Riley so unexpectedly that I nearly dropped the phone, 'and we'll have to sort something out for tomorrow.'

'Oh!'

Amazing! Did the suggestion of Mr Connor not being very pleased perhaps scare the shit out of her? What an interesting thought.

'Can you ask Mr Connor,' I found myself whispering to one of the theatre assistants over the phone a little later, 'if we can change our flights to Paris?'

I held on for the response, trying to listen to the whispering at the other end, wondering if there was nudging and eyebrow-raising going on around the operating table at my expense. I heard an exchange of voices and then the phone being picked up again.

'Mr Connor says he really needs to be on that flight. But you can change yours,' said the ODA cheerfully.

Well, thanks, Ashley. Thanks a bundle.

'If you can just manage for ten minutes while I make a quick phone call,' I told Becky, looking doubtfully at the queue already beginning to build up for early gynaecology appointments, 'I'll be able to stay till the end of the clinic, and Sylvia Riley's going to get someone to cover for tomorrow.'

'But Rosie! You can't miss your plane!' said Becky mournfully.

'I'm going to try to change the flight. Don't worry. It's no big deal.'

It was, actually, It was the biggest deal I could imagine, and if it wasn't for Ashley, and Paris, and the underwear and everything, I wouldn't have even contemplated it. For a start, I was nervous of flying anyway, and the thought of getting on the plane on my own, without anyone to talk to and hang on to during the scary bits was terrifying. And for another thing, I was miffed. Well, wouldn't you be? I mean, I know he had to get to Paris for his conference, and maybe he needed an early night or a couple of drinks or whatever in the hotel to prepare for the morning, but it might have been nice if he'd even *considered* changing to a later flight if it meant we could go together. It didn't exactly make me feel very crucial to his plans for the weekend. I went into the office, shut the door behind me and spent a pleasant ten minutes holding onto the phone listening to classical music and being told how many people were in the queue in front of me, before I finally got as far as a computerised voice telling me to press four if I wanted to discuss flight availability. After a further five minutes holding on, and almost as long trying to explain the problem to a girl with a bored voice who sounded like a work experience student, I finally got put through to yet another girl who told me without any hint of regret that the next flight she could get me on would be at twenty past eleven the next morning.

'Mum! What are you doing home?' exclaimed Stuart as I walked through the door at half past six, having stayed late to help Becky finish off the clinic outcomes.

'Don't ask.'

I put down my suitcase, put on the kettle and wished I didn't feel quite so much like crying.

'Aren't you going to Paris? Have you had a row with your friends?'

'No. I had to . . .'

'Rosie! What are you doing home?' echoed Barry, looking round the kitchen door in surprise when he heard my voice.

'I got thrown off the flight. Refused entry to France. Lost my passport. Couldn't prove my identity.'

'Don't be silly,' said Barry mildly. 'Aren't you going, then?' He brightened visibly. 'Only I was just wondering about the washing machine.'

Wondering about it? As in – does it work itself?

'What're we having for dinner?' put in Stuart. 'Can we have sausages?'

To be honest, on the way home from work I'd been feeling so pissed off about Ashley not thinking me special enough to change his flight, and so nervous about getting on the plane on my own, I'd been seriously contemplating ducking out of the whole trip, underwear or no underwear. But standing there in the kitchen waiting for the kettle to boil, looking at Stuart's face as he anticipated sausages not cooked by himself, and Barry's face as he anticipated the washing not being done by himself, I felt even more pissed off with myself for having allowed them both to become so totally and utterly selfish.

'Yes, I *am* going,' I said crossly, grabbing one mug, one tea bag, one spoon and making just the one cup of tea for myself. 'And you can cook whatever you bloody well like – whatever you were going to have if I hadn't come home. *And* work out how to use the washing machine. *I'm* going to have a Marmite sandwich and an early night. I'm going to Paris tomorrow, even if I have to *walk* there, so get used to it!'

It might have been quite a good exit if I hadn't heard Stuart whisper to Barry just as I was leaving the room:

'Probably PMT, Dad.'

Chapter Eleven

Paris in the Spring Time

'Attention please. This is a security announcement. Please do not leave baggage unattended . . .'

I clutched Natasha's old sports holdall, which was the only thing I'd been able to find that was about the right size to contain all my clothes for the weekend, even tighter in case anyone prowling the airport looking for Unattended Baggage should be in any doubt about its ownership.

I'd been in such a state of panic about getting to the airport on time, I'd left home far too early and was now the first person at my check-in-desk, waiting for it to open. The chirpy little chap who eventually opened up sang 'Good morning!' to me as if he thought I'd been there all night.

'Did you pack your bag yourself?' he asked me cheerfully, as he slapped half a dozen assorted labels on it and whizzed it backwards on the conveyor belt.

Did I pack it myself?! Trust me, sonny Jim, no other bugger was going to see the knickers I'd put in that bag!

'Boarding at ten-fifty am, Gate forty-five,' he told me with a smile. 'Have a good journey!'

10.50? I looked at my watch. It was 9.20. I had an hour and a half to kill before I could even get near the bloody plane. I thought air travel was supposed to be easy these days? I thought it was supposed to be no big deal, no more trouble than getting a bus or a train? Since when did you have to hang around a bus stop for two hours before the bus was due, or sit in a British Rail waiting room forced to drink their coffee and eat their sandwiches before being herded to the platform and finally lined up like cattle to get onto the train?

I found my way to Departures and joined the queue of travellers waiting to have our dignity removed in the various stages of (1) Passport inspection including eyebrow raising by supercilious official who wonders how you got to look so much older in so few years since the photo was taken; (2) Removal of coat, handbag, cabin luggage, keys, watch, anything on your person that could set off alarms, sirens, bells, whistles and international distress signals, before being prodded through a cattle-grid closely watched by twenty-three members of MI5; (3) A thorough frisking by large lesbian with unnatural sadistic gleam in her eye and strange obsession with your shoes; and (4) Complete evacuation of your handbag onto a table where its contents are strewn like the offerings at a Bring and Buy Sale and randomly poked, prodded and sniffed by a seedy looking little man who, without his uniform, would have been arrested within minutes and charged with nasty crimes that would keep him on the sex offenders' register for ten years.

'They're tampons,' I hissed, as the seedy looking little man in question unscrewed the top of my *Discreet Handbag Feminine Hygiene Holder* and peered into it with morbid curiosity.

'Sorry, Madam,' he replied in an unapologetic monotone, 'Random drugs check.'

If I wanted to hide drugs the last place I'd consider putting them was somewhere where I might accidentally use them during a period. I threw everything back into my bag as, bored with me, he moved on to inspect the teddy bear and dummy of the two-year-old behind me in the queue. Fair enough, I felt a lot safer getting on the plane knowing that everyone's tampon holders had been checked.

I still had over an hour before I could turn up at my departure gate. I wandered around the shops, weaving my way through excitable gangs of Stags and Hens on their way to Stag Weekends and Hen Weekends on opposite sides of the world from their Does and their Roosters, screeching with already well-pissed laughter about what they were no doubt intending to get up to on their final fling of freedom before settling down and forgetting all about it. An airport isn't a good place to be alone. Everyone seemed to have someone – a friend, a lover, a parent, a child – even a business associate would be better than nothing. Even a consultant from the hospital where you worked, who seemed to be interested in you but couldn't be bothered to change his flight for you, would be better than nothing. I queued up at a café-bar to buy myself a coffee and then, at the last minute, changed my mind and ordered a white wine. Drinking wine on my own, mid-morning on a Friday, felt dissolute and reckless – which was exactly how I'd planned to feel this weekend, when I packed my bag with that red and black underwear and before I'd had to turn up at the airport on my Jack Jones.

'Attention please!' called the disembodied voice again, making me clutch my handbag and look around me in panic. 'Would the one remaining passenger for flight B one-seven-six – *B one-seven-six* – please go immediately to Gate forty-three, where the plane is waiting to depart! I repeat, would the one remaining passenger ...'

Hands shaking, fingers suddenly stricken with a sudden onset of neurological incompetence, I fumbled in my bag, screwing up tissues, dropping a lipstick, finally pulling out the boarding card which wasn't where it was supposed to be, scrutinising it, doubting the evidence of my eyes, holding it up to the light, checking the details again, until, not totally convinced and still shaking slightly, I returned it to my bag and took a huge gulp of my wine.

'Flight one-seven-six,' said an amused voice from the next table.

'Sorry?' I looked round and found a young man with shocking blond hair and an unseasonal tan watching me over the rim of his cardboard coffee cup.

'Flight one-seven-six. Gate forty-three. Thought perhaps you didn't catch the announcement.'

'I did. Thank you. It's just that I'm flight one-seven-eight. Gate forty-five. And I thought for a minute ...'

'No. You're all right. It's an hour off yet.'

'Are you ...?'

'On that flight, yeah. Eleven-twenty, Paris.' He raised his coffee cup to me as if in salute, and immediately returned to the paper he was reading. I turned away and started stuffing things back in my bag again.

'You on business?' he suddenly called across to me.

His accent was Australian, but with enough of an edge of Cockney to show he'd been living in London for quite a while.

'Not ... exactly.' I turned in my chair and smiled back at him. 'Meeting someone.'

'OK. Staying long?'

'Only for the weekend. You?'

'Going to look at a possible new job. Hospital on the outskirts of Paris.'

'Are you a doctor?'

He nodded.

'Bugger me. Can't get away from them,' I muttered to myself, taking another swig of wine.

'Sorry?'

'What speciality? I work at East Dean. Outpatient reception.'

'Obstetrics. I applied for a job at East Dean myself! Two years ago. Got as far as the interview but ...'

Our flight was being called before we'd even paused in the conversation.

I never did like flying. I put it down to a pleasure flight my father took me on when I was a child on holiday in Great

203

Yarmouth. The fragile looking little light aircraft had shuddered and dipped its way along the coast while my father roared with appreciation and I hid my face and screamed. When we were back on the ground, my father lifted me out of the plane and I burst into a delayed flood of tears, ran back to my mother and promptly threw up down my new white holiday dress. '*I told you she wouldn't like it!*' snapped my mother, who spent the next fifteen minutes cleaning me up and the rest of the holiday not speaking to my father.

Being on a plane on my own was like a bad dream. I went through the motions – fastening the seatbelt, watching the safety demonstration, getting a drink and an in-flight magazine, closing my eyes and holding my breath while we left the tarmac and climbed up through my personal ear pain threshold and finally settled into a more or less horizontal position above the clouds – but inside, my stomach was churning with apprehension and I was desperate to have someone next to me, someone to hold my hand and reassure me or even to tease me about my fears and make me laugh. Anything would be better than the large elderly Scotsman snoring beside me, whose wife was staring resolutely out of the window looking like she was going to cry (and I couldn't blame her). By the time we landed at Charles de Gaulle I was feeling sick and weak. I made my way shakily through passport control and whilst I was waiting for my luggage I tried calling Ashley on his mobile.

'Hello?' eventually responded a very quiet, rather irritated voice.

'Ashley? Is that you? It's me! I'm at the airport . . .'

'Rosie. I can't talk now. I'm in the conference.'

'Oh. So what should I . . .?'

'Get a taxi. Hotel La Fontaine. I'll see you this evening.'

He hung up, leaving me staring moodily at my phone, wondering whether it'd be a good idea to just get straight on the next plane back to London.

'You all right? You look a bit crook.' It was Oliver, the

Aussie obstetrics registrar, heaving his bag off the luggage carousel and looking at me with some concern.

'Yeah – I'm OK. Just a bit travel sick. I'll be ... well, actually ...' I felt myself sway slightly and looked around me for a seat. 'I think I might be going to faint.'

'Here!' He grabbed me firmly by the shoulders and shepherded me through the crowds, moved a young couple off a bench seat near the toilets with a quick 'Pardon – madame est malade', sat me down and pushed my head down in my lap. By the time the whirring in my head had faded and my vision was beginning to clear, he'd brought me a bottle of water and sat down next to me.

'Better?'

'Thanks. I think so. Sorry ... very good of you ... being a nuisance ...'

'Nonsense. Sit till you're feeling better. Is your ... friend ... meeting you?'

'No. I've got to get a taxi to the hotel.'

'Which hotel?'

'La Fontaine. Do you know where is it?'

He smiled. 'Yes. Have you got luggage to collect?'

'Oh, God – yes, just a holdall. I forgot all about that ...'

'Tell me what it's like. I'll go and get it. Sit still! Keep your head down!'

Within five minutes he was back, with my bag and his on a luggage trolley.

'Will you be OK to walk to the taxi rank now?'

'Of course. Thanks for looking after me. I'll be fine now. See you ...'

'It's all right. I'm coming with you.'

Now I was embarrassed.

'There's no need. Honestly, I'll be fine.'

'I'm sure you will. But I don't see the point in paying for two taxis when we're both going to the same hotel.'

'Oh! You're staying at La Fontaine too?'

'Yep. Come on – this way!'

He took my arm and gently led me towards Customs. An

hour ago I'd been sitting miserably on the plane wishing I had someone to hold on to. I'd better be careful what I wished for in future!

By the time we'd got to the hotel and I'd taken leave of Oliver and found my room, I felt exhausted. Often the travel sickness affects me like this – once I've recovered a little, I just need to sleep it off, and normally wake up feeling completely better. Without even bothering to unpack, I took off my trousers and top and lay down on the bed. It was early afternoon and the light from the street outside was bright, but once I'd drawn the thick curtains, it might as well have been the middle of the night, and I was soon sound asleep.

I woke, eventually, completely disorientated and with a raging thirst. There was a terrible noise going on some-where near my left ear. Was it my alarm clock? But I wasn't in my own bed! Where the hell was I? I rolled over and fumbled frantically, trying to find and silence the bell that was deafening me and splitting my head apart. But just as I came near to locating it, the noise suddenly stopped and was replaced by a thunderous banging.

'Stop it!' I muttered, trying to bury my head under the pillow. 'Stop that noise, Stuart! What are you doing? Go to sleep!'

The banging got louder. I threw the pillow on the floor and sat up, staring around the room. No, this definitely wasn't my bed, and it definitely wasn't my room. I wasn't at home, was I. In a minute I'd remember where I was . . .

'Rosie! Rosie, are you in there? Open the door, Rosie!'

Ashley! Shit! Yes, of course, shit – I was in Paris! How long had I been asleep? I stumbled to the door and threw it open.

'Sorry, Ashley . . .' I thought the phone was an alarm clock and . . . oh. Oh, fuck.'

'This is Rosie, my . . . secretary,' said Ashley in a strained voice to the two pinstriped, supercilious-looking suits standing behind him. 'Rosie, why don't you meet us down in the bar ... after you've got some clothes on?'

I wouldn't have minded so much if I'd been wearing the new underwear.

English pop music from the 70s was being played softly in the bar. Ashley looked up as I walked in, and motioned with his head for me to join him. His two stodgy looking mates turned and looked me up and down. I resisted the temptation to undo my blouse and show them I'd changed the underwear.

'Sorry about earlier,' I said instead, pulling up a chair and joining them as Ashley went to get me a drink. 'I'd been asleep, you see. I suffer from travel sickness.'

They both nodded solemnly and one of them muttered something in a foreign language. The other one responded and they both laughed. Now, look, I don't care who you are or what language you speak, that's bloody rude, isn't it?

'Sorry, but I don't speak any French,' I said stiffly.

'Doctor Gucci is Italian,' Ashley told me quietly, returning with a glass of white wine, which he put into my hand. 'And Doctor Schuter is German.'

'Oh. Very pleased to meet you both,' I said into my wine glass, hating them with a vengeance.

'But they both speak excellent English, of course,' smiled Ashley.

Might be nice to use it, then, when someone speaks to you in it, instead of laughing in Italian or German. But don't mind me, I'm only the *secretary*.

'Are you feeling better now?' Ashley asked me, suddenly and to my surprise, taking hold of my free hand and squeezing it. Maybe in France, when you're with Italians and Germans, nobody cares if you hold hands with your secretary. I squeezed his hand back and smiled at him.

'A bit,' I lied.

The truth was that I still felt quite odd. I'd slept right

round till seven o'clock and despite having a shower, drinking a pint of water and taking a couple of Paracetamol, I was having trouble shaking off the muzzy head and trembly legs I'd woken up with. Served me right for sleeping in the middle of the day.

'Good. It's going to be a long night!' Ashley whispered, nudging my leg under the table with his knee.

'Ooh. I hope so!' I giggled.

Doctor Gucci and Doctor Schuter promptly chuckled nastily together again and I felt so uncomfortable I knocked back half my glass of wine in one go.

'Steady!' smiled Ashley, pressing his thigh closer to mine. 'Don't want you getting drunk! Not just yet, anyway!'

This time all three of them laughed and I began to feel like I was definitely the only one not in on the joke.

'So!' I began cheerfully, to change the subject, 'have you all had a good day at your conference, then?'

'Oh,' Ashley waved his hand dismissively. 'You know how these things are.'

Actually, no.

'I've never been to an international conference,' I told him, seeing no point in beating about the bush, 'unless you count the Welcome Barbecue at the school when my daughter had a French exchange student staying with us when she was about twelve.'

'And was it interesting?' asked Dr Schuter, apparently making a belated effort to be polite.

'No. It was awful. The burgers were burnt and it rained. And Emma – my daughter – and our French girl, Veronique, took a dislike to each other and I had to try to communicate with this girl in sign language all week. You try asking someone whether they like Toad In The Hole and mashed potato, using only your hands to demonstrate! Believe me, it's not easy.'

Ashley was laughing but the other two were looking at me as if they weren't sure whether I should be allowed out.

208

'Do you have Toad In The Hole in Germany? Or in Italy?' I added, wondering whether they were having trouble keeping up.

Quick as a flash, Ashley translated this into their respective languages and all three of them erupted into an explosion of trilingual merriment. I had the distinct impression that I was being taken the piss out of.

'Come on,' said Ashley, standing up and leading me by the elbow. 'Let's go through to the restaurant.'

Food? I'd forgotten about food. I hadn't eaten since breakfast but my stomach contracted in protest at the thought of it.

'Do we have to eat with those two?' I muttered as we were led to a table. 'I don't think they like me.'

'Of course they do!' he said breezily. 'They both fancy you rotten. Can't you tell?'

Well, maybe it's normal in some countries to come on to someone by treating them with contempt and laughing at them in an unpleasant way but I certainly hadn't come across it before.

'I'd much rather be on my own with you,' I whispered to him as we sat down at the table.

'Later, darling – later!' he chuckled gently. I saw him catch Doctor Gucci's eye across the table and give him a smile, and it took all my inbred English sense of restraint not to jump to my feet and shout 'OK, what's the fucking joke, you lot?'

Instead, I ordered asparagus and sea bass from a leather-bound menu translated to me by Ashley whispering alternate phrases of French and English seductively in my ear, sat back and sipped my wine and tried to concentrate on thoughts of the night of passion ahead of me. Unfortunately, by the time I'd finished the asparagus and got halfway through the fish, I was feeling less and less like a night of passion and more and more like a lie-down in a dark room with a cold compress on my head – despite the constant pressure of Ashley's warm leg against mine and the occasional sneaky touch of his hand on my thigh under the table.

'Are you OK?' he whispered as I put down my knife and fork without finishing the main course. 'You look a bit pale.'

'Sorry. I'll be all right. I'm just ...'

'Anxious to get to bed?' he prompted me with a grin and a wink.

'Mm' I smiled back, ignoring the leers from across the table that had become more and more overt with the increasing effects of their alcohol consumption. 'Shall we ... er ...?'

'Yes. Let's move swiftly on to dessert!' declared Ashley, sitting up straight and calling for a menu. 'Let me see now. What have we here to tempt you?'

If I wasn't feeling sufficiently tempted by the thought of Ashley naked in bed, I really didn't see how the *Crème Brûlée* or the *Tarte au Citron* were going to make a whole lot of difference. What was the matter with me? I'd only had two glasses of wine, and the travel sickness certainly should have worn off by now.

'I'll just have a black coffee,' I said, hoping it would revive me.

The coffee arrived, thick and bitter in its minuscule thimble of a cup. I ladled sugar into it and knocked it back, waiting for the caffeine to kick in. The conversation buzzed incomprehensibly around me and when Ashley's hand became a permanent fixture on my thigh, his thumb moving a little higher with every subtle stroke, I began to feel excited enough to ignore the threat of impending sickness still churning at my guts, and, leaning into his shoulder, whispered.

'Can we go upstairs now?'

At least, I thought I was whispering, but judging by the knowing looks on the faces of Doctors Gucci and Schuter, I might as well have stood up on my chair and announced to the restaurant that I was ready for a shag now and all applicants were welcome.

'Come on, then,' smiled Ashley, taking my hand and leading me towards the lifts. 'Your room or mine?'

I supposed he'd had to book us separate rooms in case anyone thought it odd for him to share with his secretary – not that anyone was bothered about such things here in Paris, it seemed to me.

'Whichever's nearest,' I said, cuddling up to him as the lift ascended to the third floor.

'Your place it is, then,' he said, slapping my arse as he pushed me gently out of the lift. His hand lingered for a while as we headed swiftly along the corridor to my room.

'You're not wearing any knickers!' he whispered, sounding more shocked than excited.

'I am,' I giggled, 'But it's a thong. And there's not very much of it . . .'

Within two minutes of stepping inside the room, I was showing him just how little there was of the thong. Within five minutes, it was on the bedroom floor along with all the rest of our clothes. And within six minutes, I was throwing up in the bathroom.

'Sorry!' I groaned, collapsing on the bed next to him, all interest in the fact that I was naked with gorgeous Ashley Connor having gone down the pan at about the same instant as the vomit.

'Was it something I said?' he asked without looking at me.

'No, it was when you were getting on top of me, you pressed on my stomach, and . . .'

'Well, sorry, Rosie – normally it doesn't have that effect on women.'

'No, but . . .' I held my stomach and groaned again. 'Oh, I'm sorry, Ashley, but I've been feeling dodgy all night. In fact ever since I got off the plane. I thought it was travel sickness but it must be something I've eaten . . .'

He rolled onto his side and looked at me contemplatively.

'Well, are you feeling better now?' He traced one nipple with his finger. 'Hmm?'

Well, quite good at this precise moment, yes ...

He moved slowly towards me.

'No! Don't kiss me, for God's sake – you'll probably die!' I'd cleaned my teeth, but well, you know. Vomiting does horrible things to your mouth.

'OK, we've done that bit already – let's move straight on ...' he suggested, beginning to sound impatient. Not wanting to risk his weight on my delicate stomach again, I rolled on top of him.

'Oh, yes, Rosie!' he muttered, becoming instantly very excited. 'Come on – now! Let's do it now ...'

And we would have done. Believe me, I was all for it. I was, if you'll excuse the crudity of the expression, gagging for it.

But just at the most crucial moment, I suddenly felt the bile rising in my throat again and his face began to blur and the room swayed and swum and I jumped off him, very inelegantly bolting for the toilet just in time. A case of gagging for England rather than gagging for it.

By the time I crawled back to bed the second time, two things had happened. One – Ashley had gone. And two – I couldn't have cared less.

In the morning, I cared a lot. I looked at the assorted jumble of clothes on the floor. I looked at the crumpled sheets on the other side of the bed. I remembered just where we'd got to before I'd had to, quite literally, tear myself away. I wasn't sure whether I still felt sick, or I was just sick with disappointment. How could this be fair? Here I was, in Paris for the first time in my life, with a gorgeous man for the first time in my life, trying to commit adultery also for the first time in my life and what happens? I get struck down by some awful disease. And where was my would-be lover when I needed him most? Mopping my fevered brow? Tenderly stroking my poor hot sweaty little

212

hands? Lovingly clearing up the vomit? Was he fuck as like. He'd pissed off out of it at the first sign of trouble. Well, OK, the second sign. It wasn't exactly gentlemanly, was it? I mean, he hadn't even stayed to see if I'd got back to bed all right. For all he knew, I might have been lying unconscious on the floor all night. And him a member of the Caring Profession! Huh!

Moving slowly in case the room still wanted to spin on its axis, I made my way to the bathroom and took a hot shower. Towelling myself dry, I looked at myself ruefully in the mirror ad thought – this was *not* how I envisaged waking up this morning – alone, deserted, sick, covered in a red rash . . .

I blinked and looked more closely into the mirror. Yes, a rash – a bright red rash – seemed to have crept up on me unawares overnight and was now covering my chest and stomach, making me look like some sort of comic character from a children's cartoon. Oh, great! Absolutely bloody fantastic. I got two nights in Paris, two nights to have my way with Ashley Sex-God Connor – the first night I puked like a colicky baby and the second night I'd be stripping off to reveal sexy black undies and the possible onset of the Plague. Well, at least it wasn't on my face. I dressed quickly, covering myself with as many layers of clothes as possible, and had just about finished when Ashley knocked on the bedroom door.

'How are you feeling this morning?' he asked, looking as if he cared.

'Not too bad,' I lied, 'considering I was lying unconscious on the bathroom floor all night.'

'You weren't!' he exclaimed, looking shocked, taking hold of my arm as if I was suddenly going to topple over.

'No, I wasn't. But I *did* feel awful all night.'

If this made him feel bad about leaving me, he certainly wasn't showing it.

'You still look pretty rough,' he said, just to cheer me up. 'Maybe a good breakfast will help?'

My stomach churned at the thought of it, but I tried to smile and look positive. I *had* to be all right today! Maybe it was all in the mind, and the rash was just . . . just a rash? A reaction to the scratchy, lacy underwear?

We went downstairs for breakfast where, joy of joys, we were immediately confronted by Doctors Gucci and Schuter, who didn't seem to have any other friends. Fortunately they'd already eaten and were just on their way out of the restaurant.

'I just have to say goodbye to Antonio and Ernest,' said Ashley. 'They're leaving today.'

'Oh dear. What a shame,' I said sweetly, nodding at them.

'Did you have a good night?' asked Doctor Gucci, looking from Ashley to me and back again with a broad grin.

'Yes, thank you,' said Ashley, straight-faced.

'Better, I think, than last year!' said Doctor Schuter, also grinning at me.

'I think so too,' Ashley replied with a smile.

'So – we'll see you next year, my friend – and maybe, who knows? Next year will be even better again, yes?'

'Certainly hope so, Ernest! I'll be looking forward to it!' replied Ashley.

All three of them laughed heartily at this, and the mad German and the mad Italian then walked off, waving and laughing as they went.

'You all seem to get very excited about a boring old conference,' I commented as we headed for the buffet table.

'Well . . . you know how it is,' said Ashley with a vague smile.

'No. I don't,' I said. But I don't think he was listening.

Two mouthfuls of croissant later, I decided I definitely still wasn't up to eating. I sat slowly sipping from a glass of apple juice, hoping Ashley wouldn't notice.

'Finished?' he asked when he eventually looked up from

his plate of ham, salami, cheeses, bread, fruit and cake.

'Yes. Thanks.'

I'd been up for little more than an hour, and already I had the feeling that I'd like nothing better than to lie down and go back to sleep. My stomach felt terrible again, and when I went to the loo with the excuse of freshening up, the half glass of apple juice came straight back up. I was actually beginning to feel quite alarmed. Maybe I really did have the Plague. What were the symptoms anyway? I'd have to look it up when I got home ...

'Are you sure you're fit for sightseeing?' asked Ashley, frowning at me when I met him the hotel lobby. 'You really do look pale.'

'Fresh air'll do me good,' I replied without much conviction.

In fact it nearly knocked me over. There was a stiff breeze blowing and I had to hold onto Ashley's arm as we staggered out of the hotel. Well, I was certainly staggering. He actually seemed to be walking OK.

'Do you need any help there? Shall I call a taxi? Or an ambulance?'

I looked round, wondering if the hotel receptionist had followed us out – and stared straight into the face of Obstetrics Oliver from Oz.

'Hello!' I smiled.

'You OK? You look even more crook than you did the other day!'

'Do you know this guy?' muttered Ashley, frowning.

'Yes – we met at the airport yesterday – he helped me when I was feeling ill ...'

Thinking about it now, I realised with increasing anxiety that Oliver was right. I felt much worse now than I did then.

'Oliver Fenton,' said Oliver, holding out his hand to Ashley. 'Pleased to meet you.'

'Ashley Connor,' responded Ashley, looking him up and down without much enthusiasm. 'Here for the conference?'

'No, just job hunting. I ...'

'Well, good luck, then,' said Ashley, cutting him short and turning to go.

'Thanks, Oliver,' I said. 'Hope you get your job.'

'Are you sure you're all right?'

'Yes – I'll be fine ... some fresh air ...'

'Come on, then, if you want to see Paris,' said Ashley. Out of earshot of Oliver, he added: 'You don't want to go chatting up every young doctor who tries to pick you up.'

'He wasn't!' I retorted, shocked. 'And neither was I! In fact, Ashley, I was bloody glad he was there when I almost fainted at the airport, because *you* sure as hell weren't!'

We walked in silence for a couple of minutes. I was so pissed off with him, I'd have let go of his arm if I didn't think I'd fall over.

'OK, sorry,' he relented eventually. 'Come on, let's not spoil the weekend by arguing.'

Oh, I see. My fault now, is it? How do men manage to do that?! But I needed him to show me around Paris, I needed him to translate French for me, and I needed him to stop me collapsing in a heap from the nausea and giddiness that was getting worse with every step.

I tried to concentrate on looking around me. This is it – Paris! I kept reminding myself. This is what I came to see. This is the famous Place de la Concorde! This is the Champs Elysees! There ahead of me is the Arc de Triomphe! I put one foot in front of the other, willing myself to stay upright, forcing myself to keep walking, to keep holding onto Ashley's arm, to try to listen to him pointing out the sights.

'Don't you want to take any photos?' he asked suddenly.

My camera was swinging, forgotten, on its strap over my shoulder.

'In a minute,' I said hoarsely. 'Perhaps on the way back.'

'Well, you might want to take some now,' he insisted, letting go of my arm to let me get the camera ready, 'because any minute now you'll get your first glimpse of the Eiffel Tower.'

But I never did see it. When he let go of my arm I slid gracefully onto the pavement, holding onto his legs all the way down. And I don't really remember anything else with any clarity until I woke up in bed on one of the medical wards of East Dean General.

Chapter Twelve

Visiting Time

The sun was streaming in the window. It hurt my eyes. I blinked and, trying to bring up a hand from under the sheet to rub my eyes, felt with surprise the pull of the tube in my arm.

'What's this?' I asked myself out loud. My voice sounded hoarse and my throat felt scratchy.

'It's just saline,' replied a voice from behind my head. 'The one in the other arm's an antibiotic. A *different* antibiotic.'

Different? How different? And why different?

I turned over, trying to see who'd spoken. The nurse smiled at me.

'You look a bit more with it than you did last night.'

'Last night?' I licked my dry lips, swallowed and tried again. 'Last night? I don't remember, really ... What day is it?'

'Sunday. Would you like a drink of water? Or a cup of tea?'

'Yes, please. Tea.' I frowned, trying to concentrate, trying to remember. 'I was in Paris. I was feeling really ill ...'

'Yes. You came in yesterday evening by ambulance. Mr Connor, the consultant, brought you in himself!' she added, giving me a look with a raised eyebrow.

'I can vaguely remember being on the plane . . .'

I'd been drifting in and out of consciousness, my head on Ashley's chest, wishing only to die every time I came to. Most of the journey was a blur – along with most of the time in Paris, now.

'What a waste!' I muttered to myself, turning away so that the nurse wouldn't see the tears of self-pity suddenly filling my eyes.

'Do you want to see your husband now?' she asked as she returned with a cup of tea and a fresh jug of water.

'My *husband*?' I stared at her in confusion. She must surely have the wrong patient.

'Yes, dear. He's outside. Been in a couple of times to see you this morning while you've been asleep.'

'How did he know . . .?' I started to ask her, but she was busy checking my pulse and fussing with the drips.

'I'll tell him to come in,' she said finally, with a smile.

'OK,' I muttered.

She turned to leave.

'Just one thing!' I called after her. 'What exactly *was* the matter with me?'

'Oh – didn't anyone explain to you? It was the antibiotic you were taking. You were allergic to it. You must have noticed the rash – you were covered in it! Severe allergic reaction. But you'll be fine now. Make sure you let everyone know – don't ever take Penicillin again, will you – it could be really, really serious!'

Shit. So much for never being allergic to anything in my life.

'But I must have taken Penicillin loads of times before!' I protested.

'Maybe not this particular one – and it was a high dose,' she commented, looking at my notes. 'Who prescribed it – your GP?'

'No. It was . . .' I stopped, alarm suddenly making me flush hot all over. I could be getting PJ into trouble here, if I wasn't careful. 'I can't remember who it was,' I finished lamely.

The nurse gave me an odd look, closed my medical records and shrugged.

'Well, we've got you on IV Erythromycin now so that should sort you out. How did you get the cut in your hand?'

'A kitchen knife. Stupid accident.'

'It should have been stitched. Why on earth didn't your GP – or whoever . . .'

'My own fault,' I said quickly. 'I didn't want any fuss.'

She smiled at me.

'And look at you now!'

'I know. Stupid. Hospital staff are the worst patients, aren't we.'

Barry came into the ward looking anxious and carrying flowers.

'Blimey,' I joked feebly, trying to sit up. 'It's not even our anniversary.'

'You gave us all a scare. The kids are beside themselves with worry.'

Not you, then. Just the kids.

'How did you hear about it?' I asked, looking down at the floor, waiting for the answer that was presumably going to deliver the final deathblow to our marriage. *How did I hear? Oh, I had a nice friendly phone call from the lover you were spending the weekend with. Said how much he liked your underwear.*

'Had a call from the hospital in Paris.'

'The *hospital* in *Paris*?' I echoed, blinking at him in surprise.

'Yes, Rosie. The hospital where you'd been whisked off by ambulance after you collapsed in the street. Don't you remember anything?'

'Not a lot,' I admitted truthfully.

'Apparently they wanted to keep you in there, but the English doctor who went with you to the hospital persuaded them that you'd be OK to fly home with your friends as long as he arranged an ambulance to meet the plane at Gatwick.'

'English doctor?' I prompted, wondering just what the hell Ashley had told Barry.

'Well – English-speaking, anyway. Had a bit of an Australian accent. Nice guy called Oliver Fenton. You were dead lucky, Rosie, that he happened to be there when you collapsed. God knows what would have happened – out there in a strange country with your girl-friends – I bet none of them speak any French – anything could have happened ...'

Barry went on at great length about the folly of having been in Paris without someone masterful and fluent in French, such as himself, to look after me, but I'd stopped listening as soon as I heard the name of my Good Samaritan. Not Ashley Connor, against whose legs I'd fallen gracefully into the gutter, against whose protective chest I'd lain semi-conscious on the flight home, under whose care I'd apparently arrived back at East Dean in the ambulance – but Aussie Oliver the Obstetrician! Oliver Fenton who'd looked after me at Arrivals in Paris when I first felt ill, who'd showed such concern when I left the hotel with Ashley feeling even more ill ... who somehow, as if by magic, had turned up in the street just as I did my dying swan act and had apparently, for some reason, taken charge of the situation.

'I wonder how he found your phone number?' was all I could think to say.

'In your handbag. He said he was sorry to have had to rummage for it, but you were out of it. Like I say – you were bloody lucky he was around, Rosie.'

Yes. Seems like an obstetrics registrar is more help than an orthopaedic consultant in a crisis, then.

'I'm surprised you've bothered to come and see me,' I said to Barry when he finally ran out of things to say about the dangers of collapsing in Paris streets when you don't speak the language. 'In the circumstances.'

He looked hurt.

'We may be having some problems, Rosie, but I think

we can still be civil to each other, can't we? I'm not a total bastard, whatever you might think of me. I could hardly think of you lying here ill, and not come to see you, for God's sake.'

'No. Thanks for coming. Sorry – I don't think you're a total bastard, I didn't mean that. If I did, we'd have split up years ago.'

'Whereas, as it is, we're going to split up now?'

'I think you were right when you said we need to talk about it. That's all I'm saying.'

He nodded silently and picked at the flowers lying on his lap.

'Give them to one of the nurses to put in water,' I said. 'Before you pick off all the petals.'

If you pick away at things too much, they're just not worth keeping in the end.

I drifted off to sleep again after Barry left. It was a restless, troubled sleep, disturbed by dreams about Paris and sudden fearful awakenings where I'd sit up in bed and gabble on about what had happened to my suitcase full of underwear. When I woke up properly, in the afternoon, I felt even more tired than before. I lay still while my eyes focused slowly on my surroundings: the thin white NHS bed cover; the pale yellow and brown patterned curtains; the wooden bedside locker with its standard supply of drinking water and tissues; the greasy-looking paper bag balanced on the edge of the locker ...

I sat up quickly and reached out for the bag. Something red and sticky was oozing out of it. I opened the bag and smiled at the sight of the two fat, sugary doughnuts inside.

'Could you do me a favour?' I called to the nearest nurse. 'When you've got a minute, could you possibly bleep Mr Jaimeen in orthopaedics and tell him I said thank you?

'So you finally woke up?' said PJ, plonking himself down unceremoniously on my bed. 'I hung around for as long as

I could – tried shouting at you to wake you but as usual, you just ignored me. You were snoring and muttering about thongs. You want to be careful who you sleep with, Rosie, talking dirty like that in your dreams.'

'Thanks for the warning,' I smiled at him. 'And thanks for leaving these,' I nodded at the doughnut bag. 'Want one with me?'

'Of course. Are you allowed, or are you meant to be nil by mouth? I thought the hand surgeons were talking about taking you to theatre?'

'Nobody's said anything. Haven't seen a doctor yet – apart from you of course!' I bit into a doughnut and passed him the bag. 'Anyway, I'm bloody starving. Haven't eaten for ages, and what I did eat I threw up.'

'So I've heard.' He ate his doughnut silently for a while, watching me. 'Sorry, Rosie – Christ, if I'd known ...'

'Don't be stupid. Not your fault.'

'You must be the only one who doesn't think it is.'

'What? Who's been saying ...?' I stopped, put my doughnut down on the bed cover and sighed. 'Ashley?'

'Who else? I was hauled over the coals almost as soon as he'd unloaded you from the ambulance. Looks like he's going to report me.'

'*Report* you?!' I sat bolt upright in bed and stared at him. 'What the hell for?'

'Unethical prescribing. You weren't my patient. I didn't write up the prescription in your notes.'

'But everyone does it! Ashley does it himself; hospital staff always get prescriptions written by the doctors ...'

'Yeah, but maybe their patients don't end up collapsing with severe allergic reactions and being rushed into hospital in Paris. Especially not when they're on a dirty weekend with a consultant.'

'PJ, that is so unfair! He can't be serious. He probably just wants to blame someone.'

'No, Rosie. He doesn't just want to blame *someone*. He wants to blame *me*. Like he always does. Think about it.'

'I'll talk to him. Don't worry, I'll explain. It wasn't your fault. There's no way you're going to take the blame.'

'If you say so,' he said, gloomily, biting into his doughnut again. 'Anyway, glad you're on the mend. Did you have a nice time in Paris apart from throwing up and falling down?'

'No, I didn't. I felt ill the whole time. I didn't even get to see the Eiffel Tower.'

'And how about the nightlife?' he asked, giving me a very direct look. 'Was that any good?'

'Ruined. Not that it's any of your business.'

'Oh, dear. Sorry to hear it!' he said, brightening visibly. His smile widened to a grin. 'No wonder poor old AC is in a grumpy mood – taking you all the way to Paris and he didn't even get his wicked way with you!'

'I'm not too happy about it myself, PJ, as it happens. I don't know what's so bloody funny about it.

'Don't you? You're not sitting where I am!'

He turned the bedside locker slightly so that its open door faced me. The shelf inside was roughly piled with the clothes I'd been wearing when I was admitted – topped by the red and black lacy underwear.

'PJ!' I snapped, feeling myself blush scarlet. 'Close that door! For God's sake! My husband was sitting here earlier on!'

'Was he?' asked PJ, closing the locker door obediently and turning it back to face its usual direction. 'Oh dear.' He looked at me sadly. 'Poor chap.'

'There's no *poor chap* about it!' I retorted, crossly. 'He's got something going on with a young girl with short skirts and no bus fares. We're on the point of separating. You don't have to feel sorry for *him*.'

'Is it OK if I feel sorry for myself, then?' he asked as he stood up and brushed the sugar off his scrub trousers.

I looked at his downcast face and felt a wave of affection for him. He'd been a good friend, despite our ups and downs especially over the old armchair thing – and now he

224

was in trouble because of me. He didn't deserve that.

'Come here,' I said, pulling at his arm.

He leaned towards me and I pulled him closer and gave him a kiss on the cheek. For a moment I held his face close to mine and felt a strange urge to stroke the back of his hair.

'It'll be all right,' I said softly. 'Don't worry.'

'See you later,' was all he said in reply. He straightened up, turned and left without a backward glance.

So much for affection. But then again, what did I expect? I'd brought him nothing but trouble lately, hadn't I.

If nothing else, it was a good day for visitors. Natasha and Stuart turned up later.

'You shouldn't have coming rushing back from Leicester!' I gasped.

'Mum, it's the Easter holiday. I came home on Friday, just as you went off on your jaunt to Paris.'

'Oh yes,' I remembered, duly chastened. How bad is that? I'd been so excited about going away with Ashley, I'd completely forgotten that my younger daughter was due home the same day. 'Sorry, Tash. I should have been there . . .'

'Mum, don't ever say that!' she returned, surprisingly fiercely. 'Emma and I were only saying last week on the phone how it's about time you got yourself a life and started going out and about more. We're not kids now. Even Stuart can look after himself up to a point . . .'

'What do you mean, up to a point? What point?' interrupted Stuart indignantly.

'Up to the point when you get into fights and get yourself rushed into hospital,' said his sister calmly.

'Well, Mum's just as bad!'

They both turned to look at me, apparently suddenly remembering the purpose of the visit.

'Are you feeling OK now?' asked Tasha, taking hold of my hand and staring at the saline drip.

'Yes, much better, thank you, love. And thanks for your concern, you and Emma, but don't worry – I *am* getting out and about more.' I looked at her thoughtfully, looked from her to Stuart and added on a sudden impulse, 'but it might not be with your dad.'

'I know,' she said, stroking my hand lightly. 'I realise that.'

'You do?'

'Don't look so surprised. We're not stupid, Mum. We've all realised things were . . . not right.'

'Have you?' Even to my own ears, my voice sounded screechy with amazement. 'But – it's not like we've been arguing all the time, or there's been a horrible atmosphere at home or anything – has there?'

'No,' said Stuart matter-of-factly. 'There hasn't been *anything*. That's the whole point.'

I stared at my son as if I was looking at a stranger. How did he, at fourteen, get to notice more about my relationship with his father than I did myself?

'You and Dad just aren't really *together* any more, are you?' said Tasha.

'Aren't you upset? I've been trying to avoid hurting you, both of you – and Emma . . . trying to carry on and pretend it was OK. It's not so very bad . . . We could probably still try . . .'

'You've managed twenty-odd years together,' she shrugged. 'God knows how anyone does that – you both deserve a medal. So why feel guilty? You shouldn't both put up with being miserable just to pretend to us kids that everything's OK.'

'Life's too short, Mum,' commented Stuart without looking up from reading the problem page in a *Marie Claire* magazine he'd picked up from a shelf in the ward.

There hadn't, up till then, been many occasions in my life when I'd felt totally gobsmacked. I'd always managed, in even the most extreme of circumstances, to come up with some sort of response worthy of the occasion, even if it was only a four-letter one. But lying there in my hospital bed, with my son reading women's magazines and philosophising, and my daughter shrugging and saying I shouldn't feel guilty about considering the break-up of her family, I couldn't do any more than swallow and cough and blink and try to keep my face from crumpling up like a bit of soggy old toilet paper.

'Don't cry, Mum,' said Tasha, handing me a tissue from the top of the locker. 'It'll all work out OK.'

'Yeah, it'll be cool,' said Stuart, turning the pages of *Marie Claire*. 'All my mates've got divorced parents. They get two holidays every year!'

In your dreams, boy. In your dreams.

And a little later in the evening, Ashley arrived.

'How are you feeling?' He sat down on the bed and looked at me speculatively. It was the look of a consultant, assessing a patient's progress. I didn't like it. I wanted him to look at me like a man assessing his lover's ability to get horny.

'Much better,' I said, trying to look seductive but fighting a losing battle with the hospital gown and the drips in both arms. 'Soon be up and about and fit for . . . anything.'

He ignored this, and the look of burning desire I was trying to give him, and instead picked up my hospital records and began reading them with a frown of concentration.

'I'm sorry about the weekend,' I said quietly. 'And for all the trouble . . . the ambulance, and the flight, and everything . . .'

'Well, it was partly thanks to your interfering young boyfriend from the hotel.'

'Oliver? How come?'

'He called the ambulance from the hotel and took you to the hospital in Paris.'

Hold on, hold on . . . I was a bit lost, here.

'The hotel? I thought I collapsed in the street?'

'Yes. So I called a cab to take us back to the hotel, and made you comfortable in the lounge. Next time I looked, you'd disappeared, and the receptionist told me you'd been taken to hospital. Apparently your friend Oliver decided, with all his wealth of experience in gynaecology ...'

'Obstetrics. He's an obstetric registrar.'

'Quite. Helps to deliver a few babies and thinks he can diagnose potential anaphylactic shock ...'

'But he did, didn't he?' I pointed out. I felt just a little bit miffed at Ashley's apparent lack of concern. Why hadn't he called an ambulance himself? Why had he just dumped me in the hotel lounge when I was semi-conscious and dehydrating? What was he doing that was so much more important than getting medical attention for me? 'I had to see a couple of the other delegates,' he explained as if he was reading my mind. 'I had important papers to pick up from somebody, and then I obviously had to check out of the hotel and ...'

'All very urgent, then,' I said sarcastically.

'I'd only left you for a couple of minutes, and I was going to drive you straight to the hospital myself. Anyway, if that idiot Jaimeen hadn't tried to play God in the first place ...' he muttered, putting my notes down sharply and turning back to look at me. 'Why the *hell* didn't you come to me about your hand?'

'I don't know ... you were busy ... he was there ...'

'Absolute bloody idiot. He should have checked you weren't allergic ...'

'Ashley!' I didn't realise quite how loud I'd shouted until I noticed the nurses looking at us. I lowered my voice a couple of decibels and continued, angrily, feeling the heat rise to my face. 'He *did* ask me about allergies, but I didn't even know myself I had a problem. It wasn't his fault! He was trying to help me!'

'Rosie, your loyalty is misplaced. He should *not* have been trying to help you, and this *is* his fault. He should, for a start, have sent you to the hand surgeons. That cut should have been sutured and you should have been on intravenous antibiotics . . .'

'So I could have my allergic reaction in the comfort of a hospital bed instead of while we were trying to get a shag in Paris?' I retorted, much to the delight of the nearest nurse. '*I'm* the only person to blame for all this, Ashley. I refused to see the hand surgeons. I kept forgetting to take the first lot of antibiotics PJ prescribed me and I let it get worse. And I didn't recognise that I was having an allergic reaction because I was too busy trying to rush into bed with you – not that you seemed to care!'

I stopped, shocked by what I'd said and by the anger, and volume, with which I'd said it – and even more shocked by the fact that I didn't regret it.

'Why don't you just make an announcement to the whole hospital about our sex life?' said Ashley, deadly quiet.

'Good idea,' I retorted, 'except that we still don't seem to even *have* a sex life!'

'And whose fault is that?'

'Well, it's *not* PJ's, is it! If that's what's bothering you, Ashley, let's pull the curtains round the bed right now and get on with it . . .'

'It seems to me that you waste a hell of a lot of energy defending that idiot Jaimeen . . .'

'He's not an idiot! I just don't want you to blame him, and get him into trouble, when he's done nothing wrong.'

'Well, I disagree with you. But it won't be my decision.'

'If you report him, Ashley . . .'

'Yes?' He held my gaze, perfectly still, one eyebrow raised, not a flicker of amusement. 'If I report him, what?'

'I won't want to see you any more.'

There was a pause – a moment's hesitation – a blinking of the eye of time, during which everything changed and moved into different directions like sand shifting on a beach as the tide turns and the ocean crashes away again on its way between the continents.

'I mean it,' I said softly, regretfully, thinking sadly of

his lean fit body next to mine in the hotel bed, and the lost night of passion, and the money wasted on underwear. 'I mean it – I won't want to see you again.'

He stood up, adjusted the sleeves of his jacket carefully and passed a hand thoughtfully through his hair.

'Well, Rosie,' he said finally with a faint twitch of a smile which didn't reach his eyes, 'I'll try not to mind too much.'

And the second man of the day walked away from me without looking back.

'Everyone's talking about it!' Becky told me with wide-eyed excitement. 'Imagine! Dumping Ashley Connor, in front of everyone in the ward!'

'I didn't dump him. Not exactly,' I said, miserably. 'I just wanted to stop him from getting PJ into trouble.'

'Well, good for you, Rosie. Bloody good for you. He doesn't deserve you . . .'

'But, Becky, he didn't even seem to care,' I whispered.

I closed my eyes and settled back into the heavy black cloud of gloom I'd been immersed in ever since Ashley left the ward the previous day. How had everything gone down-hill so suddenly? Just a few days ago I was looking forward to the most exciting weekend of my life. Now here I was, lying in a hospital bed with a locker full of unused lingerie, a marriage that was in its death throes, a husband and family who seemed quite happy to accept its demise, and a so-called lover who still hadn't made love to me and walked away without so much as a shrug when I threatened to finish with him. I could be forgiven, at this point, for having a bit of a crisis of self-confidence.

'I think he'll still report PJ anyway,' I sighed behind my closed eyelids.

'Maybe you should get your story in first, then?' suggested Becky gently. 'If you really want to help PJ . . .'

'Yes, I do want to. It isn't fair – he only tried to help me . . .' I tailed off. 'I'll have to think of the best way . . .'

'Well, you've got plenty of time to think about it. When are you being discharged?'

'Later on today, hopefully. One of the hand surgeons came and looked at this, earlier on—,' I waved my bandaged hand, '—and decided it only needed cleaning and suturing, thank God, and now I'm OK on this antibiotic I can carry on taking it orally.'

'How long have you got to be off work, then?'

'The rest of the week. Sorry, Becky. How on earth are you managing? Is Sara back?'

'No. You're not the only one to be rushed into hospital this weekend you know! It's been all drama . . .'

'Callum?'

'Yes – he was on the kids' ward from Friday till yesterday. They got his temperature down and rehydrated him and he's on the mend at home now, but poor Sara – when she phoned me on Friday night she was beside herself.'

'Poor thing – she must have been. I must give her a ring.' I felt guilty, now, for wallowing in self-pity about my non-dirty weekend when poor Sara had been so worried about her little demon child. 'So have you got a temp working on reception with you?'

'Two! Isn't that incredible? Sylvia Riley organised one herself apparently, for Friday, and then this second girl turned up this morning – it seems *someone* phoned Mrs Riley at home last night and demanded she organise cover for you for the whole week . . . she got onto the agency this morning as soon as they opened!'

'I suppose that has to be Ashley,' I said, sadly.

'Well, at least he did *that* much for you.'

'Certainly didn't do much else.'

'Never mind, Rosie. Oh, but that reminds me! Dave told me something strange about Ashley Connor.'

'Dave did? What?'

'Apparently a while ago, he turned up in the Photography Department and asked Dave if it was him who had developed your photos.'

'My . . .?' I frowned at her. 'What's it got to do with him who develops my photos?'

'He asked if he'd got the negatives. Said you'd asked him to pick them up for you. Did you?'

'No, of course not! I didn't ask him to pick up anything! As if I would!' I paused, considering this for a minute. 'Actually it's funny, you know. At first that was all Ashley seemed to want to talk about – my photography. Every time we got together he was on at me to show him my photos. I showed him some, and he kept nagging me to see some more. I thought it was quite flattering – you know, he was complimentary about them. Then he seemed to just lose interest.'

'I suppose he started taking an interest in your other attributes instead,' she teased.

'For all the good it did, yes,' I sighed again, the gloom beginning to return.

'Cheer up, Rosie. Plenty more fish in the sea. From what you were saying about Barry and the kids, it looks as if you're going to be a free woman soon.'

'I'm not sure if it's what I want. I don't know *what* I want,' I returned morosely.

'Well look, don't start worrying too much about things for now. You need to get yourself fit. I'd better get back to work . . .'

'Of course. Thanks for coming to see me.'

She stood up and straightened her skirt.

'By the way,' I added. 'What did Dave do about the negatives? Did he give them to Ashley?'

'Yes. So he hasn't passed them on to you yet? Typical man – I suppose he's put them somewhere and forgotten about them.' She looked at my face. 'I hope Dave didn't do the wrong thing, Rosie?'

'No. Don't worry. I'll get them back from him some time, I suppose. I couldn't really care less, Becky, to be honest.'

It was true. I didn't feel much like caring about anything.

But it still niggled me slightly with the beginnings of an unease that wasn't going to go away. I wasn't sure what Ashley Connor was playing at. But I had a feeling I wasn't going to like it.

Chapter Thirteen

Who the Dog Lives With (and other decisions)

I couldn't remember ever having been signed off sick before. I lay on the sofa, watching daytime television, and tried to feel guilty about the fact that I didn't really have very much wrong with me. I told myself there were probably people with debilitating serious illnesses who didn't get a week off work at the drop of a hat like this. There were probably people with chronic painful conditions of various limbs and organs who had to battle on, struggling through their daily lives without complaining or whingeing, and here was I with a little bit of a sore hand, still in my dressing gown at half past eleven and being brought grapes and magazines by my children as if I was a bona fide invalid. But it didn't matter how much I tried to rebuke myself, I was loving every minute of it. Tasha and Stuart were at home for the holidays, their friends were wandering in and out as if we were the local coffee-bar, and the house was once again full of the ear-splitting squeals of girls discussing boys and the animal grunts of boys discussing football and PlayStation II. Music and laughter echoed around the place, the dog charged in and out of rooms like a mad thing, barking and panting with excitement, and I laid back, closed my eyes, listened to it all going on around me and felt strangely peaceful.

'So what's going to happen, then?' asked Barry eventually, shattering my peace like an alarm clock going off in the middle of a lovely dream. It was Good Friday. He'd spent most of the day doing what men usually describe as 'pottering'. Back and forth he went from garden to shed, from shed to kitchen, from kitchen to garage, carrying boxes of tools and bits of wire, frowning at flower beds and window-sills, scratching his head and looking like there were serious decisions to be made. And we all knew what the most serious decision was, didn't we?

'What are we doing about this, Rosie? Are we splitting up? Because if we are, the house . . .'

'I know, I know.' The house would have to be sold. He'd get himself a little flat somewhere, I'd get myself a little flat somewhere else, Stuart would commute between us hoping for extra presents and holidays, and Tasha and Emma wouldn't ever be able to talk about 'going home' any more. I'd seen it all a hundred times. Friends, colleagues, neighbours, cousins, my brother and Barry's sister had all been down this road at least once. We'd sometimes joked that we were the only people we knew who were still clinging onto the same old original partner. Now it didn't seem very funny any more, and I suddenly knew why I'd been wrapping myself in a cocoon of peace all week, lying on the sofa and pretending to be calm and happy. I didn't want to face facts. I didn't want to deal with this. I wanted it to go away.

'I'm not sure. I don't know what I want,' I muttered.

He sat down next to me and rubbed the back of his neck, the way he always did when he was worried.

'It's not like we quarrel, or fight, or even like there's a horrible atmosphere all the time,' I said, repeating the argument I'd put forward to the children.

'No. But we don't do *anything* together, do we.'

'Are you unhappy?'

'No,' he said cautiously. 'Not really *un*happy.' There was a pause of about half a lifetime, during which we finally looked each other in the eye and must have both made the same decision, at the same time, to be totally honest now.

'But not really happy, either,' we finished more or less together.

Having decided to be honest it seemed there was going to be no stopping us.

'I've been seeing Robyn.'

'I thought so. And I've been seeing someone . . .'

'But we haven't slept together. Not yet. I know what you think but we haven't . . .'

'Nor have we. He was with me – in Paris. But . . .'

'I think I guessed that too.'

'But nothing happened. And now I think it's over anyway.'

We stared at each other, the enormity of our confessions suddenly reducing us to silence.

'There's a lot we have to deal with,' Barry said quietly.

'Yes.'

I had to deal with the fact that, despite having been naked in bed with Ashley Connor just a week ago and regretting with my whole heart not having had sex with him on account of puking my guts up at inappropriate moments – despite all this, it felt strange and somehow annoying that Barry had been lying to me all along about not seeing Robyn. That he'd admitted only that they 'hadn't slept together *yet.*' If not yet – when? Tomorrow? Next week? Had they fixed a date for it – perhaps something romantic like her eighteenth birthday or the day she passed her driving test or graduated from the Brownies? And if I found this hard to deal with, I could only presume, and certainly didn't want to ask, how strange and difficult Barry was finding it to accept that I'd lied to him about Paris: that I'd been there, not with some girlfriends but with another man – another man I hadn't even managed to sleep with and had now (perhaps) finished with.

'We have to deal with stuff like the mortgage, and the

endowment, and the life insurance policies,' said Barry. 'And who the dog lives with.'

Well, just so long as we know what the priorities are.

I went back to work the day after Easter Monday. I felt like I'd been off on a long, long holiday. People obviously *thought* I'd been off on a long, long holiday. They kept coming up to me and saying I looked well, and then looking puzzled at my absence of a tan and lack of holiday stories. (*Lovely beach but the apartment was awful – toilet wouldn't flush and we had to stand in a bucket to have a shower.*)

'Is it nice to be back?' asked Becky when things quietened down a bit near lunchtime.

'It's a relief, really,' I admitted. 'All over Easter Barry kept wanting to talk about separating.'

'Oh, Rosie.' She reached out and touched my arm sympathetically. 'I'm sorry it's come to this. But, you know, in the end ...'

'No, it's OK – I don't actually seem to be very upset about it. I think I went numb some time during the last ten years or so and I can't seem to feel anything very much. But he wants us to make decisions, and I can't really be arsed to think about them.'

'Like who moves out? Who gets what, who pays for what?'

'That sort of stuff, yes. And who the dog lives with.'

'Take him for a walk, let him off the lead and see who he runs to.'

'Knowing Biggles, he'd probably leg it in the opposite direction and never come back.' I sighed. 'I suppose it'll all sort itself out in the end. At least we're managing to stay civil to each other, if you can call grunting at each other being civil.'

'Some people might say it was normal.'

Normal? If civil grunting was normal, why were we splitting up? What were Barry and I looking for?

Something abnormal? Subnormal? Paranormal?

And talking of the paranormal, Sylvia Riley wanted to see me. I'd hardly got myself installed back behind the reception desk that morning before she'd phoned to request the pleasure of my company in her office at 12.45. Why 12.45 and not 12.30 or one o'clock? Don't you think that's calculated to make someone feel intimidated? It implies that she's got so many far more important people to see on every hour and half hour throughout the day, she's just about managed to squeeze you in and you'll have to be there *exactly* on the dot, otherwise you'll miss your slot and be sent to detention.

So there I was at 12.43 precisely, tapping nervously on her door like a first-year student expecting to be expelled.

'Come in!' she bellowed graciously.

I pushed open the door and found, to my surprise, not only Sylvia Riley majestically enthroned behind her huge untidy desk but also Long Term Sick Monica, huddled in a chair to the side of the desk looking at the floor as if mesmerised by the dust and hole-punchings and screwed up bits of yellow stick-it-notes that had missed the wastepaper bin.

'Oh, hello!' I said, surprise making me forget my apprehension about meeting the Queen. I sat down uninvited in the chair next to Monica's and tried unsuccessfully to get her to look up at me. 'Are you better? Are you back at work?'

'Monica's making a good recovery,' said Sylvia Riley in the tone of a doctor giving a press release about a significantly famous patient. 'But she still isn't fit to take on anything too stressful.'

Like speaking for herself? Or looking up from the floor?

'So are you coming back to your job?' I asked, purposely continuing to address Monica.

'No, Monica won't be coming back,' declared Sylvia without a hint of regret. 'She's come here today to hand in her notice.'

I was beginning to feel embarrassed for Monica. I hadn't felt terribly fond of her when she'd cleared off on Long Term Sickness having dumped me right in the shit with the referral letters in the brown internal envelope, but as things had panned out, I'd got over it and it was now all too evident that the poor cow had been suffering from stress or exhaustion – and who could really blame her, working as she had done for as long as I could remember, under the immediate and close scrutiny of Sylvia Riley? And it looked now like whatever little shred of dignity she might have had left after everyone in the hospital knew she'd done a runner when the heat was on, was being stripped away from her as SR spoke her lines for her like some malign celestial ventriloquist.

'I'm sorry to hear that, Monica,' I told the top of her bent head as kindly as I could.

'Yes, and *Monica* has something to say to *you*, Rosemary,' said the puppeteer, pulling the strings of the poor broken doll so that she sat up, startled, staring straight at me, her eyes wide and appealing.

'No, don't ... honestly, don't try to talk ...' I stammered, horrified almost as much by my own ineptitude as I was by Sylvia's cruelty. But Monica, without a flicker of reaction, without moving a muscle and almost without moving her lips, stated flatly and very quietly:

'I'm very sorry, Rosie.'

'There's nothing to be sorry about! Nothing happened! I don't know what you mean!' I gabbled, lying desperately, wanting only for this to stop, for Sylvia Riley to decide that enough was enough and for Monica to be allowed to slope off home to enjoy her retirement or her breakdown or whatever she had planned for the rest of her life.

'Yes, Rosemary,' insisted Sylvia remorselessly. 'Yes, Monica is very, *very* sorry that because of her actions whilst she was feeling *ill*, I was left with no alternative but to assume you were to blame for a *considerable* problem which *in fact* ...'

239

'Bollocks!'

The shocked silence was lovely. I felt so much better for that.

'Pardon?' asked Sylvia, her eyebrows almost on the top of her head.

'Bollocks!' Well, you did ask. Perhaps you didn't hear the first time.

There was a snigger from the chair next to me. I glanced round to find Monica convulsed with laughter, absolutely shaking with it, her hands over her face and funny little noises escaping from deep in her throat every now and again. It wasn't entirely normal, but it was sure as hell a lot more fun than the pale-faced, passive staring at the floor bit.

'There really wasn't any need for this,' I said, getting to my feet with as much dignity as I could manage. 'You didn't have to call me over here just to make poor Monica squirm. Don't worry, Monica – I know you didn't drop me in it deliberately. And anyway, it wasn't a *considerable* problem, it was something that got sorted out with hardly any fuss at all after *Mr Connor* spoke to Mrs Riley!'

I shot a scathing look at Sylvia as I said this. Huh! Who did she think she was – reducing a poor Long Term Sick person to a quivering wreck when she herself had so obviously capitulated in the face of a dressing-down from a consultant?

'Mr Connor?' retorted Sylvia. 'I can assure you Mr Connor had absolutely nothing to do with . . .'

'No?' I sneered. 'And I suppose he had nothing to do with you booking two temps to cover the situation on the reception desk the other week, either?'

Ha! Answer *that* if you can, you smug cow!

Unfortunately, she did. She looked me straight in the eye in a way that made me uncomfortably aware that she wasn't lying, and moreover that I'd lost the high moral ground here along with any advantage I might have assumed in the argument.

'I can assure you,' she repeated haughtily, 'that Mr Connor has *never* involved himself in your business, Rosemary.'

If it hadn't been for Monica giggling quietly and inappropriately beside me I'd have felt like slinking out of the room hanging my own head. So my knight in shining armour had never even taken up his spurs for me after all? He'd never, metaphorically, even got on his bloody horse and charged into battle. I was almost, *almost* glad I didn't get to shag him, now. The bastard! He hadn't even bothered to contradict me when I'd thanked him for his help. He'd allowed me to believe in him! He'd allowed me to fall for him! He'd *encouraged* me to make a fool of myself! I was so engrossed with my thoughts about Ashley Connor and his deception that I almost forgot about Sylvia until she suddenly stood up and looked at her watch, signalling the end of my interview.

'I'll overlook your outburst, Rosemary, and put it down to the stress you've been suffering since your recent admission to the ward,' she told me impassively.

'I'm not suffering from stress. I just didn't like what you were saying.'

'We'll consider this episode closed, then.'

She illustrated this with a snapping shut of a book on her desk, making poor Monica jump half out of her skin. I nodded towards the door and Monica scuttled out.

'What are you going to do?' I asked her as I followed her down the stairs from Sylvia's office.

'Go home, I suppose, now that's over,' she said with a sad shrugging of her shoulders.

'I mean, when you're ready to go back to work? Now that you've handed in your notice? Will you get another job at the hospital?'

She shook her head vehemently.

'No way! I'm never coming back to this place . . . it's what made me ill. I can't cope with the stress. I should have got out long ago but you know how it is . . . you think you can keep going ... then suddenly ...' She made an explosive gesture with her hands – *like a bomb going off*. I felt, suddenly, sorry and ashamed. We were working in a caring environment and yet nobody had noticed Monica struggling with a job that was causing her to slowly self-destruct.

'I hope you find something else that suits you better,' I told her with some genuine warmth. 'Something less stressful.'

'Yes.' She brightened visibly. 'I think I will, Rosie. I've applied to join the police force.'

Sometimes, '*Fucking hell*!' isn't the most polite or the most constructive thing to say, but it's the only possible response in the circumstances.

'There's another lecture next Friday,' Sara told me during the afternoon.

'Lecture?' I repeated vaguely, trying to concentrate on making a patient a new appointment before the computer logged me out of the system halfway through the attempt. '*Bloody* thing's done it again! Becky, can you get on the phone to the IT department? This is an absolute joke! Sorry to keep you waiting, Mrs Dickinson.'

'They said they'd be round to look at it this afternoon,' Becky reminded me.

'Yes, well, if they don't hurry up they'll have to bring another computer with them and sit here and help us with the queue. Why can't they ever get it working right?'

'Crap system, crap equipment. Come on, Rosie, you haven't been away that long! Remember where we work? This is the NHS ... patient care is the budget priority.'

Or is it the salaries of all the people trying to achieve government targets and get some stars or house points for the hospital?

'So what's all this about a lecture?' I started again once Mrs Dickinson's appointment was finally made.

'The monthly Occupational Health lecture. Remember we went before? *Body and Soul*?'

'Course I bloody do. It made me buy a camera, go for walks and get out more. I don't want to go to another one, Sara. I'll probably end up buying something else totally useless and starting on another totally inappropriate course of action . . .'

'I don't think it was useless or inappropriate!' she retorted. 'It's done you good!'

'How? Since then I've made a right prat of myself with a man who doesn't care about me, got myself rushed into hospital, and more or less written off my marriage. Great stuff!'

'At least you haven't been complaining about being bored, lately,' said Becky with a smile.

'Come on, Rosie – I think we ought to go. It's a follow-on from the last lecture. It's called *Change Your Body, Find Your Soul*.'

'That's a bit deep, isn't it? Who says I want to change my body? Who says I've lost my soul?' I looked down at myself. My thighs were spread over my chair like two nasty saggy pillows. My stomach strained irritably at the zipper of my trousers. 'Well, all right, no one's body's *perfect* . . .'

'And we're all searching for *something*,' said Sara gently. 'Call it soul, or whatever you like . . .'

'Oh, all right, all right!' I agreed a bit snappily. All this talk of souls and searching was making me feel melancholy. 'I'll come to the stupid poxy lecture, but this time do me a favour and don't volunteer me to answer all the questions!'

I thought about it on the way home that night. It was true the first lecture had made me feel better about myself. So what had gone wrong? I'd started off with such good intensions, taking up a new hobby, getting more exercise, trying to get a social life. I'd even cleared out my wardrobe and my underwear drawers. Now look at me – same old Rosie but with fewer clothes, a short haircut and no sex life. I'd gone to the first lecture because of being called an old

243

armchair, but now I felt even worse. Never mind an old armchair, I felt like a nasty old commode – unattractive, unloved, and shat on. I wiped a tear of self-pity away from the corner of my eye and sniffed miserably. How unfair was my life? All these years I'd been married to the same person, and then when I finally decided to be unfaithful I couldn't even seem to manage it. I didn't even think I wanted Ashley any more. I didn't even think I liked him very much. But it would have been nice to do it with him just once while I had the opportunity!

'I think it's probably best if I move out,' said Barry suddenly in the middle of *Holby City*, 'in the circumstances.'

'If that's what you want,' I said, feeling a bit sick.

'If it's what we *both* want,' he corrected me. He looked over at me and sighed. 'This is hard for me, too, Rosie. I love this house.'

'It wasn't the house you married.'

'No. But look, we can still be friends, can't we. I'll be round, to see Stuart and the girls, and the dog.'

Biggles looked up and wagged his tail happily. Seemed like everyone was happy, then. One big happy, divided family.

'Where will you go? Will you get a flat or something? How can you afford ...'

He coughed and fidgeted awkwardly in his chair. He picked up the remote control and fiddled with it as if it was strangely interesting. He'd gone a bit of a funny colour.

'You're moving in with *her*, aren't you! Christ, Barry, one minute it's all in my imagination and you're just friends, next minute you've been seeing her but not having sex, and then suddenly ...'

'Yes!' he held up both his hands as if in surrender. 'Yes, OK, Robyn suggested I move in with her for a bit ... I mean for a little while. But it's not like *that* ...'

'Oh no?' I retorted. 'I suppose you'll have separate rooms and knock on the bathroom door?'

'It's just a temporary measure,' he carried on, ignoring my sarcastic snorts and head-shakings. 'Because I haven't got anywhere else to go. And because I think, I really think, Rosie, that we ought to try living separately for a while before we rush into a decision. I don't think either of us is ready to do anything too drastic just yet.'

'I think moving in with your eighteen-year-old girlfriend is pretty drastic, Barry.'

'She's twenty-six.'

'And you're going to live with her, but still have your marriage and your family and your home waiting here for you in case it doesn't work out?'

He was silent for a few seconds, still frowning at the remote control.

'Put like that, it sounds bad,' he admitted. 'But that's not ...'

'Well, at least that's something we agree on,' I interrupted. 'Yes, it does sound bad. But if that's what you want to do, then you'd better get on with it. The sooner the better. I expect she's waiting for you.'

'Don't be bitter, Rosie. Don't be like this ...'

'You want me to give you my *blessing*?'

We stared at each other for a full minute before he got up abruptly and went up to the bedroom. I could hear wardrobe doors opening and shutting, and knew he was packing.

'I didn't expect to feel like this,' I sniffed into my third cup of coffee. Becky offered me the biscuit tin and I shook my head dismissively. 'After all, I agreed we ought to separate. I've been behaving badly myself ... at least, I've been *trying* to ... but I feel like I want to get hold of that ... manipulative little *tart* and punch her right in her stupid fucking face ... hi, PJ.'

'Is this a private therapy session?' asked PJ, glancing at Becky and sitting down on the other side of me. 'Or can anyone join in?'

'Rosie's just a bit upset,' said Becky by means of the understatement of the year.

'Shall I go for doughnuts? Or would you prefer to choke on a buttered bun?'

'No. I can't eat.'

'God, it must be bad.' He looked at me in concern. 'Not sleeping either, by the look of it.'

'No. Barry left me last night. He's gone to live with a little schoolgirl ... well, a twenty-six year old,' I amended as I saw his eyes widen. 'I mean, it's one thing to agree to separate ...'

'Yeah, I get your point. Separating means living *separately*. Not *with* someone.'

'That's exactly it!' I looked at him with relief. 'That's what I've had trouble explaining. He shouldn't have moved straight from me to her. It wasn't supposed to be about her. It was supposed to be about our own ... difficulties.'

Funny, I couldn't even remember what the difficulties were, now.

'It might have been different,' said Becky, 'if you'd wanted to move in with Ashley. I mean, with *someone*.'

'That was *never* on the cards!' I retorted, shocked. 'Never! Even before I knew he was married, I wasn't interested ... I mean, I wasn't looking for a *relationship*.'

'Just a bit of nooky,' said PJ mildly.

'Yes, if you like – yes, why don't we all be honest about it! I was only after his body! A silly, desperate old cow looking for a bit of nooky ...'

'Hey, Rosie!' PJ took hold of me by the shoulders, looking alarmed. 'Shit, I didn't mean to make you cry! Don't be silly, of course you're not desperate ...'

'Or old,' put in Becky. 'Ashley Connor's *much* older than you!'

'He isn't!' I blubbed, wiping my face on the sleeve of PJ's white coat. 'He's four years younger than me! I'm forty-fucking-four and fucking desperate and my husband's

246

shagging a teenager with short skirts and huge boobs and nobody wants me!'

I ended on a sort of howl that had Becky looking at the door of the coffee-room quickly to make sure it was shut. Probably everyone was leaning on it from the other side with their ears pressed up against it.

'Don't be ridiculous.' PJ put his arm round me and, unexpectedly, kissed me on the cheek. 'You're going to be fine. Of course people are going to want you. Look at you ...'

'Yes, look at me. A battered old armchair ...'

'I *like* old armchairs, Rosie. That's just the point. That was always the point. You should see the old chair in my room. It's huge and battered and torn and scruffy and I love it ...'

'Thanks a lot,' I muttered, determined not to snap out of my self-pity. 'Thanks so much for comparing me to something huge and scruffy.'

'No, I didn't mean ...'

'If you two are going to start fighting,' said Becky, getting to her feet and looking at her watch, 'I'm going back to the desk to relieve Sara.'

'I'll be back in a second.'

'It's OK, Rosie. It's fairly quiet now. Finish your coffee and get yourself together.'

She closed the door behind her.

'I always seem to say the wrong thing,' said PJ, taking his arm away from round my shoulders. 'Sorry.'

'I'm used to it.'

'Well, if you get lonely or upset again, and you want someone to hurl abuse at you and make you feel worse, you always know where I am.'

'That's really nice of you, PJ. I'll bear it in mind.' But I was smiling a little bit. 'If I wake up feeling sad and rejected in the middle of the night I'll bleep you, shall I?'

'Yes.'

I glanced at him in surprise.

'It was a joke, PJ. Anyway, I thought you were upset with me, the way you walked out on me when I was in the ward.'

'You were lying in bed,' he reminded me with a grin, 'Half naked, and you flung yourself at me and kissed me. You can't do that to a red-blooded young male and expect him not to get a hard-on, Rosie. I had to get out before you and the whole world noticed!'

Now I was laughing properly.

'Go on with you, don't take the piss! At least you've cheered me up, you idiot.' I sighed and went to wash my coffee cup. 'Better get back to work. By the way, you haven't heard any more about Ashley Connor reporting you, have you?'

He shrugged and looked down at the floor.

'He said he was going to talk to the Clinical Director.'

'Old Willy Wanker?'

Mr Wagner, Consultant ENT Surgeon, had worked at the hospital for about fifty years but wasn't held in a great deal of respect. The rumour was that he'd only applied for the job of Clinical Director of Surgery so that he could go to meetings instead of performing surgery now that his eyesight was going and his hands were beginning to shake.

PJ nodded and grinned at me.

'There's a story going around. Not that I believe it, of course. But people are saying you dumped Ashley Connor because he wouldn't promise not to report me.'

'People will say anything,' I replied lightly. 'You know what it's like around here.'

I went to touch his arm as I left the room, but remembered his joke about getting a hard-on and suddenly felt self-conscious and just smiled at him instead.

William Wagner's office wasn't in the least like Sylvia Riley's. It looked more like the lounge of a stately home. The carpet was a bit threadbare and the leather chairs a bit worn, but by NHS standards it was luxurious. He had a window overlooking the car park, and real curtains instead of blinds. There was a jug of spring flowers on top of the filing cabinet, probably freshly picked by his pert little secretary who looked as though she was in love with him. As she ushered me into the room, he looked up from reading a thick pile of papers and pushed them to one side with obvious relief. Maybe he didn't get many visitors.

'You wanted to see me, Rosemary?' he began. 'Paula – could you bring us some coffee and biscuits? Thank you, dear.'

'*Dear*? Fucking *dear*? Since when did secretaries get endearments tossed at them in the workplace? Paula smiled and simpered as she left the room, confirming my suspicions as surely as if she'd stepped out of her knickers and screwed him on the threadbare carpet in front of me.

'Yes – I ... er ... thanks for agreeing to talk to me,' I started hesitantly. Oh well – nothing to lose. I might as well come straight out with it. 'It's a bit indelicate, but I need to ask you something.'

'Fire away, dear.'

Oh! Obviously every female over the age of consent was a *dear* to this one.

'It's about PJ ... I mean, Paresh Jaimeen.'

'Paresh, Paresh ...' pondered the great man, looking at me blankly.

'He's one of the surgical SHOs. He's been acting up as Mr Connor's registrar.'

'Oh, yes. Yes indeed. I know the one. Go on, go on,' he said quite excitedly, as if I was telling him a bedtime story.

'Well, it's like this. Have you ... had any complaints about him?'

Mr Wagner looked back at me thoughtfully.

'I suppose you wouldn't be able to answer that,' I said. 'I expected as much. Sorry to have wasted your time.'

I was about to get up when he waved both his arms at

me as if we were playing a guessing-game and he wanted more time.

'Wait, wait, wait! I need to know why you're here.'

Well, I thought I'd made that obvious. Perhaps he was a bit more senile than people realised.

'Paresh Jaimeen,' I reiterated slowly. 'I wanted to know ...'

'Yes, yes, yes – but *why*? Why did you want to know? Do you have a complaint to make too, dear? Because if you do, your line manager is the correct ...'

'No! No, of course I don't want to make a complaint against him! That's the whole point! He shouldn't *have* any complaints made against him! He hasn't done anything wrong! And I'm the one who should know!'

At this point, the door opened and Pert Paula came tripping in with a silver tray of coffee cups, milk jug and a little silver sugar bowl. I felt even more like I was a Sunday afternoon guest at a country house party.

'Thank you dear,' he smiled at her as she blushed and fluttered and fiddled with her hair. She walked backwards to the door and I thought for one dreadful minute she was going to curtsey as she went out, but she was probably just trying not to come in her knickers.

'Have a biscuit,' said the object of her adoration, passing me the china plate with two custard creams and two digestives arranged prettily on a doyley. I shook my head impatiently.

'No, thank you, I just wanted to say ...'

'What *is* your relationship with Mr Jaimeen?' he interrupted me, dunking his custard cream carefully in his coffee and looking at me over his glasses.

'What?' I exclaimed, startled. 'Relationship? We haven't got a relationship!'

'I *meant* working relationship. Do you work together? I wondered why you felt this need to come and see me to plead on Mr Jaimeen's behalf.'

'He's a friend. And he's been good to me,' I said stoutly.

'He was good to me when I cut my hand. It was my own fault I didn't want it stitched. And nobody knew I was going to react to that antibiotic ...' I was warming nicely to my subject now. 'And he was nice to Stuart – that's my son. He didn't miss the fracture – it was Stuart's fault for not telling the truth about hitting Steven Porter. And everyone knows Mr Connor picks on him in theatre. Ask the theatre nurses! And he took all the patients' case notes home to study before he operated with Mr Connor the first time! He was up all night ...'

Mr Wagner was smiling at me.

'I think you've made your point,' he said quietly.

'So ...?' I picked up my coffee cup and took a sip. 'So, will you ...?'

'And I think Mr Jaimeen is a very lucky young man to have a friend like you.'

I felt myself go hot with embarrassment.

'That's not what this is about. I just ...'

'I know, dear. You just don't want to see someone get into trouble when they don't deserve it. And I must say that's very commendable.'

'So will you ...'

'Unfortunately, I can't do anything about the comments made by a consultant about a member of his junior staff. Those comments will remain on the record, but they're only a record of one individual's opinion.'

'But that's so unfair! He's biased against PJ! He doesn't like him!'

'That's life, dear, unfortunately, isn't it? It does tend to be unfair at times. But I'm glad you came to give me your point of view. I'll bear it in mind if your friend Paresh asks me for a reference.'

'A reference?' I repeated, putting down my cup with a clatter on its china saucer.

'Yes. As I'm sure he's told you, Mr Jaimeen won't be bothered by Mr Connor's opinion of him for very much longer. He's just accepted a new position at the London

251

Hospital. Orthopaedic Registrar. Very good move for him – he's done well. I expect you're pleased for him, aren't you dear?'

I nearly knocked Paula over as I left the room.

Chapter Fourteen

Scary Stuff

Stuart was back at school, Tasha was back at college. Life went on pretty well as before except that I had no husband. I noticed it in funny little ways. I mean, apart from the obvious ones like having lots of room in the wardrobe and lots of new experiences with the remote control. For a start, the dog wouldn't settle down. He cried when I went to bed. I moved his basket upstairs so he could hear me and feel more secure but he still cried. Stuart wanted to have him sleeping on his bed but I didn't want to start that. Then one morning I woke up and he was in bed with me. Biggles, not Stuart. He'd got under the duvet and was snoring gently with his tongue hanging out in a way that reminded me briefly of Barry. I pretended to be cross and shoo him off the bed, but the next morning when he was there again I knew this was going to be the pattern of my life from now on. Sleeping with dogs. It had finally come to this.

Then there was dinner. We kind of stopped having it. Stuart was having school dinners anyway, and now that there wasn't a man coming home hungry, poking around hopefully in the oven as if cottage pies and steak and kidney puddings like his mother used to make were going to magically materialise out of thin air, I sometimes just forgot completely about cooking anything. Stuart would prowl around the house grazing on ham sandwiches and packets of crisps, and I'd suddenly realise just before I went to bed that I hadn't eaten, and get myself a bowl of cereal.

'You've lost weight,' said PJ disapprovingly about a week later. It was the first time he'd really spoken to me since my interview with Willie Wanker. I'd told myself he was avoiding me but the truth was that *I* was avoiding *him*. If he walked past the reception desk, I pretended to be terribly, terribly busy and stressed. If we passed each other in the corridor I'd suddenly find an urgent piece of paper in my hand to become totally engrossed in as I was walking along. I didn't want to speak to him. If you were supposed to be friends with someone and they couldn't even tell you something as important as the fact that they were leaving, why would you want to talk to them at all?

This particular day, we were both, unusually, in the hospital canteen. I very rarely went there but I'd already been nagged by Sara about the fact that I wasn't eating. To tell the truth, I'd started to feel a bit ill and that morning had nearly passed out in the middle of Urology, so I'd agreed reluctantly to being sent off on a mission for proper nourishment. I was sitting miserably at a table on my own with a bowl of minestrone soup.

'Can I join you?' persisted PJ, and pulled out the chair opposite me without waiting for a reply. He lowered a plate piled high with chicken curry and chips gently to the table so that it didn't slop over the edges and commented lightly: 'I'm fuelling up for a session with Ashley Connor in theatre.'

I continued to stir my soup slowly and take the occasional sips from the side of the spoon.

'What's the matter?' he asked abruptly, putting down his knife and fork and staring at me until I met his eyes.

I wasn't going to say anything. I *so* wasn't going to say anything. But before I'd had a chance to think, to clamp my teeth together and swallow back all my hurt feelings together with the mouthful of minestrone, out it all came like a torrent of vomit.

'*What's the matter? What's the matter?!* What do you think's the matter, PJ, sitting there all smug and happy with your curry and your chips and your nice new job in the London Hospital – yes, I *have* heard about it, and were you ever going to tell me or were you going to just go, just leave and never bother getting in touch again, after all your talk about being there for me and how I should bleep you if I was lonely in the middle of the night – not that I am, not in the least – who needs a man in the night anyway? I'm sleeping with my dog and proud of it, thank you very much, and let me tell you I *like* not having to bother about dinner, I never was much good at cooking anyway and I *like* losing weight – what woman doesn't want to lose a bit of weight? So you don't have to sit there pretending to be concerned about me. No, just go off to your new job, I'm very pleased for you, but I wish you'd warned me before I made a prat of myself with Willie Wanker, what with the china cups and the custard creams it was a bit of an ordeal but I was only trying to help, and instead all that happened was . . .'

'You went to see Willie Wanker?' repeated PJ. 'About me?'

'Of course about you, you idiot – why else would I go and see him?' I sighed, running out of steam, and put down my spoon. The soup wasn't remotely appetising. PJ reached across the table and grasped my wrist. I tried to shake it free but he gripped harder.

'Rosie, listen. I was going to tell you about the job. I was, honestly. I went for the interview while you were off sick. I didn't make a big thing about it because I really didn't expect anything to come of it. As soon as I heard I'd got the job last week, I came looking for you, to tell you. But when I found you, you were crying about your husband leaving you and nobody wanting you and it just . . . didn't seem . . . very appropriate timing . . .'

He stopped and relaxed his grip on my wrist but didn't let go completely. Instead, he stroked the back of my hand

255

with his fingers, just once, very lightly and said, quietly: 'I'm sorry. I also didn't know how to tell you.'

'When are you going?' I asked equally quietly, my outpourings forgotten.

'About four weeks. Start there on the second of June.'

'You must be pleased.'

'Yes. It's exactly the job I wanted ... but sooner than I dared to hope.' He looked at me pleadingly. 'Am I forgiven? I want us to stay friends ...'

'Not easy, really, PJ, when you're working thirty miles away.'

'I'll get a long range bleep. For night times.'

I tried to force a smile.

'Don't kid yourself. I'll find someone else to bleep. Someone a bit nearer home, who can get here quicker if I need him ...'

'You mean you'll find someone else to buy you doughnuts?' he asked, pretending to look hurt.

'You bet your sweet arse I will. Doughnuts don't travel that well. They'd be stale by the time you got here from London.'

'I could have them specially delivered.'

'Yeah, right. I bet you say that to all the girls ... all the girls you leave behind.'

There was an uncomfortable silence. I got up and took my half-full soup bowl back to the counter. When I looked round, he was still sitting at the table with his plate of curry and chips.

'Eat that or you'll pass out in theatre,' I called.

He picked up a chip on his fork and waved it at me as I left.

I hadn't had to face Ashley Connor since our rather public altercation in Ward Nineteen because, fortunately for me, he was on holiday in the Bahamas during my first week back at work and had, probably wisely, not been anywhere near me since. But everyone's luck runs out sooner or later.

256

That afternoon I was talking to Trudy, his secretary, in her office when he came bustling in with two briefcases, a laptop computer and a pile of patients' notes balanced so high in his arms that he probably couldn't see me. Trudy jumped up to help him unload everything onto her desk and there we were – trapped, confronting each other like two uneasy cornered cats.

'Rosie!' he said, not meeting my eyes. 'Hi.'

'Hi,' I echoed. 'Nice holiday?'

I edged towards the door, not really interested in the reply.

'Very nice. Yes. Very pleasant. And are you ... quite well, now?'

'Yes, thank you – fine.'

This was awful. Trudy was looking at us with a puzzled smile. This stilted small talk was so incongruous when I remembered how recently it was that we were naked in bed together. I just wanted to make a bolt for it. I took another step towards the door – but at the same time, Ashley apparently had the same thought and started to head for the door himself. We ended up performing a kind of line dance routine in the office doorway.

Face your partner, skip to the right! Jump back, turn around, doh-se-doh!

'After you,' I said, looking at my feet.

'No, after you,' he replied stonily.

This was ridiculous.

'This is ridiculous!' I exclaimed, suddenly, standing still and finally looking him in the eyes. 'We can't carry on like this. We both have to work here. Sorry, Trudy – we'll get out of your office.'

We moved into the corridor out of earshot.

'I want you to know,' I told him, quickly but quietly so that it came out in a sort of a hiss, 'that I went to see Willie ... I mean, Mr Wagner. About PJ. I told him there was no cause for complaint.'

'You're entitled to your opinion, of course,' he responded smoothly, 'and I to mine.'

'But he's got the job at the London, anyway. With or without a reference from you.'

'As always, Rosie, your loyalty to Mr Jaimeen is commendable.'

He began to walk away. I felt my temper starting to rise. Perversely, now he was going, I didn't want him to. I didn't feel satisfied with the way things had ended – with a hiss and a smirk and a sneer. I wanted a row.

'And another thing!' I said, stopping him in his tracks. He turned back and raised his eyebrows at me. 'Sylvia Riley says you didn't say anything to her to help me! About the referral letters, when I was in trouble and she wanted me to tell lies . . .'

'What do you mean? No, of course I didn't . . .'

'Or when I needed her to get me a temp. So that I could come to Paris . . .'

'I presumed you'd sort that out for yourself. I seem to remember I was busy in theatre.'

'I thought you . . .' I tailed off. I'd been going to say that I thought he cared about me, but what was the point? Of course he hadn't cared about me. I knew that all along, really, didn't I? I'd been kidding myself, living in a dream world where gorgeous good-looking consultants cared about silly receptionists in boring marriages. But this wasn't a dream any more. I was wide-awake and looking at him properly for the first time.

'I used to think you were gorgeous,' I said very lightly, instead, forcing a smile. I was about to go to say that now I'd changed my mind; now I saw him as he really was – selfish and arrogant. But before I could go on, there was a movement behind us and a little cough and – trust my luck! – Heidi The Hiker from Occupational Health who must have crept round the corner of the corridor like a thief in the night, appeared at my shoulder, fixed me with a glare designed to turn me to stone, announced: 'Good after*noon*,

258

Mr Connor!' in a booming voice without even looking at Ashley, and strode off with a ferocious clicking of her heels.

'What's with *her*?' I muttered, more to myself than Ashley.

He shrugged and looked at his watch.

'Look, I have to go ...'

OK, OK, no point in prolonging this farce any longer than necessary.

'Just one more thing,' I suddenly remembered as he turned away. 'Why did you want my negatives?'

'Sorry? Negatives?' he frowned, looking at me as if he'd never heard of them. 'I don't think ... Why should I ...?'

'Oh, forget it!' I sighed, suddenly feeling an impatient urge to get away from him and get back to work. 'If they turn up, let me have them back. If not, you're welcome to them. Thanks for the weekend in Paris – well, the half of it that I remember.'

He managed a smile. I couldn't even force one. I just felt sad about the underwear.

That same evening, I was finishing up at the reception desk on my own after the others had gone home. I suppose it must have been about half past five and I was just closing down the computer when Heidi, with the same sort of stealthy approach as before, suddenly appeared in front of me, gave me what I can only describe as an evil look, and barked at me:

'Are you coming or not?'

'Sorry? What? Where?' I replied, naturally a little confused.

'To the lecture. You put your name down for it, didn't you?'

'The lecture? The body and soul thing? I thought it was on Friday? At lunchtime?'

'It's been changed. Don't you ever read your e-mails?'

'Oh. Sorry, I've been a bit busy today ...' Why was I

acting so pathetically with this woman? And why was she in such a foul mood anyway? 'I won't be able to make it, then,' I said with an attempt at assertiveness. 'Only I need to get home. My son'll be expecting me.'

'Give him a ring,' she retorted in a tone that brooked no argument. She began to walk off. 'See you in a minute in the meeting room on the second floor.'

Change of date, change of time, change of venue. With a bit of luck there'd be a change of lecturer. This one was beginning to seriously get on my tits with her aggression and her bossiness.

'What about Sara?' I called after her. 'She's gone home. She didn't know ...'

'Yes, she did. She's already told me she couldn't make it.' Nice of her to remember to tell *me*, then. 'Hurry up, we're ready to start.'

The second floor meeting room was a fair walk away, in the old part of the hospital, between a ward which had been closed down and was now being used for storing mattresses and old filing cabinets, and a disused sluice room that had been converted into an open-plan office for some junior administrators who hadn't reached the rank of deserving anything better. The administrators obviously didn't hang around after five o'clock, as the office was deserted, all the lights off and the door firmly shut. I hurried past it to the meeting room, wondering as I did, whether I was out of my mind coming here at all. I should be in my car now, on my way home to my little family (son and dog) to sit in front of the TV on my own being bored and miserable with a cup of tea and a Wagon Wheel and nobody to bother me. Instead, I was chasing along deserted corridors in this old building where the hospital ghost was reputed to prowl, rushing to take part in a lecture I wasn't even sure I wanted to go to, and why? Because I was, to be honest, just a little bit scared of Miss Bossy Mountain-Climber and didn't have the guts to stand up to her. At the thought of the hospital ghost, I shivered a little and glanced behind me as I

260

approached the meeting room door. No, no ghosts on the prowl yet. Probably a bit too early in the evening. I pushed open the heavy door and blinked in surprise. The room was in darkness. Where was everyone? Had I got the wrong place? I hesitated. I was sure she'd said the second floor meeting room. Was there a power cut or something?

'Heidi?' I called out a little nervously, stepping into the room.

The door slammed shut behind me. With a thumping heart and horrible thoughts of ghosts, I spun round, just as the lights were suddenly switched on. Heidi leaned against the door, staring at me.

'Well,' she said. 'Here we are.'

'Yes!' I tried a little laugh, to let her know I was very amused by her strange sense of humour, but the laugh came out a bit false. 'Where's everyone else?'

'It seems to be just the two of us,' she replied calmly, still leaning on the door.

'Well,' I said, trying to do the little laugh again. 'I don't think I'll bother, then, if it's all the same with you.'

I moved towards her, reaching for the door handle, but she remained where she was, her full weight against the door. I considered trying to shove her bodily out of the way, but then I remembered how fit she was. And anyway, if she was just playing silly jokes it wouldn't really be very polite to kick her in the shins and knee her in the groin. On the other hand, if she wasn't playing a joke at all ... and she didn't look remotely like she was joking ... what the fuck was all this about? Had she flipped? Was she dangerous? Was she about to go for me with a knife?

I stepped back out of stabbing range and went to stand behind the table, trying to feel surreptitiously through my handbag for the comforting shape of my mobile phone. Could I dial 999 without taking my eyes off her? Would it be quicker to dial H for home and whisper 'Help!' to Stuart when he answered the phone? He'd either think I was messing around or I'd scare the shit out of him and psychologically scar him for life. But before I got any further with my contingency plans, Heidi the Potential Homicidal Maniac produced an envelope from behind her back, waved it at me as if it was the ace of trumps in a championship game of whist, and flung it on the table in front of me.

'Have a look,' she challenged me.

Several possibilities jumped interestingly to mind. A belated Easter card? An invitation to her wedding? Her resignation (she might just want me to check the grammar for her)? I picked up the envelope and looked inside. A couple of photos – and a strip of negatives.

'My negatives?' I said, frowning at them. 'Why . . .? Did you find them somewhere or what?'

'Let's just say they came into my possession,' she said with a nasty smile.

'So . . . what are you doing with them?'

I'd lost the plot here. I was beginning to favour the theory that she'd flipped her lid.

'This is what I'm *doing* with them,' she replied, suddenly grabbing the negative strip back out of my hands, so that the envelope with the photos still inside it went fluttering to the floor. When she produced a pair of scissors out of her jacket pocket I really did begin to freak. The mobile phone was out of my bag quicker than you could blink, but my hands were shaking so much I couldn't press any keys at all, never mind make a split second decision about 999 as opposed to H for Home. But fortunately the scissors appeared to have a far more significant purpose in life than the hacking to pieces of my face or body. In the same amount of time that it took for me to lose control of my shaking fingers, drop the phone and dive under the table to retrieve it, the strip of negatives had been reduced to dozens of tiny coloured shreds that fell like fairy jewellery into a scattering on the floor.

She had, definitely, lost her fucking marbles.

'Look at the photos,' she commanded.

262

Discretion being the better part of valour, and being as she still had the scissors in her hand and a mad gleam in her eyes and I was still shitting myself, I'd stayed under the table. Trust me, I did as I was told. I reached out from under the table and picked up the envelope and slid out the photos. I looked at the first one: a print of one of my negatives. So what was the point here? She was jealous of my photographic skills? She wanted the job of processing my photos in future?

'If you'd wanted a copy of any of the pictures,' I told her, 'you only had to ask.'

'Now look at the other print,' she told me, ignoring this.

OK. Another copy of the same photo . . . but, no, it was an enlargement of just *part* of the photo. A blown-up version of the car in the foreground of the photo. Come to think of it . . .

'I don't remember that car being in the original photo,' I commented, curiosity beginning to overcome my worry about the scissors.

'It wasn't in your print. Dave cut it out.'

I stood up, put the photos on the table and stared at them.

'Yes . . . possibly he did. I remember him saying he cut some irrelevant bits out of the photographs. But what's all this got to do with . . .?' I picked up the enlargement again and studied it more carefully. 'You!'

'Yes.' Heidi smiled at me and put the scissors back in her pocket. No thoughts of stabbing just at the moment, then. In fact she looked quite friendly now she'd worked out her aggression on the negatives. 'It was my car. It was me.'

'With . . . someone else?' I was guessing now. There was the shape, possibly, of another face behind hers in the car but it was too faint and blurry to make it out. 'You were worried that I'd show the photo around the place? For God's sake! You'd have needed telescopic eyes to work out that there was anyone in the car at all, never mind see who it was . . .'

263

'But we didn't know that, did we. When we saw you aiming your camera at us ...'

'I wasn't aiming at you!' Of course, I remembered it now: the car in the woods. The steamy windows that had been wound down when I walked back past it again. The feeling that someone was watching me. Involuntarily I shivered, and at the same time I felt slightly disgusted to think I'd almost, accidentally, spied on Horrible Heidi having it off in her car with some bloke. 'I didn't even realise I'd got the bloody car in the shot! What do you take me for ... some sort of *pervert*?'

'What do I take you for?' she repeated, giving me a very odd look. 'What do I *take* you for?'

Not a hard question, you would have thought?

'I *take* you,' she said very slowly and deliberately as if she was about to reveal a profound truth – *Ladies and Gentlemen: You Will Be Amazed*! 'I take you for an adulteress.'

'Hey, hang on a minute!' I didn't come here to be insulted! Bad enough being tricked into getting shut in a dark spooky room with a freak with a pair of scissors and an irrational fear of photographs, without being called names into the bargain! '*I'm* not the one scared about being caught on camera shagging some guy in a car!'

'Maybe not. But you shagged him nevertheless, didn't you. In *his* car, after the football match? In Paris? In his office, I suppose ... that's where he takes most of them ...'

'*Ashley*.'

Stupidly, my first reaction was to look at the photo again. No, you'd never know it was him. She was probably making it up. It was probably some guy she picked up, who dumped her afterwards, and she'd have *liked* it to be Ashley ...

But there was no fooling myself like that. I knew it was true. I not only knew it, but I knew I should have known it all along.

'I didn't,' I said quietly, as if it mattered really. 'Actually, I didn't. Not in the car, not in Paris, not anywhere.'

For a moment she looked vaguely taken aback, like she'd lost her composure a little – but only for a moment.

'So you *say*. But anyway, it's academic. You've been seeing him. Everyone knows!'

I sighed. I looked at my watch. Now that I knew what this was all about, Heidi didn't bother me any more. I just felt a bit sorry for her, and wanted to go home.

'Yes, well. I'm not seeing him any more. So can we just ...'

'Don't give me that. I saw you this afternoon, outside his office – cosy little chat, lovey-dovey smiles and whispers ...'

'I was just clearing up a few things with him, actually. I'd have preferred to shout, but it might have frightened patients in the ward next door.'

'So you've finished with him? Really?'

'Yes, really. Look – I'm sorry, but I had no idea you and he were ... an item. You didn't exactly make it clear to me.' I shrugged and added: 'Anyway, I'm no more of an *adulteress* than you are. He's a married man. He's not yours, any more than he was mine.'

With this, she gave a huge sigh, sat down on a chair opposite me and began to cry – not sobbing or wailing or anything lively like that – just a few big fat tears rolling down her face. She didn't even bother to wipe them away; she just sat there letting them drip. It was one of the saddest things I'd ever seen.

'He *was* mine. He was, Rosie – long before he ever met Teresa, long before they ever got married, long before they had Harry and Jake ...'

I had my head down against the wind of my own surprise, pedalling fast to keep up with the flow of her words. Presuming Teresa to be his wife, Harry and Jake being their eight and six year old sons ...

'That's a long time,' I agreed slowly, looking at her in a slightly different light. 'You've known him a long time . . .'

'Twelve and a half years,' she said in a sort of a low moan. 'We worked together in Manchester. Whenever he moved, I moved, so we could be together.'

'And he married someone else?' I asked, incredulous. The bastard! Why was she still seeing him – still letting herself be used by him?

'You've never met Teresa, have you?' she said, ruefully. 'She's absolutely stunning. Even now, after two kids, she looks like a supermodel. Her family have money. She's gorgeous, rich, clever, a talented musician, and runs her own PR company from home. Everybody loves her. Fuck it, Rosie, even *I* love her! I can't blame him . . .'

'Does she know?'

'That we've gone on seeing each other all these years? Of course not. She thinks we're just good friends. She'd throw him out the minute she found out. It'd kill him.'

'It'd serve him right . . .'

'No. No. I couldn't do that to him.'

She shook her head. Another tear dripped into her lap. I stared at her, appalled, and on a sudden impulse, I put my arm around her shoulders. 'I'm so sorry . . .'

'Not your fault. No more than all the others . . .'

I felt my blood run cold with fury. Not for myself – I'd had my fun, despite the lack of sex, but I hadn't really *cared* about Ashley if I was honest – but for poor Heidi, who'd given up her entire life, and for his poor wife, who'd been deceived since before she'd even had the ring on her finger, and for . . . all the others . . .

'He's always had . . . others?' I forced myself to ask.

'Oh, yes, of course – what do you expect?' she smiled thinly. 'You surely didn't think you were the first? Rosie, it all started with you because he was worried about you taking the photo.'

Well, that's good for the self-esteem, isn't it?

'He'd do anything rather than risk Teresa finding out.'

Even pretend to be interested in a silly receptionist with a boring marriage. Just to get his hands on one silly photograph. Well, now I really do feel great. Carry on.

'But then, of course, he can never resist it. The older he gets, the worse he gets – it's flattering, you see, for his ego. Once he sees he's got a woman interested – he just can't leave it alone. And *you* happened along just at the right time.'

'The right time?' I repeated, weakly, not really wanting to hear this, but unable to stop her.

'Just in time for Paris.' She looked up at me as if considering whether to go on, then shook her head again and gave a tired, sorry little laugh. 'The Paris conference is an annual event, Rosie, Ashley's been going ever since he was a registrar. He always meets the same guys there. They've been friends for years.'

'Doctor Gucci and Doctor Schuter. I hated them.'

'Yes. So did I.'

'You've been to the conference too?'

'About six or seven years ago. Rosie – you are so naïve.'

'Oh, am I?' I retorted, crossly. 'What makes you say ...'

'He takes a different "secretary" to Paris every year. It's a bet, Rosie, for God's sake. He and those two idiots had a bet, years ago when they were all drunk. He bet them he could get a new woman to bring to Paris every year and that his wife would never find out. Sorry to have to tell you, but you were just the latest in a long line.'

'Better, I think, than last year ... and who knows? Next year will be even better, again, yes?'

I closed my eyes, swaying slightly, remembering. At the time, I'd felt too sick to try to make sense of what they were laughing about in the hotel. Now, I just felt sick with humiliation. How could I have been so stupid? I wasn't a fifteen-year-old schoolgirl – I was a middle-aged woman with nearly grown-up children, and yet I'd allowed Ashley Connor to make a complete and utter fool of me. And as for Heidi ...

267

'I know what you must think of me,' she was saying very quietly, looking at the floor. 'But when I saw you with him today, I just felt like I'd had enough. I had to tell you, and I knew I'd never get you to listen unless I forced the issue.'

'You certainly did that,' I agreed grimly. 'Shutting yourself in a room with someone and getting your scissors out does tend to focus their mind on what you're saying.'

'Sometimes I really think I'm losing my mind. Sometimes I think I lost it about twelve and a half years ago.'

Poor cow. Poor bloody cow, wasting her life and her love on someone so completely undeserving.

'We shouldn't let him get away with it!' I spat, getting up and almost stamping with temper. 'The bastard! The total ... rotten ... horrible ...'

'I love him,' replied Heidi, shrugging her shoulders at me helplessly.

Well, some women may not be able to help themselves. But I wasn't one of them. And never would be!

Ashley Connor, you time is up. Next year, if I have anything to do with it, you won't be taking ANYONE to Paris to show off to your unpleasant slimy friends ... because no one's going to want you! If only I could find a way to stop you!

Chapter Fifteen

No Such Thing (as a free lunch)

'Come on Rosie,' said Sara that Friday lunchtime. 'Don't pretend you've forgotten about the Body and Soul lecture.'

Forgotten? It'd be haunting my dreams for the rest of my life.

'I'm not going.' And don't expect me to tell you the whole sad story about my own personal one-to-one counselling session (with optional extra scissor therapy) with Heidi the night before last, because quite frankly I don't feel ready to talk about it.

'Are you OK? You've been very quiet,' persisted Sara. 'I really think the lecture might do you good ...'

'No.' I *so* didn't feel like arguing, or explaining, I made up an excuse. 'I've got to go to the dentist. Got a really bad toothache so I've got an emergency appointment.'

'Oh, poor you!' She seemed quite happy with this. 'No wonder you've been quiet.'

'Yes. Sorry. It hurts to talk.' I rubbed my mouth ruefully. 'Agony. Probably got an abscess or something.' Whoops, better not lay it on too thick or I'd be needing to take some more time off work. 'Or a broken filling,' I added quickly.

She gave me a worried look.

'Well, why don't you go now, Rosie, while it's quiet, and the dentist might see you earlier.'

269

'Good idea.'

I put on my jacket and wandered over towards the staff car park. Once I was out of sight of the hospital building, I slowed down and wondered what I was going to do for an hour or so whilst I was supposed to be at the dentist. It was a nice spring day, with a hint of warmth in the air. I could go for a drive, but the chances were that when I returned I'd have lost my space in the car park and would spend another hour driving around looking for somewhere to park. It hardly seemed worth it just to kill time. I got into the car, leaving the door open and opening the sunroof so that I could feel the warm breeze. Maybe I'd just sit here for a while. I should have brought a paper or magazine with me. I looked around the car. Surely I had something in here I could read?

A couple of minutes later I became aware of someone watching me. PJ was leaning on the open door of the car, a puzzled grin on his face.

'Rosie, are you planning a long drive or a holiday, or do you often spend your lunch break sitting in the car park reading the *AA Book of the Road*?'

'I'm pretending to be at the dentist,' I told him morosely.

'Too frightened to go? I could write you up for some tranqs. They can't sack me now I'm leaving.'

'No, I'm not *really* going to the dentist. I'm lying. I just didn't want to go to the lecture.'

He frowned.

'But I could do with the tranquilisers,' I added, only half jokingly.

'What's wrong?'

I hesitated. I hadn't planned on talking to anyone about this, but maybe it would help, and as PJ said, he was leaving soon. Whether he laughed at my humiliation or pitied me, I wouldn't have to bear it for long before he was gone.

'How long have you got?'

He went round to the passenger door and slid into the seat beside me.

'As long as it takes. I'm on my way to an outreach clinic at Wessington but I'm really early. If I'm late they'll just think I'm held up in theatre anyway.'

'It's Ashley Connor,' I told him very quickly before I could change my mind. I looked away as I saw his eyes darken. 'I've found out a few things. I've been a complete prat, PJ.'

He listened to the whole story without interrupting. A couple of times he tutted and shook his head, but apart from that he sat in total silence until I finished up:

'See what I mean? I feel so absolutely stupid . . .'

'Well, you shouldn't do,' he retorted stoutly. 'It's him that's being a prat, not you. He'll end up losing his wife *and* whatser-face-Heidi – *she*'s bloody stupid, if anyone is. At least *you*'re not hanging around to get treated badly for the rest of your life . . .'

'He didn't want me to, anyway,' I reminded him, my voice coming out little and hurt.

'And if he did? If he came on to you again now, what would you do?'

'Are you kidding? After making a big joke of me for his friends in Paris? I'd tell him to fuck off! I just wish I'd done it sooner!'

'Good,' he said vehemently. 'So do I.'

'He didn't even do the nice things I *thought* he'd done for me! He had nothing to do with Sylvia Riley changing her mind about those referral letters. And he didn't even make her get a temp for the reception desk so I could go to Paris! I was *sure* that must have been him . . .' I stopped, looked at PJ, who had now picked up the *AA Book of the Road* and was looking at a map of Northampton as if he found it totally absorbing, and added quietly, 'It was *you*, wasn't it.'

'Maybe, maybe not . . .'

'It was. My God, I really *am* a complete prat. Why didn't you say? Why did you let me go on thinking it was him?'

'Rosie, if you wanted to think it was him – if it turned him from an arrogant git to a Prince Charming in your eyes – who was I to spoil that for you?'

'Don't! You're making me feel worse! PJ, why would you do those things for me? Sylvia Riley must have put you through hell.'

'Nothing I can't handle, baby!' he said with a grin. 'Why? Well, I guess for the same reason you went to see Willie Wanker for *me*. We're friends, aren't we? Friends do that sort of stuff for each other.'

'Oh, PJ, why are you leaving? I'm going to miss you so much! You're the best friend I've got in this place!' I said, trying to hug him and trying not to cry at the same time. It came out a bit gurgly because of the crying, and the hug came unstuck because of the gear stick, but he just laughed lightly and kissed me on the cheek.

'You'll find someone else. You know – the guy you said you'd find to bleep in the middle of the night and bring you doughnuts.'

'Knowing my luck he'd turn out to be another Ashley Connor. I feel so sorry for poor bloody Heidi. I wish there was something I could do to make her see sense and get away from him. And to stop him taking some other silly susceptible woman to Paris *next* year to be made a fool out of.'

'He'll come unstuck sooner or later. People like that always do.'

'Well, I'd just like it to be sooner rather than later. I'd feel a whole lot better.'

'Me too,' said PJ. He glanced at his watch. 'Better get going, Rosie – will you be OK?'

'Of course. Apart from one thing.' He looked at me anxiously and I smiled. 'Don't worry. Just that I'll have to spend the whole afternoon talking like I've had root canal treatment.'

Which might have been marginally less painful than the indignity I'd suffered at the hands of Mr Ashley Connor.

*

272

Easter was a mere blink away but it was another bank holiday weekend already. Natasha had decided not to come home, as she'd only just got settled back at Leicester and she had a lot of work to do for her impending exams, not to mention an important rock concert and a couple of parties.

'Have you heard from Emma?' she asked me when she phoned home on the Saturday afternoon.

'Not this week. Why?'

'She sent me a weird text message the other day.'

'How weird?' I asked, maternal alarm bells beginning to ring.

'Said she had something to tell me. But when I tried to talk to her on the phone, she got all cagey and odd. I think Tom was there. Maybe she didn't want to say anything in front of him.'

'I wonder if they've had a row,' I mused, frowning.

'Don't worry, Mum. She sounded OK, just a bit evasive – you know?'

No, I didn't know. It wasn't like Emma to be evasive. Normally she was one of life's open books – what you saw was what you got with Emma. She didn't try to hide things. Unless . . . it was something bad . . .

'I'd better phone her,' I said, feeling another flutter of anxiety.

'OK. Let me know if everything's all right, yeah?'

'Of course. Don't *you* worry!' I added quickly.

Women! We try to share our problems, but don't want to burden those we love, so we end up weaving circles of emotional care around each other until we almost trip ourselves up on the threads. I dialled Emma's number and held my breath, counting the rings until she answered.

'Are you OK?' I demanded almost instantly. 'Tasha seemed to think you were being evasive.'

'I'm fine. She shouldn't have got you worried – there's nothing to worry about, Mum.'

'Are you sure? How about Tom? Is everything OK . . .'

'Yes! Everything's fine. Actually, I was going to phone you. Is it OK if we come over tomorrow?'

'Of course!' I sat back in surprise. Emma and Tom usually seemed to have full social programmes at weekends. Visits home were normally booked several weeks in advance so that we didn't get squeezed out by a better offer. 'That'll be really nice. Do you want to stay over for Monday?'

'Yeah, we might – thanks. Be nice if we could see Dad as well.'

'Well, I can't speak for your father, of course,' I replied a bit stiffly.

'No, of course not,' she said gently. 'I'll give him a call on his mobile, see what he's doing. See you tomorrow, then, Mum.'

I hung up feeling only slightly less anxious than before.

And then, during the evening, halfway through a particularly horrible film about aliens that Stuart had bribed me to be allowed to watch (a gift of Cadbury's Dairy Milk, plus *all* the washing and wiping up – not a bad bargain), I had another phone call that completely knocked the wind out of my sails. It took me several minutes to recognise the voice.

'Hi, Rosie. Hope you're feeling better than last time I spoke to you?'

It was an Australian accent. Young, friendly, a hint of a smile in his voice . . .

'Oliver! What . . .? How did you get my number?'

'Found it in your handbag, actually, Rosie, while you were fast asleep on a trolley in a Paris casualty department.'

'Oh, Christ, yes! You phoned my husband . . . my, er . . .' How weird. What did you call a husband who'd popped off to stay with a tart from his school? 'My . . . er . . . ex . . . sort-of . . .'

'Yes,' he intervened, saving me the dilemma, 'sorry about the intrusion into the handbag. Had to be done, really, but I didn't take any notice of any of the other stuff,

274

you know, the credit cards, tampons, condoms . . .'

'Hey!' I burst out laughing. 'I think the contents of my handbag are probably subject to patient confidentiality!'

'Sure! No worries!' He laughed along with me and, suddenly, inexplicably, for the first time for weeks I felt light-hearted and cheery, as if life hadn't just dealt me a series of blows and desertions but was full of excitement and possibility.

'Well, how are you? Are you better?' he repeated when we'd both stopped laughing.

'Yes – thanks. I spent a few days in hospital. I'd had a severe allergic reaction to some antibiotics . . .'

'Thought as much!'

'But I'm fine now. I'm so glad you've called – I think I owe you a huge "thank you" for looking after me when . . . well, when the person I was with, couldn't be bothered, quite frankly.'

'So . . . you're not still *with* . . . that person?'

'Absolutely not,' I replied firmly, suddenly very glad about it. There was a moment of silence. 'And what about you? Did you get the job in Paris?'

'Absolutely not!' he echoed with a laugh.

'Oh . . . what a shame . . . I'm so sorry!'

'Don't be. It was a long shot. I wasn't even sure if I wanted it. Not as much as I want the post I've applied for now.'

'Really? Where's that?'

'At East Dean, Rosie. I'm coming for another interview next Thursday and this time I think I'm in with a good chance. Would you let me take you out for lunch?'

'You look pleased with yourself,' Stuart said accusingly when I sat back down in front of *Alien Hell on Elm Street*. 'New boyfriend?'

'Stuart!' I reprimanded him mildly. 'Your dad and I have only just separated. I *don't* have boyfriends.'

But that didn't mean I couldn't look pleased with myself. Or look forward to lunch with Oliver.

*

'Dad's going to meet us at the pub,' said Emma cautiously, watching my face. 'For a drink.'

It was Sunday lunchtime and Emma and Tom had only just arrived. We'd barely had time to exchange hugs and hellos, the dog was still doing his welcoming hysterical circuit of the house and garden, knocking over everything in his path with his madly wagging tail, and Stuart hadn't looked up from the PlayStation. I felt another frisson of anxiety.

'You're not setting something up ... some sort of reconciliation-type meeting between me and your dad?'

'Don't be silly, Mum,' she laughed.

'And he's not bringing that girl?'

'No. He's coming alone. I just thought it'd be nice ... I don't often get to see either of you ...'

'Well, fair enough, I suppose,' I said a bit grudgingly. I guess this is part of the whole thing of being separated. You have to make a combined effort occasionally for your kids' sake.

'Come on, Stuart, turn that off!' I called sharply, looking for my shoes. 'Biggles, for God's sake calm down. Come on, then – to the pub.'

The Red Cow was only a five-minute walk away. We trooped into the bar and found Barry already at a table on his own, staring into his beer.

'I'll get the drinks. What does everyone want?' said Tom, going to the bar.

'Hi Dad!' said Emma, giving him a kiss. 'Let's sit in the garden – it's such a lovely day.'

So we trooped outside again and found a table with an umbrella. Tom brought the tray of drinks out and sat down, and we all stared at each other in expectant silence.

'Well,' said Barry eventually, 'this is nice.'

'Yes. Nice to see you. How have you been?' asked Emma. I noticed her voice had a tiny shake in it. I looked at her carefully. She was slightly flushed, her eyes bright, as if she had a fever.

'What is it?' I demanded, cutting through Barry's description of his new life in Robyn's love-nest. 'What's happened, Em?'

She returned my gaze, smiled and looked at Tom. He smiled back, and then, of course, I knew. Before she'd even opened her mouth to say the words: 'I'm pregnant!' I knew what all this was about – the news she didn't want to tell Tasha before she'd told us, the hurried visit home, the insistence on her dad being here, the excited, happy look . . .

But what about Tom?

Didn't she say he didn't want children – ever?

Didn't she say she might have to leave him because he'd never change his mind?

I hugged her, smiled with her, told her how happy I was, congratulated Tom, laughed with them both at the jokes about becoming a grandmother, but all the time an uneasy little voice in my head was asking awkward questions. He looked happy enough now, but had he really agreed to this baby? Or had she taken it upon herself to give nature a little helping hand – by way of a forgotten Pill or two?

'Come on, *Gran*, drink up and I'll buy you another one!' laughed Tom, and I smiled and pretended to find it funny.

Yes, he seemed happy enough now, with all the excitement and attention, slaps on the back and pints of beer being bought. But what about the reality – screaming kid in the middle of the night, tired mum with no time for him, no more wild nights out . . .

I hope you know what you're doing I thought, looking at my eldest daughter as she sipped her orange juice and laughed at suggestions for the baby's name. *This isn't just going to last for nine months, you know. It's for the rest of your bloody lifetime!*

'My daughter's having a baby,' I told Becky when we were

277

back at work on the Tuesday.

'Cool!' she exclaimed. 'Shit, Rosie – you'll be a granny! You'll have to take up knitting, and telling bedtime stories, and stuff!'

'Not a chance!' I retorted. 'Modern grandmothers aren't like that ...'

'Well, they don't go jaunting off to Paris with naughty underwear and blue nail varnish!' she giggled.

'Who doesn't?' asked PJ, leaning on the reception desk and looking from one of us to the other with bright-eyed interest.

'Grandmothers. Rosie's going to be a granny, PJ!'

'So?' I replied defensively. 'It doesn't mean I've got to change my life ...'

'No, of course not!' said PJ with a smile. 'You can carry on with the naughty underwear just as long as you like, Rosie!'

'Pervert!' laughed Becky. 'I always *thought* you had a thing about older women, PJ!'

It suddenly went very quiet. PJ looked at me, I looked at PJ, and Becky frowned and looked at us both.

'What have I said now?' she asked the world in general.

'Don't take any notice of Becky,' said PJ later in the coffee-room. 'I don't care about you being an older woman, you're still a very attractive old armchair ... whoops, sorry, a very attractive older woman ...!'

'Shut up!' I glared at him and picked up my coffee mug. 'You'll be telling me to stay at home and start knitting soon.'

'Well, I really think, in the circumstances, you should perhaps ...'

'PJ!' I took a sip of my coffee and watched him, over the brim, as he smiled at me across the room. I didn't feel in the mood to be teased. It was all very well my daughter having a baby – if indeed it *was* all very well – but I wasn't sure about this whole grandmother thing. I didn't really feel

278

ready for it. I was only just getting used to the idea of being a single woman again. I wanted to be young, and free, and ... all the things I'd never been while I was married to Barry.

'I'm *not* an older woman,' I told PJ peevishly. 'I'm young and free and single and ... and anyway, I'm going out with a nice young obstetrician on Thursday, so there!'

'Who?' demanded PJ at once. 'What obstetrician? Trying to book him for your daughter's delivery, Rosie?'

'No!' I returned, stung by the suggestion that this could be the only reason for me going out with a young obstetrician. 'He's just taking me out, PJ. He just happens to fancy me, surprising though that might be to you, and probably wants to shag me, so I'm going to bloody well enjoy it, if that's OK with you!'

'Well, have a bloody nice time, then!' he replied, putting down his cup and heading for the door. 'And just watch out for his forceps and his breech position!'

Very funny! I muttered to myself as the door swung shut behind him. *Idiot. Who needs him? He's leaving soon anyway. I'll do what I said – find someone else to bring me doughnuts. Maybe Oliver might be just the man for the job!*

I seemed to have stopped being a source of interest for the hospital gossips since Ashley Connor and I had stopped having anything to do with each other, so I was a bit taken aback when I gradually became aware of being talked about again. It wasn't anything too obvious – just the occasional excited burst of conversation that stopped abruptly when I entered a room, or a subtle nudge and whisper as I passed a couple of nurses in the corridor.

'I think I must be getting paranoid,' I commented to Becky and Sara that afternoon. 'I keep imagining people are looking at me. Have I got my skirt tucked into the back of my knickers or something?'

'Not a chance,' smiled Becky. 'Don't forget I was with you when you bought your knickers. No room in there for a skirt to get tucked in.'

'I don't wear *them* to work,' I retorted primly.

'I expect people are just looking at you because they like your hairstyle,' said Sara kindly.

'Or they've heard about you becoming a grandma and can't believe you're old enough!' added Becky, who was frantically trying to make up for calling me an older woman earlier on.

'OK, OK,' I said, laughing. 'Now I *know* you're being sarcastic!'

Maybe I *was* paranoid but I couldn't help wondering if the looks and nudges were anything to do with Heidi.

'I never asked you how the Body and Soul thing went on Friday?' I asked Sara tentatively.

'It was OK,' she said with a shrug. 'You didn't really miss much. She-Who-Must-Be-Obeyed spent most of the time ranting on about her drama group.'

'Drama group? What drama group?'

'She's taken over running the hospital group – you know, the one that Mousy Monica and a few of her cronies used to organise to put on a Christmas pantomime for the kids. Heidi wants to get more people to join, so they can do more performances during the year. Used the lecture as an excuse to advertise the whole thing – it was, like: *Change Your Body* (by dressing up as Snow White and The Seven Dwarfs) *And Find your Soul* (by appearing on stage looking like a twat in front of all your colleagues).'

'Well, I suppose it gives her a purpose in life,' I said weakly, hoping for Heidi's sake that she'd immerse herself so thoroughly in the affairs of the drama group that she'd *Find Her Soul* somewhere other than down Ashley Connor's trousers.

'Well, I don't doubt she'll get a few volunteers,' put in Becky. 'She's so forceful, people are frightened to say no to her. She's sent out an e-mail to everyone about it, too!'

'Has she? I haven't had a chance to read my e-mails today.'

And I didn't get a chance then, either, because the queue for Rheumatology was becoming restless and we were kept busy for the rest of the afternoon.

On Thursday lunchtime, Oliver Fenton greeted me with a kiss on each cheek followed by a hearty embrace, much to the delight of the watching eyes of Sara, Becky, several nurses, and a wheelchair patient for whom I'd just left the reception desk in order to direct him to the disabled toilets.

'Got the job! I got the job!' said Oliver, grinning all over his face. 'I start next month! Come on, let's celebrate! Get your coat, you've pulled!'

'Well done – that's great!' I responded happily. 'And it's so nice to see you again, Oliver!' I reached up and kissed him back.

'Mm – I could get used to this!' he joked, putting an arm around my waist. 'Maybe you don't need your coat after all, Rosie ... it seems pretty hot in here already!'

There was a discreet cough from the wheelchair next to me.

'Er ... excuse me ... the, er, toilets ...?'

'Neglecting your patients, Rosie?' said PJ quietly out of the side of his mouth as he brushed past me on his way to the consulting rooms. He looked back and gave me a quick grin before rushing on without a glance at Oliver.

'Friend of yours?' queried Oliver, watching him go.

'Yes. Paresh Jaimeen, orthopaedics. I'd have introduced you, if he wasn't ...' I was going to say 'in such a hurry', but I'd had to turn my attention back to the wheelchair patient before finishing the sentence, and to my surprise Oliver finished it for me, instead.

'If he wasn't so jealous?'

'Jealous – PJ?' I snorted. 'No way! He's always like that. We take the piss, have a bit of a laugh together, you know.'

'Yep!' Oliver nodded, with a smile. 'I know. Come on, then – where's best for lunch around here?'

'What's for dinner, Mum?' demanded Stuart a few hours later, with his head in the fridge and his feet in his roller boots.

'Anything you like.' I looked up from reading the paper, husband-like, at the kitchen table. Strange how, since Barry left, I seemed to have become a cross between a mother figure and a father figure, like some kind of benevolent Bohemian hermaphrodite. 'Take your skates off indoors.'

'Can I have these sausages? Can I have chips? What's this pie?'

'The rest of the frozen chicken pie from yesterday. Have what you like, Stuart. Take your skates off.'

'Aren't you doing the sausages? Can't you do chips?' He withdrew his head from the fridge and gave me a searching look. 'Don't you feel well? Is it your period again?'

'Don't say *again* like that! It makes you sound like a man. You've got a few years yet before you need to sound like one.' I sighed and turned a page of the paper. 'And anyway, it isn't. I'm not ill, I'm just full up. I can't even think about food, Stuart, so you'll just have to eat the pie or go and get fish and chips.'

'Can I eat the pie *and* get fish and chips?' he asked eagerly, holding on to the fridge door whilst wheeling back and forth across the kitchen floor.

'Yes! Take the boots OFF! NOW!'

'I'm going out!' He slammed the fridge door shut and skated out to the hall. 'Where's your purse? For the fish and chips?'

Score for the evening – 2 out of 10 for Mother/Cook/Domestic Goddess; 10 out of 10 for Cool Dude Father/Provider of Funds. I watched him skating off with the necessary money out of my purse and I turned another page of the paper with another huge sigh. The sigh had a lot to do with the discomfort of my stomach following a massive celebratory lunch with Oliver. And it also had a lot to do with the discomfort of my mind.

'I must say,' Oliver had wasted no time in telling me, over the first drink before we'd even been served with our crab pâté, 'I was *bloody* glad when you said you'd finished with that Ashley Connor. What a prat. You deserve so much better, Rosie.'

'He's a consultant at the hospital,' I warned him, thinking it a bit dangerous for Oliver to sound off about Ashley being a prat before he'd even got his foot in the Obs and Gynae Department Door. Not that I disagreed with his diagnosis.

'I know.' He smiled as he raised his glass to me. 'I hope that doesn't mean you restrict yourself to consultants?'

'Sorry?' I asked, too confused to lift my glass to him in response. 'How do you mean?'

'I hope you're not averse to going out with registrars? Cheers!'

'Oh! Er ... cheers, Oliver.' A bit belatedly, and a bit flustered, I clinked my glass against his. 'Congratulations, and, er ... welcome to East Dean.' I took a gulp of my wine. 'Of course not – I'm out with you now, aren't I?'

'You know what I mean, Rosie,' he persisted, laughing and covering my hand with his as he put his glass down. 'I don't just mean going out – I mean,' he raised his eyebrows and adopted a sexy drawl, '*Going out.*' He pressed my hand more firmly and leaned towards me across the table. 'I was hoping we might see a little more of each other later on ... if you know what I mean.'

Fortunately the pâté was delivered at that moment, giving me just enough time to try to pull myself together. How had this happened? How had we gone from being two strangers thrown together by fate in Paris a few weeks ago, to being old friends having lunch together, to the point where I suddenly now found myself being propositioned over the crab pâté? I *liked* Oliver, I felt very grateful to him for looking after me the way he did in Paris, and yes, I'd quite enjoyed the thought that perhaps he might fancy me and we might have some fun together ... perhaps leading

283

to something more interesting in due course. It was a nice thought to play with, to turn over in my mind while I was lying in my lonely celibate bed at night, listening to Biggles snoring and farting and remembering Barry without very much regret. I wasn't exactly a shy little virgin, especially since my desperate attempt to seduce Ashley Connor on his slippery leather upholstery. But to be honest I'd kind of hoped for a little more chat and a little more getting to know each other, perhaps a bit of flirting and a few nights out together, before we undressed and got down to it as if it was the only thing on the agenda.

With a sinking heart I realised, two mouthfuls into the crab pâté, that it obviously *was* the only thing on the agenda.

We ate in silence for a while. I could feel him watching me, probably wondering whether he'd said the wrong thing and blown his chances. I gave him a weak smile and saw the relief in his eyes as he smiled back eagerly, re-assessing the possibility of a shag.

Well, why not? I thought to myself as I spread the last of the pâté copiously on my bread. Ashley Connor had made a fool of me, but only because he was playing with a different set of rules from me. Oliver was at least being honest. There was nothing wrong with laying his cards on the table right from the start. I was free to say no if I wanted to. I could get up now, pretend to be offended, leave the rest of my wine and my Peppered Steak with Sauté Potatoes, and go back to work on my own with my dignity and my pride intact. Or I could throw caution to the wind and get myself laid.

'I think it'd be very nice,' I said after the waitress had taken away our starter plates and we were both looking at the table in a slightly hesitant silence, 'to see ... more of each other.'

A spark leapt in his eyes and I felt a flutter of excitement in response.

'Tonight?' he said hopefully.

'No. I've got a son at home. Let me know when you can come back again, and find somewhere we can go. I'll wait till I hear from you.'

I tucked into my steak with enthusiasm. This was a good feeling. I was in control here. I had him eating out of my hand – almost literally, the way he was devouring me with his eyes as he devoured his monkfish. I pursed my lips suggestively at him as I chewed a piece of steak and he grinned and winked at me. *Mm*, I thought happily, *I think I'm going to like this.* Straightforward sex, no nonsense, no messing around with formalities. Should be fun. What had I been worried about?

And what, you may ask, was I worried about now, sitting at my kitchen table with my stomach still full of lunch, the paper spread out in front of me and not a word of it being read? Was I having regrets? Was I changing my mind, or getting cold feet?

Come on, Rosie, this is the twenty-first century! Women are allowed to screw around now – it's not a sin, no one's gong to strike you dead or jump up in front of you and declare you a trollop. And besides, won't it be nice to get your money's worth from that new underwear after all?

The phone had rung several times before I shook myself out of my soliloquy and jumped up to answer it.

'Hi, Mum! Just calling for a chat. I'm not interrupting your dinner, am I?' sung out Emma cheerfully.

'No, I'm not eating tonight,' I said with a groan. 'Had a huge lunch.'

'Good for you,' she said approvingly. 'You need to build up your strength!'

'What for?' My head was still filled with visions of Oliver in various states of undress, in various positions of interest.

'For grandmotherhood, of course!' exclaimed Emma with an unspoken hint of 'What else?!' to her voice.

I smiled to myself. She'd be amazed if she knew what else.

'Of course,' I said lightly. 'That's *exactly* what I'm building myself up for, darling. I need a lot of strength for ... all the knitting and stuff I'm going to be doing.'

Or whatever.

Chapter Sixteen

Dressing-up Games

'Aren't you just a little bit concerned,' I said hesitantly to Barry on the phone a couple of days later, 'about all this?'

It was the third time in two days that Barry had phoned me to talk about the forthcoming grandchild. It was beginning to grate on my nerves slightly. I mean, it was good, it was commendable, it was excellent (if surprising) that he was taking so much sudden interest in the life of his soon-to-be-extended family, especially so quickly after having walked out on it. But to be quite frank, I didn't really want him phoning me three times in two days. I didn't particularly want him phoning me at all. Fair enough, a brief conversation 'en route' to talking to Stuart was acceptable; a quick enquiry about my state of health and whether the roof had fallen in since he was last in the house was only polite – but all this in-depth stuff about his pre-grandfatherly feelings just wasn't appropriate in the circumstances of our separation and his living with an under-age bimbo. I suddenly found I couldn't listen to his emotional gushing any more without wanting to douse it with the cold water of my own uncertainty.

'Concerned?' he queried. 'Why? What do you mean?'

'Do you think Tom's really as happy as Emma is about this baby?'

'Of course!' he retorted, sounding shocked. 'Why wouldn't he be? You saw how chuffed he was! What man wouldn't be proud and excited ...'

'Well,' I interrupted him before we could go off on a tangent again about men and babies and the pride of fatherhood, to say nothing of grandfatherhood, 'it's just that only a couple of months ago, Emma told me how determined he was *never* to have children, and yet here they are ...'

'I know what you're thinking,' he said smugly. 'And you've got it all wrong, Rosie.'

'Oh, have I?' I retorted, instantly annoyed. 'Enlighten me, then, if you know what I'm thinking.'

'You think Emma got pregnant by herself, don't you?'

'Kind of difficult, actually, Barry ...'

'You know what I mean. Accidentally-on-purpose. Stopped her Pill without telling him.'

'It crossed my mind, yes,' I admitted. 'I don't see how else they could have gone so quickly from him refusing to be a "sperm donor", to instant expectant parenthood.'

'We can all make mistakes, you know,' said Barry.

'How do you mean?'

'Tom and I had a talk. Man-to-man, at the bar the other day when you and Emma were discussing knitting patterns ...'

'I do *not* discuss fucking knitting patterns ...'

'No need to swear,' he said mildly. 'Tom really opened up to me about his feelings.'

Oh, yeuk. Spare me, God, please spare me this male pseudo-psychological claptrap. Next thing I knew, Barry'd be telling me he was having menopausal symptoms.

'And?' I prompted through clenched teeth.

'He told me how frightened he'd been of the commitment necessary for fatherhood, how he'd taken refuge in aggressive denial of his feelings and Emma's needs, how he'd failed to grow and develop as a man and had used his immaturity as a weapon against her natural desires for fulfilment in motherhood ...'

288

'And you're going through the menopause, I suppose?'

'Sorry?'

'Barry, what exactly did Tom say?'

'That as soon as Emma told him she was about to leave him if he didn't agree to try for a baby, he personally threw her contraceptive pills down the toilet and made love to her non-stop for a fortnight.'

'No wonder they both look knackered.'

'Don't you think it's amazing that he was prepared to admit he was in the wrong, that he was able to face up to his ...'

'Yes, Barry, I think it's wonderful. Now, did you want to speak to Stuart or what?'

Non-stop for a fortnight. Bloody hell. She *deserved* a baby after that.

The Tom-and-Emma situation wasn't the only thing that had been playing on my mind, of course. There was the question of Sex With Oliver (or, rather, the question of when and where Sex With Oliver was going to happen, it having become an undisputed fact, somewhere between the crab pâté and the steak, that it was going to happen). Oliver had phoned me the day after our lunch, to tell me that he was in the process of sorting out accommodation for himself near East Dean, in preparation for taking up his new post at the beginning of June.

'I've found a flat I like, in the town centre. Nice big bedroom,' he told me, his voice dripping with lustful insinuation. 'I'm just living in a room at the hospital where I work now, so I can afford to take over the new flat as soon as possible. Then we'll have somewhere to ... er ... meet up, Rosie.'

'Mm. Good,' I said, trying to match his enthusiasm but feeling strangely flat.

'So I'll give you another call? As soon as I've got the keys? Can you arrange for someone to have your son, so you can stay all night?'

'Oh. I don't know. I'll have to see . . .'

'I hope so! I'm looking forward to it, Rosie . . .'

I could tell he was. He sounded like he was almost on the point of orgasm, just talking about it. So what was wrong? What was missing? He was a young, good-looking man, nice, clever, good company, obviously desperate for me. Why wasn't I drooling with anticipation at the idea of falling into bed with him, the way I'd been with Ashley Connor?

At the thought of Ashley, my heart sank even lower. I didn't want to think about him. I certainly didn't want to dwell on how he must have laughed at me behind my back as I flirted and came on to him, when all he wanted was to make sure I hadn't got a photograph of him having it off with Heidi. I didn't want to remember how I'd tried to jump him in his car, or how he'd paraded me as a sick joke in front of his grubby-minded friends in Paris. Was this, then, the root of my problem? I sat down shakily at the bottom of the stairs, still holding the receiver, warm from the desperate way I'd gripped it during Oliver's phone call. Was I afraid of making a fool of myself again? Did I suspect that Oliver was only interested in me because he'd seen how casually Ashley had used and abused me? That Oliver might, in fact, just be thinking of me as a slag – an easy lay?

I think, at that moment, sitting on my own on the stairs in my empty house, trying to work up some enthusiasm for the sort of sexual encounter I'd only dreamed of before, I hated Ashley Connor more than anyone I'd ever met. I had a horrible feeling he might have put me off sex for life.

'Do you think I behaved like a slag? You know, with Ashley?' I asked Becky quietly at work when no one else was around.

'What?! Don't be daft! *He*'s the one acting like a slag – how many women does he have on the go . . .?'

'I know. But it's always a different story, isn't it, for men. It's so unfair, the double standard.'

'Not these days, Rosie. Come on, what's the matter with

you? Nobody thinks like that any more. Your marriage was more or less over when you started seeing Ashley Connor. You weren't doing anything wrong. His marriage is his own business.'

'And his affair with Heidi. And all the other bits on the side,' I reminded her grimly. It had taken me quite a few days to calm down enough, after the episode with Heidi and the scissors, to tell Becky the whole story, and her eyebrows had taken almost a week to come down out of her hairline.

'Exactly. As I say – *he*'s the one with a problem. What are you worried about? Put it behind you, love, and move on.'

'I know. I know that's what I *should* do, but I . . . kind of think . . . I might have gone off the idea of sex completely now.'

'Jesus!' said Becky, looking at me open-mouthed. 'They can prescribe something for that, though, can't they?'

Needless to say, I'd avoided Heidi like the plague ever since the day of our private Body and Soul session. Even seeing her name on an e-mail was enough to make me dive for the delete key – until I realised it was the Group E-Mail – sent to everyone in the hospital – the one the girls had told me about, appealing for volunteers for her Drama Group. And what was this? The next e-mail on the screen was a reply from Ashley Connor! What was this doing in my in-box? Intrigued, I clicked to open it and my eyes nearly popped out of my head as I began to read:

Dear Fluff
Of course I'll be there on Friday night. Would you like me in the gorilla suit or the Superman tights and mask? And don't forget I still have the collection of leather stuff. I'm looking forward to playing a domi-nant role!
Big Boy
xx

'Dear FLUFF?!' I exploded, laughing out loud so violently that Becky leaned over to see what I was reading. 'BIG BOY?!?'

'Who's that from?' she asked. 'Who's Fluff? Who's Big Boy? What's all this about Superman tights?!'

'It's from Ashley Connor to Heidi Hampton about the Drama Group!' I spluttered, wiping tears of laughter from my eyes. 'He must have hit "Reply All" instead of "Reply"!'

'How amusing!' laughed Becky. 'I saw that last week, but I deleted it without bothering to open it – I just presumed it was a BORING e-mail about Heidi's drama group ...'

'Last week?' I repeated, wonderingly. Had it really been that long since I'd checked and sorted my e-mails? We'd been busy for so long, I'd got into the habit of having a quick look at my in-box every morning before starting work, and only reading anything that looked particularly urgent. 'This e-mail went out to everyone in the hospital? Last week?'

'Looks like it! Good, eh! Make a change for *him* to be a laughing stock for a while!'

You can say that again. *Fluff* indeed! *Big Boy*? – huh! I knew differently!

It was over a week before Oliver phoned again. I was beginning to wonder whether he'd forgotten about me, or lost my number, or changed his mind. I was beginning to wonder, too, whether I'd be disappointed or relieved if he did.

'Rosie!' he began excitedly, 'I get the keys to the flat on Friday! I'll be over there for the weekend. Can you come round?'

I hesitated. This was awful. It was supposed to be fun. Hadn't I decided I was going to have sex with him for the fun of it, for the hell of it, and enjoy myself? What was I waiting for?

'Do you still want to?' he asked anxiously. 'If you don't want to ...'

What? We'd forget about it, go back to where we were, friends who'd met in Paris, who'd talked about having an affair and then changed their minds? Oh, I was sure he'd be perfectly nice about it. He wouldn't make a fuss, wouldn't make me feel silly or embarrassed or show me up in front of people at work. It would never be mentioned again. We'd be polite and friendly to each other and nobody need ever know ...

'Rosie?' he asked again. 'Are you still there?'

'Yes! Yes, sorry, Oliver. I was just thinking ... working out what the date is on Friday ... whether I've got anything planned.'

'And?'

He sounded so eager. Bless him. He sounded just like Stuart when he wanted permission to go on a school trip or out to the pictures with his mates. *Can I, Mum – please let me! Please, Mum, please say yes, I'll be good, I'll do anything, please let me ...*

'Yes. Yes, that'll be fine. Friday, then.'

'Excellent! Will you be able to stay the night?'

'I don't know. I'll have to see what I can arrange.'

'Do your best, Rosie. I'll make it a night to remember ...'

Well. Apparently that's what they all say. But how would I know?

'Stuart, could you wangle an invitation to stay at Andrew's house on Friday night, do you think?'

'Why?'

'Why? Why? So your mother can go and screw the new obstetrics registrar all night, why do you think?

'I'm going out. And I'll be staying the night with one of the girls ...'

'Oh, I see!' he said, with a knowing look. 'I get it!'

'What?' I asked, flushing with alarm. Had he read my thoughts? Did he realise what was going on? How? And how was I going to explain myself? What if he told his father? How was this going to affect the divorce? Would the judge stop Stuart from living with me because of my immoral behaviour? Would I be deemed an unfit mother? Or an unfit grandmother – banned from looking after Emma's baby, before it was even born?

'I suppose,' went on my son, smirking broadly, 'you're going to get *pissed* and won't be able to drive home!'

If only that was all.

We were drifting towards the end of May and it was beginning to really feel like summer, with less chronic bronchitis in the queues at the reception desk and more gardening injuries.

'People are *definitely* still talking about me,' I confided to Becky, having just noticed two physiotherapists turning their heads and whispering as I walked back to my post after lunch.

'I'm sure you're imagining it,' she insisted. 'What could they be talking about? Nobody knows about Aussie Oliver, do they?'

'Only you.'

Well, trust me – I haven't told a soul. Besides, no one knows who he is, yet. When does he start here?'

'Second of June – the same day PJ starts his new job at the London.'

'Out with the old, in with the new!' laughed Becky.

'But I'm going to miss PJ, in a weird sort of way.'

'Can't think why. You two never stop arguing.'

'It's only banter. He's been a good friend, really, Becks.'

'Men can't be good friends to women, Rosie. It just doesn't happen, unless they're gay. There's always an ulterior motive.'

'That's very cynical. And it's also crap. There's never been anything like that between PJ and me. We're just friends.'

'So are you coming to his farewell party? He was going on about it again this morning when I met him in the corridor . . .'

'Of course, if only he'd hurry up and make up his mind when he's having it. I'll need to make arrangements for Stuart if I'm going to be out late.'

And that would be a problem, wouldn't it. I couldn't possibly ask Stuart to stay at Andrew's again for another night. Andrew's parents would start wondering whether I was a fit mother, never mind the judge in the divorce case. It wasn't as if it was an option for Stuart to stay with his father overnight – not with him living at Robyn Red Breast's place. Perhaps Barry could be persuaded to come round for the evening – as long as he didn't bring *her* with him. I'd have to work on it.

And I *still* had the worry of people talking about me.

It came to a head when I was in the staff toilets the following day. The afternoon clincs had run late again and I was tired and ready to go home, but I hadn't had a chance to go for a pee all afternoon and I didn't think I'd make it home unless I stopped first and relieved my bladder. I'd just shut the cubicle door when I heard two more people come in, chatting. The other cubicle was occupied so they stood by the sinks and carried on their conversation. At first I wasn't really listening. I was too tired, too relieved to be both sitting down and emptying my bladder, and by the thought of going home. Gradually it dawned on me that one of the voices belonged to Hayley Gibson, the outpatient department gossip.

'I can't *believe* he's seeing *her*!' she was squealing with delighted malice. 'She's *such* a bossy old cow! Can you imagine it!'

How long do you think it's been going on?' asked the other voice. It wasn't Hayley's usual sidekick, Linda. It might have been the new little student nurse, or one of the health care assistants.

'Well, God knows. But calling her *Fluff*! I mean, can you believe it!'

They both dissolved into hysterical giggles. I almost stopped peeing with shock.

'And calling himself *Big Boy*!' added the second girl. 'Ooh, Hayley – I wonder if he *is*, you know—' they both went into further paroxysms of laughter '—a *Big Boy*!'

'Well, you know how to find out, don't you!' screamed Hayley. 'Ask Rosie Peacock!'

By now I'd come over so hot that any traces of urine left in my system must have evaporated. I sat rigid on the toilet, holding my breath, terrified that I'd give away my identity by some unwarranted cough or fart that might be recognised.

'Did she go out with him, then?' asked the younger voice in surprise. I was sure by now that it was the new student nurse, Colleen.

'Of course she did! Everyone knows that! They were absolutely *blatant* about it! He took her to Paris for the weekend and she came back BY AMBULANCE!'

'Ooh!' squealed Colleen with excitement. 'By *ambulance*! What *ever* did they get up to in Paris?!'

They both laughed again, loud and hard, whilst I sat in silent misery, wishing the floor, or even the toilet, could swallow me up.

'Well, now the whole world knows about his little *fetish*,' continued Hayley with obvious relish, 'now we all know how he likes to dress up as Superman . . .'

'They were probably trying to jump off the wardrobes, and fly through the air!'

'Or he was dressing up in his gorilla suit!'

'Yeah, and carrying her off . . . like an ape-man . . . and throwing her around . . .'

The laughter reached screaming pitch again.

'Ooh, I'm going to wet myself in a minute! Hurry up in there!' squealed Colleen.

The other cubicle door opened and the giggles were

smothered for a moment as Colleen dived for the toilet, slamming the door behind her. The sound of her urgent urination was just about drowned out by the sound of the tap running as the previous occupier of the other cubicle washed her hands and then went out.

'Whoops!' Hayley called through the cubicle door to Colleen, on the verge of laughter again. 'Did you realise who that was? Sylvia Riley! She had a face like a slapped backside!'

Great. I screwed up my face and cringed and felt like howling out loud. Was there to be no end to my humiliation? Now the story of my supposed antics in Paris would be carried around the management offices too. As if it wasn't enough to be stared at and talked about by every other fucker in this place – when I hadn't even done anything!

Suddenly I saw red. I was buggered if I was going to let this go on . . . let this ridiculous story continue on its merry giggling route around the hospital until there wasn't a nurse or a doctor, a porter or even a patient left who didn't believe I'd played dressing-up games with Ashley Connor as well as knowing I'd made an absolute prat of myself with him. I flung open the cubicle door, only just remembering in time to pull up my knickers first, and shouted at the back of Hayley's head:

'Right!'

She whirled round, her face a picture of shock and embarrassment, just as Colleen flushed her toilet and emerged from the other cubicle.

'Rosie!' they both said together on a sort of strangled sigh of distress.

'First!' I yelled, my anger and humiliation giving a one hundred per cent increase to my normal vocal volume, 'I don't play dressing up games! Not with Ashley Connor, not with anyone!'

'No, no, of course not!' said Hayley hurriedly, trying to put her arm round me in a matey, girls-together gesture of appeasement. I shook her off, vigorously.

'Secondly!' I continued, volume unabated, 'Nothing happened in Paris! I came back by ambulance because I was ill!'

'Yes, yes, OK, Rosie,' soothed Hayley, casting an anxious look at Colleen, who was hovering nervously in her cubicle doorway.

'And fourthly!' I pronounced, having lost the ability to count, along with my temper and the final shreds of my dignity, 'I *finished* with Mr Ashley Connor! I finished with him because . . .'

'Because of the dressing up?' interrupted Colleen in a frightened squeak. 'Because of the . . . animal stuff, the leather and the . . . er, gorilla?'

'I don't blame you, Rosie,' said Hayley immediately, sensing an opportunity to get on my side. 'I wouldn't put up with anything like that myself, either. I mean to say; it's one thing wanting to use a few, you know, sexual *toys* and stuff. I don't mind handcuffs too much, as long as they're those soft velvety ones from the Ann Summers catalogue. But I do draw the line at anything really *kinky*, you know, whips or chains, and well – all that gorilla malarkey, well it's a bit *weird*, isn't it . . .'

I was about to tell her to shut the fuck up. I had the rest of my speech mapped out in my mind – point number four, or five, or wherever I was up to, being that they were two stupid, thick, unpleasant little bitches who'd managed to make a piece of unlikely titillation out of an e-mail about costumes for the drama group, and who'd managed to make me the laughing stock of the hospital in the process of their unintelligent gossip-mongering. But as I stood there, mouth open ready to let rip again, I had a sudden thought. Yes, people might be looking at me and whispering and smiling . . . but it wasn't *me* who had become the real laughing stock of the place, was it? Everyone knew I'd finished with Ashley Connor by now – whether they knew the reason or not didn't really matter. If they were daft enough to think I stormed out of his life because I wasn't too keen on his gorilla suit or his Superman tights, could I help it? Who looked the biggest prats around here – me, or *Big Boy* and *Fluff*?

'Yes,' I said, giving Hayley a faint smile and watching her jaw relax with relief. 'Yes, you're quite right – it's very weird. Very weird indeed.' I smiled again, suddenly feeling a lot better. 'I can honestly say,' I added conversationally as I washed my hands, 'That I've never had sex with a gorilla in my life.'

'I didn't think you had, Rosie,' said Hayley very earnestly. 'I really didn't.'

It was Thursday afternoon before I saw PJ again.

'Can't stop, Rosie!' he called as he rushed past the desk on his way to theatre.

'I wasn't going to stop you!' I called back. 'Don't kid yourself!'

'Oh, I see! No time for your old mates now you've got your new *obstetrics* boyfriend!' He slowed down despite his apparent hurry, turned back to me and made a very rude gesture.

'PJ!' I remonstrated, pretending to be shocked. 'Oliver and I have only had lunch together.' I remembered what Oliver had said about him and added with a grin, 'Anyone would think you were jealous!'

'Anyone who didn't know better,' he agreed. 'Anyway, as I said, I'd love to stop and chat but there's a patient bleeding on the table needing me to save his life . . .'

'Don't exaggerate.'

'Well, all right, waiting for me to take a buried suture out of his finger . . .'

'Go on, then, doctor, get to it.'

'See you tomorrow night?'

'Tomorrow night?' I looked at him blankly.

'Tomorrow night, Rosie – my party! Don't mess around – you are coming, aren't you?'

'I didn't know it was tomorrow night,' I said. 'You're not leaving till next week . . .'

'But it's Bank Holiday on Monday, then I've got a week's terminal leave. I *told* you it was tomorrow ... didn't I?'

'No,' I said, faintly. 'You didn't.'

'But you can come, can't you?' he persisted, having now stopped his headlong rush to theatre completely. 'It's at my place – the other guys in the house are joining in, we're using the whole house for the party. It'll be brilliant ... Rosie? You haven't got anything else on, have you?'

'No, no, it's fine. Nothing else on, PJ.'

Nothing I can't live without.

I called Oliver that evening.

'About tomorrow night,' I said a bit anxiously.

'You can't get anyone to have your son for the night?' he guessed quickly. 'Never mind, Rosie. Can you just come round for the evening? He'll be OK on his own for a few hours, won't he?'

'Well, yes, but ...'

'It'll be fine. I'll do us something to eat, and we can just ... enjoy each other's company ... for a while. There'll be another time.'

'Well, to be honest, Oliver, I was going to say ...'

'You haven't changed your mind?' he asked quickly. 'You still *want* to ...'

'Yes, of course,' I said, realising with a shock that I was shaking my head whilst saying Yes. I bet I couldn't do that again if I tried. 'But it's just ...'

Why was I such a wimp? Why couldn't I ever say what I really meant? I should have told him that I'd rather be at PJ's party than in bed with him, with or without the added and dubious benefit of his home cooked meal. That I wasn't even sure if I fancied him, that I had a sneaking suspicion I'd lost interest in sex for life, and that if I was ever going to regain any desire for it, it wasn't going to be by grabbing the first opportunity to drop my knickers with the first horny young doctor who asked me. Obstetrician or not.

300

But no, needless to say, I wimped out.

'Of course I still *want* to come round,' I began, desperately trying to think of an excuse. 'But . . . Stuart . . . it's his Open Evening at school! I can't possibly get out of it!' I ended in a rush, mentally congratulating myself on such a good lie. 'It's very important. He starts his GCSE course in September, you know, and with his father and I separating, it's *essential* that I'm there . . . and you know how these things go on, by the time I've seen all the teachers . . . it'll be very late . . .'

'Rosie,' said Oliver in a low voice, 'I've been waiting for this for long enough now. I can wait a few more hours. I'll have the wine in the fridge, the soft lights and music in the bedroom and the condoms on the beside table. Whether it's eleven o'clock, midnight, or the early hours of the morning, I'll be waiting for you . . . ready and waiting!'

I didn't need any more graphic description. I got the picture. He had the scenario all planned out, and I was going to be a part of it. Well, who knows? Maybe I was wrong. Maybe some casual sex with champagne and music and stuff was just what I *did* need to get my libido going again. Maybe I could go to PJ's farewell party *and* go on for sex with Oliver afterwards. Why not? I was a free woman. Perhaps by the time I'd had a drink or two at the party I'd be feeling more up for it.

'OK,' I agreed, making a determined effort to sound more positive about it. 'I'll see you after the Parents' Evening, then.' Too late now to admit it was a party I was going to. 'Shall I call you when I'm on my way?'

'No need,' he purred. 'Like I say, baby, whatever the time, I'll be ready and waiting.'

It must be frustrating working in Obs and Gynae when you're that horny.

PJ had a room in one of the doctors' residences on the hospital site. Doctors with wives and families occupy whole houses, whereas single doctors share a house between four

301

of them. They have a bedsit each, and share a kitchen, lounge and bathroom. I'd ventured into a few such houses over the years, usually for an occasional social drink with someone who was leaving or getting married or had just passed an FRCS or FRCP exam. They're pretty grim. I've no doubt the domestic staff do their best, but they're fighting a losing battle against the tide of squalour generated by four desperately busy people who eat messily on the go, sleep infrequently at haphazard hours, and whose idea of personal hygiene outside of operating theatres is to hang sweaty socks on the radiator to dry them out before wearing them again. Trust me, I've seen better housekeeping in Tasha's student halls, and that's saying something. The house PJ shared with Henry, Claude and Ahmed was no exception.

'Come in, Rosie! And may I say how very lovely you look tonight, my petite English Rose!' gushed Claude, who was obviously already very drunk by the time I arrived.

'You may, if you like,' I granted, following him into the kitchen. 'As long as you don't expect me to believe a word of it.'

In fact I'd had a nightmare trying to decide what to wear. It had to be casual enough for a drinks party in a house that resembled a populated dustbin, and yet sexy enough for the encounter I was going on for afterwards – preferably without making it obvious to anyone here what I was dressed up for. Eventually I'd settled on jeans with a low-cut silky black top that I'd put away at the back of my wardrobe because I thought it was too tight for me. Well, to be honest, it *was* too tight for me. I could be in trouble if I did too much breathing.

'Hi, Rosie! What d'you want to drink ... fucking hell!' exclaimed PJ, looking up from pouring cheap white wine for three little student nurses who didn't look old enough to be out at night, never mind drinking hospital measures of alcohol on empty stomachs. If their stomachs weren't empty, I couldn't imagine where they were hiding their

302

undigested food, as they were all so completely thin, their minuscule shiny black skirts fitted them in concave curves like chair-backs. On hearing PJ's exclamation they all turned round and stared at me and I recognised one as Colleen. 'Oh, hello, Rosie,' she said, smothering a giggle which immediately set the other two off.

'Piss off,' I muttered under my breath as they tripped out of the kitchen on their stilt heels, spluttering into their wine glasses.

'You look ... absolutely ... different!' said PJ, who hadn't taken his eyes off my neckline.

'Thanks for nothing. Hello! I'm up here, PJ – I speak from my face, not my boobs!'

'Yes, well. You've got to admit, Rosie, you're showing a bit more of yourself than we're used to. Be careful how you move – one of those could come out and hit someone in the eye! Are you wearing a bra?'

'Just because you're leaving doesn't mean you can be so bloody rude and personal, you cheeky little ... hey!' I stopped in mid-insult and pointed to the kitchen window behind PJ's head. 'What's going on? I didn't know you'd invited the local circus!'

I look back on that moment as one of the most exquisitely satisfying times of my entire life. Of course, in the cold light of day, when we were all able to think about it sensibly and rationally, without the accompaniment of the shrieks of laughter, pints of beer and the general carnival atmosphere that erupted during the next few minutes, it was quite clear what had happened. Obviously, the Drama Group meeting which had been convened for that evening hadn't been well supported because of the preferred option of PJ's leaving party. In fact it had been so badly supported that only its two leading lights had bothered to turn up, and on realising that their meeting was doomed they decided to go for broke and join everyone else at the party. And why not come as they were? Hadn't someone told them the party was supposed to be fancy dress? And look how much it helped the popularity stakes that night at the pub, at Henry's birthday party, when Ashley wore the gorilla outfit! Yes, it was quite easy to see the logical reason for it all. Why would they be worried about all that silly hospital gossip about their sexual preferences? After all, *everyone* at the party was going to be dressed up, weren't they?

But when Ashley Connor and Heidi Hampton turned up at PJ's house that night dressed as Little Red Riding Hood and The Big Bad Wolf, the place was in uproar before they'd even put a foot in the door. Any street cred, any popularity points Ashley might have gained back in March by appearing as the gorilla in the midst, were lost and forgotten that evening as he went almost overnight from Pop Idol to Figure of Fun in the unforgiving minds of the East Dean staff. Without me having to do a thing, everybody around me was meting out my revenge to Mr Ashley Connor. PJ, his expression unreadable, caught my eye and winked.

'You told them it was fancy dress?' I whispered, feeling the grin spreading across my face.

He shrugged his shoulders and grinned back.

'Nice one,' I told him firmly.

Game, set and match.

Chapter Seventeen

The One Perfect Night

It wasn't really a great surprise to anyone that Ashley and Heidi didn't stay very long. Stifled laughter as drinks were handed to them, suggestive comments bordering on the obscene about the size of the Big Bad Wolf's teeth, eyes and various other parts of his anatomy, and what Little Red Riding Hood might have to look forward to when he got hold of her basket of goodies, were enough to send the pair of them scuttling off in embarrassed silence within half an hour of their arrival.

'And bloody good riddance,' I said cheerfully as I watched them leave.

'Feel better now?' asked PJ quietly, handing me another beer.

'Yep. That was brilliant! Ridicule is probably the best thing I could have wished for him. He'll hate it. He prides himself on his Mr Nice Guy image.'

'Nobody who works with him in theatre believes that for very long.'

'No.' I looked at him thoughtfully. 'He gave you a hard time, didn't he. He just didn't seem to like you. No wonder you're glad to be leaving.'

'In some ways,' agreed PJ. 'Come on, drink your beer and let's have a dance.'

The furniture in the little lounge had been pushed to the sides of the room and piled up, to leave space for dancing, and already people at various levels of alcoholic loss of inhibition were jumping and swaying around to a wildly contrasting selection of everyone's favourite CDs. I'd never seen PJ dance before.

'Move your feet!' I laughed as he flailed his arms around like a windmill, rooted to the spot.

'Can't!' he retorted. 'I'll fall over!'

He'd already had a lot to drink, but he was usually good at handling it. Whereas I . . .

'I'd better not have any more!' I remembered with a sudden shock as he brought me yet another beer a little later while I was dancing with Becky and some of the girls from Medical Records. 'I'm driving!'

'What the hell for? Don't be a party pooper, Rosie! I'll get you a cab.'

'No, no . . . it's fine, PJ.' I felt myself go hot at the thought of him calling me a cab to take me to Oliver's flat. 'I want to drive, honestly.'

He raised his eyebrows, shrugged and began to drink the beer himself instead. His eyes were beginning to look a bit glazed.

'Come here, you silly sober thing,' he demanded as the music changed yet again. 'I want to dance, and I need someone to hold me up.'

We swayed around the room together dangerously. He was leaning against me and breathing beery fumes against my ear.

'I don't really think Status Quo is quite the thing for a smoochy dance,' I reproved him gently, nudging his head away.

'Shame!' he said with a funny twisted grin.

'And I think you might need to drink some water, or get some fresh air,' I added as he stumbled over his own feet for the third time, 'or you're not going to last out the evening!'

'Let's go for the fresh air, then,' he retorted, tugging me behind him as he made for the door. 'Water is a disgusting idea, Rosie, at my own leaving party!'

It was a warm evening and there were a few other people hanging around outside the row of houses, on the communal grass strip where the residents' washing lines and dustbins were all that gave it any claim to be known as a garden.

'I've never seen you pissed before,' I remarked lightly as with a sigh he rested his back against the side wall of the house.

'I'm not *pissed*,' he protested. 'Just feeling a bit *tired* . . .'

'Yeah, right!'

'Well, I did start on the Scotch at about six-thirty tonight . . . as soon as I got out of theatre with You Know Who for the last time!'

'Good enough reason for celebrating!' I agreed, laughing with him.

'I'll miss you, Rosie,' he said, suddenly looking straight at me without a trace of a smile.

'Yeah. Me, too.'

He was such a sweet guy. We'd had such a lot of laughs together, as well as our share of spats. Of course I was going to miss him. I felt a bit sad, a bit emotional, the same as I'd feel if I was saying goodbye to any other colleague I'd enjoyed working with. That, at least, was the best explanation I could come up with for the snog.

I'm not even sure which of us started it. I know he pulled me towards him. I know he put his hands around the back of my head, rested his arms on my shoulders and just looked at me for a while as if he was considering it – but then, without any warning, as if they'd done it without either of us moving a muscle, our mouths kind of hit each other and that was it. By the time we came up for air I was gasping and trembling as if I'd just run a marathon. I hadn't kissed anybody like that since I was a teenager.

'Shit!' I said, shakily, looking down at my feet, looking anywhere rather than at PJ's eyes.

'Rosie?' he said quietly. 'You OK?'

'At least you've got the excuse of being drunk!' I tried to joke.

'Actually I feel quite sober now.'

For a couple of minutes we just stood like that, still leaning against each other. I was trying desperately to think of something witty to say to ease the tension, so that we could both laugh and nudge each other and call each other names and go back to our normal selves, our normal pre-snog selves. But I couldn't think of anything. My mind was a complete mess.

'I need to go to the loo,' I said eventually, moving away from him and straightening my hair self-consciously.

'You OK?' he repeated.

OK? Why shouldn't I be? What's a little kiss between friends?

'Sure!' I said brightly, giving him a quick smile. 'See you later.'

But instead of going to the loo I went straight into the lounge to find Becky. She was dancing with Dave to a slow number, arms wrapped around each other, eyes closed, his hand on her bum. Too bad! I tapped her on the shoulder and her eyes flew open in surprise.

'Rosie! What's up?'

'I need to talk to you! Quick! It's an emergency!'

By the time she'd followed me out to the kitchen I'd poured myself a straight Bacardi and had swallowed half of it in two gulps.

'I thought you were driving?' she said, watching me anxiously.

'Shit. So I am.' I finished the glassful. 'So I was,' I amended.

'What's up?' she repeated, very quietly, ushering me into a corner of the kitchen, away from the crowd around the drinks table. 'What's happened?'

'I kissed PJ,' I said, my voice beginning to shake again at the thought of it.

308

'So? You've kissed him before, haven't you? You've always said what good friends you are ...'

'No! Not just a kiss! A KISS!' I implored her with my voice and my eyes to understand the difference.

'A snog?'

I nodded miserably.

'A grope?' she prompted, a wicked gleam in her eyes.

'No! Becky, no, it wasn't like THAT! It was ...'

She watched my face. I sighed and took a deep breath.

'It was lovely,' I admitted. 'I wanted to do it again.'

'So much for what you said! *There's never been anything like that between us*! Ha! Told you so! Men and women can't just be friends ...'

'Stop it, Becky. We *are* just friends. This wasn't supposed to happen. I feel ... really mixed up, now.'

'Tell him, then,' she suggested, trying to look a bit more sympathetic. 'Just say you got carried away. It happens all the time at parties, nobody gives a shit. Tell him it won't happen again and you didn't mean anything by it.'

I looked at her doubtfully.

'But you did, didn't you,' she added perceptively. 'I think you *did* mean something by it, Rosie, whether you want to admit it or not.'

So much for girl friends. They never tell you anything you really want to hear.

I spent the next hour or so slinking around the house getting slowly pissed on neat Bacardi and avoiding PJ. By the time I'd run out of rooms to avoid him in, it was nearly midnight and a lot of folk had already gone home so I was running out of people to hide behind, too. Plus I was having trouble standing up. He finally cornered me at the end of the lounge, where I'd kind of flopped against an armchair, my empty glass in my hand.

'You've obviously changed your mind about driving home,' he said calmly, taking the glass and putting it safely on the windowsill.

'Home?' I stared at him, puzzled. Something didn't sound right about this. I couldn't think what it was. Home, home? Why didn't I recognise that idea?

'Oh, no!' I smiled with relief, remembering. 'I'm not going home tonight.'

PJ raised his eyebrows, as well he might.

'Well, of course, you can stay here, Rosie – it's no problem, you're very welcome, but will Stuart be OK? Have you phoned him . . .?'

'No, no, no,' I laughed, swaying drunkenly against the back of the armchair. 'I'm not staying *here* – I'm going to Oliver's place!'

Silence. I could feel PJ looking at me but I couldn't quite get his face into focus.

'Oliver's place,' he repeated eventually, stonily. 'You're going to Oliver's place.'

'Yes,' I said, starting to giggle.

'You shouldn't have had so much to drink, then,' he said. 'How are you going to get there?'

'Don't fuss!' I laughed. 'You sound like my father! Whoops!' He reached out to steady me as I started to sway again and lost the support of the armchair. Gently, he guided me round to its seat and pushed me down into it.

'I'll get you some water,' he said, no less stonily.

By the time he came back from the kitchen I'd closed my eyes and had such frightening, spinning vertigo I was relieved to open them again, if only to blink with surprise to see PJ perched on the arm of my chair, trying to feed me sips of water from a tea cup.

'I'm all right,' I slurred, sitting up and knocking the cup so that it splashed water down his shirt. 'I've got to get going. I need to call a taxi.'

'I suppose *Oliver* will be waiting for you.'

'Ready and waiting!' I giggled again, mimicking the sexy way Oliver had said it on the phone. Pushing PJ away with one hand, I staggered to my feet and made my way, slowly and laboriously, up the stairs to his room where I'd dumped

310

my jacket and surreptitiously hidden my overnight bag for Sex At Oliver's, when I arrived at the party. Trouble was, I'd hidden it so surreptitiously I couldn't find it now.

'Shit!' I muttered to myself, lifting pillows, opening the wardrobe door, crouching (with difficulty) to look under the bed. 'Fuck it! Where did I put it?'

'What have you lost?' came the stony voice again.

PJ was standing in the bedroom doorway watching me. I could focus a little better now and there wasn't a flicker of amusement on his face. I sat down on the bed, hiccuped and wondered why I felt like crying. Shit, why did I have to get so drunk? How was I going to manage sex with Oliver, in this state? What was the matter with me?

'Don't go to *Oliver*'s,' said PJ, plonking himself down next to me on the bed. He pronounced the name as if it was the most disgusting, abhorrent swear word he could think of. 'I don't want you to go. Why are you going?'

'Why do you think?' I tried to laugh, but it came out as a hiccup instead. 'Because he's *Ready And Waiting* for me, *Baby*!'

'Stop it!' He turned to me, fiercely, took hold of me by the shoulders and shook me. I hiccuped again in surprise. 'I don't know what you're playing at, Rosie, but for fuck's sake! You're doing my fucking head in! Is this some sort of game? Or some sort of test? You want to know how much I can stand before I finally crack? OK!' He let go of me and raised his hands as if in defeat. 'You win! I give up! I can't stand it any more! Thank God I'm leaving! Go and screw bloody Oliver! Screw bloody Ashley Connor! Screw every fucking guy in the hospital! I've had enough of it!'

I stared at him, shock combined with the shaking beginning to sober me up slightly.

'What are you talking about?' I said in a very timid voice.

'You *know* what I'm talking about. You *know* I want you. You *know* . . . you shouldn't have kissed me like that,

311

and then just carried on as if it was some sort of a joke, telling me you were going to screw fucking *Oliver* because he was Ready and Fucking Waiting . . . what do you think *I've* been doing all this time, Rosie? *I've* been fucking waiting, and waiting, and waiting . . . and I've been a fucking idiot because now it's too *fucking* late and you're going to *fuck* fucking Oliver . . .'

'That's a lot of fuckings in one sentence,' I said, thoughtfully, looking at the carpet. PJ didn't answer. He seemed to have run out of steam.

'I didn't know,' I said. 'You didn't say. How was I supposed to know? I thought we were just . . . friends.'

'Your bag's behind the door, if that's what you were looking for,' he said dully.

'I didn't *know!*' I repeated, turning to look at him, feeling suddenly so anguished I wanted to scream it out. 'You should have *said!*'

'I didn't think I needed to. I thought it was obvious. I could understand it if you didn't fancy me. Fair enough. I'm no oil painting, I'm not a bloody sex God like Mr Ashley *Big Boy* Connor . . .'

'Don't be stupid!'

'But I thought once you'd got over him, got it out of your system, and I thought once your marriage was over . . . I thought there might be a chance for me, to be quite honest, and the way you kissed me outside earlier on . . .'

Remembering that kiss now, I felt my legs go weak. He was right, of course. What was I playing at, trying to deny it? I'd known it all along, really, hadn't I? There'd always been more between us than simple friendship. That was why we argued, why we took refuge in insults and banter when really, what we'd both been hankering after all along was . . .

I looked at him quickly, my breath suddenly stuck in my throat.

'I don't want to go to Oliver's,' I said in a rush. 'I never did want to go in the first place. I was just trying to find out something.'

'What? Find out what?' he asked, his eyes narrowing, his breathing sounding as shallow as mine.

'Whether I could get interested in sex again. You've got me all wrong. I haven't screwed *anyone*. Not ever, apart from Barry, and most of the time that wasn't anything to write home about. I'm not some kind of desperate nymphomaniac, PJ. I can't even get laid when I try, what with leather seats, and allergic vomiting, and . . .'

'Shut up,' said PJ gently, pulling me towards him and kicking the bedroom door shut with one easy movement. 'I never thought you were a desperate nymphomaniac. It's me that's fucking desperate. Come here and let's see if we can get you interested again.'

It didn't take long to find out.

'Mum! MUM! Phone!'

Stuart stood at the front door, waving the receiver at me. I was outside cleaning the car, trying to do something energetic and useful with my hands and arms to stop them craving the feel of the body they'd spent most of the previous night caressing.

'It's not Dad again, is it?' I hissed at him, throwing the sponge in the bucket and wiping my hands on my jeans.

'No. It's some other guy,' he said without much interest.

PJ! I felt the smile come to my face as I took the receiver eagerly, my hands still dripping soapy water.

'Hi! I . . . oh! Hi. Hello.'

It was Oliver.

'I . . . oh, Oliver, I'm so sorry.' I frowned and closed my eyes, trying to think of an acceptable lie. 'But I felt ill . . . after the parents' evening. I know I should have rung you but I went straight to bed . . . a terrible headache . . . still feel a bit sick today.' I stopped and shook my head. This was awful. Why couldn't I just take a deep breath and say what had to be said? 'OK, look, I need to be straight with you,' I began again more calmly. 'I've had second thoughts. I don't feel ready. I've only just separated from

313

my husband and ... things didn't go well with Ashley Connor ...'

'That's all right, Rosie. I understand,' he said, to my immense relief. 'You probably need some time to yourself. I did wonder whether I was rushing you a bit.'

Just a bit, yes. Invitations to intercourse over the starter do tend to fall into the category of being slightly on the fast side.

'I'm sorry,' I said again. 'I thought it'd be fun, but ... when it came to it ... well, you're right – I just don't think I'm ready to rush into anything.'

Unless it happened to be one perfect night with someone I felt like I'd known forever. Because that's what it had been – perfect. And that's what it was going to remain – just the one night.

We'd started talking about it, PJ and I, that morning while we lay curled up together in his narrow sagging bed in his tiny scruffy room and listened to the sounds of his housemates getting up, making coffee, arguing and laughing amongst themselves and starting to clear up the debris of the party.

'I can't believe I nearly let you move away without ever finding out,' I murmured, stroking the soft dark hair of his chest and nuzzling up to him contentedly.

'Finding out what? That I'm a fantastic, unbelievable sex machine with the prowess of a mountain ram ...'

'That too,' I laughed. 'And that we both wanted each other ... like this. It just seems so ridiculous that we've spent over a year skirting round the subject in a state of denial.'

'Too busy being friends,' he said, kissing the top of my head with such affection that it brought tears to my eyes. At that moment, I couldn't think of anything nicer than having sex with someone who'd wanted me as a friend before they wanted me as a lover.

'That's such a lovely compliment,' I told him, returning the kiss.

314

'And just to show I really mean it,' he said, jumping out of bed surprisingly nimbly for someone who'd just spent most of the night indulging in a marathon sex session, 'I'm going to make you a nice cup of tea and run you a hot bath.'

'You're a lovely man,' I told him sincerely, grabbing his hand to stop him leaving, 'But I ought to just get dressed and get going. It's nearly eleven o'clock. Stuart will be coming home from his mate's house and wondering if I've left home for good.'

'So will I see you later? Or tomorrow?' he asked me eagerly as I climbed out of bed with a lot less agility than he had. He came up behind me and put his arms around me, holding me tight around the waist and kissing my neck. 'Come on, Rosie – when can I see you again? I've only got this week before I move ...'

'I know,' I said quietly. I pulled my top over my head and shrugged myself into my jeans. 'So let's not make it more difficult than it has to be.'

He sat down on the edge of the bed and watched me with a stricken expression as I slipped on my shoes.

'You don't want to see me again? That was it? After all this time, Rosie, I finally get you into bed and you're telling me that's *it*?' He shook his head and I had to force myself to look away from the pain in his eyes. 'Didn't you *like* it?' he tried to joke, feebly.

'You know better than that,' I told him softly. 'It was perfect, PJ. And that's how I want to remember it. I'll *always* remember it,' I added a bit shakily. 'And you.'

I turned away and started brushing my hair. I was in danger of getting soppy, of starting to cry, or telling him I loved him, or something equally yukky that I'd regret as soon as I left.

'But there's no reason for it to end!' he protested. 'It can go on being perfect! I could get even better! It could end up being ... *pluperfect*, Rosie!' He looked at me appealingly. 'Couldn't it?'

315

'How? Think about it logically. You're moving to London . . .'

'Oh, God, is that all! For God's sake, do you know how *suburban housewife* you sound? London isn't another planet! It's only just down the road! People commute that distance *every day* to work!'

'And we can commute to have sex?'

'Yes! I mean, no! Not just sex! Why do you think like that? We've got more than that going for us, haven't we?'

'Have we, PJ?' I asked him sadly, turning back from the mirror to face him. 'Maybe we have right now, at the moment. But it can't last, can it. OK, so you're only moving to London this time, but the next job might be in . . . Liverpool, or Scotland, or even the States. I've got kids, and a mortgage, and . . . I'm forty-four, PJ!' I finished desperately.

'So what? What the fuck has age got to do with it?'

'Oh, it's easy to say that when you're – what? Thirty-five? And single. But one day you'll want to get married, and have kids, and . . .' I faltered. 'All right, I'll admit it. I don't want to be dumped again. I don't want to get close to you, to get . . . attached to you, and end up on the scrap heap again when you decide it's time to move on.'

'Fucking hell,' he said sadly, taking hold of my hand, studying it for a moment and then letting it drop, despondently, as he moved his gaze to my face. 'We've only just got it together, and you've worked out how you think it's going to end. What *is* your problem?'

'I don't know. I can't explain it. I just want to keep this memory . . . precious.'

'I'm going to try to change your mind. I'm going to keep phoning you, and texting you, and e-mailing you, until I get on your nerves . . .'

'Do!' I smiled. 'I want to hear from you – of course I do. I don't want to lose touch with you . . .'

'When I move all those millions of miles away to London?' he said sarcastically.

'But I won't change my mind,' I started to add, quietly, but he smothered the words in a kiss that went on for a long, long time and left nothing else to say other than goodbye.

Barry phoned on the Saturday, again on the Sunday, twice on Bank Holiday Monday and every day the following week, finally culminating in an e-mail to me at work the next Monday morning. My patience by then was reaching its last few threads before I lost the struggle to stay polite and told him to fuck off. He seemed to phone for the most ridiculous, trivial reasons, or for hardly any reason at all. The last call had been because he wanted me to look through all the family photo albums and find out the name of a seaside resort in Devon where we'd spent a holiday when the children were toddlers.

'I was thinking what a good holiday that was,' he said, a tinge of sadness in his voice. 'I was just ... you know ... thinking about how nice it would be to go there again ... with Emma and Tom and the baby – one day.'

'Barry,' I said, edgily, 'The baby is a twelve week foetus. It won't exactly be ready to play with a bucket and spade for a while yet.'

'No, but ... you know, looking to the future, Rosie ... thinking about the past ...'

I had no idea what the hell he was talking about.

'Are you drunk?' I asked suspiciously. 'I really haven't got time for this, Barry, unless you've got something more important to tell me?'

Robyn's got her stabilisers off her bike? She's learning to do joined-up writing?

'Christ, she's not *pregnant* is she?' I added in sudden horror.

'Who – Emma? Of course ...'

'No, for God's sake, not Emma – bloody Robyn, you haven't got bloody Robyn pregnant, have you, Barry? Is that what all this soul-searching about babies and father-

317

hood is all about? You're surely not stupid enough to get the girl *pregnant*?'

There was a silence. Then:

'No, Rosie,' he said very firmly. 'No, she's not pregnant.'

When I got the e-mail, everything fell into place. It was short and to the point.

Dear Rosie
I tried to tell you this on the phone but I didn't know how to say it. I think this has all been a mistake. I want us to get back together again. I've finally realised how important the family is. And you. Please can we talk about it?
Barry
PS: I'm not living with Robyn any more. I'm in a B&B in New Market Street.

'What are you shaking your head and sighing about?' asked Sara, looking up from her computer.

'Barry,' I said dismissively. 'Can you believe it? His bimbo's kicked him out and suddenly, as if by magic, he's seen the light and decided all he really wants in life is to be back with the family ... oh, and me too, by way of an afterthought.'

'Men!' declared Sara in disgust.

'What will you do?' asked Becky.

'Do? Me? Nothing,' I said, staring at the e-mail thoughtfully. 'It wasn't me that moved out, after all. Although we did both agree we wanted to separate.'

'Would you have him back?' persisted Becky.

'No. I don't think so. What would be the point? Things would just be the same as before.'

I clicked Delete and got on with my work, pretending not to notice the looks Sara and Becky were giving each other. No, I wasn't going to have him back. What – just because

Robyn had had enough of him? Just because he was living in a B&B? That was his hard luck, wasn't it. We'd set off down the road of separation and divorce now. There wasn't going to be any turning back.

'Dad says you might be getting back together,' said Stuart without too much obvious excitement in his voice.

'Did he?' I retorted, annoyance rising to the surface like a giant burp of indignation. 'Well, he's living in a fantasy world of his own, then, because ...'

'He's living in this one crappy little room, Mum. He can't even make himself a cup of tea. The wallpaper is yellow with huge flowers and the bed's got a *yellow candlewick bedspread*!'

'Sounds awful,' I said with a wry grin. God save and preserve us all from yellow candlewick bedspreads!

'Stuart says you've got terrible wallpaper,' I said when Barry phoned later. 'And a candlewick bedspread.'

'Mm. I'd like to say the décor is sixties, Rosie, but I don't actually remember anything quite as bad as this in the sixties, myself.'

'Never mind. At least you've got a roof over your head.'

'Well, a few square feet of peeling ceiling, anyway.'

You're *not* going to make me feel sorry for you. No way, José!

'It's only temporary, surely,' I pointed out matter-of-factly. 'You'll be looking for a little flat or something for yourself, I suppose, and then once Stuart's left school, the house will have to be sold, and ...'

There was a shocked silence.

'Didn't you get my e-mail?' he asked abruptly.

'Yes. Thanks.' And I couldn't resist adding: 'So it's all over between you and Lolita?'

'It ... er ... didn't work out,' he replied tersely. 'Robyn and I had our differences.'

Yes. Mostly in the years between your ages.

'Sorry to hear that,' I lied cheerfully.

'So,' he persisted, sounding uncomfortable now, 'what did you think about . . . what I said in the e-mail? About getting back together?'

'What? Because you don't like your room? Because of the bedspread?'

'Don't be facetious, Rosie. You know what I'm trying to say.'

'You're trying to say . . . *sorry*, by any chance, Barry?'

'It was your idea as much as mine! We both agreed we wanted to separate. *You* had another guy on the go as well, you admitted it, don't make it all out to be my fault . . .'

I sighed.

'Look, we've been talking on the phone for about two minutes and we're arguing already. How the hell do you think it's going to make sense for us to get back together?'

'We could try. We could both try, really hard, to make it work. Start again. I think we could . . .'

'And this change of heart has nothing to do with Robyn kicking you out?' I retorted sarcastically.

'OK, I'll be straight with you. I was already starting to have regrets, before she . . . before we decided it was over. It was the baby that did it.'

'Baby? What baby? I didn't know she had a baby . . .'

'*Emma*'s baby, Rosie, for God's sake. Thinking about . . . you know, about our daughter having a baby; about the whole idea of the family, about the kids all getting married and having their own children . . .'

'Well, I'd like Tasha to finish at Uni first. And Stuart isn't likely to be thinking about fatherhood for a while yet . . . as long as he stays away from Katie Jenkins . . .'

'You know what I mean. Rosie, we're going to be *grandparents*. Doesn't that mean anything to you? Don't you think we ought to be grown-up enough to give it another try together . . . for the sake of the family?'

*

320

'The whole thing pisses me off, to be quite honest,' I told Becky over coffee a few days, and several similar phone calls, later. 'I'd prefer it if he said he'd suddenly realised he still loved me desperately and couldn't live without me. Even though I'd know it was a load of crap, I'd still prefer him to say that, rather than going on and on about the family and the babies everybody might have in about twenty years' time, with no mention of me whatsoever.'

'You're not weakening, then?'

'No.' I stirred my coffee and sighed, a huge, heavy sigh that felt as if half of my life was sighing its way out of me. 'No, definitely not. I don't think it's the answer. Definitely not the answer.'

'The answer to what?' asked Becky softly. But I pretended I hadn't heard.

If I was looking for answers, then what, you might well ask, was the question? Did the question, by any chance, have anything to do with what I was doing with my life – getting up every morning feeling like shit, going to work, passing the day like an automaton, going home to the TV and a microwave meal, drinking too many glasses of wine and finally going to bed with the dog? The glasses of wine were a new addition to my schedule. They'd crept into it, one at a time, building up to an average of about four a night, since the night with PJ, and there was no getting away from it, they were helping to dull the ache. The ache started somewhere low down in the pit of my stomach, rising up slowly like nausea through my diaphragm until it lodged itself as a tight ball of pain at the very top of my chest, feeling like it was going to choke me. And what, apart from the obvious difficulties of sharing the bed with Biggles and spending every night watching *Big Brother*, was the aetiology of this strange new pain that was afflicting me? Well, it wasn't anything to do with Barry and it sure as hell didn't relate to either Ashley Connor or Oliver Fenton. Any other suggestions?

I hadn't heard from PJ since the night of the Perfect Shag. He said he was going to call, right? He said he was going to phone, and text, and e-mail, and continue to pester me and annoy me until I changed my mind about seeing him again. At first I jumped every time the phone rang. No wonder Barry got short shrift whenever he called. My heart missed a beat every time my computer told me I had new mail, even though nearly all the messages were from Medical Records appealing for missing case notes, or Car Park Security telling us that someone had left their lights on, or Catering Services advertising the excellent low-fat mushroom quiche they were serving for dinner in the canteen. My spirits lifted every time my mobile phone bleeped its announcement of a text message – only to fall again on reading that I'd been specially selected – *from thousands of phone users*!!! – for a super prize, and all I had to do was text 'YES' to this number NOW ... There was only one prize I was interested in, and I'd blown my chances. I'd told him I wasn't going to see him again, so what did I expect? Why should he waste his time trying to persuade me to change my mind, when in all likelihood he'd already found someone else more accommodating, more available, more ... young, and slim, and pretty ...

During the first week, when I knew he still hadn't started his new job, I kept thinking he might just appear, unannounced, at the reception desk. He'd be busy moving into his new accommodation, and he might be coming back to East Dean to collect some of his stuff. He'd turn up with a smile and a joke just the way he always had, and we'd both laugh off the fact that he hadn't had time to call, and we'd go out to lunch together and everything would be lovely again. I caught myself sometimes, staring across the desk into space, imagining him there, and coming to with a start when the patient at the front of the queue coughed loudly to get my attention.

'Phone him!' hissed Becky. 'Text him! E-mail him! What are you waiting for?'

'Him. I'm waiting for him. It's not up to me ... I was the one who said I didn't want to see him again. I can't ...'

'Can't, can't, what are you talking about, can't?' she retorted impatiently. 'Any fool can see ...' She stopped, shaking her head.

'What? Any fool can see what?'

'Nothing. If you can't see it yourself, never mind.'

Me? I couldn't see anything. I'd lost the plot, and I never even knew what the plot was in the first place.

By the time PJ had been at the London for two weeks, it was the middle of June and I'd started meeting up with Barry to discuss our future. We hadn't made any decisions yet, but I was beginning to think he was probably right. Neither of us had anyone else in our lives. We'd had our difficulties but maybe it was true that with a bit of effort on both sides, we could put it all behind us, make a fresh start, learn from our mistakes, get along together as best we could ...

'We've been married nearly twenty-five years, Rosie,' he reminded me over a pub lunch one Sunday. 'It seems a shame to throw it all away ...'

Twenty-five years. I thought about it that night whilst I was trying to get to sleep. It would be our Silver Wedding anniversary in October. People said long marriages were an achievement, something to be proud of and celebrate. Perhaps, if we got back together, we'd have a party, invite all our friends and family round for champagne and a sausage-roll buffet. Perhaps they'd buy us silver photo frames and silver ornaments and those little silver clocks I'd always liked, to put on the fireplace. Perhaps Barry would make a speech, and propose a toast: 'To another twenty-five wonderful years together.'

Suddenly I felt a chill creeping into my bones that had

nothing to do with Biggles occupying most of the duvet on an unseasonably cold night. If I didn't get back together with Barry, what was I going to do with the rest of my life? There wouldn't be any twenty-five wonderful years, not with anyone – it would just be me, on my own, with no silver clocks and no one sleeping next to me in this bed, ever again. The realisation of my loneliness hit me like a blow to the stomach. I sat up, turned on the light, picked up the phone and was about to call Barry to suggest he started moving his things back in the next day. But I didn't dial Barry's number. Instead, I looked up the number for the London Hospital and called the switchboard there.

'Is Mr Jaimeen on call tonight?' I asked quickly, before I had time to change my mind.

'I'll just check for you . . . yes, he is. Would you like me to bleep him for you?'

A tired sounding voice answered a couple of minutes later.

'I'm sorry!' I stammered, regretting it straight away, wishing I'd hung up before he answered. 'Are you busy . . . are you in theatre, or on a ward call, or . . .?'

'Rosie!' he said, brightening up. 'No, it's fine – I was asleep in the on-call room!'

'I don't know why I'm phoning you,' I admitted, shakily, and to my horror I suddenly realised I was crying. 'But I was cold, and lonely, and there was something you once said to me . . .'

'About bleeping me in the middle of the night!' he said at once. 'And *you* said you'd find someone else . . .'

'But I haven't. And you probably *have* . . .'

'Don't be stupid. Rosie, don't cry. I'm sorry I haven't called you. Come and see me? Please – I miss you. Say you'll come?'

I sniffed, blew my nose loudly, and sighed into the phone.

'London isn't very far, you know, he added softly, '*Suburban housewife*!'

I smiled and, catching sight of my tearstained face in the dressing-table mirror, sighed again and shook my head at my reflection. What was I waiting for now?

'OK,' I said. 'OK, I'll come.'

Chapter Eighteen

Second Honeymoon

He met at the station. It was a Friday evening and we'd both come straight from work.

'Pub?' he suggested. 'There's a couple of half-decent places just down the road here. We could talk . . .'

'No. Not a pub.' I looked at him gravely. The pain in my chest felt sharper than ever. He looked even thinner, even more vulnerable and boyish than I remembered. I wanted to touch him but I kept my hands firmly in my pockets. 'Let's find somewhere to eat.'

'Eat?' he said as if he'd never heard of such a thing. 'What, as in, like, a meal?'

'Yes, PJ.' I smiled. 'I'm going to treat you to a meal. Three courses, with wine. It's what I wanted to do, a long time ago – and I didn't. I should have done. You're too bloody skinny by far and I bet you never eat properly.'

He shrugged cheerfully.

'Well, you know what us single guys are like. Microwave meals, too much alcohol, not enough sleep . . .'

'Same here,' I said quietly as we began to walk. 'Same things apply to single women, apparently.'

'You're not sleeping, obviously.' He looked sideways at me with some concern in his eyes. I can see that. Quite apart from the midnight phone call.'

I didn't answer. We walked in silence for a while.

'So how are things at East Dean? Still the same?' he asked. 'Any gossip?'

'Oh, just the usual stuff. Heidi Hampton has finished with Ashley Connor.'

'Wow! Good for her! At last!'

'Yes. Everyone's saying she was humiliated by the Little Red Riding Hood episode, but I don't think she's the type to let a bit of humiliation bother her. I've heard whispers that his wife found out about them and threatened to leave him. Heidi knew it was all over so she got in first and dumped *him*.'

'Excellent. It couldn't happen to a nastier person.'

We stopped outside a little Italian restaurant.

'How about this?' I suggested. 'You like pasta, don't you?'

'Of course.'

We were seated at a window table and chose our meal.

'This is a nice idea,' said PJ appreciatively, touching my hand. 'But I'll pay.'

I flinched as if his touch was burning me.

'It doesn't matter. We'll split the bill. Whatever. Why didn't you phone?'

The abruptness of my question obviously took him aback. He looked away, picked up his fork, played with his place mat, looked back at me and finally said with a shrug: 'Because you made it clear you weren't going to change your mind.'

'But you promised to phone *anyway*. You were going to phone, and text, and e-mail, and we were never going to lose touch . . . why did you say all that? All that stuff about keeping on and on until you got on my nerves! You would *never* have got on my nerves! Now I . . .' I wiped the corner of my eyes with the back of my hand and swallowed hard before finishing on a whisper, 'I feel like I've lost you as a friend, as well as . . . everything else.'

'No you haven't!' He watched the waitress deliver our

327

antipasti and took a gulp of his wine. 'I'm sorry. I wanted to phone you. Of course I did! I wanted to do exactly what I'd said ... I was going to pester you night and day, keep on at you, plead and beg and bother you until you changed your mind and agreed to see me again. But when I started thinking about it, I knew I was just being selfish.'

'Selfish? How?'

'The things you'd said – about not knowing whether it was going to last, about what might happen in the future, if I move away, if I move abroad, about your family, your children, your home and your mortgage ...'

'I know, but ...'

'You had a point. When I really thought it through, I knew you had a point, you had your reasons, and who was I to try to push you into something you didn't want? It wasn't fair – it was just me being selfish and trying to capitalise on ... that one night.'

'Perfect night,' I amended quietly.

'And perhaps what you said was true. If we carried on seeing each other – like you said, we'd just be meeting for sex, and it wouldn't always be perfect. One of us wouldn't be feeling quite as good as usual, both of us might be tired, or have a headache, you'd get resentful, you'd start wondering what it was all about ... you'd go off me ...'

'Or you me.'

'And we'd break up, and then we couldn't stay friends either, and we'd have hurt each other and ... I don't ever want to hurt you, Rosie.'

He put down his fork and stared at me sadly.

'Do you believe me? Or do you think I'm just another jerk-off waste of time who screws you once and moves on?'

'I was beginning to think that,' I admitted. I hadn't started eating. I stared at my plate and wondered whether I was ever going to feel like eating again. 'I've been drinking too much,' I told him flatly. 'I've got this pain, right here, it comes from my stomach and it feels like it's choking me, and the only thing that helps is red wine. I drink every night but it's not getting any better. I don't know what to do about it.'

'Change to white wine?' he suggested with a tired little smile.

I laughed. It felt good to be laughing. How long since I'd laughed? I couldn't remember.

'Can we stay friends?' I asked in a small voice. 'Please? I'll come up here to see you. I won't think like a suburban housewife. You're right – it's only a little way on the train.'

'And I'll phone. This time, I will – I promise. I'll keep in touch. Or you can bleep me again in the middle of the night. Any time. It's no trouble. I'm good at talking in my sleep.'

'I noticed!' I said with a grin.

'Eat some of your *gnocchi*, come on. Please? For me?'

'I haven't been badgered to eat since I had tonsillitis when I was four years old.'

'Then it's time you were. You look like you need nourishing. You need someone to take care of you.'

I took a mouthful and chewed unenthusiastically.

'Well,' I said at length, 'I might be getting back together with Barry.'

He looked up at me with surprise.

'I suppose I should say I'm pleased. I *am* pleased, in a way.'

'Are you? That's not altogether flattering.'

'I'm not really your *If I Can't Have You, Nobody Else Can* type, am I? I'm not up for bundling my rivals into the boot of a car and driving them off the edge of a cliff. If you two can get it together again ... if it makes you happy ...' He tailed off and pushed his plate away. 'We only get one crack at this life, Rosie. What's the point of being lonely if you don't need to be?'

'I don't know. I'm still not sure if it'll work. He's putting pressure on me, talking about the family, about Emma's baby, about making an effort ...'

'He's probably right.'

'I don't think I'll ever love him again. But I think I want things back ... things I didn't appreciate. I want someone to watch TV with and moan about the news with. I want someone lying next to me snoring and farting. I want to celebrate my wedding anniversary and have ... a little silver clock ...' I broke off, met PJ's eyes across the table and took a deep, shuddering breath. 'I think I do.'

'Everybody wants those things. It's nothing to be ashamed of. Life's made up of those little things, little comforts ...'

'And you?' I prompted. The waitress looked at me questioningly and I waved away my plate. 'What about you?'

'Don't worry about *me*, for God's sake, Rosie! I'll be all right! I'm *used* to being on my own! Who the hell would want *me* snoring and farting next to them for the rest of their life?!'

I didn't answer.

We walked back to the station and said our goodbyes on the platform, as my train was pulling in.

'But it *isn't* goodbye,' he said firmly. 'Don't cry!'

'I'm not!' I protested, my eyes overflowing. 'I'm ... not ...'

He kissed away the tears, gently at first, licking the salt as it dried on my cheeks. But within seconds we were wrapped tightly in each other's arms, kissing fiercely until I felt as if my lips would be bruised and numb for ever.

'I'm glad we had that one night,' he whispered hoarsely, as he opened the train door for me.

'Perfect night,' I corrected him with a sad smile.

The train pulled away. I waved until he was out of sight and then sat down, with a sigh, closing my eyes. A sudden bleep made me jump and sit up straight, rummaging in my bag for my mobile phone.

'*Not just perfect*,' read the message on the screen. '*Pluperfect.*'

*

330

'I was thinking,' said Barry a couple of weeks later. He was sitting in our kitchen, drinking coffee. It was a Saturday afternoon and we'd spent a couple of hours together talking about redecorating the bedroom. *If* he moved back in. 'We should perhaps go away.'

'Go away?' I repeated, looking at him as if he was mad. 'Go away? Where? When? What for?'

'Just for a long weekend. It's your birthday soon. I thought I'd take you away somewhere. Maybe one of these city breaks. Rome, or Paris, or ...' He caught my eye and amended quickly, 'No, maybe not Paris. Somewhere romantic – what about Venice? I've always fancied ...'

'Barry! You've *never* fancied doing anything like that! All the years we were together, I could never get you to go anywhere out of the ordinary ... anywhere more exotic than a couple of weeks in Cornwall ...'

'I know. I realise that. That's why I think it would be a good idea, now. I want to show you I'm making an effort, Rosie. I want things to work out better this time. I'm trying to show you I really mean it.'

For the first time for a very long time, I felt a tiny little bit of warmth spreading out from my heart and easing the place in my chest where the pain was still sitting like a hard lump of gristle.

'That's a lovely idea,' I said, gently, meaning it. 'I'd really like that.'

I almost put my arms round him, but at the last minute I held back and went to make some more coffee instead. It was still a bit too soon for arms.

PJ had been true to his word. He was phoning from time to time, e-mailing me occasionally – usually to tell me a joke, or something funny that had happened at his new job – and I responded with news of his old colleagues and an easy, bantering chat that was more like the early days of our friendship. Sometimes he'd call me at home during the evenings. If Stuart answered the phone I'd hear him laughing and talking to PJ about football, or Kylie, or the new Matrix film or even what he was doing at school, and the gentle pleasure of listening to it would make me smile, and seeing me smiling would make Stuart grin and wink as he passed me the phone. And I'd raise my eyebrows and shake my head and tell him with mock exasperation that PJ and I were just friends – and somehow even saying this would give me the warm, light, happy feeling that things were all OK again. It was as if our night together at his farewell party had never happened. It was better like that, of course. The pain in my chest began to subside and the number of glasses of wine I needed as anaesthetic was going down to one or two a night.

'You look better, Mum,' said Tasha thoughtfully over breakfast one morning. She was home from Leicester for the summer and had got herself a holiday job in Marks & Spencer. She had to be up early if she wanted a lift into town on my way to work, but it was always a struggle for her, and she normally had to choose between breakfast and make-up. On this occasion, unusually, breakfast had won because she'd been out on the piss with some friends the night before and needed something starchy to counteract the hangover. She'd no doubt be doing her make-up in the car.

'How do you mean, better? I haven't been ill.'

'No. But when I first came home,' she took a bite of toast and carried on talking with her mouth full, 'you looked ... well, a bit *strained*. A bit kind of sad. Emma and I were worried about you.'

'Emma? Emma was worried?'

It wouldn't be good for the baby. Negative vibes might be reaching him, inside the womb, making him neurotic before he'd even had a whiff of the outside world and all its evils. Poor little sod. It'd all be my fault if he was anxious and disturbed all his life.

'Well, not really *worried*, Mum – just, you know, concerned. We knew what it was all about, of course ...'

332

'You did?!' I said sharply, almost choking on my orange-juice.

'Well, obviously, it was the separation. You were missing Dad. We're both really glad you seem to be getting over it now. Getting used to being a single girl again,' she added with a smile.

'But I thought . . .' I frowned. 'I know you all said, when we split up, that you weren't surprised, you thought it was for the best . . . but I thought if we *did* get back together again, you'd be pleased.'

'Get back together?' she repeated, pausing in mid-bite of her toast. 'You're joking, surely?'

'Why? You know we're having a trip to Venice for my birthday?'

'Yes. I know.' She hesitated. 'Look, Mum, I'm not trying to interfere or anything. Perhaps the separation's done you good in a way – perhaps you and Dad *will* get on better now . . .'

'Yes . . .'

'But don't rush into anything, will you?'

'You'd like it, though, wouldn't you?' I persisted. 'And Stuart. Stuart would like it, wouldn't he – after all, he's only fourteen, he'd like to have his dad back with us, like a proper family again?'

'You'd better ask Stuart about that,' she replied, gulping down her coffee. 'But don't do it for our sake, Mum. That's all I'm saying.'

I'm not. I'm not, am I? I wish I could pretend I was that unselfish. If I'm doing it at all, I'm doing it to get a silver clock.

I did ask Stuart about it, though. He was eating his spaghetti Bolognese at the time, to be fair, and trying to watch *The Simpsons*, so I suppose I could have chosen a better time from the point of view of his concentration.

'What d'you mean, get back together?' he asked without much obvious interest.

'Like, cancelling out the separation,' I explained patiently. 'Like, your dad moves back in again and we carry on being married.'

I watched him, waiting for a reaction. Any time, no hurry, this is only the future of our family we're discussing after all.

'Is that what you want?' he asked eventually, shoving in another forkful of Bolognese.

'I thought it might be what we *all* wanted.'

'Well.' He put down his empty plate and dragged his eyes away from Homer Simpson to look at me. 'I don't know. I thought, Mum, to be honest . . .'

'What?'

'Well, it's none of my business really. But I kind of thought you liked PJ.'

'Oh, for goodness sake, Stuart!' I exclaimed crossly. My hands trembled as I picked up his empty plate. 'Just because *you* like PJ, just because you think he's cool, or whatever . . .'

'Yeah. I do.'

'Well, he was just a colleague, and now he's moved away. OK?'

'OK, Mum. Don't get stroppy about it. Yeah, fine, whatever, if you want to get back together with Dad, then I guess that's excellent. Good. Great!'

'Wonderful,' smiled Tash, who'd been listening. She put her arms around me and kissed me. 'If you're happy, Mum, then that's all that matters. Go for it.'

'I think it's wonderful,' echoed Sara a few days later. It was my birthday – Thursday 14th July – and a glorious sunny day. I was forty-five today. Halfway to being ninety. And how did I feel?

'You look marvellous,' declared Becky.

I'd had my hair cut again the night before – and recoloured. I'd really gone for broke this time, and had some red streaks added, to symbolise my new beginning.

'It's just wonderful,' repeated Sara, beginning to look dopily romantic and beginning to get seriously on my nerves. 'Like an old-fashioned love story. Two people ... worn down by the worries and cares of everyone life ... separated by fate ...'

'No, separated by Bobbin' fucking Robyn, actually,' I reminder her caustically.

'... And coming together again to renew their love ...'

'Oh, give us a break, Sara!' interrupted Becky, seeing the expression on my face.

'Thanks. I was just about to throw up,' I smiled.

Tonight, after work, Barry and I were leaving for our trip to Venice. A second honeymoon, he'd taken to calling it. I wasn't at all sure about this, as the first one hadn't been a great deal of cop and I couldn't see the sense in trying to repeat it – but I'd decided to adopt a new policy of keeping my mouth shut. It wasn't easy. For years I'd thrived on my ability to shoot anyone down with a volley of sarcasm, whether they'd hurt or offended me or merely bored me rigid. But I'd decided that if Barry and I were going to stand any chance at all of carrying off this second attempt at marriage that seemed to be reinventing itself as a love story born in Heaven, I was going to need to shut the fuck up, plaster a grateful smile on my face and let him do his best. And, to be fair, I was looking forward to Venice. Ever since the Paris fiasco, I'd lived with a little twinge of regret that I hadn't been able to enjoy my chance of a weekend away. And – do you know what else? I was ready to be pampered. One way or another, I'd had a lot going on in my life recently – not very much of it being particularly enjoyable – and I was quite happy with the idea of being wined, and dined, and taken down the Venetian canals on a gondola, being sung to and offered Cornettos. Yes, this was going to be the life! No point in crying over spilt milk ... I was going to take myself off to Venice with Barry, with my new red hair and my new underwear in my bag!

I'd made the mistake of joking about this with PJ on the phone the previous day.

'Lucky Barry,' he'd said sourly.

'Oh, it's not really like *that*,' I laughed dismissively. 'Trust me, he won't even notice it. He never looks at me, and especially not when I'm undressed. It would be really unnerving if he started now.'

'But he will. Of course he will, Rosie – that's the whole point of all this, isn't it. I'm looking at it from a man's point of view, and I can tell you, when he sees you in that underwear . . .'

'OK, PJ, let's forget it, eh?' I said quickly, beginning to regret bringing up the subject at all. The truth was that I was only taking the black and red lacy stuff with me at all because it was the only decent underwear I had and it seemed a crying shame to let it rot in the drawer until I was ninety-five years old and wouldn't be able to climb into it without assistance.

'Have a lovely time, then,' murmured PJ. 'I'll be thinking of you . . .'

But to my surprise, he phoned again that afternoon of my birthday, about fifteen minutes before I was due to leave work to meet Barry at the airport.

'I can't talk for long, PJ,' I reminded him. 'I'm just about to leave.'

'I know. Just wanted to say Happy Birthday.'

'Thanks,' I said, puzzled. 'But we did all this yesterday. You didn't have to phone again.'

'Yes. I did. I had to phone again.'

I frowned, alarmed by the tone of his voice, feeling my breath catch in my throat.

'Are you all right?'

'No. No, I'm not. I'm not all right and I'm sick of pretending I am.'

'What's the matter? Are you ill?'

'Ill? No. You *know* what's wrong with me. I want to see

336

you. Now, Rosie! I want to get in my car and drive down there *now* and . . .'

'You can't!' I protested, sharply. 'I'm going to Venice! I'm waiting for a taxi . . .'

'Don't go!'

There was a silence. I felt my cheerful mood draining away from me. This wasn't fair. Not *now*, not when I'd just got my hopes up for the future, just got my hair cut and my bag packed and started planning where to put the silver Anniversary clock.

'Don't start this now,' I told him quietly. 'It's not fair.'

'I know it's not. I know, and I'm sorry, but I couldn't go on pretending. I haven't slept a wink since you told me about Venice. I feel sick with rage thinking about you and Barry getting back together.'

'But you said you were pleased! You said it was best . . .'

'I lied. I was trying to be noble.'

'*Noble*?'

'I can't keep it up. I'm no good at being noble. I don't want you to get back with Barry. I want you to be with *me*. You didn't give us a chance. We could have found a way. I know you can't leave your home, you can't leave Stuart, but we could still see each other. I could live in East Dean and commute. We could see each other every day. I could come round every night. We wouldn't have to talk about moving in together until the time's right, until Stuart's left school, or whenever you're ready. I can't give you a guarantee that it'd work out. There aren't ever any guarantees! But sometimes you just have to take a chance in life, just take a chance, Rosie, and bite the bullet . . .'

He broke off. I could hear him breathing, very fast, as if he'd run for a bus. Run for a bus . . . and missed it just as it was pulling away.

'Well, anyway,' he continued more quietly. 'I just had to say that. I'm sorry. Sorry if I've spoilt your birthday.'

'You haven't. But I can't . . .'

'I know. I knew you'd say that.'

337

'It's too late. I've made my decision.'

'Yes. I know. OK.'

'I'll talk to you when I get back. All right?'

'OK.'

'Are you all right, Rosie?' asked Becky quietly as I put the phone down.

I swallowed hard, took a deep breath and straightened my shoulders.

'Yes,' I said, pinning my new false bright smile to my face and picking up my holdall from under the desk. 'Yes, I'm fine.'

'Your taxi's outside,' called Sara, who'd been watching the door for the past half hour and getting more excited than I was. She stood up ad gave me a hug. 'Have a *wonderful* time, Rosie.'

'Yes,' said Becky, hugging me too. I felt like a bridesmaid going off to someone else's wedding – far more fuss and emotion than the occasion deserved. 'Don't worry about . . . anybody else, Rosie. Just concentrate on having a good time. Yeah?'

'Yeah,' I smiled. I could feel the old gristly lump in my chest beginning to play up again but I knew I could swallow it back down, fight against the sensation, have a couple of glasses of wine at the airport and I'd be fine. Fine, fine, fine.

Outside the hospital entrance, two taxis were pulled up behind each other. I opened the door of the first taxi and was just about to ask the driver if he was booked for the airport, when the second driver got out of his cab and called me:

'Excuse me! Mrs Peacock? Rosie Peacock?'

'Oh!' I smiled apologetically at the first driver. 'Wrong cab.'

I turned to face the driver who'd called me.

'Airport?'

'No. Delivery for you in the cab, Mrs Peacock. If you like to follow me?'

'*Delivery* . . .?'

I put down my bag and watched as the taxi-driver opened the rear door of his cab.

'Package for you on the back seat, Mrs Peacock,' he announced grandly.

I leaned into the cab. A brown carrier bag sat in the middle of the seat. *A birthday present*! I guessed happily. How romantic of Barry to send it by taxi! He wasn't joking – he really was beginning to make an effort! Or perhaps it was one of the kids, or all of them, clubbing together for a special treat! My heart lightening with pleasure, I picked up the carrier bag, straightened up and peeked inside. The smell of sugar made me blink with surprise. Nestling together in the bottom of the bag, oozing jam and staring at me challengingly, were two round, fat, greasy doughnuts.

'Gentleman said he'd pay the fare back to London,' said the cabbie cheerfully. 'For you and the doughnuts.'

'Oh, PJ!' I muttered under my breath, staring from one taxi to the other in dismay, my heart hammering painfully against my ribs, and fighting the urge to laugh and cry simultaneously. 'You *fucking* idiot, PJ! It's *too fucking late*!'

The curtains in the hotel room were closed against the night sky, but it was a clear, warm night and we'd left the windows open and were lying on top of the duvet, listening to the unfamiliar sounds outside and planning what to do the next day. The next day, and the rest of our lives.

'Glad we're here?' he asked me, rolling onto his side to touch my cheek gently. 'Have you had a good birthday . . . so far?'

'Of course I have,' I said, happily. 'And I'm really grateful. For this . . . the hotel . . . and everything.' I laid my head on his chest and sighed. Yes, I'd made my decision now. Made it, and was going to stick to it. You could spend your whole life faffing about, wondering what to do, listening to what other people said, but at the end of the day you just had to do what you thought best and get on with it. 'We've been through a bit of a rough time, haven't we.'

'But you know what they say. It makes you stronger . . .'

'Whatever!' I laughed. 'I know it's taken me a while, but I'm sure, now.'

'Are you? Are you sure you're sure?'

'I'm sure that I'm sure that I'm . . . as sure as I'm ever going to be!'

'Well, I'm glad. We could have just drifted on, apart, but when you think you've made a mistake, sometimes you just have to – well, you just have to bite the . . .'

I put my fingers over his lips, and, laughing, finished for him:

'You just have to bite the doughnut?'

'You do, Rosie. And I'm glad you did! And I'm glad you think a couple of nights in a hotel in the West End of London is an acceptable alternative to a weekend in Venice.'

'I think it's wonderful, PJ. I think it's the most beautiful hotel in the world.'

And the world is a beautiful place. And the pain in my chest has completely gone.

When I'd called Barry on my mobile a few hours before, he was already waiting for me at the airport – and I was in the taxi on my way to London, with a bag of doughnuts on my lap.

'What do you mean – you're not coming? I've got the tickets and everything. I can't get a refund.'

'I'm sorry. I'm really sorry. But if that's all you're worried about . . .'

'No, of course it isn't. Why, Rosie? What's happened?'

'I've stopped pretending, Barry, that's all. I was pretending I wanted to stay married but I don't, not really. I just wanted an anniversary and a silver clock, and someone to watch telly with.'

340

'Well, we can . . .'

'No. No, we can't, because we'll both just be pretending. Even the kids know it. Even the grandbaby'd know it. I don't want a pretend life any more. I want something—' I sniffed the doughnuts on my lap again '—real.'

'And I suppose you've found it? With your *friend* from work?'

'Perhaps,' I said quietly, feeling my face stretch with a smile. 'I hope so.'

'Well, I'm gutted,' he said huffily. 'I might just go to Venice on my own.'

You do that, old chum. I'm only sorry Robyn Red Breast isn't going with you – you could have pushed her out of the gondola.

'Dad's gutted,' said Stuart cheerfully when he answered my call a bit later. 'He's gone to Venice on his own.'

'Good for him. Do you . . . and Tash . . . think I'm being very mean? Changing my mind and coming to London with . . . with my girlfriends . . . instead of going with Dad?'

'Nah! You'd only have given him the wrong idea, Mum. He'd have expected . . . you know. Sex and stuff.'

Christ. God forbid.

'Anyway – got to go,' he added. '*The Fresh Prince of Bel-Air*'s on. Have a great time, Mum! See you Sunday.'

'Yes, see you Sunday. Behave yourself, Stuart – don't argue with Tash.'

'OK. Oh, and . . . Mum?'

'Yes?'

'Say hi to PJ.'

We ate the doughnuts in the middle of the night, washed down with champagne from the mini-bar. Sex had made us hungry and we both bit into the jammy bit in the middle at the same time, watching each other and laughing as it trickled down our chins and stuck our fingers together and ran over our bare legs outstretched in the tangle of the sheets.

'My favourite food,' said PJ, smiling at me as he demolished the last mouthful.

'Mine too.'

And whatever happens now, however it all works out, whether this is good or bad, sensible or crazy, whether we're going to regret this pluperfect night, or remember it for the rest of our lives ... doughnuts will always be my favourite food now – for ever.